friends
to
die for

HILARY BONNER

PAN BOOKS

First published 2014 by Macmillan

This edition published 2014 by Pan Books
an imprint of Pan Macmillan, a division of Macmillan Publishers Limited
Pan Macmillan, 20 New Wharf Road, London N1 9RR
Basingstoke and Oxford
Associated companies throughout the world
www.panmacmillan.com

ISBN 978-0-230-76665-5

A CIP catalogue record for this book is available from the British Library.

Typeset by Ellipsis Digital Limited, Glasgow
Printed and bound by CPI Group (UK) Ltd, Croydon, CR0 4YY

For Jimmy
In memory

acknowledgements

With grateful thanks to various members of the Metropolitan Police Service, including the desk staff at Charing Cross station – you were all great; former Detective Sergeant Frank Waghorn, as ever; Terry Freeman for his help and wonderful stories of being a bouncer (sorry, 'security doorman'); Lt Colonel John Pullinger, OBE, formerly of The Parachute Regiment; Wayne Brookes, Anne O'Brien and everyone at Pan Macmillan for their hard work and continuing belief and support; my agent Tony Peake; and my partner Amanda, for yet again putting up with me in writing mode. Also, of course, enormous thanks to the real life Sunday Clubbers, Alan St Clair, Chris Clarke, Amanda etc., and a certain restaurant called Joe Allen and all its staff – for the inspiration and for many wonderful Sunday nights without a murderer to be seen. As far as we know . . .

prologue

Ingrid's heart was singing as she walked up the Caledonian Road. Even the inconvenience caused her by the closure of King's Cross Station due to a bomb scare could not dampen her spirits.

Security alerts of this kind were rare in London in the autumn of 1998. This was the year the Good Friday Agreement had more or less brought IRA terrorist attacks on the UK mainland to an end, and three years before 9/11 would herald a whole new era of al-Qaeda terrorism.

Ingrid had no idea just how unlucky she was to be caught up in one, any more than she realized that her luck was about to desert her completely. Her thoughts were full of the momentous decision she had made, and how her parents in Sweden would react when they received the letter she had finished that morning.

It was just gone 10 p.m. After completing her shift as a student nurse at University College Hospital thirty minutes earlier, Ingrid had as usual made her way to King's Cross underground in order to board a Piccadilly Line train to Wood Green, where she was staying for the duration of her training with a cousin of her mother's.

This accommodation arrangement had been a condition laid

down by her parents when Ingrid had expressed a wish to come to London in order to gain what she felt was the best possible nursing training at one of the city's great teaching hospitals. Most of the other young nurses shared flats or rooms, but Ingrid had been happy to conform with her parents' wishes. She knew she wouldn't have fitted in. Even in Sweden, she had always been different.

At nineteen she was still a virgin, with no interest in boys. Or girls. Her passion was the Lutheran Church, to which her mother had introduced her when she was a child. She now knew beyond a doubt that she wanted to make the ultimate commitment to her Church. She believed that was the way she could make best use of the nursing skills she was still in the process of acquiring.

And today she had written to tell her parents that when she finished her training she was going to become a Lutheran nun.

She knew that her parents would not be too surprised, although she suspected that her farmer father might regret that his clever only child would not now give him grandchildren. He would support her, though. He always did.

It was as if the act of posting the letter had made it official. Once she'd dropped it in the postbox opposite the station she was far too excited to join the other commuters milling around the bus stops and trying to hail taxis. Police manning hastily erected barriers at the station entrance were advising passengers that a limited underground service was still running from nearby stations, so Ingrid set off for Caledonian Road, the next stop on the Piccadilly Line heading towards Wood Green. She reckoned she could walk there in fifteen minutes.

The area immediately around the station was rapidly being shut off as police reinforcements arrived, so Ingrid got out her pocket *A–Z* and made a detour into Pentonville Road and along

Northdown Street into the Caledonian Road. What Ingrid's *A–Z* failed to tell her was that the Cally Road, as locals called it, was a notorious red light district. The regeneration of King's Cross had begun a few years earlier, but much of the Cally Road remained a wasteland of derelict buildings and flattened empty ground awaiting redevelopment.

Ahead of her was a road junction known as Class A Corner. It was where the prostitutes met the drug dealers in order to exchange the proceeds of one vice for the product of another.

Ingrid wore her long white-blonde hair in a tight bun when she was on hospital duty. She never found this entirely comfortable. With one hand she released the constraints of the bun, as she often did on the way home, and allowed her hair to fall onto the shoulders of the black coat covering her nurse's uniform.

Almost immediately a car pulled to a halt alongside her. The passenger window was lowered. A man's head appeared.

'Looking for business, darling?' he enquired.

Ingrid was shocked. She knew exactly what was being suggested and what kind of woman the man had taken her for. She hadn't led that sheltered a life, and she was Swedish, after all.

'No, no,' she replied, almost screaming the words, her voice sharp and high-pitched.

The man drove off at once.

Ingrid wrapped her coat tightly around herself. She was shivering. It was a cold damp November night, but she realized it was her sudden nerviness rather than the chill in the air that was causing her body to tremble.

She peered up and down the Caledonian Road. It wasn't well lit in those days. However, in the glare of the headlamps of passing vehicles, she could clearly see a young woman on the opposite side of the road wearing an imitation fur coat pulled down off one shoulder to reveal bare flesh.

A saloon car stopped alongside. The woman opened the passenger door and climbed in.

Ingrid was well aware now of the kind of district she had unwittingly wandered into. There were shadowy figures gathered on a piece of wasteland to her left, and another in a doorway just ahead. She considered turning back. But there was a brightly lit stretch of road not far away. Desperate to get home, she hurried towards it.

The blow caught her on the side of her head. She registered that she had been hit by a heavy object before falling, partly concussed, to the pavement.

She felt herself being dragged by the shoulders, somewhere away from the main road to a place where there was even less light. Her whole body hurt already, and the rough ground beneath cut into her. But she did not cry out. She was dumb with fear.

Then her assailant let go of her, but remained, apparently caped and hooded, looming above her. She tried to make out a face. The light was not bright enough. But she could see the eyes shining through the gloom. There was not a trace of humanity in them.

Ingrid cowered before her attacker. She wanted to pray but was unable to. She tried to crawl away, even though she knew it was hopeless. Her body seemed incapable of movement. She tried to beg for mercy but could not speak. All she could do was wait for the inevitable.

And a few minutes later Ingrid was dead.

one

Fifteen years later

The early Sunday supper at Johnny's Place in the heart of Covent Garden was a casual arrangement but a ritual nonetheless. Every week at five thirty the staff set up a long table along one wall at the back of the restaurant for the group that had become known as Sunday Club. As the evening wore on the friends would turn up as and when they could, with seating and table places readjusted as it eventually became apparent how many they would be.

Rather unusually, on this particular Sunday all ten of the group were present.

Tiny, a six-foot-six-inch man-mountain of West Indian descent, and his partner Billy were the first to arrive. As usual, Tiny gravitated to a place at one end of the table where his massive bulk would have room to spread. He had no hair at all on his head, which glistened like a large polished ebony orb resting atop broad shoulders, his jacket falling open to reveal an expansive chest, muscles bulging beneath his Gucci T-shirt. At a glance he looked thoroughly threatening, but his eyes were gentle.

In the seat next to Tiny, one small white hand placed

possessively on the big man's denim-clad knee, sat Billy, a diminutive City lawyer in a business suit by day and a bit of a raver at night. With his free hand Billy stroked his neat brown moustache, making sure no hair was out of place. Everything about Billy was neat and organized, except perhaps his relationship with Tiny whom he'd met at Cloud Nine, the gay nightclub where Tiny worked as a bouncer, or door supervisor, the job description preferred by the Security Industry Association of which the big man was an active member.

George, an actor more often out of work than in, arrived next. He rarely missed the weekly gathering, except during the pantomime season when he was to be found at the seaside being Prince Charming. Having made his entrance, he invariably chose to sit with his back to the wall, which was lined with theatre bills and signed pictures of celebrity clientele. From there he could see and be seen. Johnny's, a legendary basement restaurant selling extremely upmarket junk food alongside a range of rather more grown-up dishes, remained a haunt of the famous and feted, but rarely on a Sunday afternoon or evening when it more usually became the territory of weekend fathers spoiling the children they no longer saw enough of.

Tiny, Billy and George had got to know each other dog walking at Lincoln's Inn Fields, the biggest patch of green in the Covent Garden area, and the largest square in London, dating back to the seventeenth century. Tiny and Billy had a little chihuahua, Daisy, and George a Maltese terrier called Chump.

They had just ordered drinks – red wine for George, cosmopolitans for Tiny and Billy – when Michelle, a five-foot-nothing police constable, turned up. She'd met George at Shannon's gym, and they'd become work-out buddies. Actually Michelle, a pretty twenty-nine-year-old blonde with a winsome smile, had at first rather hoped for more than that, and had certainly thought George might ask her out on a date. He hadn't. Well, not exactly. But he had asked her if she'd like to join the group at Johnny's.

The proprietor, Johnny himself, a small man with a big heart and a very determined all-year suntan, was, as usual, at the piano by the door. Marlena, who had been coming to the restaurant longer than any of the others, had once remarked that she thought Johnny probably lived in his piano, stretching out on the black and white keys and pulling the cover over himself before going to sleep at night. Certainly he played the old upright most evenings, and had done for as long as anyone could remember. He stood up to give Michelle a hug and she hugged him back. Johnny greeted many of the regulars at his restaurant more as friends than clients, but it was clear he had a special soft spot for the young policewoman.

Michelle eased herself into the chair opposite George and added her name to the red wine order.

'No Carla then?' she remarked to George. 'Are we ever going to meet this paragon?'

Carla was the new girlfriend George had told them all about. Though his friends had listened to endless stories about how wonderful she was, how gorgeous, how adorable, they had yet to enjoy the pleasure of her company.

'She wants nothing to do with you rabble,' said George, grinning. His dark hair flopped Hugh Grant style over one side of his handsome forehead. His black silk shirt opened at the neck just enough to reveal a V of perfect tan. 'Anyway, I've told you, Sunday is her family day.'

'If you ask me, he's ashamed of her,' teased Billy.

'Oh yes,' responded George, pulling out his wallet and extracting the photograph they had all seen countless times: a stunning young woman with stylishly cropped peroxide white hair smiling for the camera. 'Is she gorgeous or what?' He returned the picture to his wallet with a shake of his head. 'It's you lot I'm bloody ashamed of.'

Greg and Karen, married thirty-somethings with two children, arrived next. They too were dog owners, and it was Karen, the principal dog walker, who had first met George, Tiny and Billy while exercising the family's pair of Westies at Lincoln's Inn. Nobody could remember who'd been first to suggest meeting at Johnny's, but it had been between these four that Sunday Club had been conceived a few years previously. The early evening outings suited Greg and Karen well. Karen's mum took the kids on Sunday afternoons to give the couple some time alone, and after leaving Johnny's they could still pick them up in time to pack them off to bed not too late for next day's school.

Johnny broke into a spirited rendition of 'I'm Forever Blowing Bubbles' as Greg, a dedicated West Ham supporter bustled in. Greg beamed.

'Don't you worry mate, the 'Ammers will 'ammer 'em,' he said.

The next day would see a derby game with Spurs. It was somehow typical of Johnny, no way a football fan, to be aware of that. Greg wasn't much taller than Johnny but had a big personality and walked with a swagger. He was a wheeler-dealer, a white van man who bought and sold, but his precise occupation was never entirely clear.

Karen, an inch or so taller, wore flat shoes and had a very slight stoop, no doubt caused by trying to ensure her husband didn't look shorter than her. She always gave the impression that she was keeping a bit of an eye on Greg.

Hoping her husband wouldn't pick up on her slightly wary

tone, Karen greeted George. Earlier in the week there had been an incident between them which she hoped was now forgotten. Certainly George seemed the same as ever, smiling back at her with no hint of awkwardness in his response. Karen felt relieved.

'No Carla then?' remarked Greg.

'For God's sake,' said George.

The others all seemed to arrive at once. There was olive-skinned Alfonso, with his hooded Mediterranean eyes and shiny black goatee beard, who could only be of Italian descent even though he'd been born and raised in Essex. Alfonso was a senior waiter at the Vine, arguably the most fashionable restaurant in London, and had been invited along to Sunday Club by Vine regulars Billy and Tiny.

Bob, in his fifties and the second oldest of the group, made a living as an inner-city gardener, watering and looking after other people's terraces, balconies and window boxes. He had, rather to his surprise, found himself invited to join Sunday Club when he became chummy with Tiny and Billy after they'd called him in to plant out their roof terrace and put in an irrigation system.

Ari, at twenty-six the youngest and the richest of the friends, was the son of a wealthy Asian entrepreneur and his English wife. Billy had run into him at a few work-related events and found the ponytailed young man not only strikingly attractive but also highly entertaining, and in spite of loving Tiny to bits, had rather wished Ari were gay. Which he most certainly was not. Nonetheless it was Billy who'd suggested Ari may like to come along to Sunday Club.

Finally there was the Covent Garden legend known only as Marlena, a name the others suspected she had adopted in tribute to her heroine Marlene Dietrich, although she always maintained it was her given name. Marlena, probably in her late sixties but perhaps older, was never seen without stage make-up and a spectacular blonde wig. She invariably dressed entirely in black, enlivened occasionally by a mink wrap or a mock leopard-skin throw, and adorned to excess with an elaborate display of bling. Her exact age was a closely guarded secret, and everything about her exuded a certain air of mystery. She was another Vine regular, and had originally been invited to join the group by Alfonso, whom she'd always regarded more as a friend than a waiter.

More drinks were ordered as everyone bustled to sit. Bob, like George, manoeuvred to acquire a place that allowed him to have his back to the wall, but because he had a deaf ear rather than a burning desire to see and be seen. Alfonso fussed over Marlena, whom he worshipped. Ari, always in a hurry to do everything and anything, only narrowly avoided knocking over Tiny's cosmo as he threw himself at a chair. There was Prosecco for Marlena, Hendricks with olives on the side for Ari, and a couple more carafes of red wine for the rest.

'Marlena darling, you'll never guess who we had in the restaurant yesterday,' said Alfonso, when he'd eventually sat down.

'Hey, Fonz, you sound like a bleeding cabbie,' remarked Greg.

'Just tell us, darling,' said Marlena encouragingly.

'Madonna, Madonna, my loves, and I poured her sparkling water,' announced Alfonso, waving his arms triumphantly in the air.

'Wonderful, darling,' said Marlena.

She turned to George.

'And what have you been up to this week, sweetheart?' she asked. 'Still no sign of that beautiful girl of yours, I see. What a pity!'

'I don't believe this,' said George. 'Look, I'll see if I can persuade her to join us, OK? But I do know she's with her family.'

He took his phone from his pocket and touched one key on the screen.

'Voicemail,' he muttered in an aside. Then he spoke into the phone.

'Hi, Carla darling, it's me. I'm calling from Johnny's – I'm with the gang, Sunday Club. Like I told you about. Don't suppose you can join us, can you? I'd love to see you and so would the rest of the bunch. If you can bear it, do come. Love you, baby. Kiss kiss.'

'I think I'm going to throw up,' said Ari.

'Behave,' said Marlena. 'One day some girl will be monumentally stupid enough to let you fall in love with her.'

'And when she does, I promise not to make all my friends feel sick.' Ari turned away from the table and pretended to retch.

'Oh, stop it, you're disgusting,' said Karen.

'No I'm not,' said Ari. 'I'm handsome, charming and sophisticated. My mother told me so this morning. And for the record, Marlena, there's always a queue of girls at my door and—'

'If there's any truth at all in that then they're obviously only after your money!' interrupted Michelle.

Marlena put a hand on Ari's arm. 'Do remember, darling, today's cock of the walk is tomorrow's feather duster,' she said.

Everyone laughed, including Ari. The friends were all very much at ease in each other's company, and with the banter, sometimes quite edgy, which was inclined to dominate their time together.

Menus were passed around and studied even though they all knew the contents well. But there were always the Sunday specials of course. This week grilled salmon with garlic mash, chicken fricassee and roasted pumpkin risotto.

It took some time to sort out the food order for everyone, amid plenty more noisy banter. The waiters were patient and smiley. They gave every impression of enjoying the presence of this lively and high-spirited group.

The friends had great energy when they were together. They met at Johnny's to have as much fun as possible. That was what Sunday Club was for, and why it had become a fixture in their lives.

two

It was Karen, the group's earth mother, who made the suggestion that was to ultimately have such devastating consequences. But she didn't know that then, of course. And neither did any of the other nine men and women sitting round the table that Sunday night.

'Why don't we play The Game?' Karen asked, after everyone had settled down a bit. 'We never have with all of us together here. I can't even remember if we've all actually been here together before. I suppose we must have, but . . .'

George, the actor, groaned theatrically, but the others recognized it as affectation and not a genuine reaction to the suggestion.

'Oh let's,' said Michelle, who neither looked nor sounded much like a police officer when she was off duty.

'If only you were more interesting, George, we wouldn't need to play games,' drawled the legendary Marlena.

Tiny and Billy, surely the ultimate gay men about town, concentrated on looking cool. As did Karen's husband Greg. Young Ari, whom the group regarded as being thoroughly spoiled in spite of his protestations to the contrary, tried to look bored and rather too sophisticated for such a thing. But that was normal. In fact, by and large, the group all rather liked The

Game, which involved one of them asking a question that everyone would answer in turn. It might be something playful and light, like what would they do if they won the lottery, or what had been the best holiday they'd ever had? Or it could sometimes be something that invited a more thoughtful response. What was their greatest regret? Or what would they want to be or do in life other than what they were or did?

It was Sunday Club's version of the Truth Game, but the emphasis was on entertaining conversation rather than revelation. Regardless of the subject matter, all ten of them knew they were obligated by the very ethos of Sunday Club to attempt to be amusing or surprising or shocking – preferably all three – both in their answers and in their reactions to the answers of the others. That was the whole point of The Game, though on this particular evening several of the group would fail to fulfil that obligation. After all, most people have secrets of some sort in their lives. Anyway, this was Sunday Club: nobody was going to be forced to reveal anything they didn't wish to.

Since Karen was the one who suggested The Game, custom had it that she got to choose the question. She ran her hands through her spiky red hair, screwed up her eyes, and made a big show of giving the matter serious thought.

'Has there been one great life-changing moment in your past, and what was it?' she asked eventually.

Greg answered first. Quickly. Mischievously. His pale eyes sparkling disingenuously beneath a tousled fringe of mostly blond hair which, although now flecked with grey, remained abundantly curly, and still contrived to help him retain a boyish appearance.

'When I met *you*, Karen, of course,' he said, grinning, pleased with himself.

'Oh, don't be so daft!' said Karen. But she seemed pleased too, if just a tad puzzled. With one hand she fiddled with the little steel spikes on a shoulder of her chunky black leather waistcoat. Karen dressed retro punk, but for all that she was earth mother at heart.

'No, I mean it,' Greg persisted. 'I was Jack the lad. Me and my mate Wiz were a right pair. We got up to a lotta no good, and Wiz paid the price . . .' Greg's voice trailed off, his face momentarily clouding over.

'What happened to him?' asked Ari.

'Oh, there was an accident. He died. We were at St Michael's – that school they closed down 'cos it was so bad. Nothing saintly about that place, I can tell you. We got into a bit of a gang, that sort of thing . . .'

Greg paused, clearly uncomfortable with the subject. 'But that's another story,' he continued in a brighter tone. 'Anyway, I never thought I'd want to settle down with someone. Until I met Karen. She saved my arse, really, and all I wanted was to be with her and for her to have my kids.'

'Aw,' said Alfonso.

'What a great softy you are,' said Marlena.

'That's me, darlin',' replied Greg.

It was too. Certainly as far as his family were concerned. But it was most unlike Greg to make such a public declaration. Plus he was one of those who felt almost honour-bound to play everything for laughs. It was in his DNA. He had his cockney laughing-boy image to protect, and it wasn't often that Greg let the act drop. Not for a moment. But just that morning he'd heard from someone he'd hoped never to hear from again. Indirectly. And rather obtusely. However, Greg was in no doubt that he'd been given a message. He was still sorting out exactly what that message was and how he was going to deal with it.

But it had dredged up long-buried memories of Wiz, and St Michael's, and a period of his life he regarded as the bad old days. And he knew it was unlikely to turn into anything other than bad news. For him. And even, Heaven forbid, for his wife and children.

Greg emptied his glass in one. A dribble of red wine escaped and ran down his chin, forming rivulets in his designer stubble. He wiped it away with the back of a hand.

'Soft as shit,' he muttered.

'I don't think I ever heard you say anything like that before, Greg,' said Karen, still puzzling over her husband's public declaration of love.

Greg shrugged. 'What, "shit"?'

'You know what I mean,' said Karen.

'It's the truth, babes. Changed my life in spades, meeting you,' said Greg.

'Oh, pass that sick bag,' exclaimed George. 'Seems I'm just a humble amateur when it comes to being nauseating.'

'Don't be such a dreadful old cynic,' said Marlena.

'Well, honestly,' continued George. 'I think we should make a rule here and now that meeting your bloody boring life partner isn't allowed as an answer to this question . . .'

'Who are you calling bloody boring?' asked Karen.

'I'll rephrase that,' said George. 'It's not the partner, whoever they are, who's boring. Well not necessarily . . .'

He glanced towards Karen, who pretended to throw a punch in his direction. She was actually pleased that George was teasing her, just the way he usually would. A few days previously the two of them had been helping Marlena get rid of some unwanted furniture – never easy in Covent Garden – and afterwards she'd plied the pair of them with champagne. Karen wasn't a big drinker. She'd quickly got rather drunk and George had offered to take her home. Greg had been working late. The kids were on a sleepover with school pals. Karen had made a silly pass at George. In her own flat. George, thankfully, had rejected her advances – most regretfully he'd said – on the grounds that they were both spoken for. The very thought of it now made her squirm with embarrassment, but at least George appeared to have dismissed the episode as a moment of madness. And so must she. The only thing that mattered was that Greg should never find out, which could only ever happen if she or George were to tell him. Well, she certainly wasn't going to. And George was showing no such inclination. Underneath the self-obsessed bluster, he had always seemed to Karen a kind man, and certainly without malice. She should stop worrying, she really should. It wasn't as if anything had happened.

'It's just *that* particular answer is bloody boring,' George continued, cutting through Karen's jumbled thoughts.

'Sure you're not jealous, George?' asked Ari.

'I've got my gorgeous Carla,' said George.

And thank God for that, thought Karen.

'Yeah, for five minutes if your previous form's anything to go by, Mr Slap and Tickle,' said Ari.

'Oh please,' said George.

During a previous Sunday Club session of The Game he'd made the mistake of revealing that his earliest childhood memory was his mother reading him the Mr Men books. And he'd confessed that his favourite was Mr Tickle. The friends had instantly seized on this; in view of his womanizing reputation, they'd dubbed him Mr Slap and Tickle.

'Maybe the gorgeous Carla's chucked you already. She hasn't rung you back,' continued Ari.

'Really, Ari,' said Marlena. Then turning to George, 'Take

no notice, sweetheart. But why don't you give her another call? Get the girl here and shut the lot of us up.'

George protested mildly, but ultimately agreed to try Carla's number again. With, as it turned out, the same result.

'Oh dear, I'm still getting your voicemail, baby, and I soooooo want to speak to you. Please come to Johnny's if you can. This lot are driving me mad. They're desperate to meet you. But don't be put off. They're all right, honest. All my love, baby-face. More kisses.'

After that, the entire group joined in poking fun at George.

'Listen, get off me, I'm sorry I said anything,' he exclaimed. 'Let's everybody tell the story of their true-love life-changing moment. Why the hell not?'

'Well, you won't be getting an answer of that sort from me,' said Michelle, her expression suddenly darkening. She'd been drinking quickly, knocking back the wine faster than the others, though nobody had noticed. She reached for a carafe and poured herself another glass. Her voice was hard and brittle when she spoke again.

'I haven't got a partner – bloody boring or otherwise. Mind you, come to think of it, meeting my ex was certainly life-changing. Or should that be life-destroying?'

'Bambina, bambina,' interrupted Alfonso. 'Let's not get too heavy, eh? C'mon, George, your turn. Clockwise round the table as usual. So let's see how exciting you can make your answer.'

George propped one elbow on the table, rested his chin on his hand, and made a great show of being deep in thought. Which he most certainly wasn't.

'I think it was probably my Hamlet in the final year at drama school . . .' he began.

'Yeah, it prepared you for panto and you've never looked back!' sniped Tiny.

'Oh, all right then, maybe it was my Rutger at the King's Head.'

'Your what, darling?' Marlena interjected.

'*Rutger*. Norwegian play. I was the eponymous lead. Thought you knew your theatre.'

'I do,' said Marlena.

'So, all right, it wasn't the most important play in the world, and it did only last a week in Islington, but I like to think I grew as an actor while I was playing it.'

'Oh, come on, George,' said Bob. 'Be serious. Give us a proper answer.'

'I am being serious. I'm a very serious actor. In fact every time I step onto a stage or in front of a camera it changes my life.'

'That's why he wears tights,' said Alfonso.

'I gave you an honest answer, man. I mean, I carried that play, everybody said so.'

'Butterfingers,' said Marlena, sparking another outbreak of laughter around the table.

'Oh, leave him alone,' said Billy. 'We all know you can never get any sense out of George.'

George smiled enigmatically. Or at least he hoped it was enigmatic. He had done what he liked to do, played what he considered to be his true role in life: he had entertained his friends, and at the same time wound them up a bit. He didn't mind being laughed at. He had, after all, set out to make them laugh. He enjoyed being part of the group. Although he would never publicly admit it, Sunday Club was actually very important to him. In spite of his flamboyant and confident demeanour, there was a deeply introverted side to George. He could never reveal his innermost thoughts to his friends. It wasn't in his nature. He liked to keep his hopes and his dreams to himself. He was what he was. And he saw no need to share his soul with anyone, that was all. But he sensed it was necessary to give just a little.

'All right,' he said. 'What really changed my life was learning how to deal with bullies. When I was a kid I seemed to attract bullying. And it felt like I had nobody to tell. Then I discovered that if I could make the bastards laugh it was all right. So I learned to be funny.'

'That's what you think you are, is it?' remarked Alfonso, but he was smiling.

'Yeah, there was one kid at school I taught a proper lesson to though . . .' George's voice tailed off.

'Go on then, tell us,' encouraged Alfonso.

'Oh, it's history. Hey, it must be your turn, Bob.'

Bob hesitated. He always felt he was the least amusing of the group. Sometimes he wondered why they bothered with him. George, Alfonso and Ari were sharp as tacks and being witty came as second nature to them. Tiny had a dry humour, a big belly laugh, and bucketloads of charisma. Billy, clever, cool Billy, was a natural conversationalist with a knack of almost always saying the right thing. Marlena was Marlena, legend on legs, she both looked and was extraordinary and when she spoke the entire room fell silent. Greg oozed old-fashioned cockney charm and sometimes was the funniest of them all. Karen was quieter and seemed more ordinary, but she too had a quick mind; Bob thought she was exceptionally bright and intelligent but deliberately played it down so as not to outshine Greg. Plus she was a great audience. Her laughter came easily and was irresistibly infectious. Michelle was young and so pretty she didn't really need any other attributes. Bob thought he must surely seem like a sad old man to them. He certainly felt like it that day. It should have been a special day. Always had been a special day. In the past.

Bob ran a hand over his close-shaven head; his thinning hair, once dark brown but now pepper and salt, had been cropped in that drastic way to hide the bald patches. Fortunately the look was quite fashionable.

'Spit it out, Bob,' said George.

'Sorry, it's Daniel's birthday today. His thirtieth. I'm a bit preoccupied. Probably shouldn't have come out . . .'

'We're glad you did, Bob,' said Karen.

Nine pairs of eyes, their expressions ranging from compassionate to plain embarrassed, stared at Bob. Most of them knew, more or less, why Daniel was a painful subject.

Bob had been a career soldier but had quit the army in order to bring up his only son after the boy's mother died of breast cancer not long after his birth. Danny was just seventeen and still at school when he'd fallen in love with a backpacking New Zealander, some years older. Out of the blue she'd announced that she was pregnant and on the same monumental day decreed that she was going home and taking Danny with her. Doe-eyed Dan, a bright boy who until then had seemed destined for university and a choice of illustrious careers, or so his father had hoped, went along with it at once. He would travel the world with the girl he loved and their unborn child, and nothing was going to stop him, not even the father who'd devoted his entire existence to him.

Thirteen years on, Bob still missed his son terribly. Danny's leaving had undoubtedly been a life-changing moment. But Bob didn't want to talk about that.

'It was the army, going through the first Gulf War, that changed my life,' he said. 'There was a lad killed – first death I saw. He wasn't much older than my Dan when he pissed off. I always felt I should have saved him – I mean, I was the lad's sergeant . . . Never the same after that.'

Marlena reached across the table and put her hand on Bob's.

'I'm sure you did all you could,' she said.

Bob smiled at her bleakly. 'Not enough though. I still think about it . . .'

'My old man was a squaddie,' remarked Greg, filling the silence. 'What was you in then, Bob?'

'Scots DG.'

'Hey, that's one tough outfit,' said Greg.

'The what?' queried Billy.

'Royal Scots Dragoon Guards,' said Bob.

'I thought they were all funny hats and skirts,' remarked George.

Greg turned to face him.

'Shut up, you prat,' he said mildly, then addressed Bob again.

'You were in the thick of it, then, in the Gulf, weren't you?'

'Yep, we sure were,' said Bob.

'Man,' said Greg. 'And you were an effin' sergeant. Respect, mate, respect.'

Bob smiled at him. You could see in his eyes that he was remembering something long forgotten, another life, another world.

Karen nudged Tiny. It was his turn.

'Everyone can guess mine, I expect,' he said. 'Finally accepting I was gay. I mean, who'd have thought, right?'

Tiny placed a hand on one hip and stuck out his elbow, camping it up.

The group giggled obediently.

Then Tiny turned towards Bob. The camp gone. Serious. Perhaps picking up on the mood of the night.

'And that meant losing my family, my kids – my missus never let me see 'em again – so I know how that feels, Bob. It was down to me though. I was the one who walked away.' Tiny paused. 'And then I threw in my all with this skinny little tyke.'

He wrapped an arm around Billy's narrow shoulders.

'Oh, sorry, not supposed to mention partners, are we? Tricky, though, when the fucker's sitting right by you, eh, Greg?'

Greg grinned and nodded. Karen addressed Billy then.

'So, how are you going to follow that?' she enquired.

'Well, by saying that it's much the same for me, of course,' Billy began, leaning back in his chair and looking as if he were about to make a speech.

'Is it fuck!' interrupted Tiny, his big bass voice reverberating around the restaurant, causing a nearby weekend dad to glower in the direction of the Sunday Club table. 'Would you believe I have to move out of the flat when his bloody mum and dad come to visit?'

The entire table erupted into cries of 'No!' and 'No way!'

'You're right, Tiny, nobody believes you,' said Ari. 'You're kidding, eh?'

'No, I fucking well am not,' said Tiny. 'Go on, Billy, tell 'em.'

Billy blushed and began fiddling with his moustache in earnest.

'Do I move out or do I not?' Tiny persisted.

'Well, I mean, we haven't got a lot of room, and . . .'

'Billy, you bastard, tell the truth. Your parents don't know that you're gay, nor that you live with me, do they?'

'Well, I'm sure they know, deep down,' Billy said.

Tiny harrumphed. 'Really? You've never effing told 'em!'

Billy coloured even more.

'Nor those precious fuckers you work with.'

'Well, yeah, but it's such a straight set-up at Geering Brothers; better to fit in and keep collecting the luncheon vouchers – you've always agreed with me on that, Tiny.'

'Oh yeah. And would it make any difference if I didn't?'

From around the table came cries of 'settle down' and 'domestic'.

'So after all that, come on, what is your life-changing moment, Billy?' asked Karen.

Billy didn't have an answer. He wished Tiny hadn't revealed that particular detail about their private life. It was all quite true, of course, and Billy was embarrassed. About himself, not Tiny. And angry with himself too. This was the twenty-first century, an era in which almost all the gay men and women he knew no longer felt the need to be secretive. In the UK equal rights were protected by law, civil partnerships were commonplace and same-sex marriage was surely on its way. Billy liked to give the impression of being a cool, slightly sardonic, very together, thoroughly modern guy. He was reasonably good-looking, reasonably well off financially, very successful in his work, and successful, too, by and large, in his relationship with Tiny. Billy worshipped the ground that rocked as the big guy walked on it. Which made it even more ridiculous that he did not always publicly recognize the existence of the man he loved and shared everything with.

The truth was that Billy had never managed to become totally comfortable with his own sexuality. If he had he would tell his parents, and take the risk at work too. Surely he would. But he could never quite bring himself to do so, and that annoyed and bewildered him even more than it did Tiny.

Billy, born into an achingly conventional suburban family, had been a confused and awkward teenager. He was all too aware that, although appearances were totally to the contrary, he had in so many ways merely grown into a confused and awkward man. And it infuriated him.

He didn't have the strength to be witty.

'Well, obviously my life-changing moment was meeting Tiny,' he said. 'Only I'm not allowed to say that, apparently.'

'Situation normal, then, as far as you're concerned,' said Tiny.

What Tiny had not revealed to the group was that Billy's parents were due to visit that week, and he and Billy had quarrelled about it shortly before leaving home. Tiny was still angry, largely because he was so hurt by Billy's inability to give him full recognition. That was why he'd blurted out this aspect of their life together which until now had always been just between him and Billy. And he'd no intention of letting Billy off the hook. Not yet, anyway.

'Can't quite bring yourself to tell anyone about your big slice of black arse, can you, darling?'

He softened the remark by squeezing Billy's shoulder and giving the smaller man a peck on the cheek.

Nonetheless, the tension between the two was obvious, not least because it was unusual. Karen was quick to move on around the table.

It was Alfonso's turn. The Italian, his beard immaculate, his black hair slicked back with gel, had a penchant for dressing formally and was the only man at the table wearing a tailored jacket. He always seemed to be rather out of his time, and had once been described by Marlena as a kind of debonair gigolo who belonged in 1930s Cannes. The description seemed apt enough, but nobody really knew what made the Fonz tick. They weren't even entirely sure whether he was gay or straight. Alfonso's habit, both at work and at play, was to reveal as little as possible about his private life. However, his manner was such that nobody ever really noticed.

Alfonso knew what his most life-changing moment had been. It was when his father had died when he was in his mid-teens. His mother made him promise he would never leave her. And the crazy thing was, he never had. He'd threatened to, promised himself that he would, the next day or the next week. But he'd never quite been able to do so. Every day, he trekked back to Dagenham to the little terraced house they shared; unless he was on late shift, in which case he stayed at his gran's place in King's Cross. And there were other aspects of his life that he considered to be even more embarrassing than shuttling back and forth between his mum and his gran. It didn't exactly fit the profile he was trying to cultivate, that of the most dashing waiter in London.

Sometimes he wondered how he managed to keep his dark secret from the Sunday Club. It certainly took a lot of work. Over the years, he had developed protecting his privacy into a fine art, evolving into a brilliant 'make-up' artist: tall tales emerged from him like water gushing from a bottomless well, all in the name of entertainment. So far as the others were concerned, he was perpetually caught up in the social whirl, forever on the verge of moving into a new flat, or staying with unspecified friends while he looked for somewhere new. He envied Ari, who was quite open about his living arrangements and didn't seem bothered when the gang kidded him about still living with his mum. But then, why should it bother him? Ari was much younger than Alfonso and actually had his own apartment in his parents' large and rather grand London house.

Tonight, Alfonso found he could not be bothered to come up with an entertaining diversion. And so he told the truth.

'Getting my job at the Vine,' he said.

'Oh, so so boring, darling,' said Marlena.

'Yeah, well, I haven't led the life you have.'

'Is that a veiled insult or a tragic complaint?'

'Both, probably. Anyway, it did change my life. I found out how much fun being a waiter could be. Before that, I was at the Reform Club. God knows how I ended up there, so bloody stuffy. Now I'm pouring water for Madonna.'

'Thrilling,' interjected George. 'Come on, Marlena. Brighten things up. Let's hear yours.'

'I suppose it was crashing my motorbike, if I were to tell the truth,' responded the older woman, surprising herself.

That had indeed been a life-changing moment, but not something she'd talked about nor even thought about for many years. Marlena had led a roller-coaster of an existence with many life-changing moments to choose from. A good number of those were best forgotten, but there were also plenty she liked to remember, and surely everyone had secrets? Marlena was not a woman who dwelled on the past, who allowed herself regrets. The only reason her motorbike accident had come into her mind so vividly was because of a TV documentary she had watched the previous evening. She'd been kept awake half the night by troubling dreams of the incident and its consequences. Not that she had any intention of sharing that with her friends.

'Crashing your motorbike?' queried Greg. 'You had a motorbike?'

'I certainly did. A Triumph Norton. I'd had it sprayed shocking pink.'

'Good God, when was that?' asked Karen.

'Oh, back in the Dark Ages, darling. It must be thirty-odd years since I got rid of it.'

'But why?'

'Finally grew up, I suppose. Realized it was too dangerous. I always rode too fast – but then, that was the whole point of it really.'

'I thought you thrived on danger, darling,' remarked Alfonso.

'There's danger, and then there's danger,' replied Marlena enigmatically.

27

'How did crashing your bike change your life?' persisted Karen.

'I was on my way to visit my sister in Scotland – hadn't seen her for years, we'd been brought up apart. Then fate intervened and I never made it . . .'

Marlena seemed lost in memories until Alfonso's voice brought her back to earth.

'Were you badly hurt?'

'Not really. Barely at all, in fact.' Marlena paused and looked down at the table. 'It was life-changing because it confronted me with reality and marked the end of a lot of silly dreams I suddenly knew I was never going to realize . . .'

She stopped again abruptly. There was silence around the table, unbroken until she chided the others: 'Oh come on. You've got better things to do than listen to an old woman like me make a fool of herself. Ari, what about you? It must be your turn. I'm sure I jumped my place.'

Ari looked blank.

'I don't think I've had a life-changing moment,' he said.

The truth of it hit him as he spoke. Sometimes Ari's entire existence seemed empty to him, which was perhaps why he was inclined to fill the hours with alcohol and cocaine. He made himself sip his second large Hendricks slowly. Sunday Club was a low-key evening out for Ari, but, as with George, it had become a curiously important fixture in his life. It was one of the few occasions when he tried to stay moderately sober, in order that his behaviour would not attract attention, so that he could at least appear to fit in with the others. Ari had many acquaintances and hangers-on, but few friends. He considered the regular Sunday group to be the nearest he had to friends. Not that he could face them without a pre-supper line or two before leaving home. Indeed, he couldn't imagine being out and about without that.

'Maybe that's what's wrong in my life,' Ari continued. 'Nothing has ever changed really. I even live at home. Can't match my dad, that's probably my problem. Dad came over with my grandmother in 1972, refugees from Idi Amin's Uganda. He built his business from scratch, starting with a street stall then a corner shop. Now he trades all over the world. He just assumed that I would go into the business with him, so that's what I've done, more or less. '

'Where was his shop?' asked Greg.

'Wanstead, first of many.'

'He must have been some man to have turned that into what he's got now.'

Ari nodded. 'He was only seventeen when they arrived,' he said. 'And he did it all on his own; my gran never learned to speak English and my grandfather was already dead. I haven't a clue how he did it. Beyond me, I'm afraid.'

He took a big drink of his Hendricks, and allowed the strangely aromatic gin to drown his brief moment of introspection.

'So there you are, I'm just a spoiled rich boy.'

'Yep,' said Greg.

'We love you, though,' said Karen.

'And I'd hardly describe your living arrangements as classic shacked-up-with-mum-and-dad,' said Bob. 'You've got an apartment bigger than most people's houses. That potted palm I got for you looked so bloody lost in it, I had to go back and get you a bigger one.'

'Bigger the pad, better the party,' said Ari.

'Thought you'd been banned from all of that since your arrest,' murmured Alfonso.

'It was only the tiny weeniest itsy bitsy soupçon of coke,' said Ari.

'Ummm, and when are you getting some more?' asked George.

'I didn't hear that,' said Michelle.

'You haven't shared your life-changing moment, Michelle,' said Alfonso. 'You've told us what it wasn't, but not what it is. Come on, let's have it.'

Michelle made herself smile. Though Bob wasn't aware of it, the two of them had something in common that Sunday. For both it was an anniversary connected to someone who'd caused them much unhappiness. In Bob's case the birthday of the son he felt he had lost, in Michelle's the anniversary of her marriage to the man who had abandoned her. They'd married young, and it would have been their tenth, known as the tin anniversary – which Michelle thought rather appropriate as tin was cheap and buckled easily under pressure. Like Bob, she was feeling uncharacteristically maudlin that evening. She'd thought she was over the hurt, but days like this reminded her that the pain was still with her, as it would be, she sometimes believed, for as long as she lived.

'We might not be allowed to have meeting our partner as our answer, but leaving them ought to count,' she growled. 'Or in my case, being left by the fucker.'

'Oh God,' said George. 'We are a cheery bloody lot tonight, aren't we?'

'Fair enough, Michelle,' said Karen, ignoring him. 'We all know how much it changed your life when your Phil walked out on you. New job, new town, new friends – not so much a change of life as a brand-new one, eh?'

'Too fucking right,' muttered Michelle through gritted teeth.

'Oh, come on, it's not all bad, is it?'

'No,' said Michelle. She paused for a moment, thinking things through. 'No, of course it's not,' she continued. 'And working for the Met does kind of beat being a Dorset plod. Or it would, if I wasn't stuck in effing Traffic.'

She spat out the last sentence, but then lapsed into maudlin again: 'It would have been nice to have been able to make a choice, that's all.'

'You did: you chose to come to London,' said Karen.

'Maybe. But I didn't have much choice about leaving the town I'd lived in all my life and the force I'd joined when I was eighteen, did I? My bloody ex not only moved in with his girl-friend at the end of the same street, he worked in the same bloody office as me. I could see his effing desk from mine. If I hadn't moved away, I might have damned well killed him.' She paused. 'Or her – smug bitch.'

'Surely not? And you sworn to uphold the law and all.' Marlena, full of mock severity, peered at Michelle over the rim of her half-moon spectacles.

'I dunno,' responded Michelle. 'I'd definitely have gone barking mad.'

'No danger of that now though,' said Marlena, dry as dust. 'You've certainly found sanity with us.'

Michelle managed a small smile again. 'Would have been different if my dad was still alive,' she said. 'He'd have beaten the hell out of Phil.'

'Bit of a bruiser, your old man then?' enquired Greg.

'You might say that,' responded Karen. 'He was a DI in the Met. Old style. Detective Inspector Dave English. Nobody messed with my dad, I can tell you.'

'Crikey,' said George. 'Come on, Karen. Give us yours.'

Karen didn't hesitate. She was perhaps the most straight-forward of the group. She certainly appeared to be. And, after a couple of drinks, totally caught up in the question game, she'd

more or less forgotten all about that silly lurking embarrassment concerning George. Her family was her entire world, she
told herself, and always had been. She glanced across the table
at George. Apart from that brief exchange upon her arrival he
had taken little notice of her. There was no reason why he should,
of course, and it would have embarrassed her further if he had.
She still couldn't believe what she'd done. And if George hadn't
kept his head, it would have been even worse.

'Having my children,' she said. 'My family. It's all that matters
to me. You see, when I was a kid things were pretty bad. Me
mum was always great, but . . .'

'But what, Karen darling?' asked Marlena.

Karen glanced at Greg.

He took her hand. 'Karen's dad went to prison when she
was four. He was a drinker, killed a man in a fight. Got himself
sent down and ended up dying in jail. That's why I gotta be a
good boy, eh, baby?'

'You better had.'

'That's quite a story,' said Ari. He looked around the table.
'Any of you lot know that before?' he asked.

They all shook their heads.

'I try not to think about it,' said Karen. 'It was just Greg
being so soft that got me going . . .'

'Hey, Michelle,' said George. 'Maybe your old man was the
one who arrested Karen's old man.'

'That isn't funny, George,' said Marlena.

'It's OK,' said Karen. 'I grew up with my dad inside. It can't
hurt me any more. Like I said, my children changed everything
for me. I think any mother would say the same. One minute
you're a selfish cow thinking only of yourself and your own
problems, and the next you have these little people with your
face and you realize you'd sacrifice anything for . . .'

Karen stopped, aware of Michelle's eyes boring into her. Abruptly the young policewoman rose from the table.

'Must go to the Ladies,' she said.

Her head was down as she hurried away, the high heels she liked to wear when she was out of uniform tap-tapping on the wooden floor. Karen thought she saw her shoulders begin to shake. Michelle had never made any secret of her deep-seated desire to be a mother, and how that unfulfilled longing had been her greatest regret when her marriage ended. But the woman was young enough not to be worrying about her biological clock for some years, and bright and attractive enough to surely be able to find the right man sooner or later. All the same, Karen kicked herself for being so tactless.

Though the men around the table did not appear to have noticed anything amiss, it hadn't escaped Marlena's observant gaze.

'Well done, old girl,' she murmured softly to Karen.

'Oh fuck,' said Karen.

I made my excuses as we left the restaurant, needing to be on my own. Fast. Not only that, I needed to be out in the open, to get some air into my lungs, to let myself be swallowed up by the sounds and smells of the night.

I hurried down Wellington Street and across the Strand towards Waterloo Bridge where I took the steps to the left, by Somerset House, leading down to the Embankment. The city was quiet, peaceful even, or maybe it just seemed that way compared to what was raging inside my head.

I crossed over to the riverside and leaned over the river wall near Temple Pier. It was spring high tide, and I could see the Thames lapping against the tall stone balustrades. A police barge went by, travelling at speed, sending up a sizeable wave in its wake. Water splashed against the wall and a drop or two hit my face. My skin felt so hot I was almost surprised it didn't turn to steam on contact.

I stayed there, hoping for another splash to cool me down, but it didn't come. Eventually I pulled myself away and sat on a bench under a plane tree. It was the last Sunday in February and the branches were bare, but it seemed darker and more secluded there under the tree's spreading arms. I felt in some way shielded, protected.

It wasn't a cold night. If anything, it was quite warm, one of those spells of good weather in what had been a bitter winter. I'd hoped the air would be cold enough to cool my burning skin. But it would have to have been well below zero to do that.

I sat there for ages, trying to get things straight in my head, to make some sense of the thoughts racing round my brain.

There could be no doubt, could there? Had I misunderstood? Was it possible that this was sheer coincidence, totally unconnected to anything in my past? Was I trying to make a connection where none existed?

I don't know how long I sat there, going over those words again and again. The more I thought about it, the more certain I was that, far from misunderstanding, I had finally understood.

And now that I understood, I had no choice but to act.

My skin seemed to be getting hotter until I felt as if I was on fire.

In spite of everything, against all the odds, I'd made a life for myself. Nobody knew what I was. Nor what I might have been. Even I didn't know that. All I knew was that I had been turned into a creature like no other. Like some kind of alien that passes for human. As if there was another being inhabiting my body, controlling my impulses.

Whenever I'd watch sci-fi programmes or films like Close

Encounters, *I'd see those humans whose souls had been invaded and think of them as kindred spirits. For almost as long as I can remember, I've been wrestling with that alien being within – the creature that made its home inside me, uninvited and beyond my control.*

There had been times when it all got too much and I gave up the fight, let that dark side lead me where it chose. I ought to regret those times, but I can't. It was inevitable, given the unbearable pressure, the strain of trying to contain it.

That pressure was building within me again, with every moment that I sat there under the tree. And inevitably it would be released, just as it had been in the past. Soon. I knew that. I'd known it in the restaurant, the words of the others washing over me. Somehow I'd kept up a pretence of joining in despite the voice screaming inside my head. But then, I was used to pretending, keeping up appearances.

Calm now, my skin once again cool to the touch, I got up from the bench. My mind was clear, all doubt removed. From this moment on I would be following the path of my destiny, although my route would not be as others might expect. It would be designed to create the maximum confusion before I allowed my true purpose to become apparent. But there would be no turning back. Not until it was settled. All of it. My misery avenged and my honour restored. Finally.

three

The changing rooms at Shannon's Health and Fitness Club in Covent Garden are situated at one end of the building and the swimming pool at the other. This means swimmers have to walk right past the gym along a glass-walled corridor.

George, being a bit of a show-off, rather liked that. Conscious of having caught the attention of a girl pumping hard on an exercise bike beyond the glass wall, he allowed himself a sideways peek. She had small breasts and thick legs and was not nearly pretty enough to interest him.

All the same he pulled his shoulders back and sucked in his stomach muscles as he walked. George could never resist posing. He knew he had a good body, its muscle definition emphasized by the perma-tan he maintained with regular visits to a tanning shop.

He was returning to the changing rooms having swum his regular mile up and down Shannon's lap pool. It was much cooler in the corridor than in the pool area and he had to tense his muscles in order not to shiver. Water droplets stood up on his shoulders and upper back, but he never bothered to dry off until he reached his locker. Unlike most swimmers he did not even carry a towel or a robe. He told himself that was because he preferred his towel to stay warm and dry while he shed most of the excess water during the short walk.

He also had just about enough self-awareness to recognize what an exhibitionist he was. Why bother working out if you couldn't enjoy showing yourself off in skimpy scarlet Speedos?

Fleetingly he looked down at the satisfactory bulge in the front of his Speedos and nearly bumped into two fully dressed men who were walking towards him, probably on their way to the exit. They turned out to be a gay couple George knew vaguely, and after calling his apologies as he carried on along the corridor he couldn't help glancing back. The two of them were both still looking at him, as he had known they would be. George flashed them what he considered to be his most enigmatic smile.

George frequently attracted the attention of men as well as women. He wasn't gay, but sometimes indulged in playing up to those who were, just as he rewarded the attentions of un-attractive women by appearing to flirt with them. It was the least he could do if someone was treating his body with the respect and admiration he felt it deserved.

He brushed a few strands of wet black hair from his fore-head, feeling invigorated, as he always did after his regular Thursday workout and swim. By the time he reached the changing room, on what had so far been a thoroughly unre-markable visit to the health centre, there was only one other regular present: an older man with a belly the gym seemed unable to diminish. George knew the guy by sight but had never deigned to acknowledge him. Instead he busied himself removing the safety pin and key which he'd attached to his Speedos and then unlocked the door to his locker. He reached inside for his towel.

There was no towel. George peered into the locker.

'What the fuck's happened to my stuff?' he muttered.

The older man, perched on a bench in the far corner, broke off from lacing up his shoes and shot George a curious look.

'I definitely put a towel in there and now it's gone,' said George.

He leaned forward and began to rummage with both hands. There was something at the back of the locker, but his clothes were missing. And his wallet, his door keys and his mobile phone.

'Oh fuck, all my stuff's gone!' George continued, still rummaging.

He could see a bundle of brightly coloured cloth that had been crammed into a corner of the locker.

George pulled it out, shook it, and held it up before him. It was a garment of some sort. It took the form of two large orange discs held together with black ribbon, and had matching elongated orange arms.

It was a Mr Tickle suit. George recognized it at once.

By now he had the full attention of the other occupant of the changing room, whose mouth had dropped open. George glowered at him.

The orange disc that formed the front of the Mr Tickle suit bore the image of a face sketched in black. The face smiled gleefully at George.

George did not smile back.

The man with the belly didn't stick around to offer George any assistance. He might have done so, and indeed at one point looked as if he were about to, but the openly hostile looks from the man with the Mr Tickle suit made him think better of it.

George hadn't been able to help himself. He'd been hostile to the man simply because he was there.

After the man left, scurrying through the door without a backward glance, George held the ridiculous costume up in front of him. It would surely be far too small for him to wear even if he was daft enough to try to do so.

George shivered. He was beginning to feel very cold. He wasn't sure what to do next. He supposed he should make his way to reception. But even he was not enough of an exhibitionist to be comfortable in the reception area, which had windows onto Endel Street, wearing only his skimpy Speedos. He desperately needed something with which to cover himself. He looked around the changing room. Sometimes towels were left lying about. Tonight there were no towels.

And as it was so late in the evening no further gym members had entered the changing room, nor were likely to do so, which George in any case considered to be a mixed blessing.

There was nothing else for it. He wrapped the Mr Tickle suit around his body and set off.

The trouble with Shannon's was that there were mirrors everywhere. Usually this did not bother George. Indeed, he rather liked it. This particular evening was very different.

Even before he left the changing room George had seen his reflection and was well aware of how ridiculous he looked. Not that he needed a mirror to be sure of that.

He ran up the stairs to reception and hovered at the door. Justin, who more or less ran the place most evenings, sensed his presence and turned round to face him.

Justin's long, lean slightly hangdog face expressed first surprise and then disbelief. Finally he started to laugh. George had never seen Justin laugh before. Indeed, Justin gave little indication of having a sense of humour at all. He wasn't the type. Or at least he hadn't seemed to be the type. Now it turned out he was a bit of a star in the laughing department. And the misfortune of another human being proved quite irresistible.

Great howls of laughter came from Justin. Tears of mirth

rolled down his normally pallid cheeks which turned distinctly pink. His body, long and lean like his face, bent involuntarily forward until it formed a right angle with his legs. And all the time Justin stared at George.

George stared back.

Justin kept on laughing.

'That's enough, Justin,' said George eventually.

Justin ignored him and carried on laughing.

'You're hysterical,' said George.

Justin ignored him.

'Stop!' yelled George at the top of his voice.

Justin, it seemed, was on the receiving end of his second surprise of the evening. He'd been shouted at. He stopped.

'Right,' said George. 'You can presumably guess what's bloody happened. Some bastard's nicked my clothes, my phone, my wallet, even my bloody towel. I need to use a phone, and I need something to wear. Have you got any dressing gowns anywhere?'

Justin shook his head. 'We only do towels,' he said.

George glared at him. A few months previously in a bid to cut costs Shannon's had stopped supplying complimentary towels, thus encouraging members to bring their own. And those that could still be acquired for a pound a go were little more than hand towels, in George's opinion.

'Well, get me two or three of them, then,' said George.

Justin hesitated.

'Now, Justin!' commanded George.

Justin passed George two towels. George threw the Mr Tickle suit to the ground, wrapped one of the towels around his shoulders and the other around his waist, thanking God he was just slim enough to be able to do so.

Clearly, he needed help. His first thought had been to call

Greg, who had a van and moved around central London with both speed and apparent ease. But Greg had no way of getting into George's flat. Bob, on the other hand, hopefully still had the door key from when he'd looked after George's collection of potted orchids while he was away in panto over Christmas. Without asking Justin's permission, George used the club phone to call Bob, thankful that he could remember his phone number. To his relief, Bob answered straight away. George explained briefly that his clothes and valuables had been stolen from Shannon's changing rooms.

He didn't mention the Mr Tickle suit. And after Bob had murmured the appropriate commiserations he cut to the chase.

'Look, you do still have my door key, don't you?' he asked.

'Yes, I suppose so.' Bob had obviously guessed what was coming next and did not sound very enthusiastic.

'Are you at home?'

'Yes,' said Bob.

'Well, look, could you nip round to mine and pick up some clothes for me?' George continued doggedly.

'What about that girlfriend of yours – Carla. Couldn't she do it? I'm having my supper.'

'I don't ever let the women in my life have a key to my place. It gives the wrong impression.'

'Oh, George, you're impossible.'

'Please, Bob.' George put a long drawn-out emphasis on the word 'please'. 'I'm begging you, mate.'

'I'll have to find the key first,' muttered Bob. 'It must be here somewhere . . .'

'I bloody well hope so,' said George.

'Hold on,' said Bob.

George held on. He could hear footsteps and rummaging sounds. After what seemed like ages, Bob came back on the line.

'Got it,' he said.

'Thank you, God,' said George.

'All right,' said Bob, positively enough, though George was pretty sure he heard him sigh. 'Soon as I've finished eating I'll head for your place. I should be with you in forty-five minutes or so, maybe less.'

George fervently hoped it would be significantly less but didn't think it wise to say so.

Instead he just thanked Bob, adding: 'You'll bring your key with you, won't you? My keys have gone, along with everything else. I'll need yours to get into my own home.'

'What do you think I would do with it? Throw it away?'

Bob ended the call before George could think of a suitable response.

While he waited, George sat down on one of the benches at the back of the reception area. Justin made a big fuss of clearing up the place. He picked up the Mr Tickle suit from the floor and spread it carefully over George's bare knees. The scanty Shannon's towel around George's waist didn't reach nearly that far.

'Don't want you to catch cold, do we?' Justin remarked.

George wasn't sure if Justin was being solicitous or sarcastic, but he didn't have the strength to respond. In any case the Mr Tickle suit was actually quite warm over his legs, and he was still shivering.

He fixed his eyes on the big round clock that dominated the wall above the reception desk, willing its hands to move faster. The last stragglers filing out of the gym could not fail to notice George and his Mr Tickle suit. Every single one gave him a long hard look. There was usually silence as they passed but audible tittering by the time they reached the double doors leading onto the street.

Justin began to huff and puff, reminding George almost by the minute just how long he was staying beyond his time.

George in turn reminded Justin frostily that he had been burgled from a Shannon's locker, and Justin had better watch himself as George would certainly be questioning the club's security and quite possibly filing a claim.

'In any case, what exactly do you expect me to do?' asked George. 'Trot off down Endel Street wearing a Mr Tickle suit?'

'Oh no,' said Justin. 'I wouldn't want you to look ridiculous, George.'

George watched him mince his way back to the counter. He thought Justin might be the only gay man he'd ever met who really did mince, and that the term had probably been invented for him. Whatever happened to a bit of respect for the customer, George wondered.

It was, however, well known that Justin didn't do respect. On a good day his offhand manner could be amusing. Right then George would have liked to throttle him, but his fingers were numb with the cold.

So instead he sat still and waited.

Bob arrived precisely forty-three minutes later. George knew that because he'd been virtually counting the seconds. It had been a very long forty-three minutes.

With great relief he watched Bob, holding a Tesco carrier bag, burst through the double doors. Literally. Bob caught a toe in the door jamb, dropped the bag and went flying, only just recovering his balance enough to prevent himself falling full length onto the tiled floor.

'Shit,' said Bob. Then his eyes focused on George.

'Oh my God,' he said. 'What is that you have wrapped round you?'

'What does it fucking look like?' asked George.

'It looks like a Mr Tickle suit to me. My Dan used to love those Roger Hargreaves books,' said Bob. 'Oh my God, you're wearing a Mr Tickle suit!'

'Not exactly wearing,' said George.

'Near enough,' responded Bob, starting to laugh.

George glowered at him. 'I hope those are my clothes in the bag you've thrown on the floor – and if so, do you think I could have them?' he said. 'Now!'

He realized he was snapping and had raised his voice. He couldn't help himself.

'So that's the thanks a good friend gets for bailing you out, is it?' enquired Bob. But he didn't look offended. By then he was laughing so much he could hardly get the words out. Pretty much like Justin.

'This is not fucking funny,' snarled George.

'Oh yes it fucking is,' responded Bob.

Bob kicked the carrier bag across to George, who grabbed it, removed the jeans and sweater Bob had brought, and hastily pulled them on over his still-damp Speedos. There was also a leather jacket. He slipped that on too, grateful for its heavy warmth.

Then he turned his attention back to the laughing Bob.

'I did tell you that my phone and my wallet including all my credit cards are also missing, didn't I?' enquired George frostily. 'Oh, and my door key. I shall have to spend the rest of this evening cancelling my cards and getting a locksmith in. I'm so glad you find that funny.'

Bob made a big effort to pull himself together.

'Of course I don't, George,' he said. 'It's just, seeing you – you of all people, you vain bastard – wrapped up in a Mr Tickle suit . . . well, nobody could help having a bit of a laugh, could they?'

He stifled a final giggle.

George glared at him and returned his attention to the carrier bag. He looked up at Bob.

'Tell me you brought a pair of shoes?' he enquired.

'Eh?' responded Bob. 'What?'

'Shoes, Bob. Obviously you brought me a pair of shoes, didn't you?'

'Uh, no, I'm not sure that I did, actually. I sort of didn't think of it . . .'

Bob let his voice fade lamely away.

George glowered and headed for the door, barefoot. Bob followed in silence.

George ignored Justin, who was leaning against the reception desk watching proceedings with interest.

'And goodnight and thank you to you too,' said Justin.

George still ignored him as he slammed the big double doors shut. Bob, right behind him, only narrowly avoided being smashed in the face. Bob wasn't having a lot of luck with those doors.

'Always remember, no good turn will remain unpunished,' Bob muttered to himself.

It was the middle of March, 2013, the coldest March in fifty years, and at 10 p.m. the temperature outside Shannon's was already below freezing. As George stepped onto the pavement his bare feet did an involuntary dance. It felt as if he was walking on blocks of ice. He gritted his teeth and carried on.

'Thank you, Bob, for stopping everything and helping me out,' Bob said. 'It was very kind of you, Bob. Not everyone is lucky enough to have a friend like you. I really can't thank you . . .'

George ignored Bob too.

*

Two days later, on Saturday morning, George took receipt of a large parcel sent by post. It contained his stolen clothes, his phone, his shoes, his credit cards and his door keys. Nothing was missing. There was also a card bearing a picture of the distinctive Mr Tickle. Inside was a brief typed message.

Thanks for the loan, it said. *If you could return my suit at your earliest convenience the entire Tickle family would be most grateful. You can Google my address.*

George called Bob to tell him the news. And he read him the Mr Tickle message.

'Just somebody's idea of a joke, then,' said Bob. 'Anyway, I'm very happy you got your stuff back. Do I get a thank you, now, by the way?'

'Of course you do,' said George. 'You get a bloody ginormous great thank you, mate. I sent you a note yesterday, actually. You not got it yet? A thank you and a sorry. I really am sorry I was so moody.'

'Ummm,' said Bob just a tad grudgingly. 'I suppose that's all right then.'

'Oh, Bob, honestly, you should try sitting in the foyer of Shannon's wearing fuck-all but a Mr Tickle suit. And with Justin on top effing form.'

'I'd rather not, if you don't mind, old boy,' said Bob.

'You're a good judge,' said George. 'It's weird though. You should see this parcel. Everything neatly folded and carefully packed. Do you want to come over and see it, Bob?'

'Not really, George. No.'

'Right . . .' George paused. 'I don't suppose you have any idea who pulled this stunt, do you?'

'Nope,' said Bob.

'Like you said, mate, someone who thought it was one hilarious joke,' continued George. 'Mind you, you seemed to find it pretty funny.'

'George, anyone would have found that sight funny.'

'Well, yes, I know, but—'

'No buts, you stupid bastard. You're not about to accuse me of having nicked your stuff and set you up, are you?'

'No, no, it's just . . . well, it must be one of our lot, mustn't it. Surely?'

'Why? The way you treat the women in your life, I'd say it was more likely to be one of your exes getting their own back.'

'Yeah, but only you lot know I liked Mr Tickle when I was a kid. The Game, remember?' George couldn't remember which members of the group had been present when he told them about his mum reading him *Mr Tickle* at bedtime. They hadn't played The Game the last two Sundays. The last time had been over three weeks ago, that night the entire group were together and it had ended up with Billy and Tiny getting into a domestic and Michelle storming off to the loo in tears. Hardly surprising then that nobody had suggested they play The Game again.

Realizing Bob was still hanging on at the other end of the phone, he added: 'I'm sure I've never told anyone else. And I wish I'd never let it slip at Sunday Club – Mr fucking Slap and Tickle indeed.'

'Suits you though,' said Bob, chuckling.

'You sure it wasn't you, mate?'

'Fuck off,' said Bob. 'I have better things to do than spend my time winding you up.'

He hung up.

George hoped he hadn't offended him too much. He was fond of Bob.

Then he considered what he should do next. Probably he should do nothing. But he couldn't stop himself. He was convinced all the friends would already know about the Mr Tickle incident. Bob wouldn't have been able to resist spreading the news.

Indeed, Michelle and Marlena had called the previous day to express concern and ask if there'd been anything they could do to help.

But he'd felt that both of them had been stifling laughter, particularly Marlena.

And when Michelle had asked him if he'd reported the theft to the police he'd assumed she was winding him up. But it turned out she'd been quite serious.

'Insurance, George,' she said. 'You'll need a crime number.'

Good advice, obviously, which somehow he never did get around to taking. Now there was no need to. However, the thought occurred to him that Michelle, who was after all a police officer, might have taken matters into her own hands.

He didn't think she would have done, but all the same he decided to give her a call.

She answered her mobile straight away.

'George, are you OK?'

He told her about his stuff being returned.

'Oh,' she said. 'All's well that ends well, I suppose. So it was just a stupid prank then.'

'You can say that again,' said George. 'The stupid bit anyway. Who could be that stupid, I wonder?'

'You're not accusing me, are you?' asked Michelle, just as Bob had done earlier. 'Is that why you're calling me, you bugger?'

'No,' said George quickly. Perhaps too quickly.

'I am a police officer, you know.'

'Yeah, that's why I thought of you first,' George fired back.

'Oh ha bloody ha,' said Michelle.

'Yeah. Yeah. But honestly, Michelle, I just said to Bob, I'm sure nobody outside of Sunday Club knows about Mr Tickle being my childhood favourite,' George continued, serious again. 'So it's one of our lot having a laugh. Who else could it be?'

'How do I know?' queried Michelle. 'Anyway, good job you can take a joke, isn't it?'

There was a pause.

'Yes,' said George, forcing himself to sound as relaxed as he could.

'You can take a joke, George, can't you?'

''Course I can,' said George.

'Right. Will we see you at Sunday Club tomorrow?'

'Yes. Well, maybe. I'm not sure.'

'Hope so,' said Michelle.

George did not turn up at Johnny's Place the following evening. Neither did Alfonso, who had a Sunday shift at the Vine. Nor Ari, who was on a three-line whip for a family dinner.

Among the seven who did attend there was only one topic of conversation. The prank, as they saw it, that had been played on George.

Bob told his version of the story in full, even though he'd already called most of the group. Grateful to have the opportunity to be entertaining for once, he made sure he told the story well too. By the time he'd reached the point where a half-naked George was sitting in the foyer of Shannon's wrapped in little more than a Mr Tickle suit everyone around the table was roaring with laughter. And Bob was thoroughly enjoying himself. He thought maybe he could be funny after all, provided he had a good enough tale to tell.

Tiny laughed so much he looked as if he might burst. Michelle said even though she was a copper, and technically a crime had been committed, this was definitely the biggest laugh she'd had since her Phil had walked out on her.

Marlena got the giggles and very nearly choked when a mouthful of braised lamb shank went down the wrong way. However, it was she, upon recovering some composure, who eventually counselled caution.

'I'm not sure George is taking it all that well,' she said. 'And I don't suppose it's a coincidence that he hasn't turned up today. I don't like to think of him being upset.'

'Nope,' said Greg. 'None of us do, I'm sure. It's just . . . it would be George, wouldn't it? We all know what he's like – prissy bastard. And left with nothing to wear but a Mr Tickle suit? I mean, nobody could help finding that bloody funny, could they?'

'Of course it's funny, and I've laughed as much as anyone around this table,' said Marlena. 'But one has to be so careful with practical jokes. They don't always seem like jokes to the victims . . .'

'Bloody hell, Marlena,' interjected Greg. 'George is no victim. He's George.'

That brought another laugh.

'But who is the comic genius who played this wondrous prank on the poor bastard?' asked Billy. 'That's what I want to know.'

The group stopped laughing and began to look at each other. Each face registered only blank innocence.

'Oh, come on,' said Billy. 'It has to be one of us, doesn't it? Surely. George seems certain of it, anyway. One of us on a mega wind-up. Greg, I reckon it was you. There's always a bit of edge between you and George. I reckon you thought you'd really land him in it and have a laugh at the same time.'

Greg held up both hands, palms outwards. 'Not me,' he said. 'Scout's honour.'

'Yeah,' said Billy. 'Like you were ever a bloody scout!'

Greg shrugged. 'And you were, I suppose,' he said. 'Mind you, come to think of it, would be a smorgasbord to you, wouldn't it?'

'Boys in shorts, lovely,' said Billy.

'In spite of that dubious assertion and whatever it does or doesn't tell us about your character, I presume you're maintaining your innocence in the matter in question?' queried Marlena.

'''Course I bloody am.'

Billy looked around him enquiringly. 'So is anyone owning up?' he asked, without sounding as if he expected an affirmative answer.

In turn everyone at the table denied responsibility.

'It could be our absent friends,' suggested Michelle.

'Umm, Alfonso or Ari,' mused Marlena. 'I don't think Ari has it in him, and I swear to God the Fonz fancies George gutless. Have you seen the way he looks at him?'

Karen grinned. 'Who says Fonz is gay? Not him! Come on, Marlena, your claws are showing.'

She glanced towards her husband. 'You sure it wasn't you, Greg?' she asked. 'Right up your street I'd say.'

'And that from his nearest and dearest,' remarked Bob.

'Boys and girls,' said Greg. 'If it were me, I'd shout it from the rafters. I'd be fucking pleased to bits with myself.'

'He's got a point. He'd be so full of himself, no way would he be able to keep shtum,' said Bob.

'Yep,' agreed Billy.

'I wish I'd thought of it,' said Tiny.

'Yeah,' said Billy. 'Come to think of it, any one of us would be proud to admit responsibility, wouldn't we, sweetheart?'

Tiny smiled his assent.

Marlena glanced at Karen. Karen shrugged.

'Not me,' she said. 'I reckon this is a boy thing.'

'Oh yes, and boys will be boys,' interjected Marlena, a note of ironic resignation in her voice.

'Billy and Tiny are right, there's no need to get serious. I mean, what happened to George is just funny,' said Bob, clearly not wanting to lose his own story-telling momentum. 'Big-time funny.'

Marlena turned towards him.

'Yes, Bob,' she said. 'But I somehow still don't feel entirely at ease about it.'

'Marlena's right, you know,' said Michelle. 'When you stop to think, well, you've got to wonder what might be behind a prank like that . . .'

Six pairs of eyes fixed on her.

'What are you trying to say?' asked Karen.

'Oh, take no notice of me,' said Michelle. 'It's being in the job, I expect. Can't help looking for hidden meaning and criminal intent all over the place.'

'Criminal intent?' echoed Greg. 'For God's sake, Michelle. George has got all his stuff back. This was a joke. Leaving a flash bastard like George nothing to wear except a Mr Tickle suit was, just like Billy says, an act of total comic genius. I mean, wasn't it?'

'Yes,' agreed Michelle. ''Course it was. Like I said, take no notice of me.'

four

The following morning Bob made himself tea, and as usual, except in the very worst of weather, wandered out onto his terrace to admire the urban garden he had created. It might be tiny, but it was, he felt, a significant contribution to what he regarded as an oasis in the concrete jungle of central London.

Bob lived in Bishops Court, a Westminster Council development tucked away between Charing Cross Road and St Martin's Lane, just where Covent Garden borders Soho. It was a kind of low-level park complex, unusual for a city centre, comprising three storeys of apartments accessed from shrub-lined communal walkways, and designed so that almost all had at least a small patch of their own private outside space. The lucky tenants inhabited possibly the most valuable public housing in the country. It was a good place to live. Particularly for an urban gardener like Bob.

Even at this time of year, there was colour on Bob's terrace. Yellow winter jasmine and a couple of varieties of viburnum grew in the big planters around the perimeter fence and against the wall of his one-bedroomed home, multicoloured winter flowering pansies and assorted heathers filled terracotta pots. Tubs of daffodils were just coming into bud.

His perennial and biennial summer bedding plants, mostly

pelargoniums and begonias, wintered in a glass frame in one sheltered corner. This year, in spite of persistent rain and the bitterly cold early spring, there had been little snow and ice and temperatures had only rarely dropped below zero. Somewhat surprisingly, as the climate had felt so miserable, the weather had remained temperate enough for even them to provide some ragged cheer.

Bob, carrying his favourite white china mug bearing in green the slogan 'stop and smell the roses', glanced up at the sky as he stepped onto the crazy paving he had laid himself many years previously. There was a break in the rain which had drenched the city over the last couple of weeks, and he was beginning to hope a fine spring might be on the way. Certainly this was a lovely morning. The sun shone with a still wintery brightness, and the sky was blue and clear, except for one fluffy white cloud just drifting past the Post Office Tower.

Bob prepared to savour that moment of satisfaction as he appreciated the little garden entirely of his own creation.

Unfortunately some of it was no longer there. The winter jasmine, and the other shrubs which climbed and were entangled with the fencing, the dormant vine, the tangled woody stems of the passion flower, the clematis and the honeysuckle remained, of course. But the majority of Bob's garden grew in containers of varying sizes and shapes. Several had been removed. The small plastic pots of wintering pelargoniums that had been inside the glass frame were missing, as was the little fig tree which grew in a treasured blue ceramic pot that had been made by Bob's son Daniel at pottery class.

Bob closed his eyes quickly then opened them again. Unfortunately his pelargoniums and the fig tree were still missing.

*

It was Tiny who found the note. Bob had been due to give Tiny and Billy's terrace a clear-up that morning. Tiny had phoned Bob when he failed to arrive, and, upon hearing of his friend's loss and realizing that Bob was more upset than he cared to let on, called round.

The note, encased in transparent plastic, had been stuck into the planter containing the winter jasmine, fastened to a spike the way florists attach cards to bouquets of flowers. The planter had fallen over, making it easy to miss.

'Many thanks, love Alan Titchmarsh,' read Tiny aloud.

He passed the note to Bob.

'Well, that explains it then, doesn't it,' Tiny said.

Bob stared at the note. His expression was one of total bewilderment.

'What's Alan Titchmarsh got to do with anything, for God's sake?' he asked.

'Not a lot, I shouldn't think,' said Tiny. 'Though he does get everywhere nowadays.'

'What?' Bob looked even more bewildered.

'Sorry,' said Tiny. 'Look, don't you see?'

Bob shook his head.

'It's the same joker who nicked George's clothes at the gym and pulled the Mr Tickle stunt. It must be.'

'Do you think so?'

'Sure I do,' affirmed Tiny. 'You both got spoof notes, didn't you? Yours from Alan Titchmarsh and George's from Mr Tickle. On form, your stuff will be returned to you, I reckon. Just don't do anything if you hear a noise in the night.'

Bob pulled a face.

'Come to think of it, it's pretty extraordinary that you didn't hear anything last night,' Tiny went on.

He looked around the terrace.

'I mean, whoever did this would have had to climb up here from the walkway at the front. The wall's not very high, I know, but it's not an easy thing to do, is it? There are the climbers to negotiate, for a start. Then they'd have had to pick up your plants, lower them down the other side of the wall and make off with them. Impossible to think that could be done without a bit of noise. Didn't you hear anything at all?'

'I'm deaf in one ear,' said Bob. 'And I always seem to sleep on my good side, so I hardly ever hear a thing in the night.'

'Right. Who knows that? Amongst us lot, particularly.'

'About my sleeping habits?' said Bob. 'None of you. Those days seem to be over for me.'

'But what about the deaf ear?' Tiny asked.

'I thought you all knew,' said Bob. 'Don't I always try to sit with my back to the wall at Johnny's? And you must have heard me ask people to talk into my good ear?'

'Oh yeah. Now you mention it, I suppose we do all know, though I didn't think of it until you said.'

Tiny clapped a big arm around Bob.

'Don't worry,' he said. 'I'm sure it's another prank, that's all. Sleep tight tonight, mate, and I bet you'll find your plants are back tomorrow morning.'

'I shall try to believe that, Tiny. It's just the fig tree's in a pot Danny made at school. Reminds me of the good times we had together.'

Bob looked away. Tiny thought he could see a tear in his eye.

'Trust me, I'm a bouncer,' said Tiny.

Bob had two afternoon gardening appointments which he fulfilled. He didn't mention what had happened to anyone. But Tiny, it seemed, had spread the word among the friends, and had obviously pointed out the sentimental value of Danny's handmade pot. Ari and George both phoned during the day and left messages of concern. Bob avoided their calls and did not reply to their messages. He really didn't want to talk about it. He couldn't avoid Greg, who turned up unannounced on his doorstep just as he was arriving home that evening. Greg and Karen were his neighbours, their flat only a few doors away from his in Bishops Court.

'Just came to see if there was anything I could do, mate,' said Greg. 'If you need to re-stock I know a bloke who's got a load of spring bulbs going cheap – that any good for you?'

Bob found it irritating that Greg was his usual cheery self.

'You plant spring bulbs in the autumn, Greg,' he said.

'Right.' Greg looked confused.

Bob wasn't surprised. Greg was no gardener. As far as Bob was aware, his neighbour's terrace was devoted to the cultivation of children's bicycles, a plastic paddling pool and assorted debris.

'Well, if there's anything I can help with, you just shout, do you hear?' Greg commanded.

Bob promised that he would and dispatched Greg on his way as quickly as he could, without, he hoped, seeming too rude and ungrateful. But he feared he had probably been both.

Then, realizing he hadn't eaten all day, he made himself a bacon sandwich, even though he didn't have much appetite, and watched some mindless television. He was an old soldier, for God's sake. He knew he shouldn't be in a state about a plant pot, regardless of who had made it. But he was.

While he was preparing for bed, Tiny called to ask how he was doing.

'I'm OK,' Bob lied.

'Everything will be fine, I told you. Trust me, I'm a bouncer,' said Tiny again.

Bob took a glass of whisky and hot water to bed with him and tried not to think about anything while he sipped it. But his mind was in a whirl. He couldn't sleep and, in spite of being quite sure his plants were not going to be returned, couldn't help keeping his good ear pricked for any sort of sound from his terrace. Once he thought he heard something and peered out of the window. There didn't seem to be anyone or anything out there. He mentally kicked himself for being so ridiculous. Towards dawn he dozed off for a while. He was woken by his phone ringing just before eight. The caller was Tiny.

'Any news? Have you got your stuff back?' he asked.

Obediently Bob shuffled out onto his terrace, taking the phone with him. It remained the same as the previous day.

'Nothing's changed, Tiny,' he said. 'No good fairy has visited me in the night.'

'Give it time,' said Tiny. 'Your plants will be returned, I'm sure of it.'

'You are, aren't you?' replied Bob. 'So sure you're making me begin to wonder why.' There was a sharp edge to his voice.

'Hey, come on, mate, don't start suspecting me.'

'Of course not,' said Bob.

He ended the call, a tad abruptly, and set about preparing to go to work. His first appointment that day was at 9 a.m. If it hadn't been for Tiny's call he may well have missed it. There were other people's urban gardens to tend, and Bob was not a man who liked to let people down.

Mid-afternoon, Michelle called him on his mobile, having been alerted by Tiny, and suggested, just as she had previously to George, that Bob should formally report what had happened to the police. Well, she would say that, wouldn't she, thought Bob.

'I'll help, if you like,' she told him. 'Not my beat – I've got far more important things to do nowadays, standing around on street corners waving my arms at blank-eyed bloody motorists – but I could put in a word to the right people.'

'It's only a few potted plants,' said Bob.

'You know you don't mean that.'

'Anyway, not yet,' said Bob. 'Tiny's convinced this is another prank, like the Mr Tickle one played on George, and that my stuff will come back. I want to give it a bit longer. Another night, OK?'

The truth was that Bob had already thought about calling the police but he couldn't imagine that they would be much help, or indeed that they would be at all interested, whether or not Michelle put in a word. The loss of his plants and that treasured pot in the heart of a city where proper crime, assaults, drug dealing, muggings and even murder were daily occurrences, was never likely to cause anyone much concern except him. And if the plants were returned then the incident would be regarded as another prank rather than a mindless act of vandalism.

Tiny had made a good show of being concerned, but who knew what lay behind that.

Tiny called again that evening.

'Just try to crash, man, turn that good ear to the pillow, blot out the world, and hope for the best,' he said. 'I reckon you're going to get lucky.'

Bob realized Tiny meant well. Or did he?

I knew I was clever. Ever since I was little. Only people never did seem to notice how clever I was. Which is why I've always been able to manipulate the world to suit me.

The missing plants and the Mr Tickle incident were just pranks – what else could they have been? But they were the kind of pranks that made everyone involved feel a bit uneasy. And that was my intention.

I wanted them all to be on edge, confused, growing increasingly suspicious of each other. That was my camouflage, the curtain of uncertainty behind which I could do what had to be done unseen and unrecognized. Their reactions were very important to me, and to my plan.

I wanted them laughing one minute and crying the next. They were my cover, my smokescreen. I didn't particularly want them to suffer, all except one of them, but if it was necessary – and I feared it would be necessary – then so be it.

I believed in rough justice. I wanted rough justice. And I was quite clear, absolutely clear in my mind, of my own integrity. Everything I had done so far and would do in the future was driven by the wrongdoing of others. And it had all been set in motion by one particular wrong by one particular other.

If there was going to be evil, if there was going to be cruelty and anguish, danger and destruction, then it wouldn't be down to me. I am the victim in all this, that's the truth of it. I have suffered far worse agony in my life than I could ever imagine inflicting on another human being. But I was going to try.

I had already begun, sitting on that bench by the river on the night it all started, to formulate a plan. Over the following weeks I fine-tuned it until I was sure it would deliver the desired result.

These 'pranks', these more or less harmless pranks, were only the beginning.

And so, on my knees I prayed to Almighty God to share with me the omnipotence of his wrath, the strength to cause torment beyond endurance, and the might to wreak the havoc I sought to inflict.

I am as one with God. As before so shall it be again.

Mine is the kingdom, the power and the glory, for ever and ever.

By the following morning, like magic, and exactly as Tiny had predicted, only twenty-four hours late, it seemed that all Bob's plants had been returned, replaced on his terrace almost exactly as they'd been before, along with a second plastic-encased note.

Thanks for the loan. Taken a few pelargonium cuttings. Hope you don't mind, AT.

Bob called Tiny with the good news.

'There, what did I tell you?' said the big man.

'OK. You were right. I still don't like it though.'

'Oh, come on, Bob. Where's that cockney sense of humour of yours? It was just a joke.'

'Ummm. And we don't know who's responsible, do we? Or what they may do next.'

'Look. It's not been anything serious . . .'

Bob interrupted, repeating his barbed comment of the previous day: 'You were very sure I'd get my stuff back, weren't you, Tiny?'

'I certainly was. True to form, I reckoned.'

This time if Tiny picked up on any hidden implication in Bob's remark then he chose to ignore it.

Bob paused before deciding to persist.

'Look, I'm going to ask you outright, no more pussyfooting around,' he said. 'Was it you, Tiny? Did you do it? Did you take my plants?'

'No I bloody didn't,' Tiny shot back at him. 'Hey, don't go round accusing me, mate. I was your good Samaritan, remember?'

'Ummm. Look, it has to be someone I know, doesn't it? Someone who knows me and my place well enough to be able to do this.'

'Could be anyone.'

'I don't have many mates, Tiny. George and I are both Sunday Clubbers. Looks like whoever played these tricks on us is one of the group. And somebody agile enough to climb on and off my terrace.'

'It's not very high off the walkway. Probably rules out Marlena though.'

'She could have paid someone to do it.'

'For God's sake, Bob.'

'OK. What about George then? He's fit. He's always at the flipping gym. And he's forever taking the piss out of me about my garden.'

'George has also been a victim of a prank. You just said that.'

'He could have played it on himself.'

'What? George? Put himself in that situation with only a Mr Tickle suit to wear? Don't be daft!'

'Maybe you're right. What about Greg then? He lives in Bishops, just a few doors from me. Knows his way about the place better than anyone. He came round the other night too. It could have been him.'

'Oh stop it, Bob. You'll drive yourself mad, and what's the point? No harm's been done. Whoever did this will probably own up sooner or later anyway. Proud of themselves, more than likely. Like we all said at Sunday Club, remember?'

'I suppose so,' muttered Bob.

'Good. You are coming to Johnny's this Sunday, aren't you?' persisted Tiny.

'I don't know.'

'Come on, Bob, this needs to be talked through. You need to admit to everyone how upset you were when you thought you'd lost Danny's pot, and that you don't think it's funny.'

'Well, I don't.'

'You laughed at George.'

'Yes, and I wish I hadn't, to tell the truth. The whole lot of us should have thought things through more.'

'OK then, I reckon we have to put a stop to all this. We don't want any more pranks, because we don't want not to be trusting each other, do we, mate?'

'I guess not,' said Bob.

After finishing the call Tiny phoned Greg to say the plants had been returned.

Greg giggled at him down the phone.

'Look, Bob's taking it all a bit seriously . . .' Tiny began.

'I know that,' said Greg. 'He was dead moody when I called round, and I was only trying to help. Even though I'd guessed it was another prank. And you gotta accept that it's funny.'

'Bob doesn't think it's funny,' said Tiny. 'Actually, he's very upset. You saw that for yourself. You have to remember, Greg, that he thought he'd lost the pot his kid made for him – he's never got over Danny pissing off. And you know how daft he is about his prize pelargoniums. He once told me he regarded his pelargoniums as his children now, and that they were a lot less trouble than a hairy-arsed teenager.'

Greg's giggling exploded into full-blown laughter at this.

'Oh for God's sake, Tiny,' he said. 'Now that really is funny.'

Tiny, Billy, George and Marlena all arrived at Johnny's early the following Sunday. Michelle came next and immediately expressed sympathy for Bob and unease about what she felt could be an unpleasant edge to the practical jokes.

'If you're upsetting people then that's not a joke, not as far as I'm concerned anyway,' she said.

'That's what I'm beginning to think,' said Tiny. 'And Bob certainly does.'

'Come on,' said George. 'I was made to look a total prat. But now a bit of time has passed I do realize the prank played on me was pretty funny. I just want to know who's doing it, that's all.'

'We all seem to agree it's the same person, and probably one of us, don't we?' said Michelle.

'Definitely the same person,' said Billy. 'Same MO, as they say in the best detective shows. And obviously someone who knows Bob and George, their habits, and where they live. What other link do Bob and George have, apart from Sunday Club?'

George shrugged.

'Can you think of anything, George?' asked Marlena.

George was just replying that he could think of no other link, when Greg and Karen arrived.

'Sorry we're late,' Greg said. 'Some bastard's slashed the tyres on the van. Three of 'em, for fuck's sake. Had to sort it straight away, 'cos I need to get going first thing in the morning. Gotta big job on.'

There was total silence as Greg sat down and helped himself to a glass of the wine that was already on the table. It seemed a long time before he became aware of the silence, or that all eyes were fixed on him.

'What?' he enquired, looking around.

'Whaddya mean, "what"? Isn't it obvious?' enquired Billy.

'Isn't what obvious?' Greg paused, then the penny dropped. 'Oh, no. You can't possibly think it's the same joker who took the piss out of George and Bob, can you? That was entirely different. This is malicious.'

'Yes, and it's a different MO,' said Billy, working it out like the lawyer he was. 'As you say, entirely different. But if it's not the same joker then we've got a coincidence on our hands.'

'Not really,' said Greg. 'Typical Saturday-night vandalism, if you ask me. I've lived in this manor all my life and these things happen. The van's parked in the street most of the time I'm not driving it, in residents' parking. Just my turn for a bit of bother, that's all.'

'So you really believe it was random?' pressed George.

''Course I do,' said Greg.

'No note then, like George and Bob?' queried Billy.

Greg shook his head.

'Maybe it blew away,' said Tiny. 'It's windy today.'

'For goodness' sake, no,' responded Greg. 'Look, we're market. Expect the odd knock round here. Don't we, babe?'

'I don't know,' said Karen. 'I honestly don't know. I mean, nothing like this has happened to us before, all the years we've lived here, has it?'

'Like I said, it's our turn. And I don't think it's anything to worry about. So come on, I'm ravenous. I could eat a horse. Whoops, shouldn't say that, should I – who knows what's in the burgers these days? Anyway, a horse might not be big enough.'

Greg picked up the Sunday specials menu. He tried to avoid meeting Karen's eye. She knew more about him than anyone else in the world. But even she didn't know everything.

He wanted desperately to change the subject. To move on from the matter of his slashed tyres.

'Hey, half a roasted elephant,' he said, realizing he was talking nonsense but not caring. 'Just the job. Oh no. My mistake. Half a roasted chicken. Think I'll have the spare ribs again.'

More wine was delivered, another Prosecco for Marlena, and a second round of cosmos for Tiny and Billy, while the group juggled the menus and finally ordered their meals. Alfonso, on duty at the Vine, and Ari, off goodness knows where and on goodness knows what, did not turn up. Neither did Bob.

It was quite usual for only some of the friends to be present, but none of them had really expected Bob to be there. Especially given the fact he hadn't taken the theft of his plants well and he suspected one of the Sunday Clubbers to be responsible.

Nonetheless, in spite of the awkwardness generated by Bob's absence and the unease caused by Greg and Karen's news of the damage to their van, after a bit the evening settled into a normal Sunday Club session. But that was only how it seemed. In truth, everyone around the table, including Greg, who had put on such a show of being dismissive, was uneasy.

Greg kept his head down and concentrated hard on his spare ribs in barbecue sauce, thankful that he had chosen a dish that demanded his full attention. Karen kept glancing at Greg anxiously and said little. Tiny, Billy and George all talked too much. Michelle and Marlena both picked at their food. Marlena, witty caustic Marlena, who normally had a riposte for everything, was unusually silent.

There was a common preoccupation, of course. Questions that lurked in the back of the minds of at least six of the seven assembled members of the group, or perhaps all of them.

Could those tyres have been slashed by the same person who had played pranks on Bob and George? Could it really be one of their supper club? Could that person actually be sitting at the table?

Or was Greg right, and this latest incident was just a random case of inner-city vandalism?

five

The next day Marlena, dressed in blinged black as usual, a mink cape tossed carelessly over her shoulders, wearing full make-up and false eyelashes, even though it was not yet 9 a.m., was still thinking about the previous evening when she set off for the Soho deli which was probably her favourite food shop in the world.

Marlena lived in a block of flats, converted in the seventies from a disused fruit-and-veg warehouse, at the heart of Covent Garden right by the Opera House.

'Where else?' she would ask.

She rarely strayed beyond the perimeters of the Garden.

'Why ever would I, darlings? Covent Garden is the centre of the universe,' was another of her sayings.

Her regular Monday-morning excursion to Franco's Deli was an exception. It was, after all, only a twenty-minute walk from her home, and she actively looked forward to it.

Soho was at its quietest at this time of the week, and Marlena often had the whole wonderful shop to herself. She did not eat a great deal, but she liked to tickle her taste buds with assorted delicacies. Normally her only preoccupation as she made her way through the city streets was to plan exactly what selection of delights she would treat herself to, but this particular Monday morning was different. Marlena was worried. Her life for several years now had been ordered and pleasant. She had good and interesting friends, a comfortable flat in the middle of an area she considered to be the very best place to live, and her demons had left her alone for some time.

There were aspects of Marlena's past life that would cause her a great deal of trouble were they ever to become known. But Marlena had almost forgotten that. It was all so far behind her that she had allowed herself to believe she'd got away scot-free. At her somewhat substantial age – she had taught herself to forget the precise figure – Marlena had finally found a kind of peace. Or as much peace as a woman like her could ever achieve.

But that peace had been disturbed by the series of incidents involving three members – possibly four, if you counted Karen as well as Greg – of the little group whose company she so enjoyed. It particularly disturbed her that the 'joker' responsible had yet to own up, leading to an atmosphere of distrust and suspicion among the friends.

She wasn't exactly fearful. The incidents had been fairly trivial, after all. And while she was concerned that she might be the joker's next target, she didn't believe there was anything they could do that would cause a real upset in her life. She was too careful for that. These days, people thought of her as an eccentric old woman. Her past was far behind her now and buried so deep no one would ever suspect.

Even so, Marlena couldn't stop feeling anxious.

She pulled her mink cape more tightly around her shoulders. The weather had turned cold again. As she touched the soft fur she was reminded of the only time she had felt in real danger since she'd moved to Covent Garden.

It had been some time ago, during a period of anti-fur protests. Marlena had been walking past the rear entrance of the Theatre Royal when a group of protesters, no doubt waiting for a fur-clad celebrity to emerge from the stage door, had spotted her. She'd been wearing an arctic fox wrap.

The protestors had rushed to surround her, and began pushing her, yelling insults.

'Fucking murderer!' they cried. 'Vicious bitch!' And more.

Then one of them had emptied the contents of a tin of red paint over her. And her white fur wrap.

Marlena had been stronger then, but in the face of their fury she'd been helpless. She could only cower beneath the overwhelming force of it.

Passers-by had crossed the street, pretending not to notice. Two stagehands having a smoke outside the stage door had ducked their heads to avoid glancing in her direction. Nobody wanted to mess with the angry mob attacking her.

Eventually the protestors had grown tired of Marlena and returned to their stake-out. She had hurried home, reeking of paint, tear stains streaking her face, and on the way dumped the irretrievably damaged fur in a municipal bin.

Marlena still winced at the memory. At least you could wear a fur in London again nowadays, she thought. Assuming you had the nerve. Although some people made their disapproval clear enough, the violence had stopped. And surely she had nothing else to worry about? Not really. She remained in charge of her own destiny, didn't she?

She passed through Seven Dials, made her way up Earlham Street, and came to a halt at Cambridge Circus, opposite the Palace Theatre. This was the point where Soho met Covent Garden in a tangle of merging, intertwining traffic lanes, and the morning rush hour was still going strong. Not that there really was a proper rush hour any more, Marlena reflected. Since the congestion charge had been introduced in 2000 it seemed that the traffic remained heavy all the time.

Momentarily, however, there was a tempting lull. Once upon a time Marlena would have diced with death and dashed across, but those days were over. Instead she waited – albeit impatiently, her nature not having changed with age, as it rarely does – for the little green man to appear on the traffic light opposite. Only then did she step into the street. And, although she was on red alert, half expecting something like it to happen, she was taken quite by surprise when it did.

He was upon her almost immediately. A grey, hoody-clad figure on a bicycle. His head was down. He was pedalling hard and did not appear to even glance up at the road ahead. Marlena saw him at the last moment – if indeed it was a him – and tried to take a step back out of the way. But such was her shock, it was as if she were rooted to the spot. In any case, she could have sworn the cyclist swerved towards her when she tried to move. The bicycle slammed into her side and pushed her in the direction of the stream of oncoming traffic. Its rider did not at any point appear to slow down, nor indeed give any indication that he was even aware of what was happening. He just kept pedalling, occasionally lowering a foot to the ground in order to maintain his balance.

Something caught in Marlena's clothing. Or was the cyclist holding on to her? Surely not. But it felt that way. She was dragged several yards along the street, then discarded. Or that's what it seemed like, anyway. And as she fell, full length right across the road, she watched the cyclist pedalling off down Shaftesbury Avenue without a backward glance.

Marlena's head was spinning and she realized she'd hit it quite hard. Then she saw the bus coming towards her. It seemed to be travelling at enormous speed, far faster, certainly, than the disappearing bicycle. In a split second the big red double-decker loomed right above her inert form. And from the expression on the driver's face, he had no hope whatsoever of avoiding her.

Marlena steeled herself for the impact. And for what she thought would probably be the final moments of her life.

They told her in A&E at University College Hospital just how fortunate she had been. She'd fallen in such a way that only her right foot actually lay directly in the path of the bus. Her head had dropped safely away from the oncoming vehicle. Or more or less safely. She'd given it such a crack on the edge of the pavement that she still had concussion, which was why they were keeping her in overnight. That and the state of her foot. It hadn't just been broken but thoroughly crushed by the weight of the bus.

She'd been lucky, they told her. Marlena tried hard to believe that as she struggled to make herself comfortable in her hospital bed. Her foot throbbed for England, her head ached, and her thoughts remained muddled.

It must indeed be considered lucky that she had fallen the way she had. The bus would certainly have killed her, had her head ended up under one of those enormous wheels. And Marlena was not ready to die yet. But neither did she want to live as a cripple. She was a proud and independent woman, born in the days before political correctness, when if you couldn't walk you were a cripple. And Marlena couldn't help wondering if she would ever walk again. The doctors had already told her there wasn't a lot they could do for her foot except wait for it to heal. And at her age, that sort of injury might never heal properly.

It was her toes which had borne the brunt of the pressure,

and apparently you couldn't set crushed toes in plaster. Instead they were loosely taped beneath a dressing. Every time a nerve twitched, the pain was so excruciating Marlena practically jumped out of her skin. She lay with her eyes tightly closed, willing the agony to ebb away. Marlena believed in the power of the mind. Perhaps she could turn the whole dreadful incident into a nightmare from which she would soon wake.

A voice cut through the pain.

'How are you, Marlena darling? I just wanted to make sure you were all right before I leave.'

It was a familiar voice. Marlena opened her eyes and struggled to focus on the speaker. Nothing about her body was working properly. Even her vision seemed blurred.

'They said I could have five minutes,' the voice continued.

Marlena lifted her head from the pillows and blinked.

'Alfonso?' she queried.

'Yes, darling,' said Alfonso, his voice tender and full of concern.

'What are you doing here?'

'I came along right after it happened. Don't you remember? They let me ride with you in the ambulance.'

Alfonso smiled and when he spoke again it sounded as if he was trying very hard to be reassuring.

'Somebody had to look after you, didn't they, you daft old broad.'

Marlena stared at him. The fog was beginning to clear. She remembered then. The shock of the bus running over her foot, and probably a slightly delayed reaction to the bang to her head when she'd cracked it on the pavement, must have caused her to lose consciousness for a few seconds. Alfonso had been the first person she'd seen when she came to, as she lay in the road at Cambridge Circus. He was crouched down next to her, talking into his mobile phone, asking for the emergency services. He must have reacted to everything extremely quickly. Next to him had been a man who, even in her fuddled state, she'd recognized as the bus driver. He'd been near hysterical.

'Oh thank God, she's opened her eyes! I thought I'd killed the woman. I couldn't do nothing about it, honest. She just came flying through the air and landed right in front of me wheels. Damn cyclists. They don't obey the rules everyone else does, see. They have ways of their own. They're all over the road and they don't stop at traffic lights. No, they just go straight through and drag some poor old lady with them . . .'

The man seemed to have a bad case of verbal diarrhoea. He'd been shaking from head to foot, his face white, drained of blood. By contrast Alfonso had been ultra calm. Funny how clear the memory of it suddenly was, thought Marlena.

Alfonso had used that reassuring voice from the start.

'You're going to be all right, darling, you're going to be all right,' he'd told her repeatedly. 'Just trust the Fonz. Stand on me, darling, stand on me.'

Now, in the hospital, Alfonso was still calm. Calm yet anxious. He reached out and touched Marlena's hand gently.

'Did you see what happened, Alfonso?' Marlena asked.

'Not really, I heard you scream and I saw this cyclist take off down Shaftesbury Avenue, that's just about all.'

The cyclist who had failed to stop. That was Marlena's other vivid memory.

'Did they catch him, Alfonso, the cyclist, did they catch him?'

'I don't think so, sweetheart. Not as far as I know, anyway.'

Marlena nodded and rested her head back on the pillows. She would have been surprised to receive any other answer.

'Is there anything I can do for you, girl?' Alfonso asked.

'Anyone else you want me to let know what happened? Anything you want? Anything at all?'

Marlena shook her head, very slightly because it too was throbbing, though not nearly as much as her injured foot.

'You were the first person by my side, weren't you, Alfonso?' she enquired.

'Yes, I was, darling.'

'What were you doing there?'

'I was going to work, Marlena darling. Early shift. Flippin' business breakfasts are bigger than lunch nowadays. Don't you remember? We've seen each other before on Monday mornings when you've been on your way to Soho.'

'Yes, of course,' said Marlena. 'I'm just not thinking clearly.'

'Anyway, I heard a scream,' Alfonso continued. 'That's what attracted my attention. I looked along the street, saw this woman lying in the road, the bus, and everything. So I rushed up to see if I could help. Then I realized it was you, darling. I couldn't believe my eyes: my best girl under the wheels of a bus! What a shock you gave me, sweetheart.'

Alfonso smiled at Marlena with great affection.

She managed a weak smile back.

'Good job I came along, wasn't it, darling?' said Alfonso.

'Yes, wasn't it,' responded Marlena.

She reached out again, took Alfonso's hand in hers, and squeezed it.

But her aching head was filled with unwelcome thoughts.

'You don't think we're being targeted, do you?' she asked. 'Our little group, one by one, all these things happening, and getting more serious. Not pranks any more.'

Alfonso shook his head.

'I don't know,' he replied. 'I honestly don't know. I can't believe it, though. I mean, why would anyone target us?'

'And who? That's the big thing. Who, if not one of us?' Marlena looked stricken.

'We mustn't think like that, Marlena,' said Alfonso quickly. 'We'll drive ourselves mad. Look, what happened to you could have been just an accident. In any case, the police are involved now. Two officers came to the scene. I think we should leave it all to them, and you should just concentrate on getting better.'

Marlena smiled at him again, even though she did not feel like smiling at all.

six

It hadn't gone as I had planned. I hadn't intended for anyone to be so badly injured. Not at this stage. Not yet. I would have to think again now, slow things down. Otherwise I risked revealing myself.

It was perhaps a lesson that even I could not control everything. I hadn't bargained on a bus travelling so fast – surely far too fast. But then, I hadn't given much thought to what might be behind me in the bus lane. I had made a mistake.

I would need to be more careful from here on. I had been so hell-bent on staging another incident that would give cause for concern among the members of Sunday Club that I had failed to think it through. The intention had been to keep them on edge, keep them second-guessing, nothing more. But in my eagerness I went too far.

As a result, this had turned into a matter for the police. The other incidents had been silly pranks. Even the slashed tyres would not have merited much police intervention. There was no way anyone could prove that the incidents were connected. And with each of these 'random' pranks I had been growing more confident, testing my camouflage, making sure that I would be beyond suspicion when it came time to inflict vengeance on my real target, the one who had so wronged me.

However, I had allowed myself to become overconfident, and as a result my entire plan was in jeopardy.

Somehow I needed to divert attention away from the spectacle of an old woman thrown into the path of a bus by a hooded cyclist.

I needed to come up with something that would shock and stupefy the whole group. I sought an abomination. And I believed that I had found one.

The gates of the rivers shall be opened.

Late that evening Michelle telephoned University College Hospital and somehow persuaded the staff to allow her to speak to Marlena.

She said she was away in Belfast on a training course and had just picked up a worrying voicemail from Alfonso, telling her about the accident.

'If that's what it was,' Michelle continued. 'Fonz said he saw it happen, more or less, and he reckons the cyclist rode at you deliberately. Is that what you think?'

'Oh, darling, I don't know what to think,' Marlena replied. 'To be perfectly honest, I'm just grateful to be able to still think at all. In any case, that's not what Alfonso told me. He said he heard me scream and saw the cyclist riding off, that's all.'

'Well, he probably didn't want to upset you. Particularly after all the other stuff that's been going on. I shouldn't have said anything. Just forget I opened my big mouth.'

'Do you think it hadn't occurred to me that what happened today mightn't have been an accident?' enquired Marlena. 'It is a big step, though, from a couple of silly pranks and some slashed tyres.'

'True,' said Michelle. 'And working in Traffic I see all too many cyclists speeding through red lights or riding on the pavement without a thought for any poor pedestrian who might step into their path.'

'It's as if some extraordinary lunacy descends upon everyone who climbs aboard a bicycle in this city,' agreed Marlena.

Relieved to hear her friend starting to sound more like her old self, Michelle asked about the extent of her injuries, how she was feeling, what the prognosis was and so on, before ending the call with a promise to visit the moment she returned to London.

After hanging up, Marlena lay back on the pillows and closed her eyes, trying to blot out the world. Michelle's call, although she was sure it was well meant, had done nothing to ease her state of mind. But thanks to a shot of painkilling morphine, administered into her bottom by a brisk but efficient young nurse, she slept through most of the night.

Early the following morning two uniformed police officers, who introduced themselves as Constables Perkins and Brandt, arrived at her bedside to interview her. It seemed, from the way they talked, that they were the same officers Alfonso had spoken of, the ones who'd attended the scene of the incident the previous day.

She did not confide her inner thoughts and suspicions. It was Marlena's policy never to tell the police anything more than she had to. Not even when the police officer in question considered herself a friend, as in Michelle's case. In spite of her pain and distress, Marlena had been guarded in what she'd said to Michelle the previous evening. It was ingrained in her, the result of a lifetime spent measuring her words, taking care never to unwittingly let slip some detail she would rather others did not know. She was so accomplished in this that none of her small circle of friends, and much larger circle of acquaintances, were ever aware of Marlena holding back. Indeed, with her flamboyant manner and quick wit, she contrived to give the opposite impression. The truth was that the outer Marlena, so vivacious and engagingly bold, was a totally different creature to the inner one, tightened into a knot of eternal angst.

And so it was to her dismay that she now had to deal with two officers intent on taking her laboriously through the details of exactly what had happened when she'd been hit by that bus.

Marlena kept her responses as vague as possible. In this she was helped by the fact that, as a result of the shock and concussion she had suffered, she was genuinely unclear about so much.

Perkins and Brandt asked her to describe the errant cyclist, whom they assured her they would do their best to find. Marlena thought it unlikely they would succeed. Certainly her description of a hooded creature of indeterminate sex and age was not going to be of much assistance.

Finally they asked her about Alfonso.

'Mr Bertorelli, the principal witness to the incident, tells us that you and he are friends, is that so?' enquired PC Ronald Perkins, the younger of the two policemen, a baby-faced blond who was already, and somewhat incongruously, growing a substantial belly.

Marlena agreed that it was so, and affirmed that she'd known Alfonso for several years, regularly meeting him socially.

'So it was quite a coincidence then, Mr Bertorelli being first on the scene?' continued PC Perkins.

'Well, yes, I suppose so,' replied Marlena, wondering what the heck was coming next. 'But Alfonso does work at the Vine, and the restaurant is only just around the corner. He was on his way to work. I've seen him before when I've been going to Soho. I go shopping at the same time every Monday, you see. Just the first time I've been horizontal, that's all . . .'

'All the same, a bit of a coincidence,' persisted Perkins. 'Perhaps a bit too much of a coincidence?'

Marlena stared at him. Whatever she was thinking privately, she had no intention of sharing her misgivings. Not at this stage. Not to some foot soldier of a PC anyway.

'Absolutely not,' she said, and such was the certainty in her voice that Ron Perkins did not further pursue his line of questioning, even though he looked as if he would like to.

Soon after the two officers finally departed, Marlena fell fitfully asleep. She woke to see Alfonso standing at the foot of her bed, again on his way to work, he said. Marlena did not share with him the seeds of doubt that PCs Perkins and Brandt had attempted to sow in her.

Instead she greeted him with the biggest smile she could muster.

'I'm fine,' she replied, in answer to Alfonso's anxiously expressed queries. 'In fact, I've been told I shall probably be able to go home later today.'

'That's wonderful, darling, but you can't go home on your own,' responded Alfonso at once. 'I'll get them to phone me when you're allowed to leave. We can take a cab to your place.'

'I'll be perfectly all right alone,' said Marlena. 'Besides, you mustn't miss any more time at work because of this. You'll lose your job.'

'I don't think so,' said Alfonso, who was quite convinced he was the Vine's most valuable asset.

'Maybe not, but you still shouldn't be skiving off to look after a silly old woman who fell in front of a bus.'

'You didn't fall. I saw pretty much what happened, and the bus driver was quite clear about it,' retorted Alfonso. 'You were dragged along by a mad cyclist and dumped in front of the wheels of a double-decker.'

'I didn't think you saw all that,' said Marlena. 'Not that it makes any difference. The end result is, I'm still in this state.'

'Yes, and you can't go home alone. You should have someone with you for at least a day or two. Didn't I hear you once mention a sister? In Scotland?'

Marlena's features darkened. 'If I did I must have been drunk,' she said. 'You will not attempt to contact my sister – not you, Alfonso, nor any of the others, nor the hospital.'

'All right, all right.'

'As I've already told you, I shall be just fine. They're going to give me a lesson in using crutches and then someone will put me in a taxi. I shall be fine.'

'Right,' said Alfonso.

Outside in the corridor he went straight to the nursing station and asked to be contacted as soon as Marlena was able to leave.

On the way to the restaurant he called Tiny. Marlena was right. He shouldn't miss any more work. Business was not as good as it had once been, even at the Vine. The restaurant probably carried a bigger staff than it could currently justify and Alfonso was almost certainly one of the most highly paid waiters. He'd been there for years, was held in considerable esteem by the management and by many of the regular clientele, including some of the most illustrious, but even though he still thought he was invaluable, you never really knew.

Tiny, already aware of what had happened to Marlena – as were all the group, thanks to Alfonso having spread the word the previous day – answered his phone on the first ring.

Knowing that the big man, aside from being a real favourite of Marlena's who might just be able to cheer her up a little, was usually free during the day, the Fonz asked him if he wouldn't mind collecting Marlena from UCH and taking her home. There seemed to be a pause before Tiny gave his answer.

'Sure,' he said eventually. 'Of course I'll do it.'

'Great, I'll be in touch as soon as the hospital call me,' said Alfonso.

'OK,' replied Tiny.

It suddenly struck Alfonso how distracted Tiny sounded. Not himself at all. He hadn't even asked how Marlena was.

'What's wrong, mate?' he asked. 'You don't sound right. You aren't letting all this business get to you, are you?'

'No, well . . . I'm trying not to,' said Tiny.

'Look, Greg's thing and this, well, like Greg himself said, stuff happens in inner cities. It's got nothing to do with Sunday Club, surely? Those pranks had nothing to do with this. Though I do think it might help now if whoever played them just owned up—'

'Fonz, stop,' commanded Tiny. 'I'm sure you're right. It's just, well, something else has happened . . .'

Alfonso waited for him to continue but there was silence on the other end of the line. 'What? What are you talking about?' he asked.

'It's Daisy, she's gone missing.'

'Oh my God. When? How?'

Alfonso wasn't mad about dogs, but he knew both Tiny and Billy were devoted to their pet chihuahua, and that Tiny was generally considered to be the most besotted. The spectacle of the big man lolloping around Covent Garden with his tiny dog on the end of a shiny pink lead had become virtually a tourist attraction. Certainly he and Daisy were frequently asked by passers-by to pose for photographs.

'I took her to the park as usual first thing this morning,' said Tiny. 'She was running around, like she does, in the bushes and everything. I lost sight of her for a bit and when I called her she didn't come. I wasn't worried at first. I thought she was having a poo or chasing a squirrel or something. Then after a bit I went looking for her. I scoured the park for her. There were other people there I knew, with dogs. They all joined in. We combed every inch of the place. She just wasn't there. She's disappeared, Fonz. Our little girl has clean disappeared. And with all these other incidents . . . Well, we're afraid some bastard's taken her. The same bastard who's been responsible for everything else, more than likely.'

Alfonso could hear Tiny stifling a sob. Maybe Sunday Club members really were being targeted by some unknown antagonist. And maybe it was one of their own. Alfonso could not reasonably deny the possibility. Maybe even the probability. But he continued to explore all avenues.

'Couldn't Daisy have just run off?' he asked. 'On her own?'

'She's never run off before. Never. Well, not for more than a minute or two. It's been hours now, Fonz. I'm worried sick.'

'Oh my God,' said Alfonso again. 'Do you really think someone's taken her?'

'I don't know,' said Tiny. 'I just don't know.'

'Oh shit,' said Alfonso. 'Look, don't worry. I'll get one of the others to pick up Marlena. If necessary, I'll swap shifts with someone at work and do it myself.'

There was yet another brief silence at the other end of the line.

'No,' said Tiny. 'I'll do it. Really. It'll give me something else to think about.'

'But don't you want to carry on looking?'

'I don't know where else to look, to be honest. Anyway, Billy's coming home early from work. He can take over. He may bring some new ideas with him. That's what I'm hoping for, anyway.'

'Well, if you're sure.'

'I'm quite sure, yes.'

'Maybe Daisy will have turned up by then.'

'Maybe she will,' said Tiny. But he didn't sound at all convinced.

Later that day Greg received a call from George.

'Have you heard about Marlena?' asked Greg straight away.

'Yes. It's awful. I'm so sorry. Alfonso called me last night. I should have been in touch to see if I can do anything to help, only . . .' George hesitated. 'Only something's happened. Chump's disappeared.'

'Are you sure?'

Greg was a dog person, and would have been devastated if anything happened to his and Karen's pair of Westies, but unlike George, and indeed Tiny and Billy, he'd owned dogs all his life. When he was a kid people had still just let their dogs out on the street to exercise themselves. As a rule, Greg didn't worry too much about dogs appearing to go missing. He also knew that George's Maltese terrier was a rescue dog with an unknown past.

'Of course I'm sure.' George sounded tetchy. 'I took him to Lincoln's Inn Fields mid-morning. One minute he was there at my feet, the next he was gone.'

'Couldn't he have gone off chasing something? That place is full of squirrels.'

'Yes, and Chump's terrified of them. He might be quite an old boy now, but you know what a baby he is. God knows what went on in his little life before I had him. He's scared of his own shadow. Sticks to me like glue.'

'So what happened?'

'My phone rang. We were by a wooded bit and Chump was sniffing about. I took the call because it was Marnie next door. You know how I look out for her. She can't get about much any more. She rang to ask me to get some shopping for her, but I think she was lonely and just wanted to chat. I couldn't get rid of her. When I eventually did, there was no sign of Chump. At first I thought he must be behind a bush or something, you know, doing his business. But no. I looked everywhere. No sign of him.'

'Where are you now?'

'I'm in the park. I've just come back here. I went home to make sure he hadn't taken off for there, and I've got Marnie waiting in my place just in case. So I thought it was best for me to be here. I'm making myself stay where I last saw him. That's where he'd be most likely to return to, looking for me, isn't it?'

'Probably.'

'Would you help me, Greg? Nobody knows this area like you do.'

Greg cursed. He had his own problems. But George knew he was a dog person, and Greg responded accordingly.

'Sure I will, George,' he said. 'Where are you exactly?'

'I'm by the bandstand.'

'I'll be there in fifteen.'

Greg lit a cigarette as he made his way along Long Acre. At least the walk gave him the chance to have a smoke. Karen thought Greg had given it up, but although he'd cut down he still couldn't quite kick the habit. He found his friend exactly where he'd said he'd be, right in the middle of the park sitting on a concrete step beneath the old bandstand. George looked pale and drawn.

'I don't like this,' he told Greg. 'Looks like we can be damned certain now that some maniac is targeting us lot, can't we? And it sure as hell ain't funny any more.'

'No,' said Greg. 'It's not, if that is what's happen—'

'What else can it be?' snapped George, before immediately apologizing. 'It's just that I'm in such a state. You hear about these cases of dog-napping and stuff all the time, don't you?' George continued.

'Not all the time, no,' said Greg. 'Honestly, George, the odds are Chump's just wandered off, got himself lost. He's chipped, isn't he?'

George nodded and looked as if he were about to speak again, when both men saw Billy walking towards them. Billy was talking into his phone and didn't notice them until he was practically alongside.

'Hiya, guys, you haven't seen our Daisy, have you?'

George turned even paler. Greg stared at Billy. It seemed things were turning nastier by the minute.

'Did you lose her here?' he asked.

'Yes,' said Billy. 'Tiny was walking her . . .'

He stopped dead, staring at white-faced George. Intuition struck.

'No, not you too? Not Chumpy?'

George nodded and explained how the little dog had disappeared while he was on the phone.

'Tiny said he thought Daisy was chasing a squirrel,' said Billy. 'But she's been gone for nearly six hours now. Oh my God. The Mr Tickle thing, Bob's plants, Greg's van, Marlena run over. Now two of our dogs are missing. It's too much happening to one small group of people. More than a series of coincidences, surely. No one can think that any more, can they? What the fuck is going on?'

'I don't know,' said Greg. 'But, look, George and Bob both got their stuff back with silly notes. Maybe that will happen with the dogs.'

'Even you don't sound convinced, Greg,' said Billy. 'That was before your tyres were slashed and Marlena was hurt. And this just feels nasty.'

'OK, OK, you're probably right,' said Greg. 'I never thought I'd hear myself saying this, but it probably is one for the bogeys. You should report the dogs missing.'

'Right, yes.'

George looked bemused more than anything. Billy's brain was racing, yet he couldn't think clearly.

'Where do you go to report missing dogs round here?' Billy asked. 'I know there's no police station in Covent Garden any more. Do we just phone?'

'I think we should go round, do it in person,' said Greg. 'Come on, Charing Cross is the nearest. Let's get a cab.'

'Hang about,' said George. 'Shouldn't one of us stay here in case either of the dogs does turn up?'

'Yes, good idea,' responded Greg. 'Look, why don't you two go together? The station's in Agar Street, just off the Strand. You should both go there to report what's happened. The cops may want to ask questions about your dogs that I couldn't answer. Don't worry, I'll stay here.'

'Are you sure?' asked George. 'I mean, you've always got things to do . . .'

I certainly have, thought Greg, and neither of you two would be likely to guess what sort of things, thank God. But all he said was: 'I won't budge till I hear from you or you get back, I promise.'

George still hesitated.

'What about Michelle?' he asked. 'Mightn't she be able to help?'

Greg shook his head. 'Not today,' he said. 'She's away on some course. Fonz told me yesterday. He'd hoped she might help with Marlena.'

'Right,' said George, still not moving.

'Go on, the pair of you, for Christ's sake,' said Greg.

He lit another cigarette as he watched the other two men make their way across the park to the gate on the lower west corner of the Fields. It was obvious from their body language how distressed they were. Funny what dogs can do to you, Greg mused. Big tough guys like Tiny, smooth operators like Billy, flash sarcastic bastards like George, even hard men like him – though he didn't feel that hard at the moment.

Dogs turned you to effing mush. That's what dogs did. And you never saw it coming.

Both Tiny and George were adamant their dogs wouldn't stray, but Greg reckoned where dogs were concerned there were exceptions to every rule. Years of dog ownership had taught him that there were two phrases a dog owner should never use: 'my dog never . . .' and 'my dog always . . .'.

This, however, was different. Two dogs going missing from the same park within a few hours of each other didn't sound coincidental. Especially after the events of the last few weeks. The dogs might yet be safely returned, but all the friends must be on edge now. No doubt about that. Greg was certainly on edge. His own situation was a particular one though, and he wasn't sure how it tied in with whatever else might be happening. Unlike the other Sunday Clubbers who'd fallen victim, he had a shrewd idea who was responsible for what had happened to his tyres. And he didn't see how it could have anything to do with the pranks played on George and Bob, Marlena being injured, or the disappearance of the two dogs.

Meanwhile, Karen was at home with their Westies. Greg had a sudden overwhelming desire to make sure she was all right. So he called her. And once he was sure she and their dogs were safe, he told her about Daisy and Chump going missing.

'That's awful,' responded Karen. 'What do you think's happened to the poor little things?'

'I don't know,' replied Greg.

'But it must be linked, there can't be any doubt about that, can there?'

Greg tried to sound positive. 'Look, all that matters to me is that my family's OK. And don't you worry, darling, I'll make damned sure of that.'

'I know you will,' said Karen in a small voice.

'Too damned right,' said Greg.

'But what do I do about our dogs?' asked Karen. 'They'll need to go out again soon.'

Greg cursed. He'd pledged to look after his own family but he hadn't thought about that when he'd promised the boys he'd stay in the park either until their return or until one or other of the dogs showed up.

He explained that to Karen, with apologies.

'I'm really sorry, babe, I feel I should be rushing home to take our two out, but you'll be fine as long as you keep them on a lead. And don't bring them to Lincoln's Inn. I know I'm here, but even so. Keep to the main drag – don't go down any of the alleyways. Go somewhere that's always busy: Russell Square, maybe. And if anything worries you, anything at all, call me.'

'I will,' said Karen. 'Don't worry, love. I'll be fine. And you're dead right to help those poor boys.'

Greg ended the call and checked his watch. There was something he had to do later on. Someone he needed to see. But that person didn't keep office hours. There was no need to start fretting at four in the afternoon. The boys were sure to have returned long before he needed to make a move, and even they would probably agree there was no point waiting in the park much longer. In any case, the gates would be locked once it got dark.

Greg sat on a park bench by the tennis courts, lit yet another cigarette and drew deeply. It was when he was under stress that he most felt not just the desire but the need to smoke. And this was a moment of stress all right.

He leaned back on the cold hard seat. Things were happening that he did not entirely understand. Nothing seemed right somehow. Events were taking a sinister turn. His life was going pear-shaped. He needed to figure out a way to get everything back on track again, and soon.

Tiny had collected Marlena from hospital at about the same time Billy had arrived at the park. He didn't tell her about Daisy, not at first. Marlena dog-sat for them whenever they needed a minder for Daisy, and took the little dog in when the boys went on holiday, to spare her having to go into kennels. She would be devastated to hear what had happened. And Tiny could see she was in enough distress already. He might fit the stereotype of the big brash bouncer, but Tiny had a very gentle side to him. He understood instinctively what it was like for a woman of Marlena's age to have been injured like that. Although she was putting on a brave face, as ever, Marlena had to be eaten up with anxiety about the extent of her injury, her chances of making a full recovery, whether she'd ever be able to walk about on her own again. Losing her independence would be Marlena's worst nightmare. And top of everything else, she was in pain. Tiny could see that too.

An orderly wheeled Marlena out of the hospital, Tiny alongside the chair, fussing. Once outside, the orderly helped load Marlena into the taxi Tiny hailed.

In the back of the cab Marlena clutched Tiny's arm with a bony hand.

'Thank you, darling,' she said. 'I don't know what I'd have done without my friends, particularly you and Alfonso.'

'You're most welcome, Marlena,' said Tiny. 'Though I gather from the Fonz that you initially said you didn't want or need help from anyone.'

Marlena smiled weakly. 'I think I may not have quite thought things through,' she said.

Tiny saw then that the hand clutching his arm was shaking. As if aware that he had noticed, Marlena suddenly withdrew her hand and held it, fingers clenched, by her side.

Tiny put a big arm around her. 'Don't you worry, sweetheart,' he said. 'I'll look after you.'

Marlena said nothing, but he could see the gratitude in her eyes and it unnerved him. For an old lady, she'd always seemed a remarkably tough cookie. Now that toughness appeared to have left her.

Marlena lived on the fourth floor of her converted warehouse apartment block, but fortunately, and relatively unusually in Covent Garden, Sampford House had a lift. Thank God, thought Tiny. It was obvious that Marlena was far too frail to use the crutches the hospital had supplied her with. For the moment anyway. And not even for short distances on the level. But Tiny had already planned how he would get her from the taxi, in and out of the lift and into her apartment, and it was therefore a relief that she seemed more compliant than usual.

When the taxi pulled to a halt he snatched Marlena's crutches from her, jumped out and propped them in the hallway of Sampford House, ignoring her protests.

'Right, there have to be some advantages to being the size

of a house,' he said, as he returned to the cab, and with that he lifted Marlena out, settling her easily into his big arms.

'What on earth do you think you are doing?' protested Marlena. 'Put me down at once!'

Tiny ignored her. He didn't think she meant it anyway. Indeed, he suspected she was relieved, though of course she would never admit it.

'I'm giving you a lift, Marlena baby,' he said. 'And if I was you, I'd shut the fuck up and enjoy the ride.'

Marlena laughed as he carried her through the apartment-block foyer and into the elevator. It was almost her normal laugh. Tiny was surprised by just how much he appreciated hearing it, even though he could not get Daisy out of his head.

On the fourth floor Marlena produced her door key and managed to unlock her front door whilst still in Tiny's arms. Rejecting his suggestion that he carry her through to her bedroom so she could have a lie-down, she insisted on being placed in her favourite armchair, by the window in the sitting room.

'What do you think I am, a crippled old woman or some-thing?' she enquired, twinkling at Tiny as he arranged a foot-stool for her in exactly the right position.

'I'll fetch your crutches, you ungrateful old bag,' said Tiny.

Marlena beamed her thanks at him. At least coming home seemed to have cheered her somewhat, and maybe he had played a part in that too, thought Tiny, in spite of his inner preoccu-pation with his missing pet.

At that moment his mobile rang. It was Billy. Tiny took the call at once, praying for good news. There was none. Instead Billy told him about meeting up with George and how Chump was also missing.

Tiny felt his heartbeat quicken. He turned his back on Marlena and moved away from her towards the door.

'Oh my God,' he said.

He could feel Marlena's eyes on him. He opened the door, walked out into the passageway and closed it behind him, still speaking into his phone.

'Two dogs,' he muttered, 'on the same day, and both belonging to members of our little group.'

'I know,' said Billy, and Tiny could feel his distress.

'What do you make of it, Billy?' he asked. 'And what does George think?'

'We don't know what to think,' said Billy. 'Neither does Greg – he's been helping us.'

'We have to do something. We should go to the police.'

'George and I are on our way to the police station now. Greg said he'd wait in the park, just in case.'

After ending the call Tiny carried on downstairs, on auto-pilot, to collect Marlena's crutches. His heart was still racing inside his chest when he re-entered her flat.

'What is it, Tiny, whatever has happened?' Marlena asked.

Tiny didn't want to burden her with it. Aside from being fond of dogs, and Daisy in particular, right now she was a frightened old lady with a crushed foot, and all the glitter and the bluster in the world couldn't hide that. The last thing Tiny wanted was to add to her distress. But Marlena gave him no choice.

'Are you going to tell me what's wrong or am I going to have to beat it out of you with one of these damn crutches?' she persisted.

Tiny told her.

Marlena turned even more pale than she was already.

'What's going on, Tiny?' she asked, her voice frail and bewildered. 'What in the world is going on?'

seven

George and Billy's luck did not immediately improve upon arrival at Charing Cross police station. They were mildly surprised to find one of the big wooden doors standing open, and might have been encouraged by this as they stepped into the lobby of the Agar Street main entrance.

Unfortunately, however, they were dealt with by a civilian public access officer whose never particularly good temper had that day been further frayed by learning that his services would soon no longer be required. He shouldn't have been too surprised, as the Met were in the process of phasing out civilian front-office staff in favour of a rota of serving police officers, but that didn't stop him feeling affronted. Michael Carter was a former uniformed sergeant of the old school, and even though he'd been retired from the force for several years he continued to fail to see quite how the Met could survive without him. In addition, Carter was a cat man who had no interest whatsoever in dogs. Indeed, he actively disliked them. He considered dogs to be dirty, disobedient creatures who fouled pavements and every so often lost the plot and bit somebody. Usually a child.

Nonetheless, he dutifully went through the motions of recording all the details of the two missing animals, asked George and Billy if their dogs were chipped, which they were, and said he would file a report.

'But what will happen? I mean, what can you do? Will you look for our dogs?' asked George plaintively.

Even Billy, in his state of deep distress, knew better than to believe that the Metropolitan Police Force was likely to conduct a formal investigation into the disappearance of a couple of dogs. But he too stared at Mike Carter with a hope born of desperation.

Carter looked George up and down in a pitying sort of way. However, no sympathy at all for the loss of George's dog was implied.

'We will put out a notice to all officers, dog sanctuaries and so on, according to procedure,' he said, as if reciting from a manual. 'And should the dogs be found or we discover anything at all pertaining to their whereabouts, you will be notified at once.'

George merely nodded. Billy found some spirit.

'Look,' he said. 'There's more to this than just two missing dogs.'

'Really, sir,' said Carter, sounding totally uninterested.

Billy persisted. He began to relate the series of incidents which had befallen the friends.

The Mr Tickle story caused the corners of Mike Carter's more or less permanently downturned mouth to twitch. Just a bit. Fleetingly, he glanced at George with a little more interest. By the time Billy had related how Bob's plants were taken in the night, however, Carter was looking thoroughly bored again. He raised an eyebrow at the slashing of the tyres on Greg's van, but merely muttered something about wanton vandalism, much as Greg had done in Johnny's Place.

Then Billy told him about Marlena.

'It seems almost certain she was hit deliberately by the cyclist,' he said.

'Was the accident reported to the police?' asked Carter.

'I think so. I'm not sure,' said Billy. 'Only we don't believe it was an accident, do we, George?'

George shook his head.

'Hold on a minute,' said Carter.

He retreated to a computer at the rear of the front office and began tapping away.

'I don't see how this is helping us find the dogs,' muttered George. 'That man doesn't give a toss, does he? He's made himself perfectly clear. We'd be better off out on the streets looking for them than hanging round here.'

'Let's at least wait until he comes back,' said Billy. 'If he begins to believe what we all do, we might yet get some help.'

As he finished speaking, Mike Carter returned.

'We apparently had two officers at the scene of the incident involving your friend Marlena,' he began. 'They have since interviewed her and various witnesses. I have just read their report and there is nothing in it about the possibility of deliberate intent. It is true that the cyclist didn't stop, but unfortunately that sort of reckless behaviour is not unknown on the streets of this city. And the victim said nothing about having been deliberately targeted.'

'Didn't she?' asked George. He shot Billy a surprised look.

'She must still be in shock and in a lot of pain,' persisted Billy. 'And she's an old lady. I shouldn't think she's capable of thinking straight right now.'

'No, of course she isn't. But Alfonso, our friend Alfonso who more or less saw it happen, he didn't think it was an accident,' said George.

'Ah, yes.' Carter glanced down at the computer printout he

was holding. 'Mr Bertorelli. Our officers did comment on the coincidence of his presence at the scene.'

'What the heck do you mean by that?' countered Billy. He was a corporate lawyer, quite unused to visiting police stations and dealing with situations such as this, but his legal brain had switched on automatically. 'One minute you're telling us Marlena was merely the victim of an accident, and the next you appear to be making insinuations about Alfonso?'

Carter's face was set in stone.

'I can only tell you what is in our officers' report, sir,' he said. 'And indeed I cannot go into any more detail. I will file a report on your missing dogs, as I have already told you, and make a note of your other comments, which will then be on record. But under the circumstances, there is nothing further I can do for you at this stage.'

'I do hope your report is a full one and that it will be swiftly brought to the attention of those who may feel able to take action,' said Billy, forcing himself to remain calm. At least on the surface.

George made no attempt to control his rising anger. 'For God's sake!' he shouted. 'We're a group of ten friends and now something weird, or unpleasant, or downright frightening, or even violent, has happened to six of us in less than a fortnight. Never mind the coincidence of one of us witnessing Marlena getting injured, don't you think there may have been one or two other coincidences too many in all of this?'

'I understand that you are upset, sir,' said Carter. 'But you need to calm down. Of course, if any further incidents occur, you should let us know.'

'Oh, what's the fucking point?' said George, and flounced off through the open door onto Agar Street with Billy following.

'Drama queens,' muttered Carter under his breath, making

quite the wrong assumption about George, who did a rather impressive flounce when he put his mind to it, as well as wearing tight trousers and smelling strongly of cologne. Bizarrely, Carter made the same, and in that instance correct, assumption about Billy, who was dressed in a business suit and had maintained his professional demeanour throughout, only because of his association with George. Once upon a time Carter would have had a lot more to say, and rather more loudly, but police officers and those affiliated to the force could no longer express their prejudices in public without landing in trouble. It didn't alter the fact that, so far as Carter was concerned, George and Billy were still a pair of poofs, and if he'd been dealing with two straight men he may well have been more helpful. Or at least listened more carefully.

He would have denied that, though, and believed his own denial. So he remained a diligent officer, duly filing a report on the missing dogs and including the suggestion that this might be linked to other incidents.

George, Billy and Tiny continued to look for their dogs the rest of that day and into the night. Bob, having popped round to see how Marlena was and been told by her that Daisy and Chump were missing, joined in.

The four men combed the streets, enquired in pubs and shops, and appealed to passers-by, all to no avail.

Meanwhile, after returning home to be with Karen and help her put the kids to bed in a bid to maintain some sort of normality, Greg was finally able to make his way to Soho in an attempt to see the man he'd been thinking about all day, in between trying to help his friends.

It was nearly ten p.m. before he arrived at his destination, a gambling club called the Zodiac, in the heart of Chinatown.

The entrance, flanked by a pair of Oriental heavies wearing black suits and dicky bows, who were both about half the size of Tiny and twice as menacing, was at the Wardour Street end of Lisle Street. Greg walked towards it resolutely, albeit on the other side of the road. And it was only when he was directly opposite that he paused. Then he walked on past and stopped again to step into the doorway of a closed Chinese supermarket.

His heart seemed to be beating much faster than usual. He could feel sweat forming on his forehead. He needed to calm down and work out exactly what he was going to say before entering that club. He took the last of his secret cigarettes from the packet in his pocket and lit up, checking before he did so that he still had the extra-strong mints he would need in order to conceal his misdemeanour from Karen later.

Lost in his own not entirely pleasant world, he bent forward slightly to light up, cupping his hand around cigarette and lighter. As the flame illuminated his face, he heard a familiar male voice.

'Greg? What you doing here, mate?'

It was Tiny.

Greg breathed out a lungful of smoke.

'Just popped out for a sneaky ciggy,' he said. 'Don't tell the missus, will you?'

Tiny looked puzzled. Greg guessed the big man was wondering why he needed to 'pop' this far from Bishops Court in order to smoke an illicit cigarette. But Tiny passed no comment. Of course, he had his own preoccupations.

Greg took another welcome drag. God, why was smoking so damned good, he wondered.

Tiny still hadn't spoken.

'Any news of the dogs, mate?' Greg asked him, though he

could tell from the way Tiny looked that there hadn't been. Or if there had, it wasn't good news.

Tiny shook his head.

'They've disappeared without a trace, Greg,' he said. 'Billy and I have been everywhere twice, and Bob's pitched in too.'

'Anything more I can do to help?' asked Greg, hoping that Tiny would answer in the negative.

Tiny shook his head again. 'Billy's having one last look back at the park, even though it's closed this time of night. Ari's printing up some posters and said he'll fly-post them all over the West End in the morning. Meanwhile, I'm on my way home to get the drinks poured ready for when Billy gets in. We thought we might get blind drunk.'

'Trouble is, that makes things even worse when you come round in the morning with a hangover as well as the shit that's going on,' said Greg, who was considering doing exactly the same thing.

He hugged the big man.

'Just remember, a dog's job is to break your bloody heart and worry you to death. They'll probably turn up, the pair of 'em, bright-eyed and bushy-tailed, as if nothing's happened. With or without one of those silly notes.'

'Thanks, Greg,' said Tiny, managing a small smile, even though he didn't believe a word of it.

'Now take care, yeah?'

'Yeah. You too, mate. Take care. And of the missus.'

Greg watched his friend carry on down the street, head bowed under the weight of his worries.

If only you knew, pal, he thought, if only you knew. He finished his cigarette, threw the butt down and stamped it into the ground. Then he stood for a moment, looking up the street at the Zodiac gambling club: its dimly lit entrance standing out by default among the bright lights of Soho, its name discreetly engraved on a brass plaque to one side of the doorway. This was a club of long standing and considerable reputation. It did not need to advertise. Greg watched a group of punters arrive. They looked like regulars, hurrying through the door, eager to begin their play. A tall man wearing a dark overcoat with its collar turned up left shortly afterwards. His head was down. Greg wondered how much the man had lost. The stakes were high at the Zodiac.

Greg shuffled his feet. He was nervous. And that chance meeting with Tiny had somehow further dampened an already ebbing resolution. He no longer had the stomach for a tricky and delicate confrontation, even though he'd been planning it all day.

He told himself that not only might it not be necessary, that his suspicions may have been ill founded, but also there was a risk that by going there he would only increase the danger he and his family were in.

No, he decided, he would put it off until the following day. Who knew what might have developed by then?

He shivered in the cold night air, thrust his hands deep into the pockets of his bomber jacket, and strode off down Lisle Street, heading for home.

All he wanted was to kiss his sleeping children goodnight, climb into his warm double bed and hold his wife close and tight.

Michelle arrived unannounced at Marlena's flat. She was carrying a small suitcase, the sort that fits under the seats of aircraft, and looked as if she had been hurrying.

'I hope you don't mind me coming round so late,' she said.

'My plane just got in and I rushed straight here.' She gestured at her bag. 'I wanted to see for myself how you were.'

Marlena tried to smile. Her lips stretched into a thin hard line.

'Ask me a load of questions, more like,' she said grumpily.

Michelle did a double take. 'I'm sorry,' she said. 'I'll go, if you like. You're right, of course. I did also wonder if I could help, though.'

'Oh, please don't go,' said Marlena, pushing aside her moment of pique as quickly as she'd allowed herself to display it. 'I'm sorry too. My damn foot is hurting so much its wreaking havoc with my temper.'

'Oh dear,' said Michelle. 'What about painkillers? You must have been given some. Are they not working?'

'Not nearly enough. I've already taken more than my quota for today. But to hell with that, I shall definitely be seeking oblivion at bedtime.'

Michelle smiled. 'Don't blame you,' she said. 'You will be careful though, won't you?'

Marlena smiled back. 'I am always careful, dear child,' she said. 'Even if it doesn't look that way right now.'

'It doesn't,' said Michelle. 'I presume you've had a police visit or two about this, haven't you?'

'Yes. Pair of charming young men with a penchant for the obvious.'

Michelle laughed. 'Sounds like a definition of all too many coppers I know,' she said. 'Not sure about the "charming" bit though.' She paused. 'Anyway, I'm back on duty tomorrow, and one of the reasons I've dropped in on you like this is because I thought I might gee things up a bit. It's not my beat, and even if it was I'd be regarded as personally involved so I couldn't take part in any inquiries, but there really should be a proper police investigation. Too much has happened for this all to be coincidence. You've heard about the boys' dogs, I expect?'

Marlena confirmed that she had.

'Both dogs, same place; same day, and within a couple of hours of each other. Another so-called coincidence? I don't think so.'

She asked Marlena if she'd go through the details of her collision with the hooded cyclist again.

Marlena protested mildly. 'The two constables who were at the scene and then came to the hospital made me do that, even though, charming or not, they didn't seem very interested,' she said.

'They didn't know the whole picture, did they? Anyway, there's a CID man I know who won't be able to resist this case. It will intrigue him, I'm sure. Come on, Marlena. We really can't let this go on, it's getting frightening. One more time, please. Tell me exactly what happened.'

Marlena did so, giving as thorough an account as she could, albeit a little wearily.

'And the cyclist, the hooded man, if it was a man, just rode off?' prompted Michelle, after Marlena had come to the end. 'He didn't stop?'

'No, he didn't stop. Come on, would you expect him to?' Marlena sighed. 'I'm still not convinced it was deliberate, though,' she added. 'I think that's too far-fetched.'

Michelle studied the older woman. There was an element of doubt in her voice, as if pleading for reassurance rather than proclaiming what she believed to be true.

'I don't know about that,' Michelle said, unable to offer the reassurance her friend craved. 'But I do know one thing: it's damned well time somebody found out.'

*

The following morning Michelle reported for duty at Charing Cross at 7 a.m. On the way to the station she'd encountered Ari, who, good as his word, was already fly-posting the neighbourhood. He showed Michelle one of his posters, which bore photographs of both dogs, emailed to him by their owners, and the slogan: *Missing. Daisy the chihuahua, light brown, long-haired bitch, and Chump, male Maltese terrier, white. Generous reward for anyone with information leading to their recovery.* The poster also gave the details of when and where the dogs were last seen.

'Well done, Ari,' said Michelle. 'Let's hope something comes of it.'

'Yep, let's hope.'

'You're out and about early,' she told him then added, grinning: 'I doubt you've ever been out this early before, unless you were coming home from somewhere.'

'Oh, ha bloody ha,' said Ari. 'I wanted to catch people going to work, and people walking their dogs before they go to work. They're probably the most likely to have seen or heard something.' He paused, his face falling. 'If anyone has.'

'I know what you mean,' said Michelle, giving him a quick hug.

At the station she checked what reports had been formally filed and what action had so far been taken: little or none. Then she set about contacting the CID man she'd mentioned to Marlena the previous evening.

In the dark days immediately after her transfer to the Met, still aching from the pain of her marriage break-up, Michelle had made a clumsy pass at Detective Sergeant David Vogel outside the Dunster Arms following a farewell party for some veteran uniform she didn't even know. She had been very drunk at the time, desperate to blot out her anguish at the betrayal and humiliation she'd suffered when her husband left her. With his wispy fair hair, wispy fair beard and penchant for elderly corduroy, Vogel didn't look much like a police officer; and unlike most of his colleagues that evening, he had been totally sober. As far as Michelle knew, he didn't drink. And he was rumoured to be a vegetarian. He was a man who seemed to allow himself few personal indulgences. And playing away from home was apparently not one of them. His response to her unsolicited display of affection had been to blink rapidly behind his horn-rimmed spectacles and decline, quite kindly, on the grounds that he was married with a young daughter.

Unaccustomed to the company of honourable men, Michelle had felt a total fool. But she'd been impressed too. From that night, Vogel had seemed all the more attractive to her, though she made sure to hide the fact for fear of embarrassing them both. In any case, unless she was really stupid and repeated the performance of throwing herself at him, Vogel could be relied upon not to notice. He wasn't the sort of man most women found attractive. Which, of course, with the sorry history of her wrecked marriage still ruling her every emotion, was probably why Michelle was so taken with him.

She sensed that Vogel was an unusual copper as well as an unusual man. They called him the Geek at Charing Cross, but not without grudging respect. The name was a twisted tribute to his intelligence and his ability to sift through endless layers of facts and figures and come up with connotations and conclusions that no one else could.

It turned out that Vogel wasn't on duty until noon that day, so Michelle dropped him an email outlining her concerns about the various events that had befallen her friends. She concluded by asking if he would do her the favour of having a quick look at the Marlena incident and maybe keep an eye on the missing-dogs scenario.

She then took off for another edifying day in the division she so disliked. There was a Garden Party at Buckingham Palace, and she was on point duty for the rest of her shift. That meant aching feet and zero job satisfaction: just another day in Traffic.

David Vogel picked up her email shortly after coming on duty. He read it through carefully, but at speed. His lips twitched, just as Mike Carter's had done, at the Mr Tickle story. Vogel was not without a sense of humour, though this was not generally recognized within the Met because it was so much gentler than that of his colleagues. He pondered for a moment or two. A pair of mystery pranks, an act of apparent wanton vandalism, two dogs going missing on the same day at the same place, a possibly deliberate attack on an elderly woman . . . Vogel was intrigued, just as Michelle had predicted. However, a mountain of paperwork sat on his desk. Twice as much data again awaited his attention on screen. The minutiae of a complex fraud case that nobody had yet been able to untangle. To most police officers, indeed most people, sifting through this lot would be a horrible chore. To David Vogel it was a delight. He loved paperwork. He relished the opportunity to seek out details others had overlooked. Loved discovering what lay behind an apparently meaningless jumble of bald facts and figures. Shortly before switching off his computer and heading home the previous evening, almost three hours after his shift had officially ended, he'd thought he might be close to a breakthrough. He couldn't wait to get stuck in again.

Mr Tickle would just have to wait, he told himself, with the smallest stab of regret. Besides, there might be nothing to it. The dogs would probably turn up unharmed and without explanation, as dogs did, and there might be no link whatsoever between the other events. He simply didn't have the time to do anything about it at present. He did, however, send an email to Dispatch saying that these matters had come to his notice, and asking could he please be kept informed of any developments.

At three in the afternoon, Jessica Harding, a bright young PC working in Dispatch, called his extension.

'Looks like there's been a development in that case you're interested in, Sarge,' she told him. 'Some *Big Issue* seller just found the remains of two dogs in a rubbish bin on Long Acre. He told a passer-by who called us. Apparently they've been badly mutilated.'

'Are we sure they're the same two dogs?' asked Vogel.

'Well, they need their microchips checking, assuming they have them, but the descriptions match,' PC Harding replied.

Vogel had already begun calling up the relevant report: 'A chihuahua and a Maltese terrier,' he read from his screen. 'The breeds are right then?'

'Yes,' agreed Jessica Harding. 'In as much as anyone could tell. Sounds like they're in a terrible state. Their sexual organs have been removed, their eyes gouged out, tails cut off – that sort of thing. The *Big Issue* seller went into shock and had to be taken to hospital, and, according to the response team, the man who called us wasn't in much better shape either. The chihuahua's head's been more or less hacked off and—'

Vogel interrupted. Unlike former sergeant Mike Carter, David Vogel liked dogs. He had a border collie called Timmy at home, and if anything like that ever happened to Timmy, Vogel feared what he might be capable of doing to the perpetrators.

'All right, Harding, I get the picture,' he said. He was about to end the call when a thought occurred to him. 'Has anyone notified the owners yet?'

'Not yet,' responded Harding.

'Good,' said Vogel. 'I think we should ask PC Michelle Monahan to do it. She knows them, apparently. And she knows the background to all this. They're going to be shocked rigid, whoever tells them, but she may be able to get more out of them.'

'Isn't she Traffic?'

Vogel sighed. 'She's still a police officer, Jessica,' he said. 'And she was previously in CID.'

'Right. OK. I'll tell my boss you're handling that side of it then, shall I?' asked Harding.

'Yes.' Vogel was no longer really listening.

He ended the call and, trying to ignore the queasiness in the pit of his stomach, sat and thought for a moment or two before contacting Michelle's team leader to ask if he could borrow her for a special task. Like Michelle, David Vogel didn't believe in coincidences. And he was beginning to get a bad feeling about the increasingly sinister and unpleasant sequence of events which he now felt impelled to investigate.

eight

And so it was Michelle who broke the news to the boys. She called round to see them after she'd finished traffic duty at the palace. First George, then Tiny and Billy. By then it was early evening, and she found all three men at their homes, as she had hoped.

George burst into tears and couldn't stop crying.

'This shouldn't have happened,' he said. 'Not to those dear little dogs. Whatever else is going on, this shouldn't have happened.'

Michelle made soothing noises, which was about all she could do.

'They must have suffered, they must have suffered so,' muttered George through his tears.

Michelle could find no words to argue with that. She was aware of the condition both dogs had been in when they were found, and although she tried to spare George that knowledge, her friend insisted on being told. No wonder he was so upset, thought Michelle. And she too dreaded to think what the two little dogs must have gone through before death had eventually brought them release.

Realizing that George was on the brink of hysteria, Michelle made sweet tea and forced him to drink it. The tea didn't appear to do a lot of good. She reckoned he needed something stronger. She found a bottle of supermarket brandy in a kitchen cupboard and poured him a large glass which he swallowed quite obediently. Then she sat with him.

It took more than an hour before she felt able to leave George. Even then she only did so because she feared that if she didn't go to Tiny and Billy soon, they might find out from some other source. Reluctant to leave George on his own, she popped next door to ask his neighbour, Marnie, the elderly woman George had once told her looked upon him as a surrogate son, if she'd call round and keep an eye on him.

Marnie, it turned out, was in a wheelchair – to Michelle's embarrassment, as she'd never met the woman before and yet here she was asking her a favour, albeit on George's behalf.

But Marnie, whose eyes welled up when Michelle told her as gently as she could that Chump had been killed, was eager to help.

'Oh, that poor little dog,' said Marnie. 'Don't you fret, dear. I can get next door all right in my chair. 'Bout as far as I can go nowadays without help. But don't worry, I'll look after my Georgie. He does enough for me, that boy, I can tell you.'

Billy and Tiny took the news equally badly, albeit rather more quietly. The big man shed silent tears which ran freely down his broad cheeks. He made no attempt to wipe them away. It was almost as if he was unaware that he was weeping.

'But have the chips been checked yet?' he asked suddenly.

'Well, no, not as far as I know,' responded Michelle. 'The dogs are the right breeds, though. I mean, it really would be one heck of a coincidence if it weren't Daisy and Chump, I'm afraid.'

''Course it would,' said Billy. His face was ashen. There was not even any colour in his lips. 'Stop clutching at straws, Tiny. It's our little girl.'

'All right, but I want to see her. I want to see her. Before . . .'
Tiny couldn't seem to get any more words out.

Michelle hesitated. She had told all three boys that the dogs
had been mutilated, but so far Tiny and Billy hadn't asked her
for the details.

'Look, Tiny, don't you think you'd rather remember Daisy
how she was?' she suggested.

'No, I want to see her. I want to see my Daisy,' Tiny persisted.

Michelle glanced towards Billy and imperceptibly shook her
head. Unfortunately Tiny caught her at it.

'You haven't told us exactly how Daisy died, have you,
Michelle?' the big man asked. 'Was it really that bad? Come
on, tell us what happened to her. Everything. I, for one, need
to know.'

'Well, we can't be absolutely sure,' said Michelle. She realized she was prevaricating, but couldn't help herself. 'I'm afraid
Daisy did suffer appalling injuries, but they could have
happened after her death.'

'Are *you* clutching at straws now, Michelle?'

'No. The truth is, we don't know. Perhaps there will be a pet
autopsy – I'm not sure what the form is. The dogs were stolen,
and that, coupled with the fact that they may have been subjected
to undue suffering, means that criminal offences have almost
certainly been committed. So I should think CID will push for
a full post-mortem veterinary examination.'

'Oh, for God's sake, Michelle, just tell us what you know,
tell us what happened to our dog.' Tiny, usually so softly spoken,
may have taken the initial news quietly and apparently quite
calmly, perhaps because it was no more than he had expected,
but now he was shouting.

'Right.' Nothing else for it, thought Michelle. Tiny, like
George, was evidently not to be deterred.

She told them, in the most clinical and unemotional way that she could manage, that Daisy's tail had been cut off, that her sexual organs had been removed, that her throat had been cut and her head almost severed.

'Th-that's why I think it better that you don't see her,' Michelle stumbled.

Billy's reaction was physical. He retched a couple of times then ran out of the room in the direction of the bathroom.

Tiny sat very still, staring straight ahead. Curiously, the tears stopped. Michelle thought he had gone beyond crying. She looked down at her hands clasped in her lap. Her palms were sweating. Silently she cursed David Vogel for asking her to do this, she cursed herself for agreeing to do it, and she cursed the whole vicious twisted world in which she lived.

Eventually Tiny spoke.

'Are you going to find who did this, Michelle? Are you?'

'Well, not me, Tiny, but there's a top CID man on it now, he's looking into what happened to the dogs and all the other stuff that's been going on with Marlena and everything. There'll be a major inquiry, I'm sure of it.'

Tiny nodded, a faraway look in his eyes.

'It doesn't matter,' he said.

'What? Of course it matters,' countered Michelle.

'No.' Tiny's voice was hard. 'It doesn't matter. Because if the police don't find the bastard who did this, I will. And then I'm going to do to him exactly what he did to my Daisy.'

David Vogel put the fraud case which had previously consumed him to one side. Vogel could get away with that sort of thing. His superior officers valued his unique abilities and tolerated his eccentricities. As far as was possible, they allowed his butterfly mind to flutter at will, because of the extraordinary results it produced. Vogel operated with a freedom virtually unknown, not only at the Met but within any British police force. His colleagues sometimes resented this, but most had benefited at one time or another from his particular talents. He was always willing to study a passed-on bundle of paperwork or a list of facts that had previously revealed little or nothing to those working on a case, and rarely failed to pick up on something, however tiny, of previously overlooked significance. In addition, even if his rare exactitude led to a solution that otherwise may never have been reached, Vogel showed no inclination to take the credit. His sole interest was achieving a successful conclusion.

Now Vogel's attention had, almost without him wishing it, become totally focused on the events Michelle Monahan had brought to his notice, starting with those pranks which, it seemed, were escalating into something very nasty indeed.

Vogel checked through the reports filed by the officers who had attended the scene of the alleged accident which had left Marlena injured, and also the report filed by Mike Carter when George, Tiny and Billy had reported their dogs missing.

There had to be a link, he was sure of it. But what could possibly be the motive? This group of friends, whom Michelle had told him met most Sundays at Johnny's Place, appeared on the surface to be an oddly mismatched bunch. Vogel needed to learn more about them, the kind of people they were and the kind of lives they led.

He wondered if he should join them one Sunday evening. But he didn't think he would be very welcome, even though Michelle was one of the group. And in light of the most recent events, he wondered if the Sunday evening suppers would continue.

After all, the entire group must suspect each other now. Unless they had reason to believe they were being targeted by some outsider they all knew.

Michelle had emailed him a rundown on the members of the group, giving him a summary of what she knew about each one and also how they had met.

Vogel also made the obvious checks on the implicated men and women. He started with the PNC, the police national computer, and then searched more widely on the web, googling them all and logging in to the major social networking sites, Facebook and Twitter.

Googling Ari immediately brought up a link to his father and the major multinational companies the family owned. The PNC provided further information. And a police mugshot.

The previous year Ari had been charged with and cautioned for possessing a class-A drug: cocaine. He had been arrested after attracting the attention of a pair of Traffic cops by driving his Porsche in an erratic manner. He was found to be under the influence of alcohol as well as cocaine, and was banned from driving for eighteen months.

He did not appear to have a Facebook page or a Twitter account.

George Kristos did have a Facebook page, mostly featuring pictures of himself looking handsome. According to Michelle, he was an actor, so Vogel looked him up on the Spotlight website and found an entry with several references to pantomime performances, and a publicity picture of him dressed as Prince Charming in *Cinderella* at Rhyl over Christmas the previous year.

Tiny, Billy and Bob did not seem to feature on the web, aside from their names being listed on 192.com. Marlena, known throughout Covent Garden as simply that, with no last name, was unlisted, but did appear on the electoral register under what was presumably her real name: Marleen McTavish – a detail she had apparently supplied to Perkins and Brandt only under considerable protest. Vogel found himself smiling at that.

He was mildly surprised that Tiny and Billy had no web input. According to Michelle, they were in their mid to late thirties and very much gay men about town. But she'd failed to go into much further detail about them, apart from giving a job description for them both, so Vogel didn't know that their relationship wasn't entirely out in the open, or not as far as Billy's family were concerned anyway; certainly reason enough in itself to avoid Facebook.

Alfonso Bertorelli had a Facebook page, but it registered very little activity. Indeed he seemed to have barely returned to it since first compiling it and posting a picture of himself wearing his waiter's white shirt and black pencil tie.

Karen Walker was also on Facebook and had by far the busiest entry. There were pictures of her with her husband, Greg, her children and her mother. Every part of her children's lives seemed to be chronicled: their progress at school, their sporting activities and so on. She updated her page every few days and had a substantial list of Facebook friends.

The PNC revealed that Greg Walker was the only other member of the group to have a criminal record. And his was an offence of a violent nature.

At the age of eighteen Greg had pleaded guilty at Bow Street Magistrate's Court to causing an affray. He and a group of other youths had caused a disturbance at the Brunswick shopping centre. A fight had broken out involving a local shopkeeper who'd ended up in hospital, albeit with only minor injuries. It had been alleged that the youths were part of a gang demanding protection money in the area, but this had not been proved. Greg had been given a three-month suspended prison sentence.

It was nothing much. A spoiled rich boy behaving true to form, and a son of the inner city falling foul of the law as a teenager and then apparently staying out of trouble ever after and building a solid family life for himself. Nonetheless, Vogel thought he might begin his inquiries with these two men.

There were already statements from Marlena, the most cruelly afflicted victim, and Alfonso, witness to her misfortune, on record, although Vogel, the master of spotting what others did not, intended to speak to them both again personally at some stage.

Meanwhile it was a matter of priorities. He had to start somewhere. He chose to visit the Walkers first.

The main gate leading into Bishops Court was unlocked, as it often was. Vogel climbed the stairs to the second floor. As he stepped onto the landing he could hear shouting from inside number 23.

Vogel moved a little closer, walking softly. He invariably wore slip-on Hush Puppies with rubber soles. Brown suede ones. Comfortable, practical shoes, which did not announce his presence before he wished it.

The woman's voice was high-pitched and easy to hear.

'You know something, Greg, you damned well know something, don't you? I thought you did when your tyres were slashed. Now I'm sure of it.'

The man's voice was lower-pitched and not so easy to hear. Vogel could only catch the odd word.

'Honest, doll . . . there's nothing . . . I wouldn't . . .'

Then the woman again: 'I just hope you're not up to your

116

old tricks – and don't you think for one minute I don't have a damned good idea what you were into before we got wed.'

Vogel could not catch anything comprehensible when the man replied, all he could hear was the murmur of a low voice.

He rang the doorbell. Immediately a small dog started to bark, then another. The woman answered, shooing to one side a pair of yapping West Highland terriers. There were patches of colour high on both her cheeks.

'Mrs Walker?' he enquired.

Karen nodded, already looking alarmed.

Vogel introduced himself and held out his warrant card.

The woman appeared to be mildly surprised. Vogel had grown accustomed to that. He'd once been told he looked more like an absent-minded professor than a policeman. And he'd actually been somewhat flattered. But, in truth, it would be hard to be less absent-minded than David Vogel.

Karen led him into the sitting room where the man Vogel assumed to be Greg Walker was standing by the window that overlooked the street.

'The police are here,' muttered Karen, glowering at her husband.

'Right.' Greg turned towards Vogel. His feet made a crunching sound as he moved.

'Mr Walker?' queried Vogel.

Greg didn't reply directly.

Vogel took in the scene before him, his eyes flitting around the room, registering every detail. It was clean, tidy and attractively furnished. But cold. Almost as cold as outside. He noticed that the carpet by the window was strewn with broken glass, and the largest pane in the window itself had been smashed. An icy draught gusted into the room. There was a brick in the middle of the floor.

'Did you call the police?' Greg asked Karen. He didn't sound angry, more resigned.

Vogel answered. 'No, your wife didn't call us, Mr Walker,' he said. 'Or at least, not to my knowledge, she didn't.'

He glanced at Karen enquiringly. She shook her head, agreeing with him.

'I am here as part of my investigation into certain incidents that have been reported to us by others with whom I think you are acquainted,' Vogel went on. 'I understand there was an incident concerning your van, which I do not believe you reported.'

Vogel looked down pointedly at the floor.

'Might this be another such incident?' he enquired.

Greg shrugged.

'Yes, it damned well might,' snapped Karen. 'Some bastard's thrown a brick through our window. Less than an hour ago. In broad daylight. Apart from anything else we could have been killed. If they hadn't been at school, one of the kids could have been killed.'

'Do either of you have any idea who might be responsible?' asked Vogel, mindful of the exchange he had just overheard.

'Well, I certainly don't.' Karen glowered at Greg again.

'And you, Mr Walker?'

'No. Look, we live in the middle of the city. These things happen.'

Karen snorted. 'That's what he said when the tyres on the van were slashed. You said you know about that, Detective Sergeant?'

'Yes, I do. Although I would like to take more details from you, and also about this incident.'

'Some idiot decided to toss a brick through a window, and our place just happened to be handy,' said Greg. 'That's all there is to it.'

'For God's sake, we're on the second floor,' said Karen, still obviously very angry. 'You have to really work at it to get a brick through our window, and this particular bastard has done just that.'

'So do I take it that you believe your home has been deliberately targeted?' asked Vogel.

'Yes, I damned well do,' said Karen.

'I don't,' said Greg.

'Right.' Vogel decided to change tack abruptly. It was a habit of his. Experience had shown that, when caught off guard, interviewees sometimes divulged more than they otherwise might.

'I understand you know Marlena McTavish, is that the case?' he asked.

Greg looked momentarily puzzled. 'What. Who? Oh. Yes.'

'You don't seem too sure, sir?'

'Oh no, I am. It's just, well, I'd never heard her last name. She's just Marlena around here.'

'I see, sir. Like Madonna or Cher, or Adele?'

'Very nearly, yes.' Karen joined in. 'Not Marlena McTavish, that's for sure. Is that really her last name?'

'I believe so. And it seems that her real first name is Marleen.'

'Well, that cuts through the mystique, doesn't it?' remarked Karen.

'I'm sorry, madam?'

'Oh nothing. Of course we know Marlena. Both of us. And we're appalled by what's happened to her. Aren't we, Greg?'

'Of course.'

Vogel studied the man. He looked like someone under considerable strain. However, a brick had just been thrown through his sitting-room window. And his wife looked strained too. But it was different, somehow.

'You also, I believe, know George Kristos, Robert Buchanan,

Alfonso Bertorelli, Ari Kabul, Billy Wiseman and Ronald "Tiny" Stephens?' Vogel continued, putting emphasis on the nickname.

Greg and Karen agreed that they did.

'And we know Michelle Monahan,' said Greg. 'Or as she's a cop, doesn't she even get mentioned?'

Vogel ignored that.

'So, am I also to assume that you're aware of the various other incidents concerning some of these people?' he asked.

Greg and Karen agreed again that they were.

'Can either of you think of anything that might be significant linking these people, including yourselves, or the various incidents that have occurred?' Vogel asked.

'Only that we're all friends, and that we meet most Sundays for supper at Johnny's Place,' replied Karen. 'But I expect you know that.'

Vogel nodded. 'Nothing else?'

'Well, I certainly don't know anything else,' said Karen, putting heavy emphasis on 'I', and staring pointedly at her husband.

'And you, sir?' Vogel asked diffidently.

'No, nothing,' said Greg.

'Were you both here when the brick came through the window?'

'Just me,' said Karen. 'And the dogs. They went mad, naturally. I called Greg and he came home straight away.'

'Did you look out of the window at all, Mrs Walker? Did you see anything or anyone that seemed suspicious?'

'I had a quick look out,' said Karen. 'Then I thought how bloody stupid I was being. Another brick could have been chucked in. I started to get really scared then. I just ran into the bathroom, where there aren't any windows, and called Greg.'

'So you didn't see anything?'

'Nothing, no.'

'And you didn't call the police. Can I ask you why you didn't do that, particularly if you were so scared?'

Karen flushed and glanced at Greg, whose face was giving nothing away.

'I don't know,' she said. 'I just wanted to get Greg back here, that's all I could think of.'

'And where were you, Mr Walker?'

'I was over at my lock-up, it's in one of those archways under the railway tracks at Waterloo. I rushed straight home. I'd only been in a few minutes when you arrived.'

'I see. Well, you and the other members of your family could have been hurt this afternoon, sir,' continued Vogel. 'And hurt quite badly. Do you realize that?'

'I damned well do,' said Greg.

'So I am going to ask you again, sir, do you really think this latest attack was just another random act of vandalism?'

'Definitely,' said Greg.

Vogel was puzzled. The three men whose dogs had been stolen had from the beginning made a point of their belief that there had to be a link between the various incidents befalling this group of friends.

Michelle Monahan had indicated the same. Indeed it was largely because of her suspicions in this regard, her fears even, that she had brought the matter to Vogel's attention.

Yet Greg Walker was quite insistent that he suspected no such link, and suspected no one particular perpetrator of being guilty of the two acts of vandalism directed at him and his family.

Vogel was deep in thought as he strolled along Shaftesbury Avenue and into Soho on his way to Harpo's, a club of which he was not a member but to which he was frequently invited because of his aptitude for backgammon. That night he was due to play in a small tournament there. Vogel had three passions in life: his family, his work and backgammon. Mary, his wife, had been known to suggest that the order was sometimes reversible.

There were two players in the competition that night who were particular rivals. One of them, a former women's world champion, had the knack of repeatedly knocking him out in the final stages. Over the years he had beaten her more often than she'd beaten him, but twice now she'd won in tournament finals.

As he walked, Vogel prepared himself, determined she would not win that night.

He believed that backgammon was the perfect reflection of life. The throw of the dice was entirely down to chance. Sometimes you were lucky, the dice fell well for you. Sometimes you were unlucky and the dice fell badly. However good a player you were, there was nothing you could do about that.

But what you made of those throws was entirely up to you. Your quick thinking, your assessment of the situation, the way in which you built your board, meant that ultimately, over any designated period of time and number of games, the good player would always win.

And that was exactly how life was, Vogel believed. Only losers blamed their luck.

Vogel did not often lose.

nine

It didn't matter to me who was in charge of the police investigation. This man Vogel had a reputation for being clever, at least among his colleagues. But the average policeman's concept of cleverness falls well short of mine.

I am in a different class. I have always been in a different class. And when I am intent upon a course of action there is nothing, and no one, that can stop me.

My one regret was the dogs. I was sorry about that. Genuinely sorry. I am a lover of animals and it pained me to end the lives of two creatures who had done me no harm. But the success of my mission called for drastic and unpalatable measures. It was vital that this entire group of so-called friends would now become not only suspects but also suspicious of one another on a whole new level. I needed to shock and confuse, to bring distress and hurt to them all. I wanted each and every one of them to be consumed by doubt, facing every day with a sense of trepidation as to what horror it might hold. Particularly the one I could never forgive, the one who had destroyed my life. The one I was determined to annihilate, totally and utterly.

There was more to come. So much more to come. I found that I was actually beginning to enjoying the challenge. There

123

was satisfaction, pleasure almost, to be derived from manipulating those around me.

I was in control, there was no doubt about that. I had already proved it to myself. And also, I suspected, to the Metropolitan Police. They were deaf and blind to my machinations. They had failed to see the footprints that I had left. Neither had they heard my song of death.

I did not believe that I was a monster, nor that I had ever been a monster. But I knew that, whenever it was necessary, whenever I so desired, I could divorce myself from the kind of human responses generally regarded as normal. Whatever normal might purport to be in a cataclysmic world.

I was not a monster, but almost certainly a freak. Indeed, I knew I was a freak. But not a freak of nature. I had been made into what I was by the actions of another, my life shattered by a deed which had too long gone unpunished, an act of unspeakable evil.

I was a freak, and I was a victim. But I was also strong. My suffering had made me stronger than anyone I had ever encountered.

And I was clever. So very much cleverer than I appeared to be. So much cleverer than those around me. I'd learned to live by my wits. My brain was my engine, the instrument of the destruction I must deploy. I needed nothing more than that which was within me in order to claim my just retribution.

And what will you do in the day of visitation, and in the desolation which shall come from far? To whom will ye flee for help? And where will ye leave your glory?

Vogel was in an unusually good mood when he arrived at Charing Cross the following morning.

He'd won the previous evening's backgammon tournament with rare ease. He had done so without having to meet his bête noire, the luck of the draw having gone his way. Or, in Vogel's mind, perhaps the only thing that hadn't gone his way. If anything, it had taken a little of the shine off his triumph, not having had the opportunity to overcome the opponent he most feared. Vogel believed that fears were there to be conquered.

His prize had been £400, two-thirds of the sum of the £50 entrance fee paid by each of the twelve entrants. The money, in cash of course, sat untouched in his inside jacket pocket. Vogel had won much more than he'd lost over his years of playing backgammon, but that was irrelevant to him. Except in as much as it represented victory. And that alone gave him satisfaction as he occasionally touched the bulge in his jacket with the fingers of one hand.

There was something else. He had immediately recognized one of the younger competitors, from the police mugshot he'd so recently studied, as Sunday Clubber Ari Kabul. This had given Vogel opportunity to watch, and perhaps learn, without his own identity being revealed. Kabul was knocked out in the first round and retreated to the bar where, Vogel noticed, he downed two or three large shots of a clear spirit and began chatting to a young woman. After a few minutes the pair disappeared from the room in the general direction of the toilets. The young woman was already unsteady upon her feet. They returned wrapped around each other and talking in loud animated voices. It didn't take a genius to work out that the purpose of their lavatorial visit had been the ingestion of certain substances rather than the fulfilment of other more basic bodily functions. Something the bar manager seemed also to have noticed. He approached Ari and murmured in his ear. Ari shook his head and appeared to protest. Then he led his companion to the door.

It was obvious that both of them had been asked to leave. Vogel was not surprised. It was no secret that Harpo's had almost lost its licence the previous year because of allegations of drug use and dealing on the premises. As a result, the club was cracking down on any such indiscretions.

Vogel was still thinking about Ari Kabul's behaviour when he arrived at Charing Cross more than an hour early for his shift, as was often his way. He had certainly learned something about the young Asian, albeit remaining as yet unsure of its significance, assuming it had any significance.

Kabul's brush with the law the previous year had obviously not stopped his usage of illicit substances, almost certainly cocaine. And judging from the alacrity with which the Harpo's bar manager had acted the previous evening, Vogel suspected that his habit was well known. He was only surprised that Ari was allowed in Harpo's at all. But then again, this was an extremely rich and privileged young man whose inherited position in life would frequently open doors and rarely close them.

Vogel logged in to his computer and wrote a full report of the previous day's events, including his visit to Greg and Karen Walker and his unexpected encounter with Ari Kabul. This he emailed to his immediate superior, along with a note saying that he wished to continue with his inquiries that day.

He did not wait for sanction from those above him. Instead he set off back into Covent Garden. It was not often that he took unilateral action. Usually cases came his way via the appropriate chain of command, but if something caught his attention, then he was confident his superiors would allow him to pursue it. This was not only because of his exceptional results, but also because of his detailed chronicling of everything that he did. No one was ever left out of the loop. No superior officer ever had the embarrassment of being forced to admit they didn't know what Vogel was up to, because he always told them. But that was exactly what he did. He told them, he didn't ask. And by and large he got away with it and was allowed to proceed unhindered.

At forty-one, Vogel was older than the average detective sergeant. In view of his crime-solving success rate, it was surprising that he remained in this lowly rank; whether this was his choice or that of his superiors was something of a grey area. Certainly Vogel gave little sign of being ambitious, and were he to rise up the chain of command his uniquely independent modus operandi may well have been curtailed. As things stood, it was debatable who benefited most from his highly individual situation, Vogel or his superiors.

He took a number 9 double-decker along the Strand. So far as he was concerned, an unmarked CID car was more trouble than it was worth in central London, on routine enquiries anyway. And although he had £400 in cash in his pocket, it was not Vogel's habit to waste his money on taxis, nor indeed on anything else, and taxi fares were not submissible expenses for Metropolitan Police sergeants. On another day he would have walked all the way, but on this occasion he was in too much of a hurry.

Vogel was convinced that if he did not achieve a result swiftly in this case then more people could be hurt. Perhaps even killed. And, as usual, he believed that if he didn't crack it, nobody else would.

He alighted from the bus at Aldwych, then walked up Wellington Street and Bow Street into the heart of the Garden, to the converted warehouse behind the opera house where Marlena lived. He now had a list of people he wanted to see and locations he wanted to check out, and Marlena was next on that list. After all, the incident involving her had been the most serious, as it remained the only one to have presented a direct threat to human life.

The woman, balanced precariously on her crutches, let him into her flat with some reluctance.

'I've already been through this again and again,' she said, wincing as she lowered herself into a chair in the small sitting room.

She was obviously struggling to cope with her injuries. Yet in spite of that, and even though he had called unannounced and she appeared to be alone, Vogel could not help noticing that Marlena was immaculately dressed and wearing full make-up, including, he was almost sure, false eyelashes, beneath the fringes of which she peered at him with some hostility.

'First the two uniformed chaps and then Michelle,' Marlena continued. 'You know PC Monahan, I assume?'

'Yes, I know her.'

'Well, she was so eager to get every tiny detail from me she came rushing round late at night as soon as she got back from the training course she'd been on in Belfast – diplomatic protection or something, I think – but then I assume you know all that.'

'More or less,' said Vogel. He paused only briefly before pushing on with the purpose of his visit. 'But I would appreciate it, Miss McTavish, if—'

'Please don't call me that,' interrupted Marlena sharply, glaring at him.

'But it is your name, I understand, madam,' responded Vogel. 'Although I must admit that it doesn't seem to fit very well. You certainly don't sound Scottish.'

And that, Vogel thought, was an understatement. The woman was what an actor pal of his would have called theatre grand. She sounded a bit like Donald Sinden in drag.

'I am not Scottish,' intoned Marlena. 'My father was, but he and my mother, who was English, parted soon after I was conceived. I was both born and brought up on this side of the border. Thank God. I'm only just beginning to realize I should have changed that bloody name legally, instead of just dropping it. Please call me Marlena. Everyone else does.'

'Very well,' said Vogel, trying again. 'So, Marlena, I would appreciate it if you would go through everything again with me. Tell me exactly what happened to you, what you told the police constables and what you told Michelle. I shall be handling this case from now on, and I want to be absolutely sure that nothing has been overlooked.'

With a theatrical sigh, Marlena told her story yet again.

When she had finished, it was a thoughtful Vogel who took the lift to the ground floor of Sampford House. He had already decided to change his plans. Instead of visiting other members of the group as he'd intended, Vogel retraced his steps down Bow Street and Wellington Street and took another number 9 bus back to Charing Cross.

There was something he had to check. Something that had been niggling at the back of his mind from the beginning of his meeting with Marlena. Something he hadn't expected and had found extremely disturbing.

Back at the station he got himself a coffee from a vending machine then logged in to his computer. A few minutes later he leaned back in his chair, the paper cup of coffee standing neglected on his desk. His mind was racing.

As he had suspected, there had been no Belfast training course in diplomatic protection that week, nor indeed any other training course, as far as he could ascertain. It was a matter of record that Michelle was looking for a transfer out of Traffic, and the Ulster police did run such courses for officers based elsewhere, as, for obvious historical reasons, they were regarded as leaders in the field. But not on this occasion.

In any case, Vogel soon discovered that Michelle had reported sick for the two days she had been absent from work. That too was a matter of record.

So where had she been during the period between her Sunday-evening supper at Johnny's Place and her arrival at Marlena's flat late on Tuesday evening clutching an overnight bag? It seemed highly unlikely that she had been genuinely sick. What had she been doing? Why did she lie to her friends, and presumably to her employers?

Vogel had no idea. But he planned to find out.

Neither Billy nor Tiny had returned to work since receiving the news that Daisy had died. And how she'd died.

Instead they mooched around their flat in their pyjamas alternating between floods of tears and shouting at each other.

Billy said he couldn't understand why Tiny hadn't been watching Daisy properly. Everyone knew that London parks were deceptively dangerous for dogs.

'Are you fucking blaming me for what happened?' Tiny yelled at him.

'Yes, I fucking am,' Billy yelled back. 'Our dog has probably been tortured to death and it's all your stupid fault.'

He didn't really blame Tiny though, and later, when they'd both calmed down, Billy apologized profusely and told his partner that.

'I'm sorry, darling,' he said. 'I don't know what I'm saying, honestly I don't. I just can't believe what's happened, that's all.'

Then he took the big man in his arms and told him how much he loved him.

Ten minutes later they were at each other's throats again.

'Oh yeah, you love me all right,' stormed Tiny. 'So bloody much you keep me a bloody great secret.'

'If you were me, you'd keep you a secret too,' shouted Billy, though even he wasn't sure what he meant by that.

'Yeah? And what other fucking secrets are you keeping from me?' Tiny continued. 'Sometimes I don't think I know you at all.'

'Nor me you. Seems I couldn't even trust you with our Daisy.'

Tiny couldn't take it any more. He exploded. For the first time in their relationship he hit out physically at his partner. He rocked back on his heels and threw a punch. But thankfully for Billy, although Tiny was built like an ox and threw a punch that was a bolt of steel, he wasn't fast. Billy saw the punch coming and flung himself to one side. Instead of hitting Billy's chin, Tiny's punch landed on his partner's right shoulder. But Billy went down like a sack of potatoes. He caught the side of his face on the edge of a low table. The skin split and blood ran freely. Billy cried out in pain as he hit the ground and lay for a few moments whimpering.

The very sight of him, injured and bleeding, caused Tiny to fall to his knees beside Billy, take him in his arms and beg forgiveness.

'You've hurt me, you stupid bastard, you've really hurt me,' said Billy. 'And it makes me wonder what else you are capable of.'

'Don't say that, please don't say that,' begged Tiny.

All the anger had left him now. His eyes were filled with tears again and he looked totally broken. Billy loved Tiny too much not to feel compassion for him, even as he lay on the ground wiping the blood from his face with one hand and gingerly twitching his sore shoulder muscles.

'It's all right,' he said. 'It's all right, darling, I know I went too far. I know what good care you always took of Daisy.'

'Not good enough, it seems,' said Tiny grimly. 'You will never be able to make me feel more guilty than I already do.'

And so it went on, as the two men continued to express their grief and their anger. One minute they were being loving and supportive of each other, and the next hitting out. Although neither did so physically because they both feared the consequences – Billy because he was the weaker and Tiny because he knew he was so much stronger.

At some time during the day Michelle phoned; to see how they were, she said. Tiny took the call. He asked if there was any news of a post-mortem examination on Daisy and Chump.

'I'm sorry, Tiny, but apparently the powers that be have decided there's no point,' Michelle replied. 'They say it's obvious how the dogs died. And there's all this stuff going on about not wasting public money . . .'

Tiny ended the call and told Billy what Michelle had said.

'Not wasting public money,' he repeated. 'How dare they?'

'Don't worry, darling,' said Billy, putting a consoling arm around his partner. 'We'll get the dogs' remains returned to us and ask our vet to do a private post-mortem. The bastards can't stop us doing that.'

A couple of times they spoke to George on the phone. After all, he was going through the same thing they were going through, wasn't he? Or rather, they tried to speak to George. He seemed to be in an even worse state than either of them. He couldn't stop crying long enough to formulate words.

It was a black day for all the friends. Seven of them had now been directly touched by some mysterious or at least unexplained event, ranging from the seemingly innocent and vaguely amusing to the malevolent, the malicious, and the downright evil. Only Michelle, Ari and Alfonso had not been the victim of either some kind of prank or worse.

'So far,' said Alfonso, when Ari had called him that morning.

'Yes, well, for myself I wouldn't mind something happening – something small and inconsequential that is,' said Ari. 'I think the others are beginning to suspect us three.'

'Oh, come on,' said Alfonso, who didn't believe anyone could ever seriously suspect him of wrong-doing. 'I know it's not me, and I don't believe it could be you or Michelle either. You'd have to be crazy to cut up two dogs like that. As for deliberately setting out to harm Marlena, we both adore her. And why would anyone want to do that?'

'I don't know,' said Ari. 'I'm bewildered by all of this. But it looks as though someone did set out to harm Marlena. And did you know the police have finally sat up and taken notice? Some CID buddy of Michelle's called Vogel, supposed to be a bit of a genius, he's already been to see Greg and Karen and Marlena.'

'I heard,' said Alfonso. 'Well, all I can say is I hope he sorts this mess out before, before . . .'

'Before what, Fonz?' asked Ari.

'Nothing.'

'You were going to say before someone dies, weren't you, mate?'

'Of course not,' said Alfonso.

Vogel spent the next couple of hours going over the data he had compiled thus far. He was like that. Methodical. Painstaking.

He couldn't stop thinking about Michelle and whether or not she could be involved in the unpleasant series of events he was investigating. He'd been fretting about her ever since Marlena had made that reference to the policewoman having been away on a training course he now knew had not existed.

He told himself there were a million reasons why Michelle might have fibbed to her friends. Friends told each other white lies like that all the time. If they wanted to get out of an engagement, if they felt they'd been remiss about something. Or if they didn't want to hurt someone's feelings.

But he was unable to shake off the little niggle at the back of his mind. And Vogel was a man who couldn't proceed with an investigation, or indeed anything much else in life, until he had dealt with anything that niggled at him. What were the odds against a group of friends finding themselves on the receiving end of a series of random incidents of this nature? No, either someone was targeting them or one of the group was the perpetrator, which meant that anyone whose behaviour was not entirely straightforward had to be suspect. And that included PC Michelle Monahan.

Vogel checked his watch. Michelle was on point duty and would not be returning to the station until late afternoon. He decided to fill in the time by interviewing Ari Kabul. As he was uncertain where to find him, Vogel checked the list of numbers for the group which Michelle had supplied and dialled Ari's mobile.

He was unsurprised to be diverted to voicemail and left a message asking Ari to call him back as soon as possible concerning the incident involving Marlena. He was, however, somewhat surprised by how promptly Ari returned his call and the way in which he so readily agreed to come into Charing Cross – 'for a chat', as Vogel put it.

'Anything I can do to help clear up what happened to poor Marlena,' said Ari. 'Not that I think I have any information for you, but I'll help in any way I can.'

Vogel was struck by the highly educated Englishness of Kabul's voice. He promptly gave himself a telling-off for indulging in stereotyping verging on a kind of racism. What had he expected, for God's sake? Peter Sellers doing 'Goodness Gracious Me'?

Ari duly arrived within the hour and was escorted to an interview room. Vogel noted that the young man was not only handsome and well turned out, he was also extremely self-assured and displayed no obvious signs of drug or drink abuse, nor of suffering from a hangover. Just because he had been arrested under the influence of alcohol and in possession of cocaine, did not, of course, necessarily mean that Ari Kabul had a drink problem and was a regular drug user. The sequence of events Vogel had witnessed at Harpo's the previous evening could merely have been a one-off occurrence from which Kabul had, apparently, swiftly recovered. However that wasn't how it had seemed. And, Vogel reminded himself, the effects of cocaine could be deceptive.

He stared hard at Ari, looking for dilated pupils, or even an unnatural brightness in the eyes. There was nothing, and if Ari noticed Vogel's close scrutiny he passed no comment.

He also gave no indication of recognizing Vogel. But then, in spite of his impressively swift recovery, the previous evening's excesses must surely have dulled Kabul's senses to some extent.

He answered most of Vogel's questions easily and satisfactorily enough. Was he speaking any more quickly than might be normal? Did he seem overexcited or overactive? Vogel didn't think so. Ari Kabul appeared to be quite calm and in control.

There was one question he could not answer satisfactorily. He had no verifiable alibi for the time of Marlena's incident.

'I'm afraid I was on my own, at home in bed, Mr Vogel,' said Kabul. 'I had some sort of tummy bug. I didn't go into work that day. My father was in his office as usual and my mother was out most of the day. In any case, my flat in the basement is completely separate from their part of the house, and has its own entrance, so they rarely know for certain whether I'm in or not.'

'Did you contact your doctor?' asked Vogel.

Kabul shook his head. ''Fraid not, Detective Sergeant. I just put it down to some dodgy grub at Johnny's the night before.'

Other than, perhaps, the absence of an alibi, there was nothing in Kabul's response to raise any suspicions in Vogel.

Ari seemed genuinely eager to help and concerned about the misfortunes, albeit that at least two cases were mere pranks, which had now befallen seven of the ten Sunday Club friends.

'If I think of anything that might throw any light on any of this, anything at all, I'll call you right away, Mr Vogel,' said Ari, when the policeman indicated that he had no further questions.

Vogel waited until the young man had reached the door before calling after him.

'You got home all right last night, then,' he commented.

Ari suddenly didn't look quite so self-assured. Which had been Vogel's intention.

'Were you at Harpo's?' he asked, perhaps a little apprehensively.

Obviously he had no memory of Vogel being there, but that was hardly surprising, thought the detective.

'Playing backgammon,' he said.

Ari grinned disarmingly.

'We didn't play each other, did we?' he enquired. 'Surely I couldn't have forgotten that.'

Vogel shook his head.

'Did you win?' asked Ari.

Vogel reckoned the other man was a good recoverer in more ways than one.

'I did, as a matter of fact,' he said. 'Did you?'

Ari looked puzzled. Presumably even he could remember that he'd been knocked out in the first round.

'The young woman, the one you left the club with,' said Vogel, by way of explanation.

'Ah, the lovely Kylie,' said Ari, grinning again. 'Oh yes. I won.'

Vogel remained sitting at the interview-room table for a few minutes after Ari left, pondering their dialogue. Ari was disconcertingly likeable, and obviously had a way with women, probably whether or not he was coked up. Vogel wondered fleetingly if the young man had been too helpful. But he reckoned he could drive himself crazy with that sort of thinking. And in any case Michelle Monahan was due back from point duty any minute.

Vogel couldn't help feeling a reluctance to confront his colleague. He certainly could not bring himself to do so formally, not at this stage anyway. So he hovered at the coffee machine conveniently situated in the corridor just outside the Traffic department's offices in order to contrive an apparently accidental encounter. In fact, when he saw Michelle approaching he moved so fast he almost tripped over his own feet, lurched forward and bumped into her, spilling much of the black coffee he had already acquired, but fortunately over himself rather than her. She looked surprised and a tad alarmed.

'Cup of coffee?' he enquired, dabbing ineffectively at the stained front of his faded beige corduroy jacket, but otherwise making a fairly good recovery.

Michelle nodded her assent.

'White, no sugar,' she instructed.

Vogel had been confident she would take the opportunity to spend a few minutes with him. He knew she liked him – well, possibly more than that, although he had no intention of taking advantage. He also suspected she would want to know what progress he was making on the matter she had brought to his attention, although she was probably not yet sure whether he was actively investigating it.

He told her that he had already interviewed Greg, Karen, Ari and Marlena, and that he was planning to talk to the remaining members of the group over the next day or two.

'Does that include me?' Michelle asked levelly.

'Oh, come on,' said Vogel.

'No. There's something else you want to ask me, isn't there?'

Michelle was looking him straight in the eye, her manner absolutely direct. She might once have made a pass at him but that didn't make her any kind of pushover professionally, he reminded himself. He also, either because of or in spite of the pass, remained disconcertingly fond of the young policewoman.

She spoke again before he had time to fully marshal his thoughts.

'You'd better get on with it,' she said.

Vogel felt his cheeks flush. He didn't like it when his usually clinical approach was tainted, as he saw it, by even a hint of emotion. That was when mistakes were made.

'Oh, it's nothing,' Vogel said.

'For God's sake, shoot,' said Michelle.

'W-well,' Vogel stumbled. 'Marlena told me you said you'd just come back from a course when you visited her the other night. That you'd been with the Diplomatic Protection boys in Belfast. There was no such course in Belfast.' Vogel paused. 'Indeed, as far as I can discover, there was no such course at that time anywhere, and although you have made an application to Diplomatic Protection you've not been interviewed yet, let alone sent on a course. And apparently you called in sick those two missing days.'

Michelle stared at him.

'You really have been checking up on me, haven't you?'

Vogel felt the flush in his cheeks deepening. He didn't reply.

'For goodness' sake,' said Michelle, the impatience clear in her voice. 'I took a sickie to go back to Dorset to see Phil. The tart he left me for has dumped him, which serves him right. Trouble is, I still love the rotten bastard. He called me in a dreadful state in the middle of the night on Sunday and I upped sticks and took off straight away. It was too late to apply for leave so I just went sick. And I didn't want Marlena or any of the rest of our lot to know, because I've done nothing but slag Phil off to them all. So I lied. I couldn't bear the thought of them knowing that I went running back to him at the first opportunity. I can't believe you picked me up on that, Vogel.'

'I can't help it,' said Vogel.

Michelle managed an ironic laugh. 'No, you can't, can you? You pick everyone up on everything. You dissect every detail. And that's why I asked you to look into this. So serves me right you're currently dissecting me, I suppose.'

'Sorry,' said Vogel.

'That's all right,' said Michelle. She downed the last of her coffee and binned the paper cup. Vogel was still holding his cup even though it was already empty. After all, he'd spilt most of it. Michelle turned on her heel and headed on to Traffic HQ. For a second or two Vogel watched her go. Then he called after her.

'So are you two getting back together again, then?' he asked.

Michelle glowered at him. 'I don't want the whole fucking world to know about this,' she said.

'There's no one else here,' said Vogel reasonably, gesturing with his free hand at the empty corridor. 'Are you?' he persisted.

'I don't know,' said Michelle. 'And in any case it's none of your fucking business.'

She seemed extremely angry. If she did still carry a torch for him, she certainly wasn't showing it. Or perhaps that merely added to her anger. Vogel wasn't sure. Vaguely wishing he hadn't got involved in the first place, he headed back to his desk. The trouble was that now he'd started his investigation he wouldn't be able to stop. He knew that much about himself. He wished he could but he couldn't.

He had a new email from his superior asking him to look into a couple of queries concerning his report on the fraud case. He decided to deal with that straight away, but his mind kept wandering.

Finally he gave in to temptation. He had to reassure himself about Michelle, he just had to. He called a colleague with Dorset police, Ben Parker, a man he'd trained with at Hendon many years previously whom he knew was a sergeant at the same station as Phil Monahan.

Only when he'd successfully completed that call did he feel able to return to finalizing his part of the fraud case. After that he considered himself free to return to the matter which was now constantly nagging away at him. He checked out his contact details for the rest of the friends and began to set up interviews for that evening and the next day. He arranged to meet Alfonso a little later on during the waiter's break from duty at the Vine. Bob agreed to come to the station the following morning at 10 a.m. He decided to visit the three men, whose dogs had died so horribly, in their own homes and made appointments to call on both Tiny and George the following afternoon. Billy, it seemed, was planning to return to work the next day but offered to come to Charing Cross police station as soon as he left his office.

Vogel wanted to speak to each of the friends individually, just in case there were contradictions or even minor variations in their stories which might give him some sort of lead.

He also wanted to interview Greg and Karen again, this time separately. He remained convinced that both had something on their minds which they weren't telling him, particularly Greg.

He had mobile numbers for the Walkers, but neither answered, so he left messages asking them to contact him, and wondered how long it would take them to do so.

Then he began to pack up his desk ready to leave for his appointment with Alfonso, who had suggested they meet in a Costa cafe just across the street from the Vine. Vogel logged out of his computer and closed it down. He cleared his desk of any bits and pieces that he didn't carry in his pocket, like his calculator and his desk diary, and locked them in a drawer. Vogel was naturally tidy and as meticulous with objects as he was awkward with people. His desk always looked as if nobody used it. There was never any personal paraphernalia, no photographs, no loose notes. Nothing.

He was just leaving the building when his mobile rang.

It was Ben Parker in Dorchester.

'You were right to be suspicious,' Ben began. 'I'm having a pint with Phil Monahan. I've just stepped out of the pub to call you. He's not seen or spoken to Michelle in over a year.'

'Are you sure?'

'Well yes, I think so. I enquired about Michelle as casually as I could. Phil has no reason to lie to me.'

'No, I suppose he doesn't,' murmured Vogel thoughtfully.

'And there's another thing,' Parker went on. 'The new bird's pregnant.'

'So she's not dumped him, then?'

'Seems not. She phoned while we were in the pub. I wouldn't

say it's a match made in heaven, but there's no doubt he's over the moon about having a kid. Something he always wanted, apparently.'

Vogel was disturbed by what Ben Parker had told him. Apart from anything else, Michelle Monahan seemed to have left herself without an alibi for the time of the Marlena incident, although Vogel still found it hard to accept that she needed one. But her husband surely had no reason to lie. Certainly not to Parker.

Vogel wondered if Michelle was aware that the new woman in her husband's life was pregnant. Either way, what was she playing at? She had asked him to investigate after all, so surely she had nothing to hide. But maybe that was double bluff. He still couldn't believe that the young policewoman could be responsible for any part of the unpleasant sequence of events he was investigating. Nonetheless he didn't like it, he didn't like it one bit.

ten

Greg, of course, did not really believe that the unpleasant incidents concerning his family were random acts of vandalism. Not at all. Not the slashing of the tyres on his van, nor the brick through the window of his apartment.

And he shared none of the professed doubts of the other Sunday Club members concerning who may or may not have been responsible. The other episodes, the pranks, the Marlena incident, the horrible attack on the two little dogs, they were one thing. What had happened to his van and to his home, the danger his whole family now seemed to be in, was entirely another. Greg knew who was responsible. Absolutely. He had no doubts at all.

He also knew that he had to do something about it. Fast. Unless he wanted to wait until someone he loved was hurt. And he knew exactly what he had to do. He had no choice.

Later that evening he made excuses to Karen, who was still furious with him, and set off for that Chinatown gambling club again. Karen thought she knew about Greg's past. She really didn't have a clue. And he could not share it with her. If she ever found out, he dreaded what the knowledge would do to their relationship. He also did not want his wife to live in fear. It didn't matter about him. Greg had sold out to the devil many years previously, and was prepared to take the consequences. He'd learned to live with fear over the years. Once in a while he almost allowed himself to forget. But only ever almost, in spite of it having been so long since he'd been given any real cause to remember. Although he'd become expert at concealment even from those closest to him, there had always been an abiding dread in his heart. And now, it seemed, he must face his demons again.

The same security doormen, in their dark suits and dicky bows, stood outside the Zodiac. Or if they weren't the same ones, then they were clones. Hard-faced and dangerous-looking.

But on this occasion Greg did not shuffle by and lurk around while desperately seeking the courage to go in. He knew that he must fulfil his intentions. If the latest events were anything to go by, he was probably running out of time.

So, attempting a display of confidence he certainly didn't feel, he walked straight up to the door of the Zodiac and addressed the nearest of the two doormen, explaining briefly why he was there and who he hoped to see. The man turned his back on Greg and spoke into a mike clipped to the lapel of his jacket. He was also wearing an earpiece. Greg knew he would be carrying, probably in a belt holster, a standard security-industry Motorola two-way radio linked to other security staff within the building and, most importantly, to the upstairs offices of Zodiac Enterprises.

'All right, you can go through,' the doorman said after a minute or two. 'I understand you know the way?'

Greg nodded. It had been years since he'd visited the Zodiac, but he knew the way all right. It was one of those things you never forgot. He moved swiftly through the main rooms of the club, past the usual roulette tables, the blackjack, and the fruit machines. There was also a fanton table, the traditional Chinese version of roulette involving placing bets on the number of buttons to be left beneath a bowl. Few of the clientele looked up as he passed. Intent upon their gambling, they were not interested in him, and he certainly was not interested in them. At the back was a door marked PRIVATE, outside which stood a third dinner-jacketed heavy. He invited Greg to pass through, into a dimly lit hallway, then frisked him with brisk efficiency before indicating the rickety flight of stairs ahead.

Greg duly climbed to the third floor, pacing himself, hoping he was fit enough not to arrive out of breath. The walls on either side were distinctly grubby and greasy, the carpet was stained and fraying, and the door off the third-floor landing, with its peeling paint and ill-assorted door furniture, appeared to have seen far better days. But appearances can be deceptive, and almost always were in this other, secret world. The door, which was actually steel-plated beneath its layer of bad decoration, possessed all the benefits of modern technology, including a camera eye. As Greg approached, as if by magic, it opened smoothly to reveal the sumptuously appointed rooms within. Greg stepped inside. His feet sank into plush carpet in the richest shade of purple. Opulent leather furniture and banks of computers lined the walls, one of which bore a massive flat-screen TV.

Across the room the man Greg had come to see sat behind a gleaming steel-and-glass desk. Obsequious minions, male and female, Oriental and Caucasian, flitted about the place.

Tony Kwan, third generation of a redoubtable family of Hong Kong immigrants, described himself as a businessman. But Greg knew him to be rather more than that. And quite disconcertingly so.

Kwan was one of the latest in a long line of Soho Chinese who were both frighteningly powerful and powerfully frightening.

His office, like everything else in his world, was a hidden-away place, a casually concealed oasis of style and luxury from which this one man ran a terrifying empire.

Kwan, taller than the average Chinese, very thin, immaculately coiffured and Savile Row tailored, rose from his desk, strode across the carpet, and, bowing his head slightly, took Greg's hand and shook it warmly.

'Welcome,' he said. 'I am most pleased to see you again, Gregory. It has been far too long. Welcome.'

Kwan was well known for his unfailing courtesy. Unlike Greg, and the inner-city kids who remained the bedrock of his organization. Kwan had been educated at a top English public school, and he invariably displayed the manners which perfectly complimented the accent. There were those, however, who believed that the more polite Tony Kwan was, the more dangerous he was.

'Thank you,' said Greg, licking dry lips in order to be able to speak. He hoped his voice was steady. 'I am most pleased to see you too, Mr Kwan.'

Kwan had always called Greg by his full given name – chosen by a mother who'd formed an adolescent crush on Gregory Peck which had lasted until her death – and was now the only person who did so. It still took Greg by surprise, but he responded in the manner that he knew was expected. With equal courtesy and also with formality. He was well aware that he should always address the Chinese gang boss as mister, if he knew what was good for him, just like everyone else did, even though he had first met the other man when they were both little more than boys. It was about respect. And respect was everything in this frightening other world. The world of the Triads, the Chinese gangs with international networks on a scale which made the Mafia look like the small family business Greg knew the Triad bosses more or less regarded it as. Kwan was a very important Triad boss. Greg had always been aware of that, even though it was never mentioned. Indeed, Greg had never heard Kwan or any of his associates utter the word 'Triad'.

Kwan called to one of his minions for tea, which was duly brought by a pretty young woman wearing an elegant silk cheongsam. She kept her head bowed as, with traditional ceremony, she poured the pale beverage into exquisite small bowls of finest porcelain. Greg couldn't help wondering what her other duties were.

Kwan asked Greg about the welfare of his wife and children, to which Greg responded evenly, although his nerves were on edge. He didn't like to hear the other man mention his family.

'So, Gregory, to what do I owe the pleasure of this visit?' asked Mr Kwan eventually.

Greg had known better than to attempt to lead their conversation.

'I just wanted to pay my respects,' said Greg, keeping his face as expressionless as he could and his voice level. 'And to assure you, Mr Kwan, that if there is anything I can do for you, you only have to ask.'

'Ah, yes.'

Kwan stared at Greg. He didn't seem to blink like other men. Greg was still trying not to allow his body language to give anything away, certainly no indication of the knot of fear that was tightening like a vice around his lower abdomen. But he knew he had no answer to Tony Kwan's unnerving Oriental inscrutability.

'And is there any reason, Gregory, any particular reason for you to come to me now, I wonder?' asked Kwan.

'No, of course not, Mr Kwan,' lied Greg. 'Like I said, I just thought it was time I paid my respects.'

'Ah yes,' Mr Kwan repeated. 'We appreciate it, Gregory. We want you to know that. We sincerely appreciate it.'

Greg nodded. It was not unusual for Tony Kwan to adopt the royal 'we'; no doubt he saw himself as a monarch of sorts. And although he kept a lower profile, he wielded more power than most modern monarchs.

Greg waited. He understood the ways of the Triad. So much remained unspoken.

'Thank you, Gregory,' Kwan continued eventually. 'We may well be in touch. Meanwhile, please don't worry about anything, will you?'

Greg shook his head. In spite of the fact he was worried sick about almost everything.

Mr Kwan took him by the hand and bade him farewell. But as Greg turned towards the door, Kwan spoke again.

'If there is anything I can help you with, Gregory, you will let me know, won't you?

Hard intelligent eyes stared at Greg. Kwan's voice was heavy with an inference the Englishman didn't quite understand.

He thanked the Chinese and fled.

Once outside the building he realized he was sweating profusely even though it was a cool night. And he was shaking. He bought more cigarettes from a late-night shop and lit one as he walked home, inhaling greedily, just to calm his nerves he told himself.

The meeting with Kwan had not gone the way he had expected, but then the Chinese gang boss was always full of surprises. That was part of his mystique, part of the way he maintained his power. Never the direct attack; when Kwan came at you he came from left of centre, always had done, Greg reminded himself.

Nonetheless the offer of help at the end of the meeting had

been totally unexpected, as had the manner in which it was delivered. The Triads always looked after their own, and were proud of doing so. Just as they dispensed their own retribution when they deemed it necessary. But Kwan had given the impression he believed Greg needed help with something, and that he was available to assist, which indicated that Kwan and his people were not responsible for the incidents that had so unnerved Greg. Or did it?

Greg gave himself a telling-off for being naive. It was just another smokescreen, surely?

Kwan was responsible all right. He had to be.

Greg's big regret in life was that he had ever become involved with Tony Kwan. It had all been long ago, and since then Kwan had left Greg alone, or more or less alone, for years. Until very recently.

When Greg married Karen, Kwan had told him that he respected his decision to back off and become a family man. He'd even sent round an ornate congratulatory bouquet of flowers to Karen. The gesture had thoroughly disconcerted Greg, as it had reminded him of the elaborate floral tributes prevalent at Mafia funerals. After that, there had been no contact aside from an occasional visit from one of Tony Kwan's men, just popping in for a chat. Lest Greg should forget that he would always remain beholden to the Soho gang boss, and that Mr Kwan retained the right to call on him at any time. And also a reminder of all that Kwan had on Greg. Stuff Karen had no idea about.

Greg had been a fifteen-year-old schoolboy when he'd agreed to join the Woo Sang Wu youth Triad, of which Kwan had then been leader. Like many other pupils at inner-city comprehensives in the early to mid nineties, Greg was recruited at the school gates, lured to sign up to WSW by the promise of adventure, training in martial arts and participation in mysterious secret ceremonies. He quickly became immersed in a subculture of controlled violence and intimidation, accepting without question the orders of his leader, even when this meant pursuing courses of action, always unscrupulous and sometimes quite horrible, that he would otherwise never have considered.

The involvement of WSW in the killing of head teacher Philip Lawrence in 1995, just a year or so after his recruitment, brought Greg to his senses. Ultimately it would lead to a reduction in the scale and influence of the youth Triad, but it did not impede the rise of Tony Kwan; Greg's Triad mentor ascended to a position of startling power within the worldwide network of these secret gangs. Much as Greg wanted out, that was not an option. He had a Triad past, and although he backed off to the best of his ability he'd always known he would never be able to get out. Not entirely.

Kwan had not called upon Greg to become actively involved again until around the time the Sunday Club incidents began. Two of Kwan's boys had delivered a message from the Triad boss. He had a little job he'd like Greg to do. Braver than he'd thought himself capable of being, Greg had declined. He'd sent his thanks to Tony Kwan for the offer, but said he had to think of his family now and he knew Mr Kwan would understand.

Kwan's boys had seemed relaxed about it and told him not to worry. If anything, they'd been a little too relaxed for Greg's liking. He'd been on edge from the moment he closed the door behind them. And when, a couple of weeks later, he'd discovered his vandalized vehicle there was no question in his mind as to who had been responsible.

Until his fellow Sunday Clubbers had made the suggestion, it hadn't occurred to Greg that there could be a connection between his slashed tyres and those comparatively playful incidents. And he remained unconvinced that the more serious matter of Marlena being injured and the two dogs being killed could be anything other than unpleasant coincidences.

No, Greg was quite sure the events were unconnected. There was no element of prank about the tyre-slashing and the brick thrown through his window. That had been payback for turning down Tony Kwan's proposal, a reminder that Greg could not escape his Triad past.

Over the years, Greg had thought about going to the law and coming clean about his past. As if in doing so he could erase not only the hold Kwan had over him but the memories that haunted him. But he knew it would only make matters worse. Even assuming Kwan didn't get to hear about it from his informers within the police force and silence Greg before he had a chance to testify, there was the fact that for all he was still a schoolboy at the time Greg had been over the age of criminal responsibility. The crimes he had participated in merited a lengthy jail sentence. And Greg couldn't stand that. Plus the Triads would probably see to it that he didn't survive long in prison. Either way, his kids would grow up without him being around. Like Karen, Greg knew what that was like for a child. And it wasn't going to happen to his kids.

Thus Tony Kwan's hold over Greg remained as strong as ever. And Greg now had no choice but to accept that and to act accordingly. It seemed ridiculous that Kwan still wanted him on side. But Greg understood the pride and protocol of the Triads. As with the Mafia, the big boys never let the little ones go – that was the source of the organization's power. Once they had you, you were theirs for life.

Kwan's henchmen hadn't mentioned a specific job. It was

possible there was no job. Kwan may have simply decided the time had come to remind Greg that he was still a Triad and must jump when he was told to.

Sooner or later – probably sooner – Kwan would demand Greg's services. That was a racing certainty now. And whatever he was asked to do, however dangerous, however unsavoury, Greg would have to comply.

There was no alternative.

That same evening Alfonso waited for Vogel in the pleasantly appointed coffee shop he'd suggested. He had already bagged two squashy armchairs in a discreet corner when the detective came in, ordered himself a double espresso and joined him.

It struck Vogel that Alfonso Bertorelli, who spoke English with a slight Essex accent, having been brought up and probably born in the UK, was nevertheless unmistakably Italian. He was also extremely personable and answered questions fluently, as one might expect from a senior waiter at the Vine. After all, the staff there were presumably required to make conversation with all sorts of people. But Vogel suspected that, beneath his smooth facade, Alfonso was jumpy. He even slopped some cappuccino into his saucer, something of a giveaway surely, for a man at the top of his profession.

It was understandable, thought Vogel. Taking the traditional presumption of innocent until proven guilty and assuming that Alfonso was a potential victim rather than a perpetrator, it was only natural that he would be nervy, given the circumstances.

Only three members of Sunday Club had escaped falling victim to these increasingly distressing incidents. One of those was Michelle Monahan, whose involvement Vogel found both puzzling and disturbing. On the way to the coffee shop his mind had been turning over various strategies to tackle his fellow police officer, but he had yet to come up with one that he was happy with. He forced himself to set those thoughts to one side and focus on Alfonso.

The detective began by asking about the incident the waiter had witnessed. He made Alfonso go over and over what he had seen, and questioned how he happened to be walking along the road at the exact time Marlena was struck by the hooded cyclist.

'I was going to work, for God's sake!' said Alfonso. 'How many more times?'

Vogel studied the other man carefully. The Vine restaurant was just a street away from the scene of the crime. It was not out of the question that Alfonso should just happen to be passing at the right moment. Indeed, it was a perfectly reasonable and easily explicable coincidence that he would be doing so. But Vogel didn't believe in coincidences. And there were already far too many of them in this case.

'Do you always take that route to work?' asked the detective.

He saw Alfonso hesitate for the briefest beat, before replying.

'It depends where I'm coming from,' Alfonso said guardedly.

Vogel raised his eyebrows. 'And where were you coming from that morning, sir?' he enquired.

Alfonso glowered at him. 'Home.'

'I see, sir.' Vogel glanced down at his notebook. 'The only contact details I seem to have for you are care of the Vine restaurant. Oh, and your mobile number. Could I have your home address, Mr Bertorelli, please?'

Alfonso looked down at his hands resting on the table before him, and wrapped them around his coffee cup.

He mumbled something.

'Sorry, sir?'

'I'm sort of between homes,' he said. That was, after all, his habitual reply to questions concerning his living arrangements. But Vogel didn't know that.

'I see. So you have no proper home at the moment?'

Alfonso fidgeted.

'Shall I put you down as being of no fixed abode then, sir?' enquired Vogel.

He looked the other man up and down. Alfonso was the epitome of what Vogel's mother would have described as debonair. His slicked-back black hair was stylishly cut, his olive skin glowed with well-being, the collar of his pristine white shirt protruded just an inch or two over the lapels of his expensive black overcoat. You could see your face in the shine on his shoes. The corners of Vogel's mouth twitched. It was simply too ridiculous to describe the man as being of no fixed abode, as if he were some unemployable wino.

Perhaps the same thought occurred to Alfonso.

'Number 5, Parson Crescent, Dagenham,' he suddenly blurted out.

'Thank you, sir.'

Vogel, in whose world the kind of people who worried about their image could only ever be peripheral, was puzzled. So what was wrong with Dagenham? he wondered.

'And that's your permanent address, is it, sir?' he persisted.

Alfonso looked most uncomfortable.

'Yes. Well, it's my mother's house, really. I spend a lot of time staying over in town . . .' Eyes downcast, he let his voice tail off.

'On that particular morning, sir, were you travelling to work from your . . .'

Something stopped Vogel from saying 'from your home' as he had intended. After all, he wanted to keep on the right side of Alfonso, for the time being at any rate. He certainly didn't want the man to clam up.

'. . . from Dagenham,' he finished.

Alfonso nodded. 'Yes,' he said. 'I only stay there when I'm on days. If I'm on the late shift, I usually stay in town,' he added, as if he needed an excuse for living at the place which he'd indicated was, at the very least, the nearest he had to a permanent address.

'So were you travelling to work along your usual route that day, sir?'

'Yes.'

'And what is that route, exactly?'

'I take the tube from Dagenham East to Embankment – it's straight through on the District Line – then I walk up Villiers Street to the Strand, and cut through to Charing Cross Road.'

Vogel thought for a moment. He had the kind of mind which, if he knew a place, enabled him to see the streets laid out as if he kept a book of maps in his brain. And he knew central London well. He was certainly no habitué of the Vine, but the restaurant was a famous landmark and he was aware of its location.

'In order to have been able to see the incident, or any part of it, and then to realize that Marlena was involved, and to get to her, you would have had to carry on up Charing Cross Road past the alleyway which leads to your place of work, would you not, Mr Bertorelli?' he asked.

'Only just past it,' replied Alfonso. 'Look, when I'm on earlies I often run into Marlena on Monday mornings. Well, close enough to wave to, anyway. She goes to that deli in Old Compton Street. Same time every week. Didn't she tell you any of that?'

Vogel half nodded, and thought for a moment. Marlena had indeed told him that she was on her way to Soho when she'd been injured. He further recalled from Perkins' and Brandt's report that Marlena had indicated to them it was not the first time she had encountered Alfonso whilst on her regular shopping trip. But Vogel hadn't pursued it. Maybe he should have done. He thought he'd probably been too preoccupied with Michelle Monahan.

'Once or twice we've even had a quick coffee together,' Alfonso continued, 'so long as it isn't that bugger Leonardo's shift.'

Vogel raised an enquiring eyebrow.

'He's the senior maître d'. Should be in the bloody army, except they probably wouldn't have him.'

Vogel obliged with a small smile.

'And on Monday last?'

'Like I said, I was about to turn off Charing Cross Road when I heard a scream. I hadn't seen Marlena. But I think I may have subconsciously recognized her voice. I don't know, to tell the truth. Anyway, the scream caught my attention. I looked up the road and saw this bus about to hit a woman. I heard it screech to a halt, and I saw a hooded cyclist pedalling off like mad down Shaftesbury Avenue. I was chilled to the marrow, honest I was. Something told me I had to be there. I ran up the street. And it was then that I realized it was Marlena lying in the road, so I rushed to her side.'

Vogel checked back over his notes. He was silent for a long time. Alfonso started to look more and more uncomfortable. Vogel wondered if there was a particular reason for this, but he knew better than to read too much into it. He was aware that he sometimes had that effect on totally innocent people.

'I believe you told my colleagues that you were a witness to the incident?'

'Yes,' said Alfonso.

'But from what you have just said, you did not actually see the cyclist hit your friend?'

Alfonso did a double take.

'Well, no, I suppose I didn't, but it was obvious what had happened. Quite obvious.'

'Ummm,' responded Vogel. 'To you, perhaps, but not to a court of law. You were not actually a witness at all, sir, you do see that?'

'I damn well saw that cyclist take off and the bus run over poor dear Marlena's foot,' responded Alfonso feistily. 'I was a witness to that.'

Vogel smiled one of his small tight smiles that stretched his lips to the minimum.

'Did you happen to notice the colour of the bicycle?' he asked.

'What? No. Hang on. It may have been black. It was a dark colour. Yes, I'm sure of that.'

'Do you own a bicycle yourself, by any chance, Mr Bertorelli?' he asked.

'Do I look like the sort of chap who owns a bike?' retorted Alfonso.

Vogel had to admit that the man had a point. But an elderly woman had been seriously hurt. He reminded Alfonso of that.

'OK, I'm sorry,' said Alfonso. 'I do not own, and never have owned, a bicycle.'

'Thank you, sir. And, by the way, where in town do you stay when you don't go back to Dagenham?'

Vogel saw Alfonso flush.

'Oh, here and there,' the Italian muttered.

'I am afraid you need to be more precise than that, sir. This is now a very serious inquiry and I need to know the whereabouts of everyone involved. As you are in full-time employ, I believe, at the Vine, and working variable hours, I presume you would need a regular place to stay in central London.'

Alfonso didn't answer. Vogel knew nothing of the likely habits of a man like this, but he decided to speculate in the hope of provoking an answer.

'Some sort of club, perhaps? Or a friend whose name you can give me? Or a girlfriend?'

Alfonso looked askance. It was Vogel's turn to flush slightly.

'O-or a boyfriend?' he concluded boldly, wondering if it was politically correct to make such a suggestion.

'No, no, absolutely not, I'm not effing gay, for Christ's sake!' Alfonso looked flustered. 'Listen, I stay with my nan. She has one of the last council places standing up by King's Cross. Near all those flash new developments. I stay with her. I can walk there from the Vine. Anyway, Mamma likes me to keep an eye on me nan . . .'

Alfonso looked thoroughly uncomfortable now.

Vogel decided he wasn't going to get much more out of the man. And in any case he didn't think he had any more questions. Not any consequential ones anyway.

He told Alfonso he was free to return to work. Then made his way home to the pretty little flat in Pimlico which he shared with his wife and daughter. On the bus.

Vogel's daughter, Rosamund, was already tucked up in bed and sound asleep by the time he unlocked his front door and stepped into the pink-and-white hallway dotted with prints and water-colours of old London. His wife collected them – from markets and car boot sales and jumble sales. She couldn't afford dealers and art galleries on her husband's salary. He, however, thought her collection quite splendid. Indeed, he thought everything about his wife was splendid. Mary Vogel was the sole homemaker. She was designer and decorator, shopper and cook. She even sewed the floral-printed curtains and cushion covers. Mary filled the window boxes with plants and the flat itself with flowers. Mary did everything. The result was that Vogel lived in an intensely feminine home. Partly because he was so tidy, and because he hadn't any hobbies apart from backgammon, which required no clutter, just one folded board, there was little sign of his presence in the place. Vogel didn't mind. In fact he loved the home his wife had created for them, and thought it quite beautiful. When he thought about it at all, which was only rarely.

The family dog, border collie Timmy, wrapped himself delightedly around his master's legs.

Mary, ever-patient with both Vogel's obsessive attitude to his work and the hours he kept, greeted her husband with a kiss then swiftly produced scrambled eggs on toast followed by a cup of hot chocolate, while he made an effort to talk, for just an hour or two, about anything and everything other than his job.

Vogel had, however, over the years developed the knack of chatting to his wife while his mind remained deployed elsewhere. In this instance, firmly focused on the case which was beginning to enthral him.

Alfonso Bertorelli, who'd seemed at first to be a straight-forward dandy of a man, whom Vogel still thought was possibly gay although he had so vehemently denied it, had turned out to be anything but straightforward. Vogel wondered why he was considerably more at ease talking about the traumatic event he had witnessed, or nearly witnessed, than giving details about his personal life.

His place of residence seemed to be a matter of particular sensitivity. Could it be that he was embarrassed to be still living with his mum? Vogel recalled the waiter's vehement protests that Mrs Bertorelli's Dagenham address wasn't really his home. And he'd been equally embarrassed to admit that, when he couldn't make it back to Dagenham, instead of staying in a trendy club, or with a girl or boyfriend, or even with one the group of friends in their central London pad, Alfonso Bertorelli stayed with his nan.

By the time Vogel had finished his bedtime chocolate he'd reviewed the interview with Alfonso over and over again in his mind. It had taken only cursory inquiries about his living arrangements to establish that, beneath the smooth, personable facade, the man was something of an oddball.

But did that increase the likelihood that he was the prankster targeting Sunday Club? Was he capable of a series of attacks that had escalated from harmless practical jokes to violence with shades of sadistic brutality?

Vogel continued to ponder the question as he climbed into his small but comfortable double bed alongside the wife he loved so dearly in his own rather detached way. He sank his head into a pillow delicately scented with lavender and pulled up the duvet in its pink-and-lilac floral cover, until it reached over his ears.

No, nothing about Bertorelli indicated any such thing. Yet still Vogel could not get over just how convenient his arrival on the scene of the Marlena incident had been. But there was no evidence to suggest that Alfonso was guilty of anything other than witnessing a nasty crime.

Evidence. Irrefutable evidence. That was what was needed. Vogel, who didn't much care for hunches, drifted off to sleep muttering the word like a mantra: Evidence, evidence . . .

eleven

By the time she finished her stint on point duty, Michelle's anger and irritation had evolved into full-blown fury. She couldn't believe the way Vogel had cross-examined her. She had no doubt whatsoever that he'd deliberately orchestrated their 'chance' meeting by the coffee machine in order to grill her. And it had been a tremendous shock to her to realize that he considered her a suspect – which he most definitely did, however much he might protest.

She decided to walk from Charing Cross police station to her home at the top end of Holborn in order to calm herself down a bit. But it didn't work. Taking a sickie for her own personal reasons might be an unwise career move, but it had nothing to do with Vogel. Similarly if she chose not to reveal to her friends the true reason for her absence from town, that was entirely her own business. How dare Vogel poke about in her life.

Michelle was still fuming as she unlocked the door to her studio flat in an ugly purpose-built 1960s block just off Lamb's Conduit Street. It seemed very cold inside. She shivered as she began to take off her coat. She put it back on again and then checked the heating system thermostat. Everything seemed to be in order, but the place was definitely extremely chilly.

Surely it couldn't be the damned communal boiler again? She phoned the part-time caretaker. The boiler was indeed on the blink, for the third time that year – and it was only March.

Michelle shouted at the caretaker, which she knew was small of her. It wasn't his fault. Well, not exactly. Then, roundly cursing the world in general, she made her way into the tiny kitchen off the far end of her bedsit. She wanted a drink. But she'd finished her last bottle of wine the previous evening. She remembered that she was also hungry, having skipped lunch, and opened the door of her fridge. It contained only the dubious remains of a carton of milk, a piece of cheese tinged with green and some bread so hard you'd need an axe to break into it.

Her mood darkened further. She was fed up, cold, hungry and thirsty. For a moment she considered just getting into bed with a hot-water bottle and forgetting the day. Then she thought again. She really should at least try to do something positive.

She called Marlena and suggested she come over and bring a bottle. Marlena jumped at the idea.

'Just make sure it's a decent one,' she commanded imperiously.

Michelle grinned. Marlena rarely disappointed. And Michelle knew exactly what her friend meant by a decent bottle. It had to be champagne. She checked her watch. It was just gone eight. If she hurried, Marks and Spencer in Long Acre, just half a street away from Marlena's home by the Opera House, should still be open. Their own-brand vintage bubbly was one of the few mass-market labels Marlena found even remotely palatable. Anything beyond that, however, was outside Michelle's means, until and if that long-awaited transfer to a better job, and maybe the promotion to go with it, ever came.

She had walked home still wearing her police uniform, with only a raincoat covering it. She changed swiftly into jeans and a sweater, then hailed a cab to speed up the short journey, a luxury she rarely allowed herself. Less than an hour later, carrying an M&S shopping bag loaded with champagne, chicken liver pâté, a loaf of crusty bread, a piece of decent cheese, and a few other bits and pieces from the deli counter, she arrived at Sampford House.

Marlena buzzed her in.

'Darling,' she said, by way of greeting, as she leaned on her crutches in the hallway of her flat. 'I didn't expect dinner.'

'Why, have you eaten already?' enquired Michelle disingenuously, well aware of her stick-thin friend's insistence that she rarely took solids except in company.

'Of course not,' said Marlena, appalled at the suggestion.

'Well, I'm absolutely starving, so I thought if I brought some grub you might at least have the grace to join me.'

'If you insist,' drawled Marlena. 'But for God's sake, let's have a drink first.'

Swiftly and efficiently she opened the champagne Michelle had brought and poured generous portions into large crystal glasses. Meanwhile Michelle piled the food on a tray which she placed on the coffee table in the middle of the sitting room.

As if by unspoken agreement both women at first avoided all mention of the string of incidents which was at the forefront of both their minds, which resulted in their conversation taking a rather stilted and unnatural tone.

How Marlena was feeling and the condition of her leg occupied some time. Marlena, who claimed to be much better and said she was sure she would be on her feet in no time – 'both of them, darling' – wanted to know how Michelle was getting on at work, and if she was any nearer to the promotion she so desired.

Eventually this led Michelle on to the subject which was

actually the only thing either of them really wanted to discuss that night. She told Marlena how she had sought help from the man whom she regarded as probably the best detective in the Met.

'Would that be Detective Sergeant Vogel?' asked Marlena.

'Ah,' responded Michelle. 'Has he been to see you already?'

Marlena said that he had, adding: 'I could see he was a sharp cookie.'

'He's that all right,' said Michelle, giving the words more edge than she'd intended.

Marlena glanced at her enquiringly. 'I thought that was why you went to him,' she said.

'Ummm.' Michelle couldn't help herself. 'Trouble is, now the bastard seems to have me down as his prime suspect, damn and blast him.'

'You? Why on earth would he suspect you? I mean, any more than anyone else. One would assume you would be beyond suspicion, since you're in the police and you brought the whole darned thing to his attention?'

Michelle gave herself a moment to think. She realized that she had backed herself into a corner. If she responded honestly, that would mean revealing to Marlena that she had lied about being away in Belfast on that non-existent course. And she couldn't do that. Not yet, anyway.

'Oh, I don't suppose he does – not any more than Alfonso and Ari, anyway,' she said eventually, keeping her voice as level as she could manage. 'We're the only three not to have been targeted, so obviously any police inquiry is going to focus on us first.'

'Ah, I hadn't thought of that.' Marlena clasped her hands together under her chin. 'What an absolutely ghastly state of affairs.'

'Isn't it just.' And you don't know the half of it, thought Michelle.

'Indeed, indeed. And all I can suggest right now, darling, is that we finish the last of your champers. I think I may well have another decent bottle or two tucked away somewhere.'

'As long as you think you dare risk it,' said Michelle. 'I mean, maybe I spiked the bottle.'

'Well, if you have, darling, that should solve all our problems,' said Marlena, emptying the last of the Marks and Spencer champagne into Michelle's glass.

Another bottle was duly opened. This time a claret far superior to anything Michelle would ever have acquired.

'Just a little something to go with that rather good cheese you brought with you, dear,' said Marlena. 'Mr Kips – the nice man who runs that shop in Endel Street which sells everything – gets it in specially for me. He sent round half a dozen bottles the morning after I came out of hospital, bless him. A welcome-home present, he said. Seems everyone in Covent Garden knows what happened – in as much as any of us do . . .'

Marlena allowed her voice to tail off as she poured them each generous measures. She took a long appreciative drink.

'Nothing quite like drowning your sorrows,' she murmured.

By the time Michelle finally left Marlena's apartment just before midnight she was inclined to agree. She had declined her friend's offer to open a third bottle, but consuming the equivalent of one had definitely helped. Along with the food too. Funny how a full tummy could improve your state of mind.

And so Michelle found herself feeling surprisingly positive as she began to walk home, not allowing herself the luxury of a second cab in one day and unwilling to face public transport in the early hours. Besides, she enjoyed walking in London at all times of the day and night. It was good thinking time. And after the amount of wine she'd dispatched, she hoped the night air might clear her head.

Naturally, her thoughts returned to Vogel and the investigation. He'd be sure to get to the bottom of it all, she told herself. And if he could find no sinister link between the incidents . . . well, that must mean there was no connection. But Michelle didn't really believe that. And she didn't believe Vogel was the sort of man who would write the whole thing off as random. No, he would persevere until he had everything satisfactorily accounted for.

She was still considering what path Vogel's investigations would take, and what conclusions he may or may not come to, as she crossed Southampton Row, heading into Theobalds Road.

The punch, when it came, was a total surprise. A fist smashed into her nose, its force all the greater because its perpetrator, whom she saw only at the very last moment, was riding a bicycle. She did not even register whether the cyclist was a man or a woman. His or her face was obscured. She had a vague impression of some kind of goggles or glasses beneath a grey hoody, and maybe a scarf wound round the chin of her assailant. At any rate, the lower face was covered.

The next thing she knew, she was going down like an axed tree trunk. There was blood everywhere. It was as if her nose had exploded. But at first she was too dazed to register the damage, or to notice that her handbag had been wrenched from her shoulder.

She was, however, aware of the searing pain emanating from her shattered nose. It seemed to spread across her face and right through her entire head, piercing into every nerve. She started to scream and couldn't stop.

Then suddenly, strong arms were wrapped around her, and

a soothing voice told her to lie very still, that help was on the way, that she shouldn't worry about anything.

'I'm here, I'll look after you,' said the voice. It was a familiar voice.

Michelle stopped screaming and struggled to focus. Panic momentarily engulfed her because she couldn't see clearly. What had happened? Had she been blinded? She reached for her eyes with one hand and rubbed the back of it across them. It was then that she realized that her eyes were covered with blood. And although the pain remained as excruciating as ever, it came as a huge relief when her sight cleared as she wiped the worst of the blood away.

Now she could see. She looked up into the concerned face of the man who was cradling her in his arms.

No wonder his voice had been familiar. It was Alfonso.

Vogel was sound asleep when the call came at around 4 a.m. He always slept well and took the attitude that anyone who didn't probably did not work hard enough.

He had issued instructions at Charing Cross and throughout every relevant department within the Met that he should be notified at once in the event of any incidents involving the Sunday Club members. As luck would have it, when responding officers called in details of the attack on Michelle, PC Jessica Harding was on duty in Dispatch. Two days earlier, she'd contacted Vogel when the mutilated dogs were found, and had been sufficiently intrigued by the case that, even without a written directive, she would have alerted him to the latest development. A violent assault on a serving police officer took the investigation to another level. Finding whoever was responsible for the attacks on this group of friends would now become a priority, not just for Vogel, but for the Met's top brass.

Vogel had the knack of waking up quickly, but the news PC Harding imparted caused him to awaken even more quickly than usual. He groped for his spectacles, without which he was virtually blind, and sat bolt upright, listening intently as Harding concluded her report with the news that Michelle had been taken to University College Hospital, where she was expected to be detained for the rest of the night.

Vogel's next, perhaps somewhat obscure, response was a sense of relief. This must mean that Michelle could not be responsible for the other incidents. After all, she could hardly have mugged herself. Then the pedantic nagging voice Vogel could never quite discount began to make itself heard, asking questions he did not really wish to consider. Could Michelle have arranged the assault in order to eliminate herself from his inquiries? Had she hired some lowlife to stage an attack? Perhaps the hired thug had hit her with more force than she'd bargained for. If the hospital had decided to keep her overnight, then they probably suspected concussion or something more serious than a black eye.

Given that Michelle was a police officer, there was also a possibility that the attack was connected to her job rather than Sunday Club. Working in Traffic, she didn't come in contact with the sort of violent criminals that officers in the serious crimes squads dealt with, but the anger of motorists who believed they had been unjustly treated was legendary. Could it be that someone had recognized her out of uniform and taken revenge?

'Any witnesses?' he asked.

'Yes, a passing motorist and a pedestrian,' replied PC Harding. 'It was well gone midnight but there were still a few people about. Craddick and Parsons were the responding officers. They took two witness statements, each giving more or less the same account of a hooded cyclist riding straight up to Michelle, punching her full in the face, nicking her bag and riding off.'

'Bit like the other incident with Marlena, then.'

'Yep.'

'Nobody tried to stop this cyclist?'

'Well no, Sarge. Sounds like it was the usual story: all happened so fast, and so on.'

'Anything else?'

'Well, one of the witnesses – the pedestrian – said he knew Michelle. He happened to be walking home from work and saw the whole thing. Quite a coincid—'

Vogel interrupted sharply.

'Name?' he barked. 'Do we have a name for this witness?'

'Of course,' responded Jessica Harding. There was a brief silence. Vogel assumed she was checking the report on screen.

'Alfonso Bertorelli,' the PC continued. 'Oh, isn't that one of the other names on your list?'

Before Harding had finished speaking Vogel was half out of bed, trying to dress with one hand while using the other to keep the phone clamped to his ear.

His wife propped herself on one elbow.

'Try not to wake Rosamund, won't you,' she said.

Vogel nodded, smiled, and mouthed the word 'sorry', but his mind was elsewhere.

'What address did Bertorelli give?' he asked Harding.

Harding read out the Dagenham address Alfonso had given Vogel the previous afternoon.

'And where is he now?' Vogel asked, keeping his voice as low as he could.

There was another silence while PC Harding did some more checking before she spoke again.

'His present whereabouts is unknown. According to the report, he went to the hospital, travelling in the ambulance with Michelle. When nursing staff told him she was being detained, he left.'

'And we don't know where he went?'

'Well, no. Home, I should imagine.'

'Do we know what time it was when Bertorelli left the hospital?'

Another pause.

'He was still there when Craddick and Parsons turned up to get a statement from Michelle. She'd been in a state of shock when they tried to question her at the scene, so they followed the ambulance to UCH. It would seem Mr Bertorelli left the hospital about the same time they did: around three a.m.'

'Unlikely he was going back to Dagenham at that hour.'

'Well, I don't know about that,' said Harding.

'I bloody know,' responded Vogel, rather more loudly than he'd intended.

'Shhhhh,' said his wife.

Turning to her, Vogel pulled an apologetic face. Then he spoke again into the phone.

'Why the hell didn't those two idiots stop him leaving?'

'Stop him? Why would they?'

Still holding the phone to one ear, his shoes clutched in his free hand, Vogel tiptoed out of his bedroom and along the short corridor past his daughter's room towards the kitchen. He needed coffee.

'Because he should have been brought in for formal questioning, at the very least,' he said. 'Not only is Alfonso Bertorelli one of these Sunday Club people, he was also the star witness when Marleen McTavish was knocked down by a hooded cyclist. Didn't Craddick and Parsons realize that? Didn't anybody in

Dispatch check it out? It's all in the system. Every detail. I've made sure of that.'

Harding mumbled something incomprehensible in response.

'We need to find Bertorelli, and we need to find him fast, before he has a chance to dispose of any evidence,' Vogel went on. 'I think I know where he'll be: at his nan's place, King's Cross. Full address already on file. I'm going over there. I'll need back-up. You don't have a response unit nearby, do you?'

'Hold on,' said Harding. This time there was a silence lasting three or four minutes before she spoke again.

'There'll be a patrol car outside your place in ten minutes,' she said. 'DC Jones will meet you at King's Cross with a second team.'

Alfonso was wide awake when he first heard the wail of a siren, some time approaching 5 a.m. he thought. He was indeed at his nan's place, and had arrived there shortly before 4 a.m., having walked from the hospital just along the Euston Road. He hadn't bothered going to bed because he knew there was no hope of getting any sleep that night.

Instead, for reasons he was later unable to explain to himself or anyone else, still wearing his black waiter's trousers and the white shirt stained with Michelle's blood, he had lain down on the velveteen sofa in his nan's front room. The night was chilly. He was shivering with cold, but did not even think about digging out a sweater or a blanket. The TV in the corner was tuned to a bad movie, but Alfonso was not really watching.

His family were all devout Catholics. He had taken one of his nan's several crucifixes off the wall and was clutching it to his chest. He could not explain why he was doing that, either.

Alfonso's mind was racing, replaying the events of the last few days, particularly the attacks on Marlena and Michelle and the injuries they had both suffered. He'd been told at the hospital that Michelle would require plastic surgery to repair her face. But it wasn't only the extent of Michelle's injuries that had left him in a state of shock. He couldn't stop thinking about his own situation. Now only he and Ari remained unscathed, as it were. And if that wasn't enough to draw the finger of suspicion, Alfonso had been in the immediate vicinity of the two most brutal incidents.

The two officers who'd arrived while the ambulancemen were attending to Michelle had been unaware that it was the latest in a series of incidents. When they asked what had happened, he told them that he'd been walking home from the Vine when he heard a woman screaming. His name was already on the police computer because of the statement he'd given about the attack on Marlena. The similarities between the two attacks would not go unnoticed. Particularly when they came to the attention of that CID man with the intelligent eyes. He had already seemed suspicious of Alfonso when they'd met for coffee the previous evening. How would he react when he learned that Alfonso had been witness to a second attack? Detective Sergeant David Vogel did not strike Alfonso as a man who would be prepared to accept a single coincidence, let alone a double one.

The wailing siren seemed to be very close now, loud above the noise of the TV. Perhaps it was more than one siren. Alfonso wasn't sure. They couldn't be coming for him, could they? Not yet. Not that quickly. He jumped up off the sofa and ran to the window overlooking the street.

Tugging the heavy brocade curtain to one side, he peered out. He couldn't see a police car and neither could he hear one any more. Maybe it had passed by. He tried to reassure himself that was what must have happened, but in his mind's eye he pictured the patrol car parking up outside, and police officers climbing the concrete staircase to the walkway that ran along the 1950s council block to his nan's flat. He had after all, under protest and against his better judgement, given DS Vogel the full address.

He stood by the window of the third-floor maisonette, listening and watching for less than a minute. It seemed longer. Part of him wanted to run away, to escape from it all, but he had nowhere to run to.

When he heard the hammering on the front door, it came almost as a relief. Bang, bang, bang. Then a male voice calling out – not Vogel; this voice was harsher and much harder.

'Police, open up. Police. Open up!'

On autopilot, Alfonso did as he was told. He walked into the hall and opened the front door. Several police officers burst in, including a woman in plain clothes, another detective, Alfonso assumed. One of the male uniformed officers grabbed his arms and held them firmly behind his back. Vogel followed, his manner far less aggressive, those intelligent eyes sweeping over Alfonso.

'Mr Bertorelli, DC Jones and I need to question you further in connection with the attack on PC Michelle Monahan a few hours ago,' Vogel said. 'I understand you were a witness to this attack and that you travelled to University College Hospital with PC Monahan. Is that the case?'

Alfonso agreed that it was. 'I was walking back here,' he continued lamely.

'Isn't it rather a long walk, Mr Bertorelli?'

Alfonso shrugged. 'I do it in about forty-five minutes,' he said. 'The only exercise I take is getting to and from work.'

'I see,' said Vogel, in the unmistakable tone of voice of one who clearly did not. 'Well, sir, I should warn you that there are certain formalities we must now proceed with, and that I have a warrant to search this property.'

Alfonso had been half-expecting this, but he was stunned all the same. He knew he wasn't functioning properly and felt as if he would probably never function properly again.

'Is there anyone else here, Mr Bertorelli?' asked DC Pam Jones.

'What?'

It was hard for Alfonso to answer the simplest of questions. Nothing was registering in his brain. There was only thick fog inside his head. He should have been prepared, but he wasn't. Not at all.

'Y-yes,' he stumbled. 'My nan. She's in bed. Asleep.'

'Right,' Vogel interjected. 'Heavy sleeper, is she?'

'Yes. I suppose so. She's poorly. The doctor gives her pills. Why?'

'Because I thought we'd made enough noise to wake most people up, Mr Bertorelli,' persisted Vogel. 'Now, perhaps you'd like to rouse your nan and bring her down here. Might give her less of a shock than one of these chaps bursting in on her.'

Vogel gestured vaguely in the direction of his and DC Jones' uniformed escort. In their equipment-packed tactical vests they certainly looked frightening to Alfonso. He nodded. Subdued. Submissive. He began to make his way towards the door that led out to the hall, aware that one of the constables seemed to be planning to accompany him.

Suddenly Vogel ordered them to wait, then took a step towards the second door off the sitting room, which led directly into the kitchen, and pointed at a washing machine in the far corner. It was running.

'Doing a wash, are you, Mr Bertorelli?' queried Vogel. 'At this hour in the morning?'

Alfonso shook his head. He looked puzzled.

'Maybe Nan put it on, before she went to bed.'

'Long cycle, unless your gran keeps extremely late hours,' said Pam Jones, pointedly checking her watch. The time was 5.10 a.m.

Alfonso shrugged and made his way upstairs, followed as he'd thought he would be by a uniformed PC. When he returned, Vogel was still standing in the kitchen doorway staring at the washing machine.

'Nan's on her way down, she's just getting dressed,' Alfonso said.

Vogel didn't respond. The machine appeared to be in spin mode now. As if on cue, it came to the end of its cycle and stopped. Vogel opened the door and pulled out a small bundle of damp washing, letting it fall to the floor. He sifted quickly through and pulled out a grey hoody.

'No DNA left on this, I shouldn't think,' he muttered.

Then he held the garment up and showed it to Alfonso.

'Yours, sir, I assume?' he said.

'No,' Alfonso replied, in a high-pitched voice he didn't recognize as his own. 'I've never seen it before in my life.'

'I see, sir. So how do you suppose it got into your grandmother's washing machine?'

'I have no idea.'

'Might it belong to your grandmother?' Vogel's voice was heavy with irony. 'Wears hoodies, does she?'

'Of course not.'

'Right. So you've never seen this hoody before, and yet it's being washed in your washing machine in the early hours of the morning.'

'My nan's washing machine,' Alfonso responded.

'Mr Bertorelli, I advise you to think very carefully before

you make any remarks that might be regarded as facetious,' said Vogel. 'I surely don't have to remind you what a serious matter this is.'

'Look, I'm as bewildered as you are,' Alfonso began.

Then he stopped. One of the uniformed officers searching the property had entered the room and was whispering something in Vogel's ear. The detective sergeant looked stern when he spoke again.

'Mr Bertorelli, do you remember when we met yesterday I asked if you owned a bicycle?'

'Yes.'

'And what did you reply?'

'No. No, I don't own a bicycle.'

'Mr Bertorelli, PC Sanderson here has just found a black bicycle in your grandmother's storeroom downstairs. Not only that, the bike is wet, indicating that it has recently been used, probably within the last few hours as the rain only started shortly before midnight.'

There was no colour left in Alfonso's face. He didn't speak.

'So, are you sure you don't own a bicycle?' Vogel repeated.

'I told you. No.' Alfonso's voice was now a barely audible squeak.

'Then who do you think it might belong to?'

Alfonso shook his head. There were tears in his eyes.

'How old is your grandmother, Mr Bertorelli?' asked DC Jones.

'S-she's eighty-nine.' Alfonso stumbled badly over the words.

'And she's not in the best of health?'

Alfonso agreed that she wasn't.

'So it is unlikely the bike is hers?'

'It's definitely not hers.'

'Definitely not,' repeated Vogel. He appeared to be on the

verge of saying more, but he was interrupted by the return of PC Sanderson, who had left the room again.

Sanderson was holding a black leather handbag in one gloved hand. He passed it to Vogel, who glanced inside, withdrew a small folded case and opened it so that Alfonso could see. The case contained Michelle Monahan's warrant card.

Alfonso made an involuntary gulping sound. He looked close to collapse.

Vogel stared at him with icy eyes. 'Alfonso Bertorelli, I am arresting you on suspicion of assault and robbery,' he said. Then he began to recite the statutory caution: 'You do not have to say anything. But it may harm your defence if you do not mention when questioned something which you later rely on in court. Anything you do say may be given in evidence.'

As he spoke, Vogel became aware that Alfonso was not looking at him. Instead his gaze was fixed somewhere beyond Vogel's left shoulder. The detective turned. An elderly woman, wearing a thick knitted cardigan over a nylon nightdress, was standing in the doorway. She looked very frail. Her hands were shaking and her face was ashen.

'What have you done, my boy?' she asked. 'Mio caro, mio caro, what in the name of God have you done?'

twelve

When George tried to call Alfonso later that morning he got no reply from his mobile. George was unaware, of course, that the other man was in custody at Charing Cross nick.

After several attempts to contact his friend, and having had no success by mid-afternoon, George called the Vine on the staff number. Another waiter George knew vaguely told him that Alfonso hadn't turned up for his lunchtime shift. Neither had he contacted the restaurant.

'Leonardo is fucking furious,' said the waiter. 'If you hear from Fonz, tell him to get his arse over here pronto – and he'd better have a good excuse ready.'

Alfonso never skipped work. Everyone knew the Vine was his life. George was at a loss as to what he should do next. Then Tiny called, apparently even more distraught, if that were possible, than he'd been over Daisy. His words came tumbling out in a muddle.

'George, did you know Michelle was mugged last night? Alfonso's been arrested. They think he did it. He's locked up in Charing Cross nick, and he phoned Billy, but Billy's not that kind of lawyer, it's all right though, he's trying to get him a criminal lawyer to sort everything out. Oh, what are we going to do, George? What the heck's happening, I mean who's going to be—'

'Hey, calm down,' interrupted George, sounding none too calm himself. 'Has Alfonso actually been charged with anything?'

'Yes,' said Tiny. 'I mean no. "Arrested on suspicion of" – that's different, isn't it?'

'I think so,' said George. 'I'm no expert. But if that is the case, presumably we should be able to get the Fonz out on police bail. You know, like all those journos mixed up in that phone hacking thing. That's what happened to them, wasn't it? They were on police bail for months before it was even decided whether to charge them or not.'

'But, George, what if he did it? What if Fonz mugged Michelle and attacked Marlena? What if he was the one who killed Daisy and Chump? Billy says the police found Michelle's handbag at his place, and a bike he claims isn't his. But what if it is? What if he's guilty?'

'Tiny, for a start you don't believe Alfonso would ever harm Marlena, do you? He idolizes the woman. I've always thought he was a bit in love with her. Getting on for obscene, given the fact that she's an old—'

'Oh don't, George, please.'

'Sorry, I didn't mean to say that. I've been trying to call Fonz all day. Wanted to know if he'd come with me to see Marlena, 'cos I didn't want to go on my own . . . It never occurred to me . . . Wow, I'm just in shock, I suppose.'

'I know that feeling. But the fact is, someone hurt Marlena. And Michelle. I called her right after Billy told me about Fonz. She's just out of hospital. She answered her phone, but she could hardly speak. Apparently her nose has been smashed to bits and she'll need to have an operation to reconstruct it. Maybe more than one op. George, what is happening to us? You didn't even ask how Michelle was.'

George did an audible double take. 'No. Oh fuck. I'm sorry, mate. I don't know why, I assumed from the way you were talking that she hadn't been hurt at all. I just thought her handbag was snatched. That's terrible, what you're saying. And she's so pretty too.'

'Do you want to come with me to visit her later?'

'Yes, of course. But are you sure she'll want visitors if her face is in that sort of state? I know I wouldn't.'

Tiny said he'd call Michelle first.

On his arrival at the custody suite of Charing Cross police station Alfonso had been searched, his fingerprints and a DNA sample taken, his clothes, his watch and the contents of his pockets taken away in sealed bags as evidence. Dressed in the white paper suit he had been given to replace his clothes, Alfonso felt as if he was living a nightmare. In between interviews he was detained in a police cell. There was no natural light in the small room, which was furnished only with a blue plastic-covered bench bed and a lavatory in one corner. He didn't know how long he'd been in there. He was so shaken by the whole experience that he'd completely lost track of time. But despite his confused state, his story did not vary.

'I know it's another coincidence, I'm not surprised you don't believe me,' he said. 'But I'm telling the truth. I was just walking home to my nan's place. I couldn't believe what I saw. I went to help Michelle, didn't I? You've taken my clothes away. What's the point? It's obvious they're going to be covered in Michelle's DNA. There was blood everywhere. She was screaming with pain. I held her in my arms.'

As always, Vogel listened carefully. On the one hand,

Bertorelli's story made sense. And on the other hand it made no sense at all.

It was, as his suspect pointed out, quite obvious that Michelle's DNA would be found on the clothes Alfonso had been wearing. But the grey hoody had been thoroughly washed and was therefore unlikely to yield any traces of forensic evidence. Despite both items having been found at his grandmother's flat, Alfonso continued to maintain that he had never seen the hoody or the bicycle before, unless they were, as seemed likely, the property of the cyclist he had caught only a fleeting glimpse of both when Marlena was injured and Michelle mugged. So far as he could recollect, he had never touched Michelle's handbag.

'So why did we find these items at your grandmother's?' Vogel asked.

'I have no idea,' said Alfonso. 'Someone must have planted them. If I were guilty I wouldn't have left all that stuff lying around to incriminate myself, would I? Surely you can see that?'

'My understanding is that it is not generally known that you stay with your grandmother. So who among your colleagues and friends and acquaintances would know where she lives?'

'I don't know. Maybe I was followed. And maybe I was followed when Michelle was mugged too. Someone waited until I was nearby, then attacked her. To set me up. That's all I can think of.'

'Mr Bertorelli, don't you think that's a little far-fetched?'

Alfonso lowered his head into his hands, and spoke through his fingers.

'Why would I hurt Michelle?' he asked. 'Or Marlena. Why would I want to harm them? They're my friends.'

And that, thought Vogel, was the million-dollar question: Why? What possible motive could Alfonso Bertorelli have?

Indeed, if these crimes were linked, as they surely must be, what motive could anyone have?

Shortly after midday, Christopher Margolia, a Nigerian-born criminal lawyer recommended by Billy, arrived at Charing Cross police station fully prepared to intervene on behalf of his new client, Alfonso Bertorelli.

The Eton- and Oxford-educated Margolia was, Alfonso realized straight away, a very good man to have on your side.

Margolia pointed out calmly but forcefully to Vogel that his client's claims were quite plausible. He could well have been followed and the incriminating evidence planted at his grandmother's house. All other evidence against him was circumstantial, the lawyer said.

'We are proceeding with our inquires, Mr Margolia,' responded Vogel doggedly. 'The items removed from the home of your client's grandmother are being forensically examined and we are awaiting laboratory reports on those items, along with the clothes your client was wearing at the time of his arrest.'

Margolia was persistent. 'You may have the right to keep my client overnight, Detective Sergeant Vogel, but unless you charge him, which I very much doubt you will be in a position to do, your time will be up tomorrow morning and I shall insist upon his release.'

Around mid-afternoon Vogel extricated himself from a further interview with Alfonso, which seemed to be getting nobody anywhere, and retreated to his desk in an attempt to think things through. Yet again. There was a lot to think about. He wanted to go over every statement, every jot of evidence again and again. He had to make absolutely sure nothing had been overlooked. It was his way.

He had no sooner started than he was interrupted by Detective Inspector Tom Forest. Vogel didn't like to be interrupted when he was thinking, but as Forest was his superior officer he didn't have a lot of say in the matter. Particularly as it was Forest who had ordained that Vogel was to be permitted to have his own way, so long as he continued to deliver results. Improving the department's clear-up rate was paramount, even though it secretly irked Forest to deal with a subordinate whose emails and reports he struggled to comprehend. For his part, Vogel thought Forest unintelligent and pedantic, but he knew that it was largely because of Forest's attitude, which even went to the extent of the Detective Inspector covering for Vogel on occasion to his own superiors, that he retained the possibly unique freedom he enjoyed within the Met.

Fired up both by his eternal obsession with targets and the desire to swiftly bring to justice the perpetrator of a violent crime against a fellow police officer, Forest appeared to be taking, true to form Vogel thought, an overly simplistic approach.

'Well done, old man,' said Forest. 'Got it sorted, then. Seems you were quite right about those incidents being linked, and now you've got the bastard, eh? Damn good show.'

Vogel stared at Forest through red-rimmed eyes. This had already been a long, hard, and mentally taxing day. Vogel was running on empty. Being woken at 4 a.m. and deprived of his full seven or eight hours' sleep did not suit him.

'I'm not so sure about that, sir,' he said mildly.

'What do you mean?' bristled Forest. 'Bang to rights, I heard.'

'We're still waiting for the forensic results. We've fast-tracked fingerprinting but the DNA will take days,' Vogel reminded his superior.

'But that's all just a formality, surely,' continued Forest. 'I mean, you can't seriously think all that stuff was planted. The bike, the handbag, and that hoody?'

'The suspect says so.'

As if on cue, DC Jones walked into the room. A large chunk of her longish brown hair had escaped the bun at the nape of her neck demanded by police regulations. She looked flustered.

'We've just got the fingerprint results,' she said. 'No match for Bertorelli's prints on either the bike or Michelle's handbag.'

Vogel frowned. Forest caught him at it.

'For goodness' sake, man, he wiped his damn prints off, didn't he? The bike and the bag were found on his grandmother's property – the place he had returned to after the mugging.'

'Yes, sir, and the bag was covered with Michelle's blood,' responded Vogel. 'How did he clean off his prints yet leave the blood behind?'

'He must have worn gloves so that there'd be no prints. And what about the washing machine – running in the middle of the night with the hoody in it. Evidence was being deliberately destroyed. Bertorelli *has* to be guilty.'

'Perhaps, sir.'

'*Perhaps?*' Forest was turning puce. 'Vogel, your own report stated that Bertorelli told no one about living with his mother and grandmother. That being the case, how would anyone have known where to plant evidence, let alone actually have done so?'

'He told us he must have been followed to his grandmother's home, sir.'

'Of course he bloody did, Vogel. And what about the co-incidence, yet again, of his conveniently timed arrival at the scene of the crime?'

'He said that was a set-up too, sir.' Even as he spoke, Vogel was aware how ridiculous it sounded.

'Every bloody criminal claims they've been set up! It's the oldest line in the book,' blustered Forest. 'Look, we're talking about a violent attack on a police officer here. And a woman officer at that. Do you not understand? This is one of our own, Vogel. We have to act and we have to act fast. Otherwise it looks damned bad, both to the public and within the force. So get this joker bloody charged as soon as, will you?'

'I don't know, sir. I really need to think it through.'

'You know what your trouble is, Vogel?'

'No, sir,' said Vogel.

'You do far too much bloody thinking,' roared Forest.

It turned out that the bicycle found in Alfonso's nan's store-room had been stolen from outside the Royal Opera House the previous evening, the chain attaching it to a lamppost having been effectively severed. It was just possible that Alfonso had finished his shift at the Vine, somehow discovered that Michelle would be walking home from Marlena's, stolen the bike, pursued her to Southampton Row where he attacked her and then stashed the bike somewhere, only to return for it upon leaving the hospital and, for some inexplicable reason, riding it to his nan's place. Vogel thought it highly unlikely.

And so did the Crown Prosecution Service.

Early the following morning Vogel presented the facts in painstaking detail to Forest, and also to a CPS representative. The CPS man shared Vogel's doubts, agreeing that the very presence of so much unsubstantiated evidence was in itself suspicious. Having crossed swords with Christopher Margolia in the past, he was also of the opinion that every piece of evidence and every witness would be subjected to rigorous cross-examination, and the prosecution would collapse at the first hurdle if they were foolish enough to bring a case against Mr Bertorelli on the existing evidence.

Ultimately, in spite of what Alfonso feared was such strong evidence against him, and regardless of DI Forest's blustering, it was decided not to charge him with any offence. Not yet, anyway.

Eventually a furious Forest agreed that Alfonso should be released. Under habeas corpus they could, as Margolia had pointed out, keep him for only thirty-six hours.

And so at 11.30 a.m. Alfonso was told he was free to leave, and his paper suit was replaced with clean but used clothes from the police store since his were still being forensically examined.

Full of fear and uncertainty, and smarting from the indignity of wearing someone else's clothes, an ill-fitting tracksuit at that, he began to wander the streets aimlessly.

How long would it be before the police might come to get him again? he wondered. How long would it be before all the forensic and DNA tests came through, and would they make things better or worse? It was obvious that his clothes would be covered in Michelle's DNA, considering he'd held her in his arms until the ambulance got there. Unaware that the results of the fingerprinting of Michelle's bag had already been delivered, and that no prints of his had been found, he wondered whether he had unknowingly touched Michelle's bag, either at the scene of her attack or on some previous occasion. Could he have moved it across the table while in Johnny's, picked it up from the floor or off the back of a chair, or merely handed it to Michelle? If so, it might bear his prints. Though the innocent possibilities were endless, there was no telling what the police would make of one more piece of evidence stacked against him.

He felt weak. Almost too weak to continue walking. He was right outside a pub. The Dunster Arms, according to the sign Alfonso didn't even glance at. Maybe what he needed was a strong drink. Or several. Alfonso opened the door and entered.

The Dunster was an unpromisingly shabby hostelry in need of a coat of paint outside and some major refurbishment inside, although Alfonso barely noticed that either. Despite its drab appearance, it provided better service and refreshment than he might have expected, even boasting a fancy coffee machine. The Dunster Arms was, by virtue of its close proximity, the hostelry favoured by staff of Charing Cross police station, but Alfonso didn't know that or he would have avoided the place. An old-fashioned television set was tuned to a cricket match somewhere sunny. Alfonso registered that the players were wearing rather garish outfits, then looked away. He was not interested in cricket or indeed anything much else right then.

There was, at that hour of a Saturday, only one other drinker in attendance, and he neither looked like nor indeed was a police officer.

Alfonso ordered a double espresso and a large brandy, which he downed in one swallow. Although he liked his wine he was not a big drinker and the neat fiery alcohol went straight to his head. The sensation was extremely pleasant, given the ordeal he had just endured and the muddled state of his brain. So he ordered another, which he also drank straight down. And then a third.

'Gotta bit of a thirst, mate?' enquired his sole fellow drinker. The man was propped on a bar stool to Alfonso's left. He had a sallow complexion, bad teeth, and one of those bulbous noses which come from years of alcoholic overindulgence. He was the sort of character Alfonso would normally have run a mile from.

On that day, his head spinning, he took a step closer, ignoring the stale sweaty smell the man exuded, and climbed with some difficulty onto the bar stool alongside him. The alcohol had loosened Alfonso's tongue and his need for human compan-ionship, any human companionship, was overwhelming.

'I'm not thirsty, I just want to get drunk,' he said.

The man with bad teeth looked him up and down. 'You're not the only one,' he said.

'What are you having?' enquired Alfonso.

'Just a small Scotch,' the man with bad teeth replied.

Alfonso ordered him a large one and himself another large brandy. His new best friend returned the favour. Then Alfonso ordered yet another round. He had never drunk that much brandy in his life before, certainly not all in one sitting and in the middle of the day.

After only a short time the bar began to rotate around him and he would probably have fallen to the floor were it not for his new companion grabbing him in the nick of time. A waft of sour breath engulfed Alfonso. He didn't even notice. Leaning heavily against the bar he managed somehow to lift his brandy glass to his lips. The double espresso remained untouched.

'You all right, mate?' asked the man, in the manner of someone not really expecting an answer.

'Dush it look like I'm bloody all right?' replied Alfonso.

The man didn't respond.

'I've been framed, I've been bloody framed, I've just spent a day and a night in the nick and I'm bloody innocent, I tell you, bloody well innocent.'

'Aren't we all, mate?' said the man with bad teeth.

Later that day, around mid-evening, Marlena answered her intercom. A familiar voice enquired after her well-being and asked if she would like a visitor.

Marlena was pleased. She'd been feeling depressed. Her foot hurt and her head was full of unwelcome thoughts. Obviously she realized she might be in danger, given the recent attacks on the friends. But while Marlena had her reasons for fearing spectres from her past, she could see no reason why anyone currently in her life would wish to harm her.

She invited her caller up and buzzed the front door open.

The visitor had brought a bottle of rather good champagne, already nicely chilled, and after Marlena, still hobbling on crutches, led the way into her sitting room, opened the bottle at once and poured generous measures into a pair of crystal glasses standing on the sideboard.

The visitor then carried one of the glasses across the room to where Marlena was sitting in her usual chair by the window, and placed it on the table by her side. Marlena picked up the glass and took a long leisurely sip.

'Lovely, darling,' she said, a broad smile stretching across her face. Then she raised her eyebrows enquiringly. 'You're not drinking, sweetheart – don't you want any?'

'Later.'

'Well, you'd better be quick.' Marlena mischievously wiggled her glass, which was already half-empty. 'You know vintage Bolly is my favourite.'

She smiled up at her visitor, who remained standing and was still wearing a full-length raincoat and gloves.

'Oh, do make yourself at home. Sit down and take your coat off. It's not raining, is it?' She glanced towards the window.

'I thought it might, that's all,' said the visitor, making no move either to remove the coat or to sit.

Marlena took another drink. 'Please sit down and have a drink, you're making me feel uncomfortable,' she said.

'In a minute. Aren't you enjoying the champagne?'

'Yes, darling . . .' Marlena paused mid-sip, looking thoughtful. 'Though it seems a little drier than usual. But it's wonderful. A real treat.'

'Good. I'm very glad. I think it's important that the last drink one has should be a special one, don't you?'

'I should say so—' Marlena stopped abruptly as the words sank in. Her smile froze on her face.

'What?' she asked.

'Oh, you know, as an alternative to a last supper I suppose there's nothing better than a bottle of decent bubbly. I knew you'd appreciate it.'

Marlena was sitting very still, unable to believe her ears. This couldn't be serious, surely? It just couldn't be.

'Stop it,' she instructed. 'I realize you are making some sort of joke. A very bad joke under the circumstances, but a joke all the same. It's not funny though, so just—'

'I'm not joking.'

'Oh, don't be ridiculous!' Marlena spoke with a lot more certainty and authority than she actually felt.

'Please don't call me ridiculous.'

The familiar voice no longer sounded the way it usually did. There was steel in it.

Marlena felt a chill run down her spine. Was this for real? The eyes staring at her across the room were cold as ice, their gaze unblinking and full of hatred.

She glanced desperately around the room, looking for her phone. Stupidly she'd left it on the table in the hall when she'd hobbled out there to open the front door. The horrible thought occurred to her that even if it were here by her side it was highly unlikely that she would be allowed to make a call. She thought she would try though. Maybe she could get out into the communal lobby, picking up her phone on the way, and even if she wasn't given time to use it, perhaps someone might hear her if she shouted for help.

Grabbing a crutch, which she waved at her visitor in as threatening a manner as she could muster, she launched herself on one leg across the room, heading for the hallway.

She didn't make it.

Her visitor moved towards her in an almost leisurely fashion. An extended foot cracked into the front of her one good leg, tripping her with easy efficiency.

Marlena crashed to the floor, the crutch flying out of her grasp. Her head collided with the corner of the sideboard, cutting open her forehead. Blood gushed from the wound, but Marlena seemed more concerned that her elaborate blonde wig had been knocked to one side, revealing a head bearing only a scant growth of wispy grey hair. Nobody ever saw Marlena without her wig. She tugged at it with one hand. It was an automatic response. Her attacker leaned forward, pulled the wig off entirely, and tossed it carelessly aside.

'Don't, please don't,' she begged.

Marlena knew what she must look like. A pathetic, bald old woman pleading as much for the last vestiges of her pride as for any other kind of mercy.

'It's an improvement,' said her attacker, as if reading her mind. 'You don't look like a drag queen any more. I really thought you would have a little more hair, though.'

Marlena's humiliation was almost as great as her fear. She realized she was crying. Tears mixed with blood ran down her face. Angry at this loss of dignity, she struggled to push herself upright. Her limbs refused to obey her. What little strength she possessed had disappeared. She knew now that she would not escape, yet still she couldn't stop trying. By force of will she managed to get on one knee, and was groping for support from the sideboard in order to pull herself upright when the punch came.

A fist hit her straight in the face, smashing her nose. Just like

Michelle, she thought, as she fell back to the ground, blood and goo from her shattered nose now mingling with the blood from her injured head.

Again she tried to rise to her feet. But this time her attacker had no need to intervene. She quickly collapsed, her head spinning alarmingly. With surprising clarity, she realized that this was not due to the blow she had taken to the head.

She slumped, spreadeagled on the ground, a blubbering wreck. Though her mind remained lucid, her limbs failed to respond when she tried to move. It was as if her body no longer belonged to her. She remembered the taste of the champagne. Drier than usual, she'd said. She of all people should have detected that there'd been something wrong with it, something added. But perhaps she had merely tasted what she expected to taste.

She looked up into the eyes of her attacker and saw only emptiness. No compassion, obviously. No pity. But it was worse than that. There really was nothing there but emptiness.

It was at that moment that she knew for certain she was going to die. But even as the awful fear gripped her, she could not possibly have guessed how. Not then. Not yet.

She tried to speak. It was hard to get the words out. Her attacker kicked her in the ribs. Casually. For the hell of it, she thought. She tried to scream but no sound came. Then a second kick, this one totally winding her.

She managed to gasp just one word.

'Why?' she asked.

Her attacker crouched down over her, smiling. The most terrifying smile she had ever seen.

'Don't you know?'

Marlena shook her head, her poor bloodied, almost bald head. She hadn't the faintest idea.

'Well, I think everyone has the right to know why they are going to die, don't you?'

The voice was mild, almost conversational. The story it then related came as a total shock. For several minutes the voice wafted over her, reminding her of something she had done many years ago.

Her attacker, it seemed, had been the victim of her actions. Unwitting actions, she wanted to explain. She had been stupid, reckless and irresponsible. But she'd meant no harm. In her panic, she hadn't stopped to think about the hurt she'd inflicted. Her attacker had not come here to listen to her explanation, her pleas for forgiveness. The drug she'd been given made it impossible for her to speak. Her mind remained clear though. She realized that what was happening to her was revenge. The ultimate act of revenge. She saw now that one of the hands which rested lightly, almost gently, on her upper body, held a knife with a long, slightly curved blade.

'You should prepare yourself to say goodbye, darling,' said her attacker, placing a heavily sarcastic inflection on the term of endearment Marlena always used so freely. 'But it will be a prolonged goodbye, so take your time.'

A terrible shudder ran through Marlena's body. She so wished she could lose consciousness now. Just slip away.

Her attacker used the knife to cut a strip of material from the hem of the silk blouse she was wearing, forced open her mouth, slotted the strip of material between her teeth and tied it tightly in a knot behind her head.

'There, we don't want you making a noise and disturbing the neighbours, do we?'

The voice was soft and all the more menacing for it. Marlena, half-choking on the makeshift gag, virtually incapable of move-ment, could do nothing but stare in wide-eyed horror as the devil loomed over her and, using the knife again to cut into the fabric, tore her skirt and undergarments from her body.

'I will discover thy skirts upon thy face. I will show the nations thy nakedness, and the kingdoms thy shame,' said her attacker, hissing out the words. 'I will cast abominable filth upon thee, and make thee vile, and will set thee as gazing stock.'

Marlena's eyes had become fixed only on the shimmering point of the knife, which was directed at her lower abdomen.

She was sure by then that she knew what was about to happen.

Yet when her legs were thrust apart and the vicious blade entered her there, brutally invading her most intimate parts, the sense of shock as the steel sliced through her flesh and thrust upwards deep into her inner being, was every bit as overwhelming as the physical agony. And that was unspeakable.

The drug which had been added to Marlena's champagne is sometimes used to lessen pain in childbirth. It could do little to combat the terrible suffering she endured at the hands of her assailant before death finally claimed her.

thirteen

It was the Sampford House caretaker who found Marlena's body.

Paddy Morgan, a tiny sinewy man who in his youth had been a national hunt jockey until a bad fall in his first Irish National put paid to a promising future, had been in the habit of calling on Marlena every morning since she'd been injured. He took her a newspaper, along with any other necessities she required: milk for her tea, the occasional loaf of bread or whatever small snack she might request.

He usually left it until after eleven before ringing her doorbell. Marlena was a night bird, and even in the state she was in, still in pain, and unable to go out at night, Paddy knew that she was likely to be up until the small hours reading, listening to the radio or watching TV. And she wouldn't open her front door to anyone, not even Paddy, until she was fully made up and properly dressed.

So on this tragic Sunday morning Paddy at first felt no particular sense of alarm when he couldn't raise Marlena. He checked his watch and saw it was not yet quarter to eleven. Paddy was in the habit of having a pint or two at the Nag's Head of a Sunday lunchtime. And he wanted to get to the bookies in time to put a fiver on a mare he fancied in the 2.30

at Plumpton and then watch the race on the betting shop TV. But he had a load of stuff to get through first. That's why he'd called on Marlena a little earlier than usual. He liked to make sure she was OK before finishing his routine chores, putting out the rubbish, cleaning the main hall, and so on, which he was required to do every day of the week, Sundays included, by the management of Sampford House. He almost always spared the time for a bit of a chat, which he knew Marlena appreciated, particularly since she'd been more or less housebound. Besides, she was interesting. A good story-teller. And Paddy had the Irishman's congenital delight in sharing a decent yarn.

When Marlena failed to respond to her doorbell, Paddy decided to complete his chores first. After he'd finished, he came back and rang Marlena's doorbell again. When there was still no response he called her name several times. Becoming increasingly anxious that she might have fallen and further injured herself, he decided to use his pass key.

Paddy was half-expecting some kind of crisis as he stepped into the flat. But nothing could have prepared him for the sight which greeted him.

The door to the sitting room stood wide open. At first Paddy was so stunned he could not quite register what he was seeing. Involuntarily he moved forward into the room. As he did so, he slipped and went down on one knee. He used his hands to stop himself falling further but the wood laminate floor was covered in a kind of wet slime. His hands slid along out of control and Paddy ended up lying full length on the floor, his face just inches from Marlena's.

It was her blood that had caused him to fall. And Marlena's face, covered in the stuff, bruised and swollen from the blow she had received to the nose, bore an expression that was to haunt Paddy for the rest of his life. Her lips were drawn back, in spite of the gag between her teeth, into a dreadful gaping leer. Her eyes were wide open and even in death Paddy could see the agony and sheer unadulterated terror in them. He tried to move away, but his gaze was drawn down over Marlena's body. Her clothes had been shredded, and there seemed to be hardly anything left where her lower abdomen should have been. Her legs were apart, and scattered across the floor between them were pieces of what appeared to be internal organs. Obliquely, somewhere in the back of his mind, Paddy was reminded of the offal tray at the butcher's.

Somehow he managed to scramble to his feet, involuntarily lifting his hands to cover his face. As he did so, he realized that they were coated with blood. Whimpering in fright, he dropped them to his side and backed out of the room.

By the time he reached the front door he had started to retch. He threw up in the doorway but didn't stop running. He ran down the stairs, out into the street, possibly moving faster than he had since the racing accident that had injured his back and twisted the ligaments in his right knee beyond repair. All he knew was that he had to get away from the nightmare he'd stumbled into. He was past realizing that, as he ran, he was screaming. Screaming uncontrollably and at the top of his voice.

At the sight of the screaming man, covered in blood and vomit, passers-by crossed to the other side of the street. They either dismissed him as some sort of lunatic or were simply afraid to come near. Or maybe a bit of both.

Still retching, Paddy stood on the pavement outside Sampford House, desperately trying to control himself enough to use his mobile phone. He knew he ought to raise the alarm, but he couldn't stop retching and clutching at his chest. It was another Sampford House resident, returning from church to find Paddy apparently drunk on the doorstep, who finally extracted from him a brief, if hysterical, account of what had happened.

Two uniformed constables arrived at the scene within minutes, having been on patrol nearby when Dispatch put out the call. The older, Fred Martin, was a career bobby intent on giving the impression he'd seen it all, although he turned absolutely ashen when he first saw Marlena. The younger of the pair, PC Brad Porter, took one look, fled outside and, like Paddy, was unable to stop himself vomiting, though he did at least manage to reach the street.

The two constables were soon joined by a team of scenes of crime officers. Suited and booted in head-to-toe Tyvek coveralls, they set about erecting the usual crime scene defences and taking photographs of the body and its surroundings.

Vogel was at his desk when Forest delivered the news. So long as PC Michelle Monahan's attacker remained at large, even those who normally took Sunday off, like Tom Forest, were on duty. And the DI was not in a good mood.

'The bastard's done it again,' he stormed. 'And this time he's killed.'

Vogel was momentarily puzzled. Then the penny dropped.

'Who's been killed? Is it one of the Sunday Club group?' he enquired.

DI Forest tersely related the circumstances of Marlena's death, as reported by Constables Martin and Porter.

'Damned nasty, by all accounts,' he said. 'Poor woman had been butchered, absolutely butchered. The caretaker who found the body was covered in blood, head to foot. Apparently he fell over . . .'

Forest paused.

'So much blood he slipped on the floor.'

His voice was matter of fact, but Vogel could tell that Forest had been shocked by what he'd been told. He felt his own stomach start to churn.

'Anyway, plods on the scene have arrested the poor bastard. Right thing to do, of course. State he's in, he has to be treated as a suspect. Can't have him wandering off when he feels like it. He didn't bloody do it, though, we both know that, don't we?' Forest was seething with anger now.

Vogel grabbed his coat and was heading for the door before his superior had finished speaking.

'Get back here, Vogel!' shouted Forest. 'You're going nowhere.'

'Shouldn't I be at the scene, sir?'

'I said get back here!' roared Forest.

Vogel decided he'd better do as he was told. For once. He returned to his desk, tossed his coat over the back of his chair and sat down again.

'But I know more about what may have led to this than anyone else, sir,' he persisted.

'So why did you let it lead to this? You should never have let that bastard Bertorelli go.'

Vogel noted the choice of words. One thing was already clear: Forest was not about to accept the blame if it turned out that Alfonso Bertorelli had committed murder within hours of his release from police custody. Already Vogel was being set up to carry the can.

'We didn't have any choice, sir,' he pointed out. 'We didn't have enough hard evidence to charge him.'

'Yes, well, it looks as if he wasted no time in striking again. The press are going to be all over this like a rash. I simply cannot believe—'

Vogel interrupted what he considered to be unnecessary

rhetoric. 'Whoever did this must have blood all over him, sir,' he said. 'If we check all the CCTV in the area, we should be able—'

This time Forest interrupted Vogel.

'Not *we*, and certainly not *you*, Detective Sergeant,' he announced. 'This is murder. I've called in an MIT. DCI Nobby Clarke is on the way from the Yard.' Forest paused. 'Met Nobby Clarke, have you, Vogel?' he asked.

Vogel shook his head.

'Right, well, latest in a long line of high-fliers,' muttered Forest. He smiled fleetingly as if at some private joke, then continued: 'The DCI will want to interview you. Make sure you're available to answer questions, but other than that, keep out of it, do you hear?'

Forest was no longer smiling. He shouted the last few words then turned around sharply and stomped off in the direction of his office. He'd been happy to support Vogel while he was getting results, but that support had clearly been withdrawn in light of what he considered to be a fatal blunder on the detective's part.

'Yes, sir,' said Vogel quietly, addressing Forest's retreating back.

Murder Investigation Teams were the force's specialist homicide squads. There were thirty-one MITs operating in the London area, consisting of between thirty and forty staff, both police and civilian, led by a detective chief inspector.

It was standard procedure for an MIT to be called in to take charge of a murder investigation such as this, even if there was no question of mishandling by officers who had been previously involved in events that may have led to the murder. In this case, Vogel feared, questions would be asked about the handling of such events. In particular, the arrest and release of Alfonso Bertorelli. And those questions would primarily be directed at him.

He didn't care. Neither, at that moment, did he care about Forest's instruction to leave well alone. He had every intention of disobeying the direct order of his superior officer. He was going to visit the scene of the crime, regardless of any possible consequences. And that was that.

Vogel's hands were trembling and he had broken into a sweat by the time he arrived at Marlena's flat. He had visited several murder scenes in his time and seen more than his share of dead bodies. It never got any easier for him. He didn't experience nausea like some police officers he knew. He was in no danger of being sick, like young PC Porter. Vogel's reaction was almost entirely mental, but it had physical repercussions in that he so dreaded his own response he felt like a gibbering wreck even before he'd come face to face with the reality.

In this case he feared he was about to confront the worst case of violent death he had ever encountered. And he was right. The sight which greeted him through the open door of the sitting room, as he stepped into the hallway of Marlena's apartment, was far beyond anything he'd ever seen before. Almost before he had time to react, he found himself marvelling that the human body could contain so much blood. And he automatically registered that the dead woman's indescribably horrific wounds had almost certainly been sustained while she was still alive, otherwise the projectile bleeding would surely have been significantly less. It looked as if the entire sitting room was splattered with blood, and in some places, on parts of the floor, there were puddles of the stuff.

Vogel stood very still, making himself breathe rhythmically. The distinctive stench of death had hit him straight away. And something else. He looked down. He'd only just avoided stepping in the pile of vomit deposited by Paddy Morgan.

He turned his attention back to the scene before him. He took in that the SOCOs were already at work, and this helped because it lent a certain air of normality even to this most abnormal and aberrant circumstance.

Few of Vogel's colleagues, if any, knew of the demons he had to overcome, for he displayed no obvious reaction to dealing with deceased human beings. His head was swimming and his stomach had begun to churn. He still didn't reckon he was going to vomit, but as he surveyed the remains of Marlena McTavish it crossed his mind that if ever there was going to be a first time, this would be it. He'd never passed out at a crime scene either, but a wave of light-headedness warned him that this might be the first time for that too. He rested a hand against the wall just in case.

One of the SOCOs looked up at him with weary eyes.

'If you're going to touch anything, Vogel, put your damn gloves on, will you?' he instructed. 'And don't you dare come any further into this crime scene without getting suited up.'

'Sorry,' said Vogel, feeling like a complete idiot.

He stepped back into the doorway and almost collided with the Home Office pathologist, Dr Patricia Fitzwarren, almost unrecognizable in her crime scene coveralls.

'Out the way, Vogel,' she commanded.

Vogel obeyed, suddenly conscious of how the entire Metropolitan Police Service seemed to regard him as a nuisance, forever getting in the way, until they wanted something that only his particular talents could deliver. Would they still require his services after this? If Forest's attitude was anything to go by, the blame for Marlena's murder would be laid at his door. After all, it was his failure to gather sufficient evidence that had resulted in Alfonso Bertorelli being released.

Vogel looked at the cruelly mutilated body in front of him. 'Sorry,' he said, bowing his head.

He watched as Dr Fitzwarren knelt at the side of the victim and began her preliminary examination. The SOCOs, meanwhile, were busying themselves collecting samples of blood, searching drawers and cupboards, photographing the scene. There was almost total silence in the room. Vogel realized that he wasn't the only one who'd been badly affected by this murder. There was none of the usual banter between the SOCOs. It was as if the barbarity of the crime had struck them dumb.

Before taking his leave, he surveyed the room one last time. The shockwaves that had been surging through his body seemed mercifully to have subsided, allowing his brain to function at something approaching its normal capacity.

There was a lot to be learned from studying a crime scene. Not just in terms of forensics, but in building a picture of what had taken place in that setting. He started by studying the front door. It didn't look as though the killer had made a forced entry to the apartment. Vogel's gaze shifted to the room in which Marlena's body lay. There seemed to be at least one clear footprint in the blood on the floor. Careless, he thought, as he studied the room. In spite of the manner of the death, little seemed to have been disturbed in the apartment itself. No furniture had been overturned, and there was no obvious sign of a struggle. All of this indicated that the woman had known her attacker. But that was what he and everyone else, including Forest and probably by now DCI Clarke, had expected, was it not?

A bottle of Bollinger champagne, about two-thirds full, stood on the sideboard. Alongside it was a crystal glass, almost full of what must now be flat champagne. It looked untouched. A second glass, nearly empty, stood on a little table next to the armchair by the window. Judging by the worn appearance of the seat and cushions, this had almost certainly been the chair most often used by the dead woman.

Vogel backed out towards the communal hall, registering as he did so an entryphone just inside the door to the flat.

There were people in the corridor he hadn't noticed before. But then, on his arrival, he had been far too preoccupied with thoughts of what he might be confronted with at the scene of the crime. PCs Porter and Martin, the two officers who had been first to respond to the 999 call, were standing alongside a man Vogel presumed to be the caretaker who'd found the body. This man, grey-faced and trembling, sat slumped on the floor leaning against the wall. His face, hands and clothes were covered in blood and vomit.

He confirmed that he was Paddy Morgan and that he had indeed discovered Marlena's body.

'To tell you the truth, I don't think I'll ever get over it,' said Paddy.

'I know, I know,' said Vogel. And he did know, more than Paddy Morgan could have guessed.

'Now they tell me I've been arrested. Why? I never hurt anybody, I've not done anything.'

Vogel made soothing noises. 'We have to eliminate you from our inquiries, Mr Morgan,' he said. 'I am sure it will prove to be just a formality. You're covered in the dead woman's blood and—'

The caretaker gasped. His eyes filled with tears. His head lolled forward onto his chest. Vogel could have kicked himself. He needed the man lucid.

'What I mean is, you are carrying evidence on your clothes and hands,' explained Vogel. 'We need to have you checked out. As soon as that's done, we'll get you taken care of. A doctor will take a look at you to make sure you're OK. You've had the most terrible shock.'

Paddy agreed weakly that he had.

Vogel uttered a few more reassuring platitudes, then tried to elicit some information that might help with his inquiries.

'What's the security like here?' he asked.

Morgan looked up, startled, as if he feared he might be held responsible for the killer gaining access.

Vogel tried to reassure him. 'What I really want to know is how difficult would it be for an intruder to get into one of these flats?'

'Well, it shouldn't be easy,' said Morgan. 'I'm not always here – it's only a part-time job – but I'm here every morning, and the front door is permanently locked with a double Balham. The glass is armoured. And there's an entryphone linked to every flat. There's been no interference – you'll have seen that yourself on your way in. Sometimes people, particularly delivery men if they can't get a response from the flat they have a delivery for, use the intercom to ring others for access to the building. But the residents know better than to let anyone in they don't know. And even if someone did manage to get into the building, all the flats have front doors with peepholes, security chains, double locks – you name it.'

Vogel nodded. It was much as he'd thought. 'So the only way to get into one of these flats is to have the householder invite you in, is that it?'

'I suppose so, yes.'

'You don't think it likely then,' Vogel continued, 'that an intruder could have broken into Marlena McTavish's apartment?'

'Well, no. Like I said, there's no sign of a break-in. I'm sure I would have noticed.'

Vogel glanced round, looking for cameras.

'Is there any CCTV here?' he asked. 'Outside the front door perhaps?'

The caretaker shook his head. 'It's been talked about but a lot of residents didn't want it. They like their privacy too much.'

Vogel nodded. There were CCTV cameras all over Covent Garden, of course, but none would probably be of much help if it were not possible to identify suspects actually entering Sampford House.

Vogel thanked the man. Then he stuck his head back through the door of the flat.

'Any idea of time of death yet, Dr Fitzwarren?' he enquired.

'I've only just got here, Vogel. What do you think I am – a miracle worker?'

'That's exactly what I think,' replied Vogel hopefully.

The pathologist grunted.

'I just want to know if it's likely the deceased was murdered more than twenty-four hours ago,' Vogel persisted. 'It's important. We may need to act fast to prevent the killer striking again.'

'Ummm. Well, Vogel, she's certainly not been dead for more than a day, judging from her body temperature, but I need to get her back to the lab before I can tell you anything exact, as you very well know.'

'Thank you all the same,' said Vogel. 'And the manner of death?'

Dr Fitzwarren looked at him as if he were a moron.

'I think she may have been stabbed, don't you, Vogel?' she asked.

'What about the murder weapon?' enquired Vogel, ignoring the sarcasm heavy in her voice.

'A long-bladed knife, I should think, in light of what seems to have been done to the poor woman.'

'And what exactly has been done to her?' persisted Vogel.

Fitzwarren gestured to the bloodied masses on the floor between Marlena's legs, the stuff Paddy hadn't been able to help himself comparing to an offal tray at the butcher's.

'The internal organs have been roughly hacked out of the body. Can't be certain, given the damage, but I suspect we're talking reproductive organs.'

She pointed at a small lump of dark red tissue, sliced partially open, lying by Marlena's left knee.

'That looks like her womb to me,' she said.

Vogel felt his knees buckle.

Again he fought for control. There was another question he needed to ask, even though he could hardly bear to hear the answer.

He gestured at the blood all around the room.

'Am I to assume from all this that the organs were removed while the victim was still alive?'

Dr Fitzwarren paused in her examination and looked up at Vogel.

'Oh yes, Sergeant Vogel. When it started anyway. This woman was alive when the knife cut into her. She bled to death. Not much doubt about that.'

Vogel could take no more. He headed for the door. Outside, the caretaker was now standing more or less upright, hand-cuffed to a still-green PC Porter.

'You should get this man back to the station. Have him processed, then arrange for him to see a doctor,' said Vogel.

'I'm just waiting for MIT, Sarge,' said Porter. 'DI Forest said I had to stay here till they arrived. I can't wait to get out of this place, I can tell you. If I—'

'Yes, that's enough, Constable. You have a man in custody, right?'

'Yes, Sarge.'

Vogel glanced towards Paddy. He didn't think there was the slightest chance that the Irishman was guilty of anything more than muddying a crime scene. At least he looked a little calmer now. He might even be up to thinking more clearly.

'Are you sure there's nothing else you can tell me, Paddy?' he asked.

The caretaker shook his head.

A thought occurred to Vogel, a question he should probably have asked earlier.

'When did you last see Marlena alive?'

'Oh, that would be yesterday morning,' Paddy replied at once. 'I came round with her paper as usual, just gone eleven. She answered the door and we had a little chat like we always do.'

'And there was no sign of anything wrong?'

'Oh no, there was nothing amiss, then, I'm sure. She invited me in. I had a quick cup of tea.'

'So what time did you leave her?'

'I suppose it must have been half past eleven, maybe a bit later.'

Vogel walked slowly along the corridor towards the lift. He had a great deal to think about.

If Marlena had been lying dead in her flat for more than a day, Alfonso Bertorelli could not have been responsible for her death because he had been detained at Charing Cross police station.

But now it seemed, even before a full post-mortem examination had been conducted, that the caretaker could confirm Marlena had been alive at 11.30 a.m., or thereabouts, the previous day. Alfonso Bertorelli had been released from custody at 11.23 a.m. Vogel had signed the release papers and he remembered the time exactly. He always remembered figures exactly.

So, he told himself as he waited for the lift to arrive, he had to accept that Bertorelli would have had opportunity to kill the woman.

There was something else forcing its way to the surface of Vogel's memory. An unsolved case dating back to his early days in CID. He was still mulling it over when the lift doors opened. Out stepped two young men and an older woman, much taller than either of her companions, who was wearing an expensive-looking tailored black trouser suit. Although none of the three were in uniform it was obvious to Vogel that they were police officers.

'And who the hell are you?' asked the woman. Her body language made it clear that she was in charge.

Vogel told her. 'You're MIT, I assume?' he said.

The woman nodded curtly. 'These officers are DCs Wagstaff and Carlisle,' she said. 'And I'm DCI Clarke.'

So that was what lay behind Forest's knowing smile, thought Vogel. Nobby Clarke was a woman.

'Now, how about telling me what you're doing at my crime scene?' DCI Clarke continued. 'Your reputation precedes you, Vogel, but that doesn't mean you can trample all over one of my cases without my say-so.'

'Sorry, ma'am,' said Vogel. Then he tried, to the best of his ability, to explain his presence, glossing over the fact that he had deliberately disobeyed an order from his superior officer.

'I thought because of the knowledge I'd gained in my previous inquiries, both concerning the deceased and her group of friends, that I might be of some use, ma'am,' Vogel said. 'I mean, I hoped I might be able to contribute.'

Clarke grunted.

Vogel cleared his throat. He decided to be bold. After all, what did he have to lose?

'Also, ma'am, the case brought to mind the murders of two young women in the King's Cross area, around fifteen years ago. It was pretty rough around there in those days, as I'm sure you know, ma'am. One of the victims was a prostitute, out plying her trade. But the other was a student nurse from Sweden who almost certainly had no idea that she'd wandered into an area known for its vice trade. Both were killed in exactly the same way, ma'am: strangled, and then stabbed repeatedly in the same part of their body.'

Vogel paused. He was afraid that he sounded coy, and wondered if this was because he was addressing a woman. Surely not? Clarke was a top homicide cop. Nonetheless he was struggling to say the words that would accurately describe what had happened to the two women. And indeed to Marlena.

'Go on, Detective Sergeant,' instructed Clarke, her impatience evident.

Vogel coughed again.

'Their reproductive organs were removed from their bodies, ma'am,' said Vogel. 'Which is what seems to have happened to the victim in this case.'

'I see,' said Clarke. 'Right, thank you, DS Vogel.'

Vogel knew he was being dismissed. He stepped into the lift, unaware of DCI Clarke's thoughtful eyes following him, his thoughts entirely occupied by those two unsolved murders.

At the time of the King's Cross murders, the Met had feared some kind of crazed serial killer was at large. But fifteen years had passed without any further killings that fitted the same profile. Not in London, at least. And nowhere else in the country, as far as Vogel knew. Despite mammoth resources being thrown at the inquiry, the police had failed to come up with a single clue as to the killer's identity. Neither case had ever been closed. Technically at least, police inquiries into the murders were still ongoing. Vogel had not been involved in the investigations into the earlier murders nor had he attended the crime scenes, but as part of Forest's drive to improve clear-up rates he had been asked to review the case files.

Vogel felt a terrible foreboding as he stepped out onto the street. Despite the age difference between the victims, there was that one striking similarity between the King's Cross murders and the killing of Marleen McTavish. The sexual organs, the womb and ovaries of all three women had been hacked from their bodies.

But Marlena, unlike the earlier victims, had not been strangled beforehand. Her internal organs had been ripped from her body while she was still alive, and she had bled to death. That was what Dr Fitzwarren had said, wasn't it?

That being the case, Marlena had died slowly. Vogel shuddered at the thought. The poor woman would have been in mortal agony for what must have seemed like an eternity.

fourteen

When my work was done, I dissolved into the night. It was something I had always been able to do. I knew how to cover my tracks, how to disappear without trace. My feet were winged. My soul was free. There would be no blood-covered, raincoated murderer on the streets of London, no easy target for the CCTV cameras to focus upon.

I was the Houdini of death. I was the messenger from Hell, and after I had wreaked my vengeance it was as if I evaporated into thin air, leaving little more than a ghostly presence.

Everything had gone according to plan. Moreover I had found a strength and a will beyond my own expectations. I'd wondered if I might falter, but even though the blood and gore exploded from her living body with far greater force than I had anticipated, I did not waver. Quite the reverse. As I watched her face twist in agony, as her life's blood washed over me, my resolve grew ever stronger, so that the power of my arm achieved greater magnitude with every stroke, and the thrust of the knife grew ever bolder and more incisive.

I had a memory, of course, a kind of gene memory, of how to cause great pain without myself being consumed by it. I knew what I was capable of because of what I had done before.

Because of all that had been forced upon me. In childhood and beyond.

But this had been a step further. An extraordinary new experience. From the moment I had learned the truth, my entire being had been focused on this ultimate act of revenge. I had lain awake at night, imagining what it might be like to carve into a living body and feel it tense and try to escape the agony I was inflicting, to be able to stare into the eyes of my victim as the life slowly ebbed from them . . .

The reality had exceeded my imaginings.

On his arrival back at the station, Vogel was summoned to DI Forest's office. This was no more than he had expected. After all, he had blatantly disobeyed orders.

'I've had DCI Clarke of the MIT on the phone,' began Forest, glowering at Vogel. 'Apparently you went behind my back and blundered into her crime scene.'

'Sorry, sir,' said Vogel, keeping his voice level and his face as expressionless as possible. He'd assumed Clarke would make a formal complaint about his unauthorized appearance.

'I've supported you, Vogel,' continued Forest, quivering with rage. 'I've given you a free hand, let you do things your own way. And this is how you repay me.'

Only because of the results I've delivered, only because of what I do for your crime figures, that's why you support me, you pompous prat, thought Vogel.

'Yes, sir, sorry, sir,' he said.

Forest grunted. 'However, it seems you must have been blessed at birth.'

'What, sir?' Vogel wasn't following this.

'DCI Clarke tells me she was impressed with your knowledge

of the case and with your suggestion that there could be a link with two unsolved crimes. "The man's a thinker," she said.'

Forest continued to glower at Vogel, as if he had delivered a thoroughly damning insult rather than passing on a remark most people would take as a compliment. 'Anyway, she wants you on her team as Assistant SIO.'

Vogel's jaw dropped.

'Seems her usual number two's just taken early retirement.' Forest sniffed. 'Not bloody surprised.'

Vogel waited to see if any further explanation might be forth-coming. It wasn't.

'I haven't got the rank, sir,' he said eventually.

'You have now,' replied Forest with a distinct lack of enthu-siasm. 'As of this moment, you're Acting Detective Inspector Vogel. Clarke's already fixed it with the top brass at the Yard. Moves fast, that one. And what she wants, Nobby Clarke gets. She is the golden girl, after all. Wonderful crime figures . . .'

Forest's eyes glazed over for a moment, before he came to and shook his head somewhat sorrowfully.

'I see, sir,' said Vogel, who wasn't entirely sure that he did.

He did know that an inspector's salary, even if it didn't prove to be permanent, would be extremely useful right now. Although Vogel had never actively sought promotion, nor even known whether he really wanted it, his personal financial responsibilities had been rising of late. He couldn't wait to tell his wife. He was only human.

'Right then, get on with it,' continued Forest, his usual bluster restored. 'Clarke wants you hands on, Vogel. She's given orders for Bertorelli to be arrested straight away, and she wants you to lead a team of the MIT chaps and bring the bastard in. A squad car's outside waiting, Vogel. Oh, and from now on you report to her. Right?'

'Right,' said Vogel.

Alfonso Bertorelli was not at his grandmother's home in King's Cross, as Vogel had hoped he would be. Instead the arresting officers found merely a frightened old woman who spoke poor English but managed to tell them that her grandson had gone to work.

'My boy, he say he just want to carry on as normal . . .'

Clarke had simultaneously arranged for a CID man and two uniformed officers from Dagenham nick to go to Bertorelli's mother's address. They found nobody at home, perhaps backing up by default the grandmother's claim.

Unless Bertorelli had done a runner, thought Vogel. Leaving two officers to search the premises, he asked for more back-up to meet him at the Vine.

It was by now nearly four in the afternoon. As this was a Sunday, the restaurant was still full. Most of the remaining lunchers were on puddings, coffee, and in some cases brandy or liqueurs, when they became aware of police activity around them.

Alfonso was delivering iced Scandinavian berries with warm chocolate sauce to table fifteen when two uniformed PCs relieved him of the dish and steered him towards the door.

Chocolate sauce slopped onto Alfonso's pristine white shirt and several berries fell to the floor, which the waiter only wished would open up and swallow him. He tried to shake himself free of the grasp of the officers.

'What am I supposed to have done now?' he asked. 'I'm an innocent man, do you hear?'

'Just step outside, please, sir,' instructed Detective Constable Jones, who was right behind the two PCs. They had positioned themselves on either side of Alfonso and had each firmly grasped him by the upper arm.

'At least will you let me walk out of my restaurant without being manhandled?' asked Alfonso. 'I'm not going to try to run, am I?'

The two uniformed officers looked at DC Jones, who glanced around the busy room. Outside, several more police officers waited. DC Jones nodded slightly to the PCs, one of whom released his grip on Alfonso while continuing to steer him to the door. The second officer kept one hand lightly resting on Alfonso's arm, just in case.

Vogel had remained outside, letting the woodentops and DC Jones do the dirty work. He stood on the pavement opposite the door to the Vine, watchful as ever. When Alfonso emerged, Vogel stared at him with impassive eyes. Jones and the two PCs stepped away from Alfonso, allowing Vogel to confront him one to one.

'Alfonso Bertorelli, I am arresting you on suspicion of the murder of Miss Marleen McTavish,' Vogel began. 'You do not have to say anything—'

Vogel stopped abruptly. He could see he wasn't going to get to finish the caution until later.

Alfonso looked as if he'd been hit by a truck. His face turned ashen, his eyes glazed over.

'Marlena,' he murmured, his voice little more than a whisper. 'Marlena . . .'

Alfonso's body began to sway.

Vogel stepped forward, arms outstretched. Other officers also reached out towards the arrested man. All of them were too slow and too late.

Alfonso dropped like a stone onto the pavement.

*

They took him to UCH for a check-up. Alfonso came round almost as quickly as he had passed out, and his only injuries appeared to be a grazed hand and a sprained wrist, but Vogel was taking no chances. Whatever the outcome of the next couple of days, he didn't want the result undermined by some technicality that would create a legal loophole through which a killer could escape.

While waiting to be given the all-clear to detain Alfonso for interviews, Vogel learned that the officers searching the grandmother's home at King's Cross had found a pair of bloodstained Adidas trainers in one of the bins outside the back door of her block. Size nine. The same size apparently as the small collection of shoes in Alfonso's bedroom.

This was a potentially highly incriminating discovery. Vogel had little doubt that the blood on the shoes would prove to be Marlena's. He did, however, as when Alfonso had previously been arrested, have doubts about the location and manner of the discovery of the trainers. Alfonso Bertorelli didn't strike him as unintelligent. Would anyone, having committed murder, dump a pair of incriminating bloodstained trainers in the bin at his place of residence? Or one of his places of residence. It would seem to be an act of total stupidity. Particularly when the perpetrator in question had already been arrested on suspicion of previous, doubtless connected, offences.

On the other hand, Vogel was well aware how those responsible for criminal acts could panic when the enormity of their actions overwhelmed them. Particularly where crimes of violence were concerned. And most particularly when it came to murder. Any murder. But surely all the more so when the murder had been as brutal as this one.

However, to question Bertorelli's guilt for no other reason

217

than the sheer weight of evidence against him would be perverse, even by Vogel's standards.

Nobby Clarke and her MIT had installed themselves at Charing Cross police station and a cell had been made ready for Alfonso by the time Vogel was able to return there with the arrested man.

Alfonso was processed in the custody suite, his personal possessions and his clothes taken from him as before, even though this time Vogel did not expect them to necessarily provide evidence. He was then offered a cup of tea. Everything by the book, said Vogel, who countered his eccentricity in certain areas by acting with almost obsessive adherence to regulations in others.

While this was going on, Clarke summoned Vogel to the office which had been temporarily assigned to her. The DCI had a real presence about her, Vogel thought, emphasized by her height and her stylish appearance. Her dark blonde hair, its length pushing the limit of Met regulations, fell nearly to the collar of her sharply tailored jacket. Her manner was confident and authoritative without being imposing or domineering. She welcomed Vogel to MIT, told him she was looking forward to working with him as her number two, then cut to the chase.

'Everything does now point to Bertorelli,' she said. 'But the more we can interview out of him the better. And you should know what the search team have found at Marlena's apartment.'

Vogel looked at her enquiringly.

'There was a suitcase under her bed containing memorabilia from her time in Paris. Back then, she was known as Madame Lola. And it appears she ran an upmarket brothel.'

'Wow!' said Vogel.

'Indeed,' Clarke agreed. 'There were photographs both of her and various clients. A very elite clientele, from the look of it. We've been on to the French police. As you'd expect, they knew all about Madame Lola. They lost track of her twenty years ago after she fell foul of the mob. Word had it she'd got overambitious, decided to try her hand at a bit of blackmail. Only she chose the wrong victim. When she suddenly disappeared, the gendarmes weren't sure whether she'd gone to ground or been buried six feet under it. Turns out she must have fled the country.'

'So is it possible someone from her past has caught up with her, ma'am?'

Clarke nodded. 'Must be a possibility, I suppose. But she came back to the UK, reinvented herself, has lived in Covent Garden ever since, and there seems to be no question of her having set herself up as a madam again. Made plenty of dosh before, apparently. No, why would anyone from her Paris days come after her twenty years after the event? It must be Bertorelli. We already have hard evidence, don't we? I just wanted you to be aware of what we've learned about Marlena, that's all.'

'Thank you, ma'am.'

Vogel stood up to leave. When he reached the door, DCI Clarke called after him. Vogel turned to face her.

'Listen, Vogel,' she said. 'Would you stop calling me bloody ma'am. This is MIT, we're not a bunch of provincial woodentops, and you're my assistant SIO. Call me Nobby, for Christ's sake.'

Vogel gulped. He could not imagine calling any woman Nobby, let alone his rather impressive superior officer.

Clarke seemed to be waiting for him to respond. He didn't know what to say.

'Oh, all right, then,' she continued eventually. 'Boss will do. Anything but bloody ma'am.'

'Yes, ma— I mean boss,' said Vogel.

DC Jones was hovering in the corridor ready to take the first interview shift with him.

'Pam, do you know why the boss calls herself Nobby?' Vogel asked.

'Isn't it to do with the clerks in the City wearing top hats in the old days? People took to calling them nobby and it stuck. So if your surname's Clarke, you're liable to get called Nobby. Thought you'd know that, guv.'

'Yeah, but I thought it was just men. I've never come across a woman called Nobby. What's her real first name?'

'Nobody knows,' replied Pam Jones. 'Apparently she hates her given name and won't let it be used.'

'Dear God,' said Vogel, his thoughts immediately turning to a famous fictional detective. 'Hasn't anyone tried to find out?'

'Carlisle and Wagstaff have a real thing about it. They've checked her out big time – the electoral register, everything. She's always Nobby Clarke. They even managed to get hold of her driving licence. Nobby Clarke.'

Vogel found himself smiling. His new superior officer was certainly different.

He turned his attention to the matter in hand as he and Pam Jones approached the interview room where Alfonso Bertorelli was waiting for them. The Italian had tried to get Christopher Margolia, the criminal lawyer previously called in via Billy, to be by his side, but it seemed Margolia had jetted off to Prague for the weekend. A duty solicitor had been duly provided.

Nothing Clarke had told Vogel made him any happier about the Bertorelli situation. Quite the reverse, in fact. But neither did he believe that Marlena had been the victim of some mobster hitman. He just hoped, as he sat down opposite Alfonso, that the ensuing interview would prove to be fruitful. Who could

tell, the man might even confess, and that would solve everything. But Vogel didn't think so, somehow.

'To begin with, Mr Bertorelli, could you please take us
through your movements after you were released from police
custody yesterday?' he asked.

Alfonso looked a wreck. His eyes were red-rimmed as if he'd
been crying. His response took Vogel by surprise. He made no
attempt to answer the question, instead he took off on a tangent.

'I loved Marlena, she was probably the most important
person in the world to me, after my mamma and my nan,' he
said. 'How dare you accuse me of murdering her? I wouldn't
have harmed a hair on her head.'

'Mr Bertorelli, I have merely asked you to account for your
movements—'

'Yes, on the day Marlena was murdered. You've arrested me,
for God's sake, for murdering her. Me! I can't even think
straight.'

'You must try, Mr Bertorelli. If you are innocent, then help
me prove that. I'm going to ask you again. Would you please
take us through your movements on the day that you were
released from police custody?'

Alfonso took a deep breath.

'I don't know my movements,' he said. 'After you lot released
me I walked for a bit and then I went into a pub. I think I had
a bit too much to drink. I must have done. I lost most of the
day. I just wanted to blot everything out.'

'What was the name of the pub?'

Alfonso held his hands out in a despairing gesture.

'I don't know,' he said. 'I didn't look. I just wanted to drink.'

'Well, do you know where the pub was, the street perhaps?'

Alfonso shook his head.

'OK. Do you remember what direction you were walking?'

Alfonso shook his head again.

'Not really, towards Soho, I think, but I can't be sure. I was trying to clear my head. I just walked around for a bit, without taking any notice of where I was.'

'Right. Do you have any idea how long you walked for before going into this pub?'

'I'm not sure of that either. A while. Twenty minutes. Maybe more.'

'And you were on your own?'

'Yes.'

'So you were drinking alone?'

'I didn't have anyone with me, did I? Of course I was drinking alone. Who would have wanted to drink with me? Me, the prime suspect.'

'Did you speak to anyone?'

'I don't know. I don't remember. Maybe. I'm not sure.'

'What about the landlord, or whoever was serving behind the bar?'

'Well, I ordered drinks, so I must have spoken to someone behind the bar, I suppose.'

'But no conversation?'

Suddenly Alfonso mustered a bit of attitude.

'Oh yeah,' he said. 'I had a chat about my morning. "I've just come out of the nick. They think I've mugged a young woman police constable." You know the sort of thing. Oh yeah, I had plenty to chat about.'

Alfonso put a heavily sarcastic emphasis on the word 'chat'.

Vogel studied him wearily. This wasn't helping, and he suspected Alfonso knew it. He ignored the sarcasm and continued.

'And after that, after you left the pub, what did you do then?'

'I don't know. I suppose I was drunk.'

'You don't remember anything else that you did that day?'

'No.'

Alfonso looked as if he didn't care. As if he had given in.

'Do you remember returning to your nan's place?'

Alfonso shook his head. 'I remember waking up there though, in the early hours of this morning.'

'And then what?'

'What do you mean, then what? I felt like shit, obviously. Because of what had happened and because I'd got wasted. But I decided the best thing was for me to carry on as usual. I was on lunchtime shift at the restaurant, and on Sundays lunch is always extra busy. I thought going to work might keep me sane and I was pretty sure nobody there knew I'd been arrested. Not the first time. I'd asked my nan to call me in sick, hadn't I.' He paused. 'They bloody know now though, don't they? The rest of the bloody world, too, I expect. And this time I'm facing a murder charge. I didn't bloody do it, do you hear? I didn't bloody do it.'

Alfonso's voice rose to a near hysterical shriek.

Vogel carried on, keeping his own voice calm and level.

'So you decided to go to work as usual. But from what you have told us, if you really were so drunk that you couldn't remember what you did yesterday, then you must have had one heck of a hangover this morning, didn't you?'

Alfonso nodded.

'I just said that.'

'Yet you went to work?'

'Best thing to do with a hangover – work through it. Besides, I didn't have to be in till almost midday,' said Alfonso.

'Are you a big drinker, Mr Bertorelli?'

Alfonso shook his head.

'Only on special occasions,' he said, his voice heavy with sarcasm again.

Again Vogel ignored it.

'I didn't think you were, you don't have the look of a drinker.'

He paused. Sometimes if you left a silence interviewees would feel obliged to fill it. You could learn a lot that way, Vogel believed. But Alfonso made no attempt to fill the silence.

'So, you are not a big drinker and yet you got so drunk that you remember nothing from the moment you entered a pub you do not remember the name of until you woke up at your nan's place in the early hours of this morning, is that right?'

Alfonso nodded. The man looked ill. It was hard for Vogel to think of him as a cold-blooded murderer. And whoever had killed Marlena would have had to be cold-blooded in the extreme. Lacking any normal human feelings, Vogel thought. But if Bertorelli was innocent he was doing nothing to help himself.

Vogel terminated the interview and told Alfonso he would be taken to a cell to await further sessions, and would almost certainly be detained overnight. The other man seemed to sway slightly in his seat. Vogel hoped he wasn't going to pass out again and made a mental note to remind the custody team to keep a close eye on him.

Of course, Alfonso had already spent a night in a cell, following his earlier arrest. The first time, for someone who'd never been near a police cell before, was always a nasty shock. Now he faced another night in police custody. And he now knew all too well what it was like. Vogel had been told the smell was the worst thing. The mix of disinfectant and sweat and urine. That and the total lack of privacy. En suite, the regulars were inclined to joke. But there was really nothing very funny about a toilet in full view of the slot in the cell door.

*

224

Wagstaff and Carlisle, the two DCs Vogel had first met when they'd arrived at the scene of Marlena's death with DCI Clarke, were sent to check out the pubs within a thirty-minute walk of the nick. It was another cold wet day. As MIT officers, Nick Wagstaff, a bespectacled and prematurely grey young man, and Joe Carlisle, who would have been darkly handsome if he didn't almost always look moody, both considered themselves rather above such routine foot-soldier activity. They were not best pleased.

'Dunno why they couldn't have put a couple of woodentops on this,' grumbled Wagstaff.

'Bastard's probably lying through his teeth, anyway,' muttered Carlisle. 'And even if he did go in a pub, he could have been walking in bloody circles from what he said. How many pubs do you reckon we're going to have to check out?'

Wagstaff had a computer printout of local public houses in his hand.

'At least twenty,' he said.

'And we can't have a single bloody drink,' responded Carlisle.

The tenth pub they visited was the Dunster Arms, which seemed to them a rather insalubrious hostelry in need of a deal of TLC. As they were only temporarily based at Charing Cross the two officers were unaware that it was a regular haunt of a number of their police colleagues. And it was actually a busy and curiously popular little place, with relatively low overheads, which provided a fair income for its landlord who escaped from it to play golf in Portugal as often as he could. He was currently away. His stand-in, Jim Marshal, a retired landlord himself, was behind the bar. Wagstaff showed Marshal a mugshot of Alfonso.

'Have you ever seen this man in here?' asked the detective.

'Don't think so,' responded the stand-in.

'It would have been yesterday, lunchtime, and perhaps

through the afternoon,' persisted Wagstaff. 'Were you behind the bar then?'

Jim Marshal nodded, looking down at the picture.

'Definitely not seen him, not yesterday anyway,' he said.

'How can you be so sure?' asked Carlisle.

Marshal jabbed a stubby finger at Alfonso's black goatee beard. 'Pretty distinctive, isn't he?' he said. 'Anyway, I never forget a face.'

'How many times have you heard that?' muttered Wagstaff as he and Carlisle continued down the street to the next pub on their list.

'Not for the last time, that's for sure,' said Carlisle. 'Come on, let's get this over with. Then perhaps we can have a pint or two ourselves.'

During the course of that evening the two officers dutifully visited every one of the twenty pubs on their list, and drew a complete blank. No one remembered seeing Alfonso Bertorelli at any time on the previous day.

'Just what I bloody expected,' said Carlisle. 'We've been handed this Bertorelli on a plate, trussed up like a chicken with all the trimmings. Trust our new assistant SIO not to be satisfied though. Typical of the nit-picking bastard, from what I've heard.'

'Yeah. No wonder they call him the Geek. He prefers problems to solutions. And if there aren't any he invents them.'

The two men continued to grumble cheerily as they made their way back to the station.

Meanwhile, at the Dunster Arms, Jim Marshal was hoping he would never see either detective again. Because the stand-in landlord had not been behind the bar the previous day. He had deliberately lied to the police officers.

Marshal, something of a serial philanderer, was in the middle of an extremely messy divorce. The previous morning his neighbour at the marital home in Ealing, from which Marshal had been barred for several months, had phoned to say that his wife was in the process of dumping all his personal belongings into a skip on the driveway. Clothes, books, his stamp collection, and his fishing gear. The missus had warned him that was what she was going to do if he didn't move his stuff out pronto, but Marshal, reduced to sleeping on the sofa of an old friend whose patience was beginning to run out, had nowhere else to keep it. In any case, he still owned half the marital home, and he hadn't really believed his wife would carry out her threat.

More fool him, he reflected. Anyway, upon getting the bad news he had called on a Dunster Arms regular, already in attendance as usual, to step behind the bar while he rushed to Ealing in an attempt to salvage his belongings. He'd promised the man double money if he would run the bar until his return. The man knew what he was about, having managed a number of pubs in his time. He had also been sacked from at least two of them for putting his hand in the till. Marshal knew that the Dunster's landlord would never leave him in charge again if it were revealed that he'd let such a character run the bar, however pressing his reasons. Particularly on a Saturday. And Marshal needed the money, desperately. He was unlikely at his age ever to get a proper full-time job again, and he had lawyers to pay.

Marshal, basically an honest man except in his dealings with women, didn't feel comfortable about what he'd done. But he'd not had a choice, he told himself. He'd had to lie.

The first results obtained from forensic examination of the trainers found in the rubbish bin outside Alfonso's nan's house, which had been fast-tracked in view of the seriousness of the crime, came back the following day just before noon. They were much as expected. Alfonso's fingerprints were all over the shoes. There were no other prints. And the size and tread of the trainers matched exactly the footprint that Vogel had spotted at the crime scene.

The DNA results from the blood spattered on the shoes would not be delivered for several days, but Vogel had little doubt that it would prove to be Marlena's blood.

Vogel had decided not to mention the bloody shoes to Alfonso until he'd received the fingerprint results. Then, along with DC Jones, he interviewed Alfonso for the second time, and challenged him strongly.

This time Alfonso, appearing even more agitated after a night in the cells, was accompanied by Christopher Margolia, his lawyer of choice, who had returned late the previous night from his trip to Prague.

'It seems certain that the trainers found in the bin at your nan's are yours. They match a footprint found at the murder scene, and we are confident that the blood on them will prove a match with that of the victim,' Vogel said.

Alfonso looked bemused.

'I didn't put any trainers or shoes of any kind in the bin,' he said. 'At my nan's? Why would I? If I were guilty of anything I'd dump the shoes I'd been wearing as far away as possible from my nan's or anywhere else I stayed, wouldn't I?'

There were obvious similarities with the circumstances of Alfonso's earlier arrest. And his last remark echoed Vogel's own thoughts, but that wasn't nearly enough to prevent what was fast becoming inevitable. Vogel said nothing. This time Alfonso did fill the silence.

'What makes you think they're my shoes anyway?' he asked.

'They're the right size, and they were found at your place of residence,' Vogel recited patiently.

He placed a photograph on the table at which Alfonso was sitting.

'But why don't you tell me,' he said. 'Are these your trainers?'

Alfonso looked down at the picture. His face had been pale before, now it was like parchment.

'They l-look like mine,' he said eventually. 'An old pair of Adidas I've had for years. I don't wear them very often. I should have thrown them out really . . .'

Vogel put another photograph on the table. This time a shot of the footprint clearly marked in the blood on the floor of Marlena's sitting room.

Only the side of the woman's head was in the picture. Nonetheless Vogel saw the other man flinch away from the image before him.

'You may or may not be aware that this is a footprint from an Adidas trainer,' said Vogel. 'It's rather distinctive, is it not?'

'Is it? I don't know. I don't go around looking at the bottom of people's feet too often.'

Again a flash of what Vogel was beginning to realize was Alfonso's natural sharpness. His customary mild wit and deftness of speech had been pretty much stamped out by then, but Vogel could still detect something remaining of the more usual Alfonso Bertorelli.

It was time to fire the next broadside.

'You should also know that we've had the results of the fingerprint check made on these trainers,' Vogel continued. 'They are covered in your prints.'

'B-but, if they're my trainers they would be,' Alfonso stumbled. 'Somebody must have stolen them. I've told you: I'm being framed. You have to see that now. Whoever dumped all that stuff on me before – the bike, the hoody, Michelle's bag – they must have taken my trainers then returned them. I'm being set up again. Someone's out to get me. It's obvious . . .'

Alfonso's bottom lip began to tremble. For one awful moment Vogel thought the man was going to cry. He so hated it when that happened.

'I think my client needs a break,' interjected Margolia.

Vogel addressed the lawyer directly. 'Look, let's just see if we can clear all this up as quickly as possible, for everybody's sake, shall we?' he asked.

'Please proceed with care, then, Mr Vogel,' murmured Margolia.

Vogel inclined his head very slightly. He didn't want any more interruptions. He had further questions to ask, to which answers were urgently required. He made his voice as gentle as possible.

'Mr Bertorelli, when you were previously arrested at your grandmother's home you were asked to check if anything had been stolen, either belonging to you or your grandmother, were you not?'

'Well, yes, but . . .'

'And you said that nothing was missing, didn't you?'

'Yes, but I'd forgotten about those old trainers. I didn't even know they were at my nan's. I can't remember when I last wore them even.'

'It would seem that you wore them on Saturday evening, Mr Bertorelli, when you visited your old friend.'

Alfonso's lower lip was trembling again, and this time he lost control. He began to cry, his shoulders shook, an animal-like wail filled the room. Briefly, Vogel looked away.

'For the record, you do not know that, Mr Vogel,' said Margolia.

Vogel ignored the lawyer and made himself stare straight at Alfonso, trying to keep his face expressionless.

'Mr Bertorelli, how do you feel about women?' he asked, remembering the man's reaction when he'd suggested he was gay.

Bertorelli stopped crying. 'I like women,' he said.

'Do you?' A sudden thought had occurred to Vogel.

'Yes. I'd never hurt a woman, if that's what you're getting at.'

'I was rather more interested in your relationships with women. Have you ever had a real relationship with a woman, Mr Bertorelli?'

'What? Of course I have.'

'Have you ever actually had sex with a woman?' Vogel continued mercilessly.

'That's enough, Mr Vogel,' thundered Christopher Margolia.

Bertorelli looked horrified. Shocked to the core. But in spite of his lawyer's intervention, he answered the question.

'Of course I have,' he said again, and once more started to weep hysterically.

Vogel was not convinced. Could Bertorelli be the oldest virgin in town? Was that one of his secrets? And, if so, how relevant was it? Had the man grown to hate women because he'd never had a woman of his own, never had an intimate relationship? Was that what had led him to kill? But why Marlena?

There could be no doubt that Marlena had invited her killer into her home. And she'd been drinking champagne with him, or her; champagne which the murderous visitor almost certainly brought along as a gift. A fatal gift.

Forensics had reported that substantial traces of gamma hydroxybutyrate had been found in Marlena's almost empty glass at the crime scene. GHB is a central nervous system depressant, not unlike the more common date rape drug Rohypnol, but it comes in a clear liquid form, thus making its presence in a translucent drink like champagne less detectable, in spite of its slightly salty taste.

Alfonso Bertorelli was not a big man. Vogel considered that he would not be a particularly strong man. But a dose of GHB would render a much younger and fitter woman than Marlena incapable of resisting assault. She would have been unable to do much more than watch as unspeakable atrocities were committed on her, until, mercifully, her life finally ebbed away . . .

Vogel realized that he had drifted off. He turned his attention back to the present, and to the man sitting opposite him, who had started to weep again.

Alfonso had no verifiable alibi for the approximate time, or for any time after 11.30 a.m. on the day Marlena had met such a vicious and violent death. The team had been unable to confirm that he had visited a public house, and even if it were to be proved that he'd been drinking in a pub he may well still have had time to murder Marleen McTavish. He may not have been as drunk as he'd suggested, or indeed, not drunk at all.

The evidence against Bertorelli in connection with this and the other incidents seemed to be growing day by day. Vogel might still think some of it a little too neat, a bit too convenient, but if someone was framing Alfonso Bertorelli then they were making an extremely good fist of it.

And Bertorelli, who'd lived in London or thereabouts all his life and might well have been staying in King's Cross with his nan at the time of the two murders there fifteen years earlier, really wasn't helping himself. He just kept repeating that he had no idea where he'd been during the period when Marlena was killed.

Vogel could no longer prevent the inevitable. DCI Nobby Clarke was very different to his previous boss, DI Tom Forest. She did not bluster. It was hard to imagine that she would ever rush proceedings or cut corners in order to obtain a conviction that might later prove to be unsafe. Clarke was thoughtful and highly intelligent. It was no accident that she was the golden girl of the Homicide and Serious Crime Squad. But she had, understandably, started to push Vogel. The evidence against Bertorelli was substantial and further forensic reports were likely to add more weight. Indeed, Vogel could not even explain to himself why he was still reluctant to charge the man. Ultimately, Clarke told Vogel she could see no reason for further delay. Unless Vogel could come up with a damned good reason why not, she wanted Bertorelli charged.

Wearily Vogel got to his feet and looked down at the quivering wreck of a man before him. A man for whom, whatever the outcome of the chain of events Vogel was about to put into motion, life would never be the same again.

'Alfonso Bertorelli, I am charging you with the murder of Marleen McTavish,' he began, his voice very soft.

Alfonso stopped crying again for a moment. He focused red-rimmed eyes on the policeman.

'I didn't do it,' he said. 'I'm innocent.'

Then he collapsed onto the table, his shoulders heaving, great noisy sobs filling the room.

fifteen

The friends had learned of Marlena's horrific murder the previous afternoon. Tiny had spent much of Sunday morning trying to call her to see if she fancied Sunday Club, and to offer to get her to Johnny's Place, but, of course, he received no reply – until around 2 p.m. when DCI Nobby Clarke answered Marlena's phone.

The terrible truth quickly became apparent. Tiny and Billy between them called the rest of the group. Everyone expressed shock and disbelief. They were even more shocked to learn that Alfonso had again been arrested, this time on suspicion of murdering Marlena.

Then on Monday afternoon came the official announcement that Alfonso had been charged.

Tiny and Billy saw it on Sky News and again phoned around the other Sunday Clubbers.

'If it wasn't so fucking serious, I'd think it was an April fool,' George told Tiny.

'What?' responded the big man.

'It is the first of April,' replied George.

'For fuck's sake, mate,' remonstrated Tiny.

'All right, all right. But how could anyone believe the Fonz would harm his beloved Marlena.'

Tiny ended the call. None of their group wanted to believe Alfonso would have harmed Marlena. But somebody damn well had. She was dead. And although the details were not yet known, she had apparently been killed in a particularly horrific way.

A disjointed and disturbing week followed, during which Alfonso appeared at Westminster Magistrates' Court and could be seen in press photos and on the TV news, head bowed, being loaded into a police van en route to Brixton Prison, where he was to be remanded in custody.

It was towards the end of the week that Ari, the only member of the group other than the arrested Alfonso not to have suffered from some kind of incident or attack, decided he wanted to see the others, that it might help if they got together again to talk. So he set about trying to organize supper at Johnny's Place for the following Sunday.

Previously there had never been any need for organization. There had always been an easy relaxed air about their gathering; the table at the far end of the basement restaurant would be laid and waiting for however many of the group turned up.

Ari had realized that if the friends were ever to meet up again – and for reasons he could not fully explain he thought it was important that they did so – then someone would have to not only do some planning, but also some persuading.

Since the sinister chain of events had engulfed the friends, Ari had become increasingly dependent on coke. And it wasn't coincidence. He hoped that he could get it under control; the last thing he needed was a repeat of the incident at Harpo's, which, to make matters worse, had been witnessed by DI Vogel. So far his father didn't seem to suspect. And Ari needed to keep it that way.

Nonetheless he indulged in a hefty snort of the white stuff

before beginning to make his calls. George was first on the list. And Ari didn't receive a particularly warm reception from him.

'To tell you the truth, Ari, I'm a bit scared of us all getting together. I've already had my dog tortured to death and my friends are falling like flies. In any case, I'm probably going out with Carla.'

'For God's sake, George, bring her to Johnny's. Don't you think it's time we all met her?'

'Have you taken leave of your senses, Ari? I can't think of a worse time to bring her.'

'Oh fuck,' said Ari. 'You're right. Who'd want to get mixed up with us lot right now. I'm sorry, George. But it would be great if you could make it. I think it might help if we all sit down together to talk things through. Those of us still able to be there, that is . . .'

'Look, I do see where you're coming from.' George seemed to be relenting. 'I'll be there if I can, all right?'

'Great,' said Ari. He paused. 'I can't believe Alfonso did this though, can you?'

Ari could hear George sigh at the other end of the line.

'I don't know what to believe any more, mate,' said George.

The remaining friends were equally unenthusiastic.

Bob said he didn't feel like going out anywhere at the moment, particularly not to Johnny's.

'Couldn't you think of somewhere else for us to meet up for this therapeutic chat?' he asked. 'It's not as if Covent Garden is short on restaurants.'

The truth was, Ari hadn't even considered another venue.

'We always meet at Johnny's,' he said lamely.

'There's no "always" about it any more, is there?' commented Bob.

Ari could think of no reply to that.

'Look, I'll think about it,' said Bob.

Disappointed with the reactions he had so far encountered, Ari took a bottle of Hendricks from his freezer and sent a couple of shots of neat alcohol to join the chemical mix already whizzing around his brain before making any further calls.

Greg told Ari he had a big job on and was working 24/7, and anyway he wasn't sure Karen could make it because her mother was away and wouldn't be having the kids that Sunday.

Ari was getting fed up with the knock-backs. And the coke had, as usual, shortened his temper and lengthened his courage.

'You're just making fucking excuses,' he told Greg tetchily.

'What if I am, mate?' Greg answered. 'What if I am? Far as I know, you haven't been mugged or had a brick through your bleedin' window, 'ave you?'

Then he hung up. Ari felt terrible. The coke was beginning to wear off. He regretted having been temperamental with Greg, and as was often the case at this stage in the proceedings, knowing that he was heading for a big low, he regretted having taken the cocaine in the first place. Ari was well aware that he was the only one of the remaining friends not to have been the victim of something. Until Alfonso had been charged, Ari had wondered, obviously, how many of the group suspected him. He'd tried to put himself in their shoes. They had all suffered to some degree, and he had not. Even if they didn't suspect him, they probably didn't like him very much any more. Ari decided that was it. He wouldn't call anyone else. Sunday Club was over. Dead as Marlena. The thought made him shiver.

Then Greg called back.

'Sorry, mate,' he said. 'We're all on edge, aren't we? I'll come if I can. And we'll see if we can get a babysitter so Karen can come too. You're probably right. It might do us all good.'

Ari felt much better after that. He changed his mind again.

He would continue to try to round up the group. He called Tiny and Billy. Billy answered the phone. And finally Ari got the sort of response he'd been hoping for from the beginning.

'I think we'd like to meet up,' Billy said quietly. 'It's been a tough time and it's far from over yet. You're right, Ari. There's a lot for us to talk through. We still don't know what it's all been about, and we need closure, don't we? I'll have to check with Tiny, but I reckon we'll be there.'

'I'm glad,' said Ari.

'Oh, and we've got a little bit of good news,' said Billy.

'Great,' said Ari, who was beginning to wonder if there was any good news left in the world.

'Tell you when we meet.'

'Right,' said Ari.

Then he made the final call, the one he had always thought would be the most difficult.

'Are you mad?' hissed Michelle. 'Do you really think I want to show my face to anyone, the state I'm in? It's been over a week now and I still look like roadkill.'

'Look,' countered Ari stoically, 'I just didn't want you to feel left out, that's all.'

Michelle's response was waspish.

'Oh, I don't feel left out, I can assure you, Ari,' she said. 'But no doubt you do.'

And so Ari, the first to arrive, wearing his best jeans and vintage leather jacket with the biker studs on the collar, really had no idea who else would turn up at Johnny's Place eight days after Marlena's murder. It was five fifteen. Early. Even for Sunday Club. Ari had been on tenterhooks all day and couldn't wait. He paused at the door to the basement restaurant then ran down the steps as if he wanted to get in there before he changed his mind. Johnny was at the piano playing 'Someone to Watch Over Me'. Ari was aware of the gentle irony. Nobody seemed to have been watching over him or any of the others for some time now. Johnny glanced up and looked as if he was about to stop playing to speak to Ari. Ari hurried by. He couldn't make casual conversation with Johnny, and neither did he have any wish for a more serious discussion with anyone other than the surviving members of his now devastated group of friends.

As he made his way across the room he noticed Justin, the counter attendant at Shannon's gym, another Johnny's regular, sitting with an unattractive older man. This was Justin's usual sort of companion and undoubtedly well-heeled, thought Ari, who had never liked Justin and usually felt rather superior to him. After all, Ari was from one of the wealthiest and most established Asian families in the country, although he tried quite hard not to let it show. On this particular evening Ari just felt conspicuous and vulnerable. He looked away from Justin, determined to avoid any possibility of eye contact, and the heat rose in his cheeks as he approached the familiar table by the rear wall.

It stood empty, but was laid for ten as usual. Ari felt a stab of irritation. Hadn't the staff grasped that there were no longer ten friends who might attend? One was dead, horrifically murdered, one was in jail, accused of being her killer, and one had such a bad facial injury she could not bear to be seen.

In spite of the hefty snort of coke he'd ingested minutes earlier, Ari's courage almost deserted him. He was suddenly overwhelmed by a desire to make a run for it, and it was only the arrival of a waitress at his side, asking if he would like a drink, that averted a hasty departure. Habit took over. And innate good manners. Ari placed an order. He asked for a beer with a vodka chaser, one of his favourite combinations of alcohol, and sat down on the nearest chair, reflecting that it might well be possible that he would find himself sitting there on his own for the entire evening. Even Billy and Tiny weren't certainties. Tiny might not have reacted the way Billy did to the prospect of meeting up at Johnny's again.

Ari downed his beer almost in one swallow, tossed back the vodka shot, and ordered a pair of replacements straight away. His nerves were jangling. He needed to relax, but he couldn't. The minutes passed. He knew he was early, but historically most of the friends turned up before six. Though he tried to convince himself they were often later, it did nothing to dispel the fear that he was about to spend the evening alone.

Then Bob arrived, his face pinched and strained, hurrying across the room just as Ari had done, not looking around him. Bob managed a small smile and ordered a beer, Corona, the same brand Ari was drinking, but without the vodka chaser.

'Don't really know what I'm doing here,' Bob muttered. 'Just couldn't stay away, I suppose.'

'I'm glad you've come, anyway,' said Ari.

George was next, handsome as ever in a tan bomber jacket over a cream linen collarless shirt. But Ari could see the tension in his eyes as George stretched out his arms for a hug, and his fingernails had been bitten almost to the quick. Ari was certain he'd never seen them in that state before; George's nails had always been well manicured and immaculately presented, just like the rest of him. No one in the group, it seemed, was immune to the pressure and anxiety which Ari was beginning to feel quite crushed by.

George hugged Ari hard and spoke into his left ear.

'Well done, mate,' he said. 'You were dead right, you know. This could do us all the power of good.'

Ari smiled edgily, unsure how to respond. He decided, probably unwisely, on what he too late realized was a rather pathetic stab at the old banter.

'No Carla then?' he queried.

George frowned. 'Don't you ever know when to stop?' he asked.

'Sorry,' replied Ari, mentally kicking himself.

This was an evening requiring tact and compassion, mutual understanding and shared sympathy. The last thing it needed was a cheap and flimsy attempt at humour.

The rest arrived within minutes; almost, to Ari's surprise, the entire remaining group. Tiny and Billy first, then Greg and Karen. That only left Michelle to make up the full complement, but Ari had never really expected her to come. He knew she must be hurting mentally and physically, her shattered nose and swollen face doubtless still aching and sore, her state of mind wounded and fragile. Perhaps more to the point, she had made it clear she had no wish to show her damaged features to the world.

And so there were seven of them. Seven diverse people who had once been such good friends, albeit somewhat casual friends, suddenly quite uncomfortable with each other. Hardly anybody spoke at first. There was the kind of awkward silence at the table that had never existed before. They were all too aware of the curious stares and mouth-behind-hand whispers of other diners in Johnny's that Sunday evening.

Their fate, because that was surely what it had become, was common knowledge now. Most of the other regulars at the restaurant must have been aware of what was going on. News travels fast and comprehensively in Covent Garden, an area of London which retains so much of the village about it, in spite of being at the apparently racy heart of a cosmopolitan city. And there'd been substantial media coverage. The story of

Marlena's brutal murder and Alfonso's arrest had been in all the papers. Not only had he already been charged with two serious offences – the attack on Michelle and Marlena's murder – but there were hints of more to come. Even the most cautious and bridled press of the après Leveson era had found ways to make it tantalizingly clear that a rare and tasty tale of yet-to-be revealed intrigue lurked beneath the bald statements of police and prosecution.

Ari thought there were more people in the restaurant than usual at that time on a Sunday. There were certainly more people that he didn't recognize. He wondered if he and the others had become macabre tourist attractions, if there were people in the restaurant who'd been drawn in by the lure of a visceral thrill from seeing those touched by a high-profile murder.

Ari glanced around that familiar table at six strained faces, and had no doubt that he looked every bit as strained. He suspected everybody wanted to talk about Alfonso, to discuss whether or not he really could be a murderer. But nobody seemed to want to broach the subject which was surely at the forefront of all their minds.

It was Ari who had called them together. Fuelled by false white courage, he'd more or less summoned them. He was unsure now if he'd been right to do so. At the very least he should have listened to Bob and chosen a different venue. But now they were here, Ari felt it incumbent on him to lead the way, to help them talk to each other again, to at least attempt to get things back to how they had been before. Not that it ever could be the way it had been before. But, perhaps, Ari thought, he and his friends could attempt a new beginning.

'I-I just wondered how everybody was?' Ari enquired eventually, starkly aware of what a lame remark that was.

Greg jumped straight in. 'Personally I'm bloody marvellous,' he snapped. 'I don't suppose the boys miss their dogs at all, we don't 'ave to worry about Marlena any more, and Michelle's new nose'll probably turn out to be better than the old one.'

Ari looked down at the table. The other four men sat open-mouthed, staring at Greg. Karen placed a hand lightly on her husband's arm.

'Sorry,' said Greg.

There was another silence. Then one of the waiters, not chatty like they usually were at Johnny's but clearly embarrassed and every bit as stilted and awkward in his behaviour as the seven friends sitting round the table, arrived to take their order.

Food was duly chosen, albeit with little enthusiasm, and more drink ordered.

Then Billy spoke.

'Actually, Tiny and I do have a bit of good news,' he said.

Oh yes, remembered Ari. Billy had mentioned that on the phone. Ari glanced at Billy questioningly. Hopefully almost.

'About the dogs . . .' began Billy.

'Oh yeah, been stuck back together and resurrected, have they?' asked George.

Tiny winced.

'For fuck's sake, don't you start, George,' said Karen. 'I thought we were here to talk, to listen to each other, to help each other understand . . .' Her voice faltered and she broke off, fighting back the tears.

'I think we might be here a long time for that,' muttered Bob.

'Tell us then,' said Ari, still looking hopefully at Billy.

'Well, you know we arranged a post-mortem examination on our Daisy and on George's Chumpy, after the police said there was no point. Turns out they were wrong. From our point of view, anyway. We finally got the results. Our vet's been away . . .'

Billy glanced at George. 'Sorry, George, we were going to call you. Then we thought, well, we'd be seeing you tonight, better to tell you in person, and everybody else too.'

'OK, go on then,' said George sulkily.

'The post-mortem showed that the dogs were killed by a lethal injection, an overdose of barbiturate – the same way vets put animals down. They were only mutilated after they were dead. Chances are Daisy and Chump died peacefully in their sleep. So we know now they didn't suffer. Isn't that great?'

'I think "great" may be a bit of an exaggeration, but it is a relief to know they didn't suffer, or not the way it seemed they had anyway,' said George.

'Yes, it must be,' said Karen. 'I know how I'd feel if it was our Westies.'

Bob looked thoughtful. 'I don't understand it though. Why would anyone evil enough to do all the other stuff that's happened show mercy to a couple of dogs?'

'And a funny kind of mercy at that,' said Tiny. 'Poor little devils are still dead.'

'Yes,' Bob continued. 'But someone went to the trouble of killing them painlessly and then making it look as if they'd been tortured to death. Why? To frighten the rest of us? To make George, Tiny and Billy suffer even more?'

'Who knows?' said Tiny. 'Anyway, I suppose we have to accept now that it wasn't a someone. It was Alfonso.'

'He never did like dogs,' said Karen. 'I've heard him grumble about dogs pooing all over the streets and their owners not clearing up after them.'

'Long way from that to dismembering 'em,' said Greg.

Tiny winced again.

There was yet another silence. Alfonso's arrest was the subject they had all wanted to discuss but couldn't bring themselves to. It remained difficult for any of them to find the right words.

'I still can't believe it,' said Karen eventually.

'Me neither,' responded Billy. 'But I spoke to Michelle yesterday, and she said the word at the nick is that he's definitely guilty. The evidence against him is overwhelming.'

'But what does she think?' said Greg. 'I mean, she was mugged. Punched in the face at close quarters. Has she told anyone whether she saw her attacker's face? Did she think it could have been the Fonz? At the time, I mean. Did you ask her that, Billy?'

Billy's attention was momentarily diverted. Johnny had abruptly stopped playing the piano, midway through a melody. The silence in the restaurant, interrupted only by one or two half-strangled gasps, was deafening.

Billy glanced across the room.

'Why don't you ask her yourself?' he said. 'She's here.'

Michelle was indeed making her way across the room. Johnny had stood up and taken a step towards her, his face full of concern. She ignored him. Her stride was uncertain and she even bumped into a chair as she approached the Sunday Club table.

But it was the sight of her face that had caused the other diners to gasp. The whole of it was swollen and discoloured. Her nose was twice its usual size, multicoloured and twisted. It wasn't so much broken as smashed. Although the friends knew that to be the case, none of them had seen her since the attack. The severity of the damage therefore came as a tremendous shock.

Ari recovered first. He jumped to his feet, reached out to Michelle with both arms and hugged her.

'I thought you weren't coming,' he said. 'We're just so glad to see you, darling, aren't we, guys?'

Everyone around the table murmured agreement and words of greeting.

'I changed my mind,' said Michelle, sitting down heavily on the chair Ari pulled out for her. 'I suddenly wanted you all to see what the bastard did to me. To see the state I'm in.'

Karen, the only other woman at the table, understood at once.

'It's awful, darling, horrid, but you will get better,' she said.

'Not without major plastic surgery,' countered Michelle.

'I'm sure there are surgeons out there who'll make you as good as new,' Karen persisted. 'Even prettier than you were before, you'll see.'

'Don't fucking patronize me, Karen,' Michelle snapped.

'I wasn't, darling, honestly . . .'

'We all feel for you, honey,' said Bob. 'And we're so glad you've come.'

'Yep, I thought you'd enjoy a freak show,' said Michelle.

Karen placed her hand over Michelle's. 'You know that's not how we see it,' she said. 'We feel for you – we're your friends.'

'I thought Alfonso was my friend,' said Michelle. 'And he did this to me.'

With her free hand she gestured towards her ruined face. Above the shattered nose her eyes were narrow bloodshot slits in mounds of discoloured flesh. One seemed to be permanently watering from a corner.

'Are you sure it was Alfonso?' Greg seized the opportunity to ask the question he'd voiced earlier. 'Did you think it was him at the time?'

'That's not the point, and of course I'm bloody sure,' said Michelle. 'He's been charged with assaulting me, hasn't he? And murdering Marlena. I'm a copper, remember, I know exactly how good a case has to be before someone gets charged with murder. The police and the prosecution service don't get that wrong – well, hardly ever, whatever the bloody public think.'

Michelle's voice had risen. Not only were all of the friends staring at her but everyone else in the restaurant too.

'Evidence,' she continued, banging her hand on the table. 'When you charge someone with murder it's because you've got fucking evidence. That's why Alfonso's banged up in Brixton nick. Fucking evidence.'

Her words were not exactly slurred, but there was something wrong with the manner of her speech, her diction not as clear as usual. Karen wondered at first whether the blow to her face had affected Michelle's ability to speak clearly. But Ari, being more familiar with the effects of drink and drugs, suspected otherwise.

'Look, don't upset yourself, we all want to help you,' he began, trying to sound as soothing as possible.

'Don't upset my fucking self! You all want to fucking help, do you?' Michelle spat out the words, her voice louder than ever. 'How can anyone fucking help? I'll never get a man now, never have a fucking baby . . .'

Tears formed in her narrowed eyes and began to run down her face. Her mouth twisted in anguish. The men around the table were almost squirming with embarrassment. Tiny reached for Billy's hand. Bob and Greg exchanged bewildered glances. Ari wished the meticulously distressed floorboards of Johnny's Place would part and swallow him up. Indeed swallow the lot of them up. He now regretted having organized this meeting, this impossible attempt at a reincarnation of a past which was gone forever.

Karen stood up, walked round to Michelle's side of the table and wrapped both arms around her.

'It will be all right,' she persisted. 'It will be. We will get through this. All of us. And most importantly we will look after you, make sure you get through it.'

Michelle began to sob loudly. All eyes in the room were now fixed upon her. The tears did not last long, less than a minute certainly, but it seemed like forever to the rest of the group.

Then she stopped crying, as suddenly as she had begun, and sat up straight in her chair, obviously making a huge effort to regain her self-control.

'I'm sorry,' she said. 'Whisky mixed with painkillers, I'm afraid. Quite a cocktail, eh? I knew I'd had too much of both. I knew I shouldn't have come. On the other hand, the only reason I'm here is courtesy of the whisky and the pills and the Dutch courage they gave me. Now all I've done is make a fool of myself.'

'No, you haven't. And yes, you should have come, you really should,' said Ari. 'I mean it.'

Michelle smiled wanly. 'Order me some coffee, will you. Strong coffee.'

Ari asked a waiter for a double espresso, which was delivered with alacrity. No doubt the staff were eager to see the restaurant return to something approaching normality. Johnny was playing the piano again with a loud thumping rhythm, far removed from his usual sensitive touch on the ivory keys. You could feel the tension in the air, no longer just at the Sunday Club table, but throughout the restaurant. Ari wondered what it would be like not to feel anxious any more. Indeed he wondered if he would ever stop feeling anxious. He suspected the rest of them around the table were going through the same thing, and like him they had forgotten what it was to wake up in the morning without a feeling of apprehension at what the day might bring.

Michelle drank the coffee in one go and asked for another.

'Tiny and Billy were just telling us a bit of good news when you came in,' said Ari, who, having instigated an occasion which was in danger of turning into a circus, was desperate to maintain at least a semblance of ordinariness.

Michelle uttered one high-pitched shriek of mirthless laughter. But there was to be no repeat of her earlier hysterical outburst.

Instead she fixed a cool stare on the boys. 'Really?' Her voice was enquiring but icy.

Tiny fidgeted. It was left to Billy to repeat the account of the post-mortem results.

Michelle did not respond. Ari supposed that given what she had been through, and indeed what they had all been through with Marlena's murder and Alfonso's arrest, the fate of two dogs was of small concern. It had seemed curiously significant to him though.

Billy carried on speaking, as if he didn't know how to stop, filling the silence.

'There's more.' He turned to face George. 'Did you know that your Chumpy was poorly, George?' he asked.

George shook his head, as if puzzled.

'Apparently he had cancer of the liver.'

'He never showed any signs of being ill,' said George.

'Well, he soon would have done,' Billy went on. 'According to the autopsy, Chump would have died within weeks. I don't know whether that helps, but I thought you'd like to know.'

George stared at Billy for several seconds before answering.

'Thanks, mate,' he said eventually. 'I think it does help a bit. Yes.'

'At least you know he didn't have long to live anyway. That's the problem for Tiny and me: Daisy was so young, barely four years old. We feel we should have protected our little girl, been able to save her.'

Michelle continued to stare at Billy in that icy way.

'And do you think maybe you should have protected Marlena?' she asked, her words clearer now, her voice quieter. She seemed suddenly quite calm. Ari found that even more disconcerting.

'Maybe even protected me,' Michelle went on. 'Or is it just the bloody dogs you're concerned about?'

Billy flushed. Tiny squeezed his hand. His voice too was very quiet when he spoke.

'You know better than that, Michelle,' he said. 'Billy and I would have done anything in our power to protect you and Marlena, to save her life, to prevent your attack. And we are well aware that losing our dog must seem a very small thing compared with all that's happened to you. Of course we realize that it pales into insignificance compared with the loss of human life. Any human life, but particularly our friend, dear Marlena. But Daisy meant a lot to us, and we were just glad to learn she didn't suffer the way we thought she had. That's all.'

Michelle's face softened. 'I'm sorry, Tiny. I do understand really, it's just hard to . . .' She broke off, started again: 'Like I said, I shouldn't have come. I'm going to leave now. I'm so sorry.'

And with that she rose abruptly from the table and half ran towards the door.

'But you haven't eaten anything,' Ari called after her.

'At least let me take you home,' shouted Bob.

Michelle stopped in the doorway and turned to face them all.

'No, no, I want to be on my own,' she said. 'Just leave me alone.'

Johnny stood up from the piano. 'I'm putting you in a taxi,' he said firmly.

The remaining friends watched in silence. They all knew Johnny would do that for any of his clientele whom he felt needed help. But Michelle was special to him, no doubt about that, and he had made no secret of how upset he had been by what had happened to her.

Johnny put a protective arm around Michelle's waist. She did not protest. He steered her towards the stairs, where she turned and glanced towards the Sunday Club table one last time.

And then she was gone.

sixteen

Back in her little studio flat Michelle went to bed, even though it was not long after eight o'clock, and cried herself to sleep. She was still under the influence of her earlier excess of whisky and prescription drugs, and both her mind and body felt empty and exhausted. Fortunately, sleep came with merciful ease and speed.

However in the cold early hours Michelle woke with a start. Her head was no longer woozy. Her thoughts were suddenly crystal clear. She hadn't been around the table with the others for long, but it had been long enough. The policewoman in her had picked up on something during that brief conversation, and now it was seriously troubling her.

As she went over it in her mind, she began to think again about what had happened to her. She had total recall, the events of that night still vivid in her mind. As she replayed the scene, re-examining each detail, a new train of thought was beginning to form. She found herself questioning whether it really had been Alfonso who'd attacked her.

Her eyes turned to the digital clock on her bedside table, its luminous numbers flickering slightly in the gloom. It was 2 a.m. She lay for a while, quite still, staring sightlessly at the ceiling.

Alfonso Bertorelli had been charged with Marlena's murder

and her assault because of the weight of evidence against him. That was what she had told the group around the table. The police don't make mistakes with murder charges, she'd insisted. And most of the time that was true. But sometimes mistakes did occur. Could it be that this was one of those sometimes?

Greg had asked her whether she'd thought at the time that it was Alfonso who'd punched her in the face.

She hadn't answered the question. The truth was, she didn't have a clue.

Her head was buzzing. She should leave this to Vogel and his team. Michelle knew she was too involved. She was a victim. If you were a victim, you could not detach yourself. You couldn't sift through the facts with anything like the required objectivity. The way Vogel always did. She trusted Vogel, didn't she? No one was more meticulous than him, no one less likely to leap to conclusions. She had to trust Vogel.

Although she was so very wide awake Michelle still felt exhausted. She told herself she should try to get back to sleep. That if she could only sleep until dawn, things might straighten themselves out. Her doubts might resolve themselves without her doing anything about them.

She turned over on her side and shut her eyes. But sleep was not to come. Instead of the oblivion she craved, she lay in her bed tossing and turning, thoughts racing through her mind. After what seemed like a very long time, though it was actually only twenty minutes or so, she gave up. Sleep was not going to come, and there was nothing she could do about it, except perhaps repeat the previous day's overgenerous doses of whisky and prescription drugs. But now that this idea had taken over her brain, she doubted that such measures would have any effect.

She climbed out of bed, wrapped a dressing gown around

her shoulders, made herself tea in the little kitchen and took it to the window at the far end of her room, the one that overlooked Theobalds Road. She glanced at her watch. It was just gone three now. Still the middle of the night. But there was an intermittent flow of traffic on the street below her. Central London never sleeps. A couple of black cabs, one with its light on, rolled by. A motorist in a four-wheel drive sounded his horn at a cyclist who stuck two fingers up at the retreating vehicle and hollered some incomprehensible abuse.

Michelle's nose was beginning to throb again. She wondered how long it would be before that throbbing began to ease. The numbing effects of the painkillers had totally worn off, and the pain was back with a vengeance. Aside from being distressing in its own right, the throbbing was a constant reminder of the sorry state of her face and the horrible reality of her injuries having been caused by someone she cared about.

She made her way into her tiny bathroom, removed the bottle of painkillers from the mirrored cabinet on the wall, and swallowed two of them, the correct dose this time, filling her tooth mug with tap water to wash them down.

She hoped they would do the job well enough, because she was determined not to deaden her brain for the second day in a row. She needed all her wits about her if she was going to make sense of the thoughts buzzing around inside her head.

It could be nothing. The brief snippet of conversation probably didn't mean anything, she told herself. If it had, surely it would have triggered an immediate reaction from her the moment the words were uttered? But then, sitting there in the restaurant surrounded by the unscathed faces of her friends, she'd been oblivious to anything beyond her own misery. Moreover she'd been far too befuddled by drink and painkillers to react immediately to what she'd heard. Maybe she wasn't too bad a cop after all, even if she was stuck in Traffic, because something had filtered through, something had lodged in her subconscious. And now it had shifted from the back of her mind to lodge firmly at the forefront.

She wandered back to her chair by the window, switching on the radio on the way. As usual it was tuned to BBC Radio 2. Michelle liked Radio 2. She knew it was a bit naff to admit to enjoying something so middle of the road, but she didn't care. There was something wonderfully unchallenging and restful about Radio 2.

The kind of music somebody at the BBC had chosen as suitable for the early hours wafted over her as she gazed out of the window. She recognized the distinctive notes of Acker Bilk's trombone playing 'Stranger on the Shore'. It had been a favourite of her father's. Michelle's eyes filled with tears. She so wished her police officer father, the inspiration behind Michelle's choice of career, were still alive. He would know what to do. He had always known what to do.

Outside, a group of migrating clubbers, three young men and two girls, made their way noisily along the pavement, laughing and talking loudly. Bizarrely, Michelle was reminded of the good old days of Sunday Club. At first glance the little troop sashaying its way along Theobalds Road, so much younger, so much dafter, and no doubt popping E and God knows what else to keep themselves awake, could not have been more different from her old group of friends. But it was the way these kids were with each other, their obvious closeness, their ease in each other's company, verbally and physically, as they joshed and teased, linked arms and patted backs and shoulders. Surely that was the way she and the other Sunday Clubbers had once been, before everything went wrong.

She ran through them all in her mind: Marlena dead; Alfonso

in jail; Ari, seemingly desperate to restore what could never be restored; Greg, no longer able to maintain his upmarket-barrow-boy act; Karen, frightened for Greg, as she probably always had been, missing the way he'd been in the past, anxious about their future, and that of their children; Bob, always inclined to be depressive, now sinking irrevocably into his own malcontent; Tiny and Billy, mourning their lost dog and a lost way of life, but still with each other to cling to; George, unfathomable as ever, but with despair in those dark handsome eyes.

And her? Where did she stand in all of this? Michelle made another mug of tea, pouring boiling water and cold milk over a solitary tea bag, muttering disconsolately to herself as she did so. So far as the group were concerned, Michelle Monahan had been striving to rebuild her life in the wake of her divorce, and young enough and pretty enough and ambitious enough to make a success of it. Wasn't that the way they'd seen her? The truth was, she'd been far more broken by sorrow than anyone realized. Except, ironically, the husband who had betrayed and then deserted her.

All Michelle had ever wanted was to be a mother. But her attempts to conceive a child had ended in false alarms, an ectopic pregnancy and three miscarriages. And then came the diagnosis of early-stage cervical cancer. She'd been forced to have a hysterectomy in order to survive. Her bosses and colleagues in the force had no idea; she'd told them that she was in hospital for something entirely different, and begged her husband never to reveal the truth. It seemed to Michelle that the loss of her womb had robbed her not only of the chance of becoming a mother but also of her womanhood. And she couldn't bear to be an object of pity. Her husband had promised it would be their secret, their sad secret. As far as she knew, he had at least kept that promise, the only one of all that he had made. After he left her, she'd questioned whether he'd ever been faithful to her. Whatever the case, she doubted he would have walked out if she had been able to give him a child. Now she'd learned that he was expecting a baby with the new woman in his life. While she, all alone, battered and beaten in more ways than one, would never have a child of her own. With her shattered face and shattered dreams, it was doubtful she would ever again have a man of her own either. Not one she wanted, anyway.

She shivered. It was the beginning of the second week in April, but the days were cool and wet and the nights still very cold. The heating in her flat continued to play up. Sitting for so long by the window, with only a light dressing gown over her Marks and Spencer's pyjamas, she was thoroughly chilled, although she'd only just noticed her discomfort because she was so preoccupied. With Marlena, and the rest of them, and with her own fractured state, both physically and mentally.

She switched on the small electric fire she'd bought the last time the heating had broken down, carried her mug of tea over to the sleeping area and put it down on the bedside table while she pulled on jeans, thick socks, a T-shirt, a shirt over it, and a warm sweater.

Even before her face had been wrecked, Michelle had come to the conclusion that the only thing she had left in life was the job. In Dorset she'd been a detective constable, but after the divorce there was no way she could face working alongside the husband who'd abandoned her. She'd never have taken the job in Traffic, but it was all that was on offer at the time. Plus it was the Met, and she'd been promised it wouldn't be long before an opportunity would present itself for her to return to CID. That was two years ago, and here she was, still stuck in the department she loathed. Even a switch to mainstream uniform would do. Anything but Traffic.

And then Vogel had started delving into her affairs, doubting her explanation as to why she had pulled a sickie. Checking her out as if he wasn't sure what she might have done or might be capable of. She knew then that not only would her hope of a transfer be destroyed but with it any hope she had of rebuilding her life.

And so she'd lied to him. Lying to the Sunday Club crowd had been one thing. She hadn't thought that it would matter. She hadn't known that there was someone out there determined to hurt them. She hadn't considered for one moment that she too might become a victim. At that stage it had still been possible that Marlena's accident was just that, that the earlier incidents had been childish pranks. With each new incident, even the abduction and killing of the two dogs, she'd tried to tell herself that this was just a chain of random, unconnected events, the sort of thing that could only happen in a place the size of London.

Michelle had lied to Vogel and to Sunday Club for reasons, deeply personal reasons, that had nothing to do with the frightening chain of events unfolding around her. She'd lied because of the lengths to which her longing for a child had driven her.

She and Phil had been about to adopt a child when he dropped the bombshell that he was leaving her. The adoption authorities had immediately withdrawn their support. Michelle had pleaded with them, pointing out that single-parent adoptions were no longer uncommon. Their response had been that her new status as a single parent wasn't the problem. It was the turmoil surrounding her marriage break-up that was the issue.

In desperation she'd turned to the Internet, researching every possible avenue to getting a child. That was how she'd learned about a ground-breaking operation, still largely experimental, that might make it possible for her to give birth: a womb transplant. Her own doctor had advised that, in her case, such an operation would not only be exceedingly unlikely to succeed, or certainly not to the extent that would allow her to safely carry a child to full term, but, with particular regard to the effect of the hysterectomy that had been forced upon her, would also be highly dangerous. He'd refused to forward her for any such treatment under the National Health Service. Refusing to admit defeat, she had sought out a Harley Street consultant who was an expert in the field. Though she had no idea how she would finance such a major medical procedure, she'd been determined to find a way. However, the Harley Street man had delivered the same prognosis, advising her that no reputable doctor would be prepared to undertake such an operation on a woman with her medical history.

So Michelle had gone back to the Internet and found a dodgy Indian surgeon who was as famous for his lack of scruples as for his undoubted brilliance. He'd originally trained in London but had been struck off the UK medical register following a high-profile case that had resulted in the death of a patient. Since then, the surgeon's maverick approach had led to him being banned from practising not only in Britain but throughout most of Europe, and many other parts of the world. Apparently he was motivated not so much by financial gain as a sincere belief that the type of operation he was performing, while still in its infancy at the moment and therefore subject to a degree of trial and error, would ultimately revolutionize obstetric surgery. In his eyes, that justified the use of human guinea pigs. Even the manner in which he acquired the wombs that he used in his transplant operations had come, rather chillingly, under scrutiny. Michelle knew all this, and yet she was prepared to take the risk. He was, after all, her only hope.

Aside from the obvious danger she would be exposing herself

to if she allowed him to operate on her, a risk which she considered to be her business and no one else's, there was the question of legality. As a serving police officer, she was jeopardizing her career as well as her life. She hadn't cared though. The moment she'd learned that the surgeon had travelled incognito to Switzerland where he was preparing to examine potential patients, she had dropped everything and jumped on a plane to Zurich. So far as her bosses were concerned, she was absent through illness. So far as her friends were concerned, she was on a training course.

Ironically, it had all been for nothing. Even that notorious renegade of the medical profession had refused to operate on Michelle. Then, after her meeting with him, she had returned to her Zurich hotel room, switched on her phone, and found a series of voicemails from her friends about the attack on Marlena. From that point on the horrors just kept on coming: the abduction and killing of the two little dogs, Vogel's suspicions about her, the attack that had left her face in ruins, and finally Marlena's murder.

Now there could be no doubt that the Sunday Clubbers were being viciously targeted. Most likely by one of their own.

Until last night, Michelle had been convinced that Alfonso was the culprit. Guilty as charged. Vogel was a meticulous man, Michelle reminded herself for the umpteenth time. He did not make mistakes. And he certainly didn't make mistakes in a murder inquiry.

Oblivious to Vogel's doubts about the case, she found she was beginning to harbour doubts of her own. In an effort to shrug them off, she took another sip of her tea, then lay down, fully clothed, on her unmade bed. In spite of her anxiety she drifted off to sleep. It was a fretful, restless sleep, but when she woke she was surprised to see bright wintery sunshine streaming through the east-facing window above her kitchen sink. Her digital alarm clock told her that it was now 8.05 a.m.

Her first impulse was to reach for the phone to call Vogel. Then she changed her mind. How could she discuss the case with him, share her doubts with him, when he continued to harbour suspicions about her? Nor could she tell him the one thing that would lay those suspicions to rest: the truth. Even now, there was no way she could bring herself to reveal the details of her trip to Zurich. Aside from the dubious legality of what she had planned, it was all too intimate, too personal, too likely to invoke pity.

No, she could not expose herself to that. In any case, she had probably got it all wrong. The case against Alfonso seemed rock-solid, she couldn't be certain that what she'd learned the previous evening would make any difference. True, it raised questions about another member of the group, but did it undermine the evidence against Alfonso?

She had replayed the attack on her over and over again in her mind and was certain that her assailant had been male. Though the features had been hidden behind glasses and a scarf, the sheer power of the punch told her it had to be a man. Besides, assuming that the perpetrator was a member of Sunday Club, there were only three women in the group. One was dead, one was her – and she was guilty of nothing except desperation – and the third was Karen. Michelle could not, even in her wildest nightmares, consider Karen capable of such extremes of violence – nor did she have the strength. Thanks to her colleagues at Charing Cross nick, Michelle was aware of details concerning Marlena's death that had not been made public; the force with which the murder weapon had been driven into her friend's body indicated a degree of physical strength that was beyond most women.

No, it was definitely a man, it was almost certainly one of the friends, and her suspicions were beginning to focus on one particular friend. Although, as with Alfonso, Michelle had no idea what possible motive he could have.

It was too soon to share her suspicions with anyone. There was too little to go on at this stage. She needed to know more, to confirm to her own satisfaction that she was on the right track. The only way to do that would be to conduct her own inquiries. She knew it was unwise, but that wasn't going stop her, just as it hadn't stopped her flying to Zurich to meet her dodgy doctor. Michelle wanted to talk to this man. Even if Vogel were to take her seriously, he didn't know this man the way she did. Faced with a policeman, his answers would be guarded, careful. She on the other hand was a friend; he wouldn't even realize he was being questioned. What's more, she had the first-hand knowledge to trip him up in any lies. No one was better placed to force him to incriminate himself. If indeed he were guilty.

For the first time since her hopes were dashed in Zurich, she felt buoyant and confident of her abilities. She realized she might be putting herself in danger, but planned to reduce the risk by arranging to meet him in a public place. A breakfast meeting in Costa or Starbucks, perhaps; somewhere he would not dare to attack.

An involuntary shiver ran through her at the memory of the cyclist bearing down on her in his hoody and dark glasses. That had been a public place; even late at night there had been cars and pedestrians in the vicinity, and still it hadn't saved her from that punch in the face. It had all happened too fast for anyone to react.

Michelle did try, momentarily, to talk herself out of her own plan. One half of her urged caution, but the other declared that she was in any case battered and broken and probably eternally childless, so what did it matter if she lived or died?

She checked her watch. Just after 8.30. She picked up her phone then put it down again. To hell with it. Better to arrive without warning. More dangerous, perhaps, but surely more likely to bring results. She doubted he would have left home yet. With luck, she would catch him as he made his way out, invite him for coffee. That way she wouldn't have to actually step inside his place. She'd better hurry though, because there was one other visit she needed to make before she confronted him.

She hurried to the bathroom, and covered her battered face with a thick layer of pancake make-up. Then she put on dark glasses and a baseball hat with a long peak which she pulled down over her forehead. She hesitated for just a moment before removing from the cupboard by the front door a small leather case, which she slipped into her coat pocket, then hurried downstairs.

Vogel had been at his desk in Charing Cross police station for a couple of hours, still battling to come to terms with his doubts. He had MIT chaps all over the place trying to build a stronger case against Bertorelli, but nothing they'd come up with so far seemed to quell his misgivings.

His peace of mind was further shaken by a call that came through shortly after nine. It was his old friend Ben Parker in Dorset.

'Look, mate, I've been mulling this over ever since I heard about that woman who's been murdered on your patch,' he began. 'It's probably nothing, and I'm hating myself for this, but I guess I just can't keep shtum any longer . . .'

'For God's sake, Ben, spit it out. I'm in the middle of a murder inquiry here.'

'OK, OK, look, that night I got wasted with Phil Monahan on your behalf, he let it slip that Michelle'd had a hysterectomy. He said she'd been knocked sideways, was never the same afterwards, knowing she couldn't have a baby. Anyway, he swore me to secrecy, because he'd promised her he wouldn't let anyone know. Said it was the least he could do. But, well, when it came through the old grapevine how that poor bloody woman had been cut up . . . Oh, I know it's ridiculous. Just shoot me down in flames, will you?'

Vogel thought it was ridiculous, but was unnerved nonetheless. He ended the call and cursed silently. It was obvious what Ben Parker had been getting at. Michelle Monahan might have become so unhinged that she'd developed a lethal grudge against women with the necessary biological equipment to produce the children she could not have.

But Parker didn't know about the mugging that had left Michelle far too badly beaten up to have launched an attack on anyone. Even if she hadn't been injured, Vogel could not believe she would be crazy enough or vicious enough to butcher another human being the way Marlena's killer had. And why, if envy was the motive, would she have chosen a victim way beyond child-bearing years, a woman who had no children? Surely her target would have been Karen, the only mother in the group.

No, he did not for one moment think that Michelle Monahan could be guilty of Marlena's murder, but Parker's call had stirred up his misgivings about her furtive behaviour, the lies she'd told to cover her absence from work. There had to be a rational explanation. Colleagues who'd been in touch with her said she was still in a bad way after the mugging, so he'd put off having another talk with her. Once she was recovered, though, Vogel would talk to her again. Make her tell him the truth.

In the meantime, his focus had to be the case against Alfonso Bertorelli. If he could only find a more damning piece of evidence, something that would silence those niggling doubts that kept troubling him . . .

The results of Michelle's first call, at a Covent Garden address not far from her eventual destination, made her all the more determined to follow through with her plan. She had the bit between her teeth now and was in no mood to let concerns about her safety stand in the way. If she started thinking like a victim, worrying about danger all the time, she might as well kiss her career in the police goodbye. The only way to conquer fear was to push yourself through whatever barriers it tried to throw up, consequences be damned.

The communal front door to the apartment block where he lived had been propped open, presumably by the driver of a courier van who was busily loading parcels onto a trolley ready to wheel them into the entrance hall. She flitted through unnoticed and quickly climbed the stairs. There was no response when she knocked on the door of his flat. She waited, knocked a second time. Again, no reply. He must be out already.

Seeing an opportunity she had not previously anticipated, she hesitated only a moment before coming to a decision. Fresh out of training college, she'd learned one of the most valuable lessons of her career from a soon-to-retire copper of the old school. The illicit art of lock-picking wasn't a skill the force looked favourably on, but her instructor insisted it would stand her in good stead. He'd been so impressed with her natural talent for the task that on his retirement he'd presented her with a gift: the small leather case in her pocket, packed with a selection of the best tools for the job. Michelle had seldom made use of it, but she remained rather proud of her ability to crack simple locks without leaving a trace.

The lock on the closed door which faced her was an elderly Yale. She set to work. It took her less than a minute to successfully open the door. She stepped inside and looked around, wondering where to begin her search. After all, she didn't even know what she was looking for. And a part of her still held out that there was nothing to be found.

Noticing a desk on the far side of the room, she crossed to it, opened one of the drawers, and began to rummage through.

Then she heard a noise behind her. A door opening. A footstep. She turned to see him standing, half naked, just inside the room, dripping water everywhere. He must have just emerged from the bath; if it had been a shower, she would surely have heard it. As he lurched towards her, his face contorted with rage, the small towel he had draped around his waist fell to the ground, leaving him naked. For a second or two they both froze. The look on his face told her he was every bit as shocked and confused as she was, and just as frightened.

As she stared at him, transfixed, Michelle knew with absolute clarity that her suspicions had been right. This was the man who had killed Marlena, who would kill her if she did not get out of here this minute. So she turned, heading for the front door as fast as she could. He hurled himself sideways, making a grab for her, but he managed only to grasp her new shoulder bag. He tore it from her, breaking the strap. Then he seemed to step back, almost as if allowing her to escape. She half threw herself down the stairs, sprinted through the main door out onto the street and took off at a run, as fast as she could, her baseball hat falling unnoticed onto the pavement beneath her feet. She put a couple of blocks between herself and the apartment building before pausing to look back. She couldn't phone anyone. Not easily anyway. Her new phone had been in her bag. She thought about approaching a passer-by for help, but decided her best option would be to head for Charing Cross police station, a couple of streets away. There couldn't be a much safer place than that.

Nobody seemed to be following her. But then, he had been naked. He wouldn't come after her without first pulling on some clothes, would he?

She leaned, panting, against a wall on the corner of St Martin's Lane and Brydges Place, struggling to catch her breath. Her damaged nose made it difficult for her to breathe while running.

Brydges Place is a narrow pedestrian alleyway, overshadowed on either side by tall buildings, and surprisingly little used at the St Martin's Lane end. It offered an effective shortcut to the police station. While Michelle was wondering if this was a shortcut she dared use, or if she should take the safer albeit longer option of the main drag, she felt a blow in the small of her back. A gloved hand was clamped over her mouth. Unable to make a sound, she found herself being pulled into Brydges Place. She could see people just a few feet away, but he'd been so quick and strong and assertive that nobody seemed to have noticed what was happening.

She began to struggle, but her strength was no match for his. The hand over her mouth was half smothering her. Why didn't someone come into the alleyway? If someone didn't come right this minute it would be too late for her; unless she could remove the hand that was blocking her airway, she'd soon lose consciousness. Her mind was extraordinarily lucid – just as Marlena's had been, though she didn't know that. So this is it, she thought. I'm going to die at his hands.

Strangely, the worst part was knowing that she would die

without learning the answer to the question that had plagued her all night.

Why? Why had any of this happened? She knew now what he was, and had seen in his eyes how he must see himself. But why had he suddenly turned on his friends, inflicting such sadistic cruelty on people who had trusted and cared about him? Why?

It was her last thought. She felt an almighty blow to the back of her head. A searing pain cut through her body. Strong hands gripped her neck, squeezing the life from her. Then she was gone. Dead in his arms.

At last, too late, a pair of chattering office girls turned into the alleyway, heading for their place of work.

He shifted her weight, twisting her round so that she faced him, her dead body pressed close to his deadly one. Then he buried her face in his shoulder and lowered his hooded head, careful that his flesh did not touch hers, so that her features were concealed.

The two girls passed by without giving him, or poor dead Michelle, a second glance. She and her murderer looked every bit like a pair of lovers locked in a clinch.

He watched the girls retreat, their backs silhouetted against the brightness beyond the alley. There was a kind of alcove to his right, formed by the entrance to an old fire escape. He let Michelle's body fall softly into a heap against its graffiti-covered yellow doors.

Then, he walked calmly away, his footsteps quiet and unhurried, until he was lost in the anonymous hubbub of the city.

seventeen

The sight of a fellow human being slumped against a doorway in central London is sadly an everyday occurrence. The homeless, the drunk and the drugged, refugees and runaways, the mentally unstable, the physically infirm, the temporarily embarrassed and the permanently hopeless, are eternally attracted to the capital's heaving melting pot. They seek refuge in the archways that surround our major railway stations, beneath bridges and viaducts, in the doorways of office and apartment blocks; they lie on the pavement by heating outlets, and are to be found sheltering in alleyways and dark corners throughout the metropolis. Their presence, frequently comatose, attracts little or no attention. And so it was that upwards of forty or fifty pedestrians, some using Brydges Place as a shortcut and some heading for the Two Brydges members' club and the old pub next to it at the Bedfordbury and Chandos Place end of the alley, made their way past Michelle's body without giving her a second glance, let alone stopping to investigate.

It was a pair of young mothers from the suburbs, in London on an away-day, their children in the care of their own mothers, who stopped to check on her, almost two full hours after Michelle had been killed. They took in the swollen face and the staring eyes and reached out to touch skin that was already cold. With trembling fingers one of them then dialled 999.

Vogel was taking an early lunch at a vegan cafe just off the Strand when the news reached him. He was told that the first officers on the scene, being from Charing Cross police station, had recognized Michelle and put a call in to Dispatch to report that one of their own was down. Vogel at once abandoned his stuffed organic tomatoes with brown rice and headed to the crime scene. He could not, in any case, have eaten any more of his food. He felt sick.

It took him less than five minutes, half walking and half running, to get there. He passed the police station on the way. The fire exit gateway where Michelle's body had been discovered was a few yards from the end of Brydges Place, almost within sight of the back door of the station. Somehow, that made the discovery of her body all the more shocking. The SOCOs were already at work. The scene was cordoned off and several uniformed officers were ensuring its authenticity and keeping the public at bay. Vogel, though he hated it, duly kitted himself out in a Tyvek suit before approaching Michelle's body.

He reckoned he wasn't going to need the expert guidance of the pathologist, whom he was assured was on her way, to ascertain how Michelle had died. The signs of strangulation were obvious. You could see the marks of the gloved fingers that had been wrapped around her neck and pressed into her flesh. These were surrounded by puffy discoloured skin. But then Vogel noticed that the hair on top of Michelle's head was matted with blood. He leaned forward for a closer look, careful not to touch anything. Already the indefinable odour of death was emanating from the corpse. He thought there might be an indent in Michelle's skull, but he wasn't sure. The distorted face seemed to grow bigger, its death-induced deformity more clearly defined, as he examined it. He felt his head begin to swim, that familiar sinking feeling. He wasn't sure if his body was swaying, but he certainly felt as if it was. As soon as he'd seen enough he closed his eyes to shut out the sight before him, turning away so as not to attract the attention of the SOCOs, and straightened up.

The sight of a corpse almost always affected him deeply. But this was a fellow officer, a young woman Vogel had grown fond of. A young woman he now believed he had let down. And fatally so. He felt weak as a kitten.

He made himself stand very still, with his legs slightly apart and feet firmly planted, waiting until he was sure that he would not fall over before opening his eyes again. The world around him was no longer spinning, which was a good sign. Making a conscious effort to breathe deeply and evenly, he moved away from the cordoned-off area of the crime scene.

His lips were parched and his head had started to ache. He knew it made no sense, but he couldn't help feeling responsible for Michelle's death. He thought of the courage it must have taken for her to approach him when these troubling incidents first began. Despite being eaten up with embarrassment over that silly pass she'd made at him, she'd come to ask for his help. She might still be alive if only he hadn't made it quite so clear that he considered her a suspect.

Only that morning, he'd listened to Ben Parker suggesting that she might be capable of a brutal murder, and instead of leaping to her defence he'd sat there methodically calculating whether it were possible.

And now Michelle had been murdered. Proving her innocence in the most terrible way possible. If only he'd gone to see her, warned that she could still be in danger and to take extra care.

He blamed himself totally, but he knew he must dismiss such

thoughts from his mind. Nothing he could do now would bring Michelle back, but at least he could make amends by bringing her killer to justice.

The killer may have used his hands and not a knife on this occasion, but Vogel was convinced that Marlena McTavish and Michelle Monahan had been murdered by the same man. Sunday Club was at the root of it all, it had to be, yet despite the hours he'd spent questioning the various members he still had absolutely no idea what the motive might be.

Unlike Marlena's killing, which had been carefully planned, Vogel thought Michelle's murder had been committed on the spur of the moment, provoked by he knew not what. Fear maybe? Had Michelle, knowingly or unknowingly, been in a position to expose the killer's identity?

She might still be alive if he hadn't bowed to pressure from his superior officers. He'd been swept along in the general wave of euphoria at the arrest of Alfonso Bertorelli, even though he had never, in his heart, believed Bertorelli to be guilty. He wondered if his head had been turned by his secondment into MIT and the attentions of DCI Clarke. Vogel hoped not.

He glanced back at the small ribboned-off piece of London. He watched the SOCOs step aside to allow Pat Fitzwarren through. The pathologist was intent on getting quickly to the corpse. It was always different when a police officer had died. Vogel was too preoccupied to greet her properly, merely nodding acknowledgement of her 'good morning' with a distracted nod of his head.

He knew some of his colleagues might cling to the belief that they had Marlena's killer in custody, that Michelle's death was in no way connected to the events surrounding Sunday Club. But that was a coincidence too far. No, this was all the work of one man. And clearly that man was not Alfonso Bertorelli.

If there was one good thing and only one good thing about being locked in a police cell, reflected Vogel drily, it proved a cast-iron alibi.

There was no point hanging around the crime scene any longer. He had work to do. And, he felt, people to protect. The friends were falling like flies. He could not fail another.

Vogel's mobile rang as he was hurrying back to Charing Cross. The caller was DC Wagstaff.

'The boss wants a full report from you soonest, guv,' he said. 'We're all gutted here. Just can't believe—'

'I know.' Vogel cut him short. He didn't need to be told what the atmosphere would be like in the station.

'Tell Clarke I'm on my way,' he said.

'Another thing, guv,' continued Wagstaff. 'Some bloke's turned up in the front office, says he's got information about Bertorelli. Something about an alibi. He's not very clear. And he stinks of booze, but—'

'Put him in an interview room,' interrupted Vogel, who reckoned any possibility of clarifying the Bertorelli situation was worth investigating.

The man awaiting him, who said his name was Charles Timpson, had bad teeth, a drinker's bulbous nose, and smelled not only of alcohol but also stale sweat. He actually seemed sober, but, as indicated by Wagstaff, was not particularly coherent.

It took Vogel some time to gather the gist of what Timpson was trying to tell him.

'So you recognized Alfonso Bertorelli from a picture in a newspaper, and you think you were drinking with him in the Dunster Arms on the day that Marleen McTavish was murdered, is that it?' Vogel asked.

'I'm bloody sure I was,' muttered the man. 'My wedding

anniversary, see – not that I have a wife any more. She kicked me out years ago.'

'Right, so can you remember what time Mr Bertorelli arrived at the pub?'

'Not exactly, but I was watching the cricket on TV. The IPL. I've got nothing better to do, so I go to the pub most days and watch whatever sport they've got on. It hadn't been on long – the early games start at eleven thirty. I'm not mad about blokes playing cricket in their pyjamas, but there you go . . .'

Vogel let Timpson ramble on about cricket while he processed the relevant information. It appeared Bertorelli had gone straight from the station to a nearby pub, exactly as he'd claimed.

'Can you remember how long you were drinking with Mr Bertorelli?' Vogel asked.

'Oh, most of the day.'

'Any idea what time he left the pub?'

'No. But I didn't go till around seven. I know that because the second game had just ended.'

'And Mr Bertorelli was still there?'

'Yep. He'd fallen asleep. 'Course the regular landlord wouldn't have stood for that. Nor Jim Marshal. But it was only Micky behind the bar that day.'

'How on earth can you remember so much if you'd been in the pub all day?' Vogel demanded. 'You must have been well plastered.'

'I can always remember cricket,' Timpson said, taking umbrage. 'And that Bertorelli, well, he just looked out of place. I could tell he wasn't a drinker. I was sort of keeping an eye on him.'

'I see. Why has it taken you so long to come forward with this information, Mr Timpson?'

The man looked sheepish. 'Well, I've been on a bit of a

bender,' he said. 'Haven't been sober for a week or so. I have a newspaper delivered at home every day, 'cos I do the horses, you see. But I'd been too pissed to look at 'em. It was only this morning that I saw the report about the murder and the picture of the man who'd been arrested. I knew I had to come and give a statement.'

'Thank you, Mr Timpson,' said Vogel. 'Thank you very much indeed.'

And that clinches it, he thought to himself, as he made his way to Nobby Clarke's office to give her his now delayed report. He hoped she would agree that the delay had been worth it.

Vogel was about to knock on the door of the office temporarily assigned to Clarke, when he was intercepted by DI Forest, bristling with indignation.

'What the hell is going on, Vogel?' Forest demanded.

In no mood for the DI's posturing, Vogel replied, 'Perhaps you wouldn't mind stepping out of the way. I need to report to my SIO.'

Forest had positioned himself so that he was blocking the door to Nobby Clarke's office. Instead of moving aside, he barked, 'Tell that flash bitch Clarke she needs to get this sort—'

At that moment the door behind Forest opened to reveal a sardonically smiling DCI Clarke.

'Thank you for your input, DI Forest,' she said quietly.

Forest glanced anxiously over one shoulder. His ruddy complexion had turned even redder. DCI Clarke was a good six feet tall, Vogel reckoned. And, in the heeled boots which accompanied the tailored trouser suits she invariably wore to work, she towered over Tom Forest.

Vogel's wife was tall. She'd told him that a lot of short men were intimidated by tall women, even if they wouldn't admit it, particularly if the women were in a position of authority over them.

Forest certainly looked intimidated. And serve him damn well right, thought Vogel.

'Yes, oh, yes, well, as long as we all pull together, I'm sure we will get the right result,' Forest blustered.

'Perhaps if you'd let my assistant SIO pass,' said Clarke, her face expressionless, 'we could get on with achieving the right result that much quicker.'

'Yes, right, yes.'

As a flustered Forest departed, Clarke shook her head sorrowfully.

'We were at Hendon together, you know,' she told Vogel as she ushered him into her office. 'We used to call him Einstein. And now he's a DI. Not changed a bit, though.'

She sat down behind her desk, and gestured for Vogel to take a seat. 'There's nothing worse than losing a fellow copper,' she sighed.

'No, boss, there isn't,' agreed Vogel.

'What do you make of it?' she asked.

'Clearly Mr Bertorelli couldn't have killed Michelle Monahan. And it now looks as though he's got an alibi for the day Marlena was killed . . .'

Vogel told her about Charles Timpson and the statement he had given. The DCI made a disparaging remark about the quality of Wagstaff and Carlisle's pub check, and told Vogel to send them back to the Dunster Arms to verify Timpson's story.

'We probably need to drop all charges against him,' said Vogel. 'I shouldn't think the CPS will want to know after this.'

'All charges?' she queried. 'I agree it's impossible for us to proceed with the murder charge, but what about the earlier mugging of PC Monahan? A considerable amount of incriminating evidence was found at Bertorelli's place of residence, was it not? The hoody, the bike, and even Michelle Monahan's handbag.'

'Yes, just as we found a pair of his old trainers covered in Marlena's blood when we went to arrest him for her murder, a murder he now has an alibi for,' Vogel pointed out. 'Bertorelli has always maintained that those items were planted at his gran's. Forensics could find no trace of his fingerprints on the bike or the bag, which was why the CPS didn't want to charge him after PC Monahan was mugged.'

'So now we have to accept that he was telling the truth about being set up?'

'Right, boss. And the blood-spattered trainers could only have been planted by the person who murdered Marlena.'

Clarke sat pondering this for a moment. 'You think the same person is guilty of all these crimes involving the Sunday Club people, don't you, Vogel?'

Vogel agreed that he did.

'But the killings of Marlena and PC Monahan each followed a very different MO – how do you account for that?'

'Marlena's murder was premeditated. He had it all planned: drugging the champagne, taking along one of Bertorelli's trainers to incriminate him, presumably making sure he had a change of clothes because his own would be covered in blood . . . it was all carefully set up to make sure that he would get away with it.'

The DCI was listening intently, she nodded for him to continue.

'Michelle was killed in broad daylight a short distance from this police station. Not the ideal time or location if you're planning a murder – far too much risk of being seen. That tells me he was in a hurry. It could be that Michelle had seen something or remembered something that would put him at risk, so he had to act fast to silence her. Maybe she was on the way here, and that's why he killed her where he did.'

Clarke did not respond immediately but sat weighing up everything he had told her. Vogel waited in silence, enjoying the novelty of a superior officer who took the time to mull things over.

'There is an alternative scenario,' she said. 'This latest killing could just be a terrible coincidence. But it would be so great a coincidence that I don't think it's worthy of serious consideration.'

Vogel was relieved to hear it. 'So we're looking for a serial offender, a double murderer. Right now he's still at large, and we don't know who he is or why he has done what he's done. We need to find him, and fast, boss.'

'We've made a bad mistake then, over the arrest of Bertorelli, haven't we?' she said. 'If we hadn't, Michelle Monahan might still be alive.'

Clarke looked quite bereft. And Vogel noted her use of the word 'we'. Under Forest's watch, it was a given that blame would be shifted down the chain of command. Vogel had never been one to pass the buck, not downwards, sideways, or up. If things went wrong he never took the attitude that it wasn't his fault because he'd only been obeying orders. No. Vogel was a Jew whose immediate family had only just escaped Nazi Germany before the holocaust. There was a great-aunt who had died in the camps, and a number of distant cousins who had suffered unspeakable atrocities at the hands of those whose ultimate excuse had frequently been that they were only obeying orders. Vogel couldn't accept that. Not for others and not for himself. He felt that the actions of every police officer involved in the

Sunday Club investigations had contributed in some degree to the death of Michelle Monahan.

He was wracked with guilt about the part he'd played. He'd been too busy fretting over discrepancies in her bloody diary, which was all it had amounted to, and as a result he'd failed to see the bigger picture. Worse, he'd allowed Alfonso Bertorelli to be charged with murder and assault even though he doubted the man was guilty of either crime. That was the bitter truth. And Vogel was beside himself with grief and inner fury. However, as was his way, he let none of this show.

'If mistakes were made,' said Vogel, 'they were mine more than anybody else's.'

Clarke looked him in the eye, holding his gaze for a few seconds before responding. 'We're a team here, Vogel. Whatever went wrong is a team responsibility. And it certainly won't do any good dwelling on it. So let's move forward, shall we?'

Vogel nodded his agreement.

'Right, we'll drop the charges against Bertorelli and release him from custody,' she said briskly. 'But I want him told that our inquiries are ongoing and he could be called back in for questioning at any time. OK? Meanwhile let's get the rest of the Sunday Club bunch picked up. No messing. One of them has probably killed a cop, so I say we arrest the lot of 'em, soon as. Don't give 'em any warning. And I want their homes turned over.'

'Yes, boss,' said Vogel.

He turned and walked stiffly from his superior's office, keeping those unwelcome emotions locked inside him. In order to maintain his outer calm he made a resolution, something to carry him through until this matter was resolved.

He would not rest until he had found the man who had killed Marlena and Michelle. He would find the bastard and bring him to justice. He would avenge the deaths of the two women and he would also avenge the injustice that had been inflicted upon Alfonso Bertorelli.

Vogel walked straight through the MIT room, pausing only to pass on his superior's instructions to arrest the remaining members of Sunday Club. Having assigned a team of officers to carry out each arrest, he turned his attention to Wagstaff and Carlisle, who looked suitably ashamed when confronted with Timpson's evidence and immediately set off for the Dunster Arms to confirm it. Finally Vogel proceeded through the lobby to the back door which led onto Chandos Place, the one that was almost opposite Brydges Place, where Michelle had been killed. He looked the other way.

Within a couple of hours there would be an endless succession of interviews to conduct, but first he needed some fresh air and a few minutes alone. He walked briskly down Agar Street and across the Strand, heading for Embankment Gardens. There he found a park bench, amongst beds of tulips and daffodils now in full April glory. Making sure he was alone, he bowed his head, and allowed the tears to flow freely down his pale cheeks.

eighteen

A pair of City of London coppers apprehended Billy at his place of work. Tiny and George were arrested at their homes. They picked up Greg in his lock-up over at Waterloo loading cases of dodgy whisky into the back of his van, and they tracked down Bob to the luxury block of flats at Clerkenwell where he regularly attended to both the plants in the public areas and several of the privately owned terraces and balconies. Karen was apprehended as she returned home with shopping for that evening's supper. Ari was found in the lobby of the Dorchester where, with his father, he was entertaining a Swiss Banker and a Saudi sheikh to a light lunch.

Their arrests had been executed so quickly that all seven of them claimed to be unaware of Michelle's murder until this was revealed to them by their arresting officers, and each appeared shocked to the core.

They were taken to Charing Cross police station where they were to be interviewed separately, waiting in between times in individual cells. First they were processed in the custody unit. Their clothes and personal possessions were removed and they were fingerprinted and DNA-tested according to procedure. A small amount of cocaine was found in a pocket of Ari Kabul's jacket. That held no interest, in itself, for Vogel, but it was possible that its presence might prove useful.

By the time all seven were brought in Vogel was once again looking his usual cool, calm self, and concentrating his legendary brain on the matter in hand instead of dwelling on the consequences of earlier failings.

The question that was bugging him most was why Marlena and Michelle had been murdered, rather than by whom. He was quite sure that if he could only find the answer to the former, the latter would automatically fall into place.

Vogel, once more accompanied by DC Jones, conducted the first interview with Ari. Before he could get a question in, Ari had one for him. He was no longer as self-assured or amenable as he'd been the previous time they'd met, but then nobody had died when Vogel had last spoken to Ari Kabul, and he hadn't been arrested and hauled into a police station.

'I suppose you think I'm guilty of murdering Marlena and Michelle as well as everything else that's been going on because nothing's happened to me,' Ari blurted out. 'Because I'm not one of the poor bloody victims.'

Vogel was very quiet, his manner more in keeping with an inquisitive schoolteacher than a police detective.

'I can assure you, Mr Kabul, that I have drawn no such conclusion. You are here to help us with our inquiries, that's all.'

'I thought I'd been arrested.'

'A technicality, at this stage,' said Vogel. 'After Michelle's body was found we wanted to get you all here as—'

'At least we know Alfonso didn't do it.'

'Mr Kabul, I cannot divulge information about an investigation which is still ongoing.'

'No,' Ari interrupted again. 'But it's damned obvious Alfonso couldn't have killed Michelle if he was banged up in here. Which he was.'

Vogel ignored the remark.

'Mr Kabul, could you tell me where you were between the hours of eight and ten this morning please?' he enquired.

'I was with my dad at the Dorchester, where you damn well picked me up in front of everybody.' Ari's voice rose. 'Can you imagine the bad time my dad's going to give me?'

'I think that may be the least of your concerns,' said Vogel. 'What time exactly did you arrive at the Dorchester?'

'I'm not sure. About twenty past eight I think.'

'And was anyone else with you up until ten o'clock or thereabouts, or were you just in the company of your father?' asked DC Jones.

'You have to be joking,' said Ari. 'You think my dad would choose to while away the morning with me? We had a breakfast meeting with some City people at eight thirty, followed by a couple of other meetings over coffee, and then the lunch – which you guys know about because you interrupted it, didn't you? It's something Dad does. Intensive entertaining, he calls it. Gets a lot of stuff over with all at once.'

'I see. And before eight twenty?'

'What do you think? We were travelling to the Dorchester from home, weren't we? In Dad's car. So his chauffeur can back me up on that, though if you think my dad would give me a false alibi then you just don't know him.'

Vogel stared at Ari. How he wished he could read minds. Sometimes he almost felt he could when he was really concentrating on interviewing a suspect. But not with this guy. He was unable to get beyond Ari's chippy responses. The difference in the man since their last encounter was so marked that Vogel couldn't help wondering whether the personality change was a sign of guilt. He noticed that Ari's hands were trembling. Was it just a case of nerves, or was it an indicator of dependency on the substance found on him, or any other substances he might be addicted to?

Vogel decided on a two-pronged attack.

'Mr Kabul, are you aware that when you were searched this morning on entering police custody we found a considerable quantity of cocaine in the pocket of your suit jacket?'

'Oh yeah, yeah,' said Ari.

'Mr Kabul, are you also aware that we could charge you with possession of an illegal drug?'

'I thought you were investigating a murder – two murders now,' said Ari.

'Indeed. However, your attitude leads me to believe, Mr Kabul, that you are not cooperating with us fully. It is possible that you need time to reflect upon your position. Were I to charge you with possession of an illegal substance, that would give me the opportunity to detain you here for considerably longer than otherwise. Do you understand?'

Ari bowed his head. When he spoke again it was without any of his earlier attitude.

'Detective Inspector, I am all sorts of things – a spoiled rich boy, probably, a bit of a druggy, definitely, and sometimes a bloody fool – but I am not a violent man. I've never knowingly hurt anyone in my life and I certainly didn't kill Marlena or Michelle. Why would I?'

And that, thought Vogel, was the crux of the matter. Why would Ari Kabul or any of the friends have committed double murder?

None of the initial interviews lasted long. Vogel had one immediate aim, which was to check alibis and therefore hopefully narrow down the list of suspects. He was also aware that the homes of all seven of those arrested were being searched while they were detained at Charing Cross. Vogel wanted evidence. He had no time at all for guesswork and inspired hunches which turned out to be anything but.

Karen was the next to be questioned. She cried through most of her interview. When she was asked who might be able to pick her children up if she were still detained by the time school was out, the crying turned into gut-wrenching sobs. She did, however, manage to say that her mother would look after the kids and to supply contact details.

She was also quite clear about her own whereabouts at the time of Michelle's murder. And she stopped crying for long enough to make sure Vogel was clear on that too.

'Same as always,' she said. 'I took the kids to school. There are loads of other mums who will have seen me. Afterwards I went straight to Tesco. Nine till one, every day, I do a shift on the till.'

Then she started crying again and her words became jumbled. Vogel could only just make out what she was saying.

'Greg . . . my Greg . . . is he here?'

Vogel told her that he was.

Karen looked up at him, both fear and pleading in her swollen red eyes.

'He's a good man, my Greg,' she said. 'He doesn't mean no harm, honestly. Don't be too hard on him, will you?'

Vogel stared at her.

'Mrs Walker, I am conducting a murder inquiry,' he said. 'My only immediate consideration is to find out who killed PC Michelle Monahan. We have also reopened our inquiries into the murder of Marleen McTavish. Now you are beginning to sound as if you are afraid that your husband had something to do with one, or both, of these murders. Is that the case?'

Karen's eyes widened. 'No,' she said. 'No. How could you think that? How could anyone think that of my Greg?'

And then she burst into tears again.

Billy claimed to have been at work at the offices of Geering Brothers, and told Vogel he had arrived just after 8 a.m., as usual.

'Your guys picked me up there, for God's sake,' he said. 'Did they think I'd just popped in for coffee and a chat? Ten hours a day I'm in that place, minimum. Sometimes I get out at lunchtime, that's all, and not for long.'

'I am just trying to eliminate you from our inquiries, Mr Wiseman,' said Vogel. 'You must see how important that is both for you and for us.'

'And now I suppose you're going back to Geering's to check whether I'm telling the truth?' demanded Billy.

'We will do whatever is necessary to confirm your where-abouts at the time in question, yes, sir,' said Vogel.

'In which case I might as well kiss my fucking job good-fucking-bye, mightn't I?' said Billy. 'Mind you, I suppose the damage has already been done – two fucking great plods coming to get me. You could have phoned. I'd have come in. I'm not a criminal.'

'I'm sure you're not, sir,' said Vogel, deadpan. 'We have certain procedures to follow in a murder investigation, that's all.'

Tiny claimed to have left home soon after Billy had departed for work, and taken the tube to Uxbridge at the end of the Bakerloo line.

'I was checking out a litter of cockerpoos we found on the net,' he said. 'Billy and I are thinking about getting another dog.

We're trying to move on.' He paused. 'Or we were, 'til this happened.'

Once Vogel had learned what a cockerpoo was – the progeny of a cocker spaniel and a poodle – he began to establish the timing and logistics of Tiny's professed journey.

'It's about fifty minutes each way on the tube,' said Tiny. 'And I guess I spent a couple of hours at the other end, time I'd walked to and from the house where the puppies are. It was twenty minutes or so from the station.'

'Do you know what the time was when you arrived at the house?'

'Yes. Nine o'clock. Well, actually it was a few minutes before. My appointment was for nine o'clock. I was early. I just waited around for a bit outside.'

'And what time did you get back to central London?'

'I'm not sure. Around noon, I think. I did some food shopping in Marks on the way home. I guess I'd been in about an hour when the heavy brigade arrived.'

Vogel nodded. He mulled this over for a moment before putting his next question.

'Mr Stephens, as members of a group of friends who have been the victims of an increasingly nasty succession of crimes culminating in murder, you and your partner had been through a very traumatic time. You had lost your dog in most distressing circumstances and, as you say, you were trying to move on, so you were looking for another dog, and you were going to perhaps choose one. I understand that. But I find it rather odd that your partner did not accompany you on such an important mission.'

Tiny was no longer meeting Vogel's steady gaze. The big man looked down at his hands.

'Billy's always busy,' he said. 'He works very long hours. So it makes sense for me to check things out. I found those dogs advertised on the net. I didn't know anything about the people who'd bred them, or about the dogs, 'til I went out to Uxbridge to see them. If I hadn't liked the set-up, if it had turned out to be a puppy farm or something, then I wouldn't have needed to waste Billy's time. I wasn't planning to actually buy a dog without him seeing it first, without his say-so.'

Vogel was silent for a moment. He had an idea forming.

'Mr Stephens, did your partner know that you were going to Uxbridge to look for a new dog?'

Tiny wriggled in his seat.

'Well, not exactly, no,' he said eventually. 'I mean, we'd talked about it, but he didn't know I was actually looking.'

'So Billy thought you were at home this morning. He didn't know you had gone to Uxbridge?'

'No – you see, he didn't think he was ready for a new dog. He didn't think either of us was—'

Vogel interrupted. 'Mr Stephens, I'm not interested in whether or not you and your partner acquire a dog, I just need to establish your whereabouts at the time of Michelle Monahan's death.'

'I told—'

'Yes, and you've also told me that your partner, the man you share your life with, thinks you were somewhere else entirely. You had better give me the details of the people you visited in Uxbridge and you'd better hope they back your story up.'

Vogel felt sure that the man's alibi would prove to be genuine. It was almost too absurd not to be genuine. However, this didn't particularly please the detective. He was beginning to run out of suspects.

George was interviewed next. Vogel remembered him as being the most cocky of the friends. Now George Kristos didn't look cocky at all. His eyes were red and, like Ari Kabul, his hands were shaking.

'I can't believe another one's dead, not Michelle, she was so lovely, so young and pretty and everything, and now it's all starting again, and it can't be Alfonso who did it because he was in jail, but none of us ever thought he could be capable of murder, not me anyway, and he'd never have hurt Marlena, certainly not her, he worshipped her you see, so—'

'Mr Kristos,' Vogel interrupted sternly.

George stopped talking. His eyes were open almost unnaturally wide. His jaw was slack. Vogel thought he looked like a scared rabbit caught in headlights.

'Mr Kristos, I need to establish your whereabouts earlier today,' Vogel continued. 'Could you tell me please where you were between the hours of nine and eleven?'

'Right, yes, of course.'

George seemed almost eager to help. And, unless he were guilty, why shouldn't he be? thought Vogel. Those suspects who were innocent must surely want to see the killer found every bit as much as he did. Aside from the fact that they would all be under suspicion until the culprit was found, in the absence of a motive there was no way of predicting who the killer's next victim might be.

'I was with my neighbour, Marnie. Well, first of all I went to the shop and got some fresh bread and a couple of Danishes. She likes Danishes, you see. I go round every morning when I'm not working. We have breakfast together and I tidy for her and keep her company for a bit.'

'What time did you leave your flat and what time did you arrive back at this Marnie's?'

'I went out soon after eight, and I don't suppose I was gone more than twenty minutes. I was with Marnie by about half past eight. I always get there quite early or she starts to fret.'

'And what time did you leave Marnie?'

'Oh, it must have been eleven o'clock. Very nearly anyway.'

'You stayed with this elderly woman for two and a half hours? I must say, that is extremely neighbourly of you, Mr Kristos. Indeed, some might say excessively so.'

George coloured slightly and mumbled something incomprehensible.

'If you have something to say, Mr Kristos, it would help if you spoke up, please.'

George nodded. 'Well, it's embarrassing. But actually Marnie's daughter, well, she pays me to look out for Marnie. Only Marnie doesn't know, you see.'

'I don't see, Mr Kristos. Perhaps you could explain.'

'Well, Marnie's daughter, she lives in Ealing now, smart house, young family. All of that. She isn't up for running into Soho every day to see to her old mum, and Marnie certainly wouldn't be up for living in Ealing. No way. Not that she'd ever be invited.' George shook his head sadly.

'So in effect this is a job?' Vogel asked. 'Looking after your neighbour is paid employment for you. Is that what you are saying?'

'Kind of, yes,' responded George, still stumbling slightly over his words, his face bright red now. 'I do all sorts of work when I'm not acting, which is most of the time, unfortunately. I do maintenance round the building where I live, I work in a theatre box office sometimes. I mean, I can turn my hand to all sorts of things, and I have to. So, yes, looking out for Marnie is a job, I suppose, it helps towards paying the rent.'

'And you go in every morning at about the same time, and always for what, two or three hours?' asked DC Jones.

George nodded. 'Yes. Only, well, you see, nobody knows. None of the others. Not my girlfriend either. Nobody. I mean, it's not very cool, is it? Chap like me, a paid carer for an old girl like Marnie. I'm ever so fond of her and that, but . . .'

George's voice tailed off. There was a kind of panic in his eyes.

Vogel stifled a smile with difficulty. This was a murder investigation, yet George Kristos was more anxious about his cool image than establishing his whereabouts at the time of the crime and enabling himself to be eliminated from police inquiries.

After George, it was Greg's turn. He said that he'd spent the entire morning in and out of his van delivering crates of whisky all over West London, and beyond, into Surrey and Middlesex. He'd made an early start. He'd got to Chiswick at about half past eight, then gone on to Ealing, Acton, Hounslow, Twickenham, and further west, he said, to Kingston, Staines and Slough. On the way back he'd made deliveries to more central addresses in Barnes, Putney and Clapham before returning to his Waterloo lock-up to reload. He claimed he'd been planning to spend the afternoon making more deliveries, some nearby, in Waterloo itself, and various riverbank addresses, as well as Covent Garden, Clerkenwell, and maybe north to Camden, Hampstead and Highgate.

'Then you lot came and that was the end of that,' he said.

'I take it you have a record of your movements, Mr Walker?' asked Vogel.

''Course I bloody do,' snapped Greg. 'Most of the places I deliver to someone answers the door and takes the stuff in. Sometimes the householder, sometimes caretakers, porters, cleaning ladies. Sometimes I go next door to a neighbour if there's no one in. They all sign for it, don't they? My clipboard's in the van. I'd have shown it to your boys if they'd given me half a chance. But they were in too much of a bloody hurry to strong-arm me down here, weren't they?'

'Mr Walker,' said Vogel, 'I'm quite sure you weren't strong—'

Greg cut him off. 'That's as maybe, but I heard my missus crying earlier. Sobbing 'er heart out, she was, and don't tell me it weren't her because I know bloody better. Whaddya think you're doing, making a doll like her cry? Never hurt a fly, my Karen.'

'Mr Walker, two women have been murdered, a police officer, my colleague, and an elderly lady, both, I believe, friends of yours. Both were violently attacked. I have to make whatever inquiries I deem necessary in order to find whoever has committed these dreadful crimes and, in each case, bring him . . .' Vogel paused, 'or her, to justice. And I am afraid that means questioning every member of the group of friends Michelle and Marlena were part of. Almost everyone in that group has recently been the victim of some type of incident, ranging in severity from malicious pranks to murder. Those of you who are innocent of any wrongdoing could be in extreme danger. That includes your wife. If she is innocent, as you say, then I must do everything in my power to establish her innocence and to ascertain if there is anything she knows, albeit unwittingly, that might lead us to the guilty party. And if she or anyone else is upset by being questioned, well, so be it.'

Vogel glanced to the side and saw DC Jones staring at him. Vogel coughed, clearing his throat noisily to hide his embarrassment. He was aware that he was not conducting this interview in a professional manner. Nor strictly according to procedure. He didn't have to explain himself to anyone. Least of all to a suspect.

Greg was also staring at him. And it was he who broke the silence.

'You're right,' he said, taking Vogel by surprise. 'I'm not thinking straight. You gotta do what you gotta do to find this bastard. It's not the Fonz, we know that now. He couldn't 'ave killed Michelle anyway, right?'

Vogel nodded.

'Yeah, so the bastard's still at large. My Karen could be next. Any of us could. And Michelle, I can't believe she's dead. She was that pretty and full of life always.' He broke off. 'I mean, not that it makes any difference, that stuff. My Karen, well, she'll be crying about Michelle as much as herself.'

He looked directly at Vogel.

'Anything you want to know, anything I can do to help, guv,' he said.

'You can tell me about your own relationship with Michelle.'

'We were friends. Not close friends, like, but good friends. Just part of a group that met every Sunday really . . . but you know that.'

Vogel nodded. He did indeed know that, and he was sick of asking the same questions and getting the same answers. He felt he was getting nowhere. All he could hope was that the boys doing the searches, and the various forensics results they were awaiting might give him some of the answers he needed. In the meantime, he could only continue to go through the motions. The answers continued to be repetitive.

Greg got on very well with Michelle. No, there had never been any ill feeling between them. And no, he could think of no one with a grudge against her.

'Except maybe her old man, Phil, another copper. Did you know she was married to a copper, and that they're separated?'

Vogel nodded.

'Yeah, he ran off with some woman Michelle always referred to as "that tart".' Greg grinned. 'She was always going on about him. No love lost there, either way round.'

Vogel sighed. The team had already checked out Phil Monahan. Vogel had asked for that to be done as soon as he'd heard about Michelle's death. He now knew that Monahan had been on duty since 8 a.m. that day and had spent most of the morning at his desk in Dorchester CID. He certainly would at no stage have had time to nip up to London, murder his estranged wife, and nip back. Even if he'd had any desire or inclination to do so.

The final interviewee was Bob.

'Of course I can prove I was at Chatham Towers all morning,' he said. 'Twice a week I go there and it takes me 'til early afternoon. I get there about eight and I don't usually leave 'til after two. I know the people who go off to work early, and I do their terraces first. Then I do the public areas. The place is usually deserted by nine o'clock, you see, because it's all professional people, lawyers, accountants, City workers, that sort of thing. So I don't get in anyone's way. Before I start, Pete – that's the porter – he always makes me a cuppa.'

'And he did that this morning?'

'Yes. We take a bit of a break, sit down in his little room in the basement, have a chat. Then I get stuck in again. There's a lot to do at this time of year on the terraces and outside, clearing the last of the winter stuff, putting in the spring bedding plants and so on. And in the foyer, well, they always like it to look tip-top with a bit of colour, so I'm constantly replacing plants, usually just rotating them, you know. I don't like to throw living things out. I bring them back to my place if I can find the room, put them in my cold frame if I need to, give 'em a bit of TLC—'

'Yes, yes,' interrupted Vogel impatiently. He didn't need a lecture on horticulture, and if he'd been less wearied by the lack of progress he probably wouldn't have let Bob go on as much as he had. He did his best to persevere.

'So how long did you and Pete spend together drinking tea this morning?'

'Oh, about twenty minutes, I suppose,' said Bob.

'And then you worked on the public areas. Was this Pete with you then?'

'Some of the time. He has a desk in the foyer, but he has various jobs to do. He can confirm that I wouldn't have had the chance to nip off and murder little Michelle Monahan.' Bob shook his head sadly. 'Look at me,' he instructed. 'Do you really think I've got it in me to murder somebody?'

'You were in the army, Mr Buchanan, you have been to war.'

'A long time ago. And one thing that did was to make me never again want to have anything to do with the death of another human being. If I'm the best suspect you can come up with, then I'd say you haven't got very far with this investigation.'

Vogel was inclined to agree. Stoically he carried on with his questioning.

'What about when you went into the various flats to work on the private terraces? Pete wouldn't have been with you then, would he? Presumably he wouldn't have even known which flat you were supposed to be in.'

'What do you mean "supposed to be"?' asked Bob, showing a bit of spirit. 'Anyway, I was in and out of my van all morning, wasn't I? They let me park it in the courtyard round the back. I'm forever shifting plants about, fresh topsoil, fertilizer, tools and stuff, aren't I? And I have to pass Pete's desk every time, don't I?'

*

Vogel watched as Bob was escorted back to his cell. It wasn't like him to feel so confused. He was also becoming frustrated. Every one of the seven appeared to have a solid alibi for the period during which Michelle was killed. And this left the policeman no further forward.

He felt as if he were groping his way through a thick and impenetrable fog. And he was getting nowhere fast. Just as Bob had implied.

Vogel sat for a moment, staring into space, aware of DC Jones watching him anxiously. Then he pulled himself together and marched into the MIT room, trying to look purposeful. Perhaps there would be news from the search teams or forensics. Also there might be word from the officers looking through CCTV footage, starting with the streets around Brydges Place, where Michelle's body was found, and then moving further afield.

Two murders had been committed and the murderer must have left clues. That was Vogel's simple logic. Criminals make mistakes. Eventually. Sadistic killers leave a trail. It was up to him to uncover that trail and to follow it to its conclusion.

nineteen

In between my turns in the interview room I waited quietly in my cell. I could not believe they had not yet discovered me. Wasn't it obvious by now that I was the perpetrator? Many times throughout my life I'd wondered if I was the only person in the world who wasn't stupid. This was just another example. I could always manipulate people, make them believe what I wanted them to and do what I wanted them to do. It was as if God had given me some rare and dangerous talent, a genuine sixth sense, in exchange for what he had taken away.

But nothing could ever make up for that.

I have experienced guilt. I am not a sociopath. I have feelings, not just for myself, but for others too. I'd even felt a certain sense of remorse when I had to dispense with Michelle Monahan. Not much, it's true. She'd always annoyed me. At first it had amused me to be wining and dining with a police officer, and her so blissfully unaware of my history. But she was just too pretty and perky, too bright and vivacious. It made me want to slap her. I was jealous. Boy, was I jealous. She had everything going for her, yet after she'd had a few drinks she would start to moan about her wicked ex-husband and her ruined life. There was nothing wrong with her life. She had a career. And her looks. Men seemed to fall at her feet. Even I'd found her attractive, and that was the most annoying thing of all.

Nonetheless I regretted her passing. Strange, really, that I found myself almost mourning her death, as if I hadn't been responsible for it.

It had been quite different with the bitch. I felt no regret for her passing. I'd carved into her and removed her organs much as a butcher would clean out the insides of a pig, leaving little more than a bare gaping cavity. It pleased me that I had been efficient, quite casually efficient. I'd felt nothing for her. Indeed, as I'd watched the bitch's life blood flow, spilling across the floor, puddling at my feet, I experienced only a sense of release.

I had lusted after vengeance for so long, never imagining that it would one day come within my reach. So, when I severed the bitch's genitalia and plucked out her womb, I had felt, more than anything else, triumphant. I had finally been avenged.

Once it was done, and the bitch was dead, I considered, then, taking my own life. After all, thanks to her, it had always been a total disappointment to me. When I was younger I would sometimes wake up in the mornings and feel a fleeting moment of hope at the thought of a new day. Then I would remember my own reality. Every day is the first day of the rest of your life, they say. It could never be like that for me. Every day of my life I had to bear the legacy of what the bitch had done, what she had turned me into – a wretched apology for a human being, a damaged, empty shell.

Marlena. So wonderful, so funny, such a character. Everyone loved Marlena. Even I had loved Marlena, hadn't I? Before I'd learned the bitter truth.

My one regret was that I hadn't killed her sooner. It offended me that she had lived so long, unscarred by what she had done. She'd claimed, in her dying agony, sputtering through the gag I *had made for her, that she hadn't realized the damage she had done. Begging for mercy – she who had shown none! She'd thrown me aside, leaving me to suffer, not just then but for the rest of my life. Self-preservation had been her only concern. She'd had no thought for me – until the day I finally caught up with her.*

Oh, I had given her exactly what she deserved. I took my time, let her know what it was to feel pain as I sliced into her skin. My God had ordained that she be delivered unto his faithful servant. He guided my hand as I hacked out her womb, the very symbol of motherhood, which had no place within her.

I had destroyed her just as she had destroyed me.

Michelle, on the other hand, met a quick and relatively pain-less death. She brought it on herself. If she hadn't invaded my privacy, sneaking into places where she was not welcome, it wouldn't have happened. But she left me with no alternative. Had I not acted, she would have revealed me – for what I am, as well as for what I had done. And it was the prospect of the former which distressed me far more than the latter. There are worse things than being branded a murderer. A prison sentence would be as nothing compared to what I had endured. But to have the world know what lay behind the facade I had spent so many years crafting and constructing? I could not face that. No, that I could not allow. Therefore Michelle had to die. I knew I shouldn't reproach myself for what she had forced me to do. She had got what she deserved.

Now I must wait, as I have waited in the past, careful to give nothing away. That detective, Vogel, he was supposed to be clever, wasn't he? I half expected him to burst into my cell at any moment and declare that he was ready to charge me with double murder. If he were really clever, possibly other murders too. But time passed. I knew that, if no charge was brought, I could only be kept in custody for thirty-six hours. Unless a magistrates' court allowed a brief extension. And therein lies a most curious aspect of British law. In order to protect the innocent, the guilty share all manner of privileges.

I knew that while I sat in my cell, Vogel's minions would invade my home, sifting through my belongings, trying to find evidence against me. Their search would be in vain. I had covered my tracks well. I'd had to move fast, thanks to Michelle Monahan sticking her nose in. I could have detained her when I surprised her in my flat, and dispatched her there. But that would inevitably have left evidence. I was too clever for that. Instead I snatched her bag, knowing it would contain her phone. I didn't want her dialling 999 or summoning help from any other quarter. It took me a matter of seconds to pull on a hooded tracksuit and gloves and run after her. On the way out I had the presence of mind to snatch up the iron I had been using earlier and throw it, along with Michelle's handbag, into my sports bag which hung on a hook by the front door.

I caught up with Michelle easily. The damage I'd done to her nose made it difficult for her to breathe, which in turn prevented her running as fast as she otherwise might. Her home was too far to run to in her condition, so I'd calculated that she would head for her place of work, thinking she would be safe there. Driven by fear, prey will instinctively scramble for the lair. And so I had set my course accordingly, aiming to intercept her at the entrance to the narrow alleyway, trusting in the Lord to deliver her to me and to ensure that we would be alone. And He did. But I'd had to be fast. One blow with the iron and she fell back into my arms. It had been so easy then to place my gloved hands around her neck and squeeze the life out of her.

My skin had not touched her skin. The point of the iron must have dug into her skull as it was tinged red with her blood.

I took it away with me in the sports bag. I was certain I had left no traces on her body, no DNA and certainly no finger-prints. It was possible that a microscopic thread or two from my tracksuit could have adhered itself to her clothes, and that modern forensics might detect this. But that tracksuit was about to disappear, along with the iron. The meticulous planning I had done in preparation for Marlena's demise stood me in good stead now. I had a mental checklist already in place, means of disposal already worked out.

The fact that this was a cleaner kill simplified matters. After I dispatched Marlena, my outer garment – the raincoat buttoned to the neck which had puzzled Marlena, though not for long – had been covered with blood. Before leaving her apartment I'd removed it and placed it, along with Alfonso's trainers, now covered in Marlena's blood, into a sturdy plastic bag that I then dropped into a sports bag. Even in central London, someone wearing a blood-soaked coat would attract notice. Underneath my raincoat I'd been wearing a hooded tracksuit. Hoodies are God's gift to the criminally inclined. There may be CCTV on every street corner in London, but in a hoody your anonymity is guaranteed. I'd walked for some time, in ever increasing circles, until I came to the pub by the river, not far from Southwark Bridge. An insalubrious hostelry, but perfect for my present needs, being unprotected by video security and with a gents' toilet that can be accessed from a side hallway without going through the bar. There I changed into the clothes I'd been carrying. Alfonso's incriminating trainers went into a plastic carrier so that I could return them to him later. Everything else I had worn when I killed Marlena was now in the sports bag, along with three bricks. I left the pub, walked to the middle of the bridge and leaned over the parapet as if looking down into the water. It was dark by this time, but I took the time to make sure no one was watching and that no vessels were passing below. Then I dropped my bag into the water.

I didn't have a change of clothes on hand when I dispatched Michelle Monahan, but fortunately my credit card was in the pocket of the tracksuit pants. I drew £200 from a cash machine so I would not leave a trail of plastic. Then I bought a T-shirt from one of the tourist stalls on Trafalgar Square, a hoody – naturally – from another store, jeans from somewhere else, and so on and so on until I had everything I needed.

Then I made my way to the public toilets near Embankment tube station. It wasn't an ideal venue because there were bound to be CCTV cameras in the area, but I hadn't the luxury of time on this occasion. Keeping my hooded head lowered, I entered the cubicle and dressed in the new clothes. The old clothes went into my sports bag, along with Michelle's handbag, the plastic bags that had contained my new purchases, and the iron, which would make a most effective weight.

I pulled up the hood of the sweatshirt and walked to the middle of Waterloo Bridge. There was no time to go further afield or to wait until dark, which made it a risky undertaking, but no one seemed to pay any attention as I dropped the incriminating evidence into the Thames, where it was immediately swallowed by the fast-flowing current.

It was a shame that, thanks to Michelle, all the meticulous work that had gone into framing Alfonso would now be wasted. When I thought of the hours I'd put in, all for nothing, I found myself wishing Michelle were still alive so I could punish her for the nuisance she'd caused. Knowing that Marlena and Alfonso usually crossed paths on a Monday morning – you'd think it was his idol Madonna or some celebrity, the way he gushed about their weekly 'chance' encounter – I had pedalled along Marlena's route through Covent Garden for three successive Mondays until finally the timing came together and Alfonso appeared just as she made to cross the road at Cambridge Circus. I hadn't bargained on a bus approaching the junction just at the moment I'd ridden my stolen bicycle straight at her, but it had turned out well in the end. The 'coincidence' of Alfonso being first on the scene had aroused the suspicions of both Marlena and the police.

I had thought to frame him for the first attack on Michelle by leaving her handbag at his grandmother's flat. Provided the 'mugging' occurred after he finished his shift at the Vine, I was confident he would have no alibi. Ironically, Michelle's comings and goings were so unpredictable that I was still struggling to devise a way to keep track of her when by chance I saw her emerging from Marks and Spencer's in Long Acre and followed her to Marlena's place. While I waited for her to emerge I scoured the surrounding streets for another bike to steal, then lay in wait. When I slammed my fist into her face as she reached the junction of Theobalds Road, I had no idea Alfonso was so close at hand. Truly, God was with me that night. He stands by my shoulder in all that my adversity has driven me to. And he that doeth the will of God abideth for ever.

While Alfonso toddled off to the hospital with Michelle, I had all the time in the world to plant the evidence that would guarantee his arrest. Not his conviction – not at this stage. If he hadn't been released from custody as soon as the requisite thirty-six hours had passed, I would have had to defer my plans for Marlena. But no, everything proceeded as He had ordained.

Until Michelle ruined everything with her prying and probing, leaving me no option but to dispose of her at a time when Alfonso, locked up in a police cell, had the most impeccable of alibis.

After disposing of the bag of clothes off Waterloo Bridge I'd *gone home and cleaned the place thoroughly, wiping every surface Michelle might have touched. Not that it would have been a disaster if I missed the odd print. After all, we were friends, what could be more natural than Michelle having visited my flat?*

There was nothing in my flat to arouse suspicion, nothing to indicate to the police that I was not the man I claimed to be.

For if they were to discover my true identity, even that bumbling Detective Vogel would be capable of piecing it all together.

twenty

Vogel spent most of the latter part of the afternoon in the evidence room. The teams searching the homes of the friends had seized a considerable selection of items including computer equipment, cameras and assorted paperwork. Specialist officers were in the process of checking the contents of hard drives and memory sticks, but so far nothing of significance to the case had been found.

Tiny and Billy had a penchant for gay porn, nothing heavy duty though. Bob had signed on to a lonely hearts site, but had engaged in little activity, not even arranging a single date. George's computer contained a considerable number of photographs of attractive young women, but the pictures were innocent enough.

The personal possessions removed from the group in the custody unit had also been bagged and filed. These included phones, wallets, notebooks and even a couple of non-electronic diaries.

Vogel paid particular attention to the contacts directories in the phones and diaries, and the contents of the wallets.

On each phone Vogel picked the first few numbers from the list of numbers most frequently called and checked them out. The recipient of the first call he made from the numbers on

Greg's list sounded most disconcerted to hear from a police officer. That, however, did not surprise Vogel. He'd already checked the number against the police database and discovered that it belonged to an importer of goods whose shipments were often dubious in origin. While distinctly shifty, it seemed unlikely that these dealings had any connection with the case under investigation.

Similarly, Ari's list of favourites included a well-known drug dealer. That held no interest for Vogel either.

Calls to numbers on the favourites lists of the other five detainees revealed nothing of obvious interest. Vogel planned to put a team onto a more thorough examination of all seven phones and their records, but before handing over had a quick glance down the full contacts directories just in case anything leapt out at him. Something did. It was an entry on Greg's phone for a Tony K. Vogel realized he might be jumping to conclusions, but there was an 0207 287 prefix, which he knew identified it as a Soho number. He hesitated for a moment then pressed dial. An educated voice with just the hint of an indefinable accent answered on the second ring.

'Zodiac Enterprises.'

Vogel ended the call. So Greg had Tony Kwan's office number listed on his phone. It was difficult to imagine what connection Kwan would have with the friends, or, indeed, with all that had befallen them. But Greg knew him well enough, or had at least had sufficient dealings with Kwan, to include him on his contacts list. That might just be the most interesting piece of information so far.

Kwan was a notorious gangland figure, and although nothing had ever been proven he'd been implicated in murders in the past. Even so, Vogel considered him an unlikely suspect. Tony Kwan was ruthless, a deadly adversary who would eliminate a rival or enemy without compunction, but he went about his business efficiently, taking care to ensure that it was conducted without attracting the attention of the authorities. This was not his style. If he'd been behind these killings, the bodies would never have been found.

However, the fact that Kwan was listed on Greg's phone was enough for Vogel to recall Greg for interview. He asked him how he knew Tony Kwan.

'I don't,' said Greg quickly. Rather too quickly, Vogel thought.

'Mr Walker, Tony Kwan's phone number is listed on your phone,' said Vogel wearily.

'Is it?' asked Greg. 'Oh yes, I remember now. I sold him a few crates of malt whisky a while back. They like their whisky, the Chinese.'

'And that was enough for you to enter his phone number in your personal contacts list?'

'More business than personal. I like to be able to keep in touch with my customers, never know when they might want to place another order.'

'And you have had no other dealings with Mr Kwan?'

'No. Why would I?'

I have no idea, thought Vogel, but I'd stake this year's backgammon winnings that you bloody well have, big time.

'Mr Walker, you do know who Tony Kwan is, don't you?' he asked.

''Course I do, Chinese businessman, ain't he?' said Greg ingenuously.

Too irritated to argue, Vogel sent Greg back to his cell. Then he recalled Karen Walker for interview. This could be interesting, he thought.

'Mrs Walker, did you know that your husband has an association with a man called Tony Kwan who is believed to be a high-ranking member of the Triad crime organization?' Vogel asked.

Karen looked shocked to the core.

'Oh my God,' she said. 'No, no, of course I didn't know.'

Then she burst into tears yet again.

After that Vogel turned his attention to the wallets, diaries, notebooks, and other pocket and bag paraphernalia belonging to the arrested seven. The contents of George's wallet proved of interest to Vogel. Tucked into the flat section at the back was a photograph of a striking young woman with cropped white-blonde hair. Vogel removed it and studied it carefully. He held it to the light from the window. The face triggered some memory that he couldn't quite put his finger on. She seemed familiar, yet he had no recollection of her name or where he had encountered her. Had he come across her in the course of a police investigation, either as a perpetrator or a victim? Vogel screwed up his eyes and concentrated hard. Try as he might, the answer eluded him. Perhaps his mind was playing tricks on him, trying to create connections where none existed. It had happened in the past, in investigations where the lack of a breakthrough had left him feeling as if he was clutching at straws.

Nonetheless, he decided it was cause enough to reinterview George Kristos.

He placed the photograph which had caught his attention on the interview-room table so that it faced George.

'Could you please tell me who this is?' Vogel asked.

George looked irritated rather than uneasy.

'It's my girlfriend,' he said.

'I see, sir. Would you mind telling me her name?'

'Carla. She's called Carla. What the heck does she have to do with any of this? She's never even met any of the Sunday Clubbers.'

'All the same, I should very much like to talk to her.' Vogel opened his notepad. 'I'll need her full name and address.'

'Carla Karbusky. I don't have her address.'

Vogel's antennae wiggled, instantly on the alert.

'Are you telling me you don't have your girlfriend's address?'

George shifted in his chair. He looked uncomfortable.

'She's Polish, she's not been in the country very long. She stays with friends.'

'I see. Does she work?'

'Yes, I think so. I'm not sure. She wants to study over here, as a mature student, only she hasn't got a college place yet.'

'You don't know very much about this girlfriend of yours, Mr Kristos, do you?' Vogel persisted.

George blushed. 'I know all I need to know,' he muttered.

Then he attempted what seemed to be a sort of knowing leer, as if indicating that his comment was a reference to matters sexual. Vogel didn't think it worked very well.

'Where did you meet her?' he persisted.

'I just bumped into her in the street,' said George. Then, as if realizing that he sounded wary and defensive, he switched gear and became effusive: 'Literally. We collided. She dropped her bag. I picked it up and asked her if she'd like to have a cup of coffee. One thing led to another.'

George leered again.

Vogel stared at him.

He reached for the padded envelope on the table in front of him and tipped out George's phone, still in its polythene evidence bag. Slipping on a pair of latex gloves, Vogel removed the phone and held it out towards George.

'Presumably you have Carla's phone number?' he enquired.

George frowned.

'Naturally.'

'And so you have it listed in your phone?'

George hesitated for a split second. Or did he? Vogel wasn't sure of anything any more. Then George nodded.

Vogel searched for an entry for Carla. There did not appear to be one. He frowned and held out the phone across the table again.

'Then perhaps you would point her number out to me, Mr Kristos,' Vogel instructed.

'Scroll down,' said George. 'Go to G.'

Vogel did so. George pointed at an entry. Vogel was puzzled by what he saw.

'Mr Kristos, this number is not listed under the name of Carla or Karbusky. It is simply listed as GF. Could you explain that to me, please?'

'It's obvious, isn't it?' said George chippily. 'GF for girlfriend.'

'I see, and is there any particular reason for that manner of listing?'

'I'd have thought that was obvious too,' said George. 'When you get through girlfriends at the rate I do, it's easier to list 'em that way. I just change the number. Don't have to bother with a new name or anything like that.'

He looked pleased with himself.

Vogel didn't know what to make of him. Was the man being serious? And was his behaviour suspicious or was it simply a display of rather unpleasant bravado?

'So you consider yourself to be something of a ladies' man, do you, Mr Kristos?'

'Obvious again,' said George, this time smiling what he presumably thought was his charming smile.

He might be a good-looking bastard, thought Vogel, but

he wondered that any woman would be interested in someone who appeared to be so lacking in charm, manners and any kind of respect for women.

While continuing to stare at George, Vogel dialled the number for GF. The call immediately switched to voicemail. Vogel tried again. Same result.

'All right, Mr Kristos, you can go back to your cell. But rest assured we will continue to check out your Carla Karbusky.'

George just carried on smiling. It seemed to Vogel the kind of smile that indicated that the bearer reckoned he knew something you didn't.

He was beginning to wonder about George Kristos. But he reminded himself that just because the man was an arrogant ratbag it didn't necessarily follow that he was a murderer too.

Vogel was determined to keep the seven for as long as possible. Certainly for the full thirty-six hours allowed without a court appearance. And so they were detained in police cells overnight.

Potential evidence submitted for forensic examination had been fast-tracked, and Clarke had drafted in extra computer forensic officers to fully examine the impounded technical equipment.

Vogel suspected it was rather too much to hope for that his double killer might be not only a sadist but also the kind of sicko who took photographs of his victims or kept an electronic diary of his activities. However, a copper could dream. At the very least they might turn up a fresh lead. Because Vogel was fast running out of leads.

He made his way down to the interview room to start a second day of interviews feeling thoroughly disheartened. He'd hoped by this time to have narrowed down his list of suspects. Instead, he was beginning to wonder if he shouldn't widen the field, work further on the possibility that the killer was not one of the seven friends.

One by one, he reinterviewed the seven suspects. In reality, he was playing for time, keeping the group in custody while the search teams and forensic experts combed through their homes and belongings, desperately trying to find some scrap of useful evidence.

That ploy came to an end with the arrival of Christopher Margolia, now acting on behalf of Billy and Tiny, and May Newman, a headline-grabbing criminal lawyer with a penchant for suing the police for wrongful arrest, who'd been hired, apparently to Ari's surprise, by his father.

While Mustaf Kabul was more than happy to allow his son to face the music unaided when confronted by drug-related charges, when a murder charge loomed it seemed he was prepared to bring in the best lawyer his money could buy.

Margolia, who'd also agreed to act for the other four detainees, and Newman made a formidable team. Newman cited just about every human rights act since Habeas Corpus, or so it seemed to Vogel, and promised dire consequences if her client was not released forthwith. Margolia followed her lead, as indeed he had in court on numerous occasions.

Vogel ultimately had no choice but to comply. The six men and one woman who had been arrested on suspicion of the murder of Michelle Monahan were released on police bail at 5 p.m. precisely that afternoon.

'Looks as if we're going to have to cast the next wider,' said Clarke. 'Get the team out interviewing friends, associates, contacts – the works. Tell them I want no stone left unturned.'

Vogel could see she was getting twitchy. He was too. A double murderer remained on the loose, while the best MIT team in

London, led by a DCI with an exceptional reputation, appeared to be achieving little beyond running around in circles.

'Did you get any hits from HOLMES – homicides matching the MO of Marlena's murder?'

The Home Office Large Major Enquiry System had been set up in the wake of the Yorkshire Ripper investigation to allow rapid and accurate cross-referencing of information between regional police forces. Details of Marlena's murder had been fed into the system, but the only matches had been the two women murdered in King's Cross fifteen years earlier.

'Just the two cases we already knew about,' Vogel told her. 'I dug out the files again and it was as I remembered: the reproductive organs of both victims had been hacked out, and unlike Marlena they had been strangled beforehand. Ari Kabul would have been eleven years old in 1998, which effectively rules him out, but the others could still be in the frame.'

'Fifteen years is a hell of a long interval. Chances are, whoever was responsible is either dead or got taken out of general circulation in some other way, maybe locked up for another crime. Even so, make sure the team keep an eye out for any connections between our boys and what went down in King's Cross. You never know . . .'

Back in the MIT's incident room, Vogel assigned one of the sharpest young DCs, Steve Parlow, the task of following up on the Carla Karbusky lead – if indeed it was a lead and not another dead end. There continued to be no answer from the contact number George Kristos had supplied for her, which had turned out to be a pay-as-you-go phone. This made tracing the owner more difficult, but Vogel was confident that Parlow would eventually succeed. He wanted the young woman found, if only to give him some respite from wracking his brain trying to figure out why her face seemed so familiar.

Meanwhile, he drew up a list of known associates of the friends and ordered that they be brought in for questioning. This included, of course, Johnny the piano-playing boss of Johnny's Place, Cathy the maître d', and several other Johnny's staff, some colleagues of Alfonso's from the Vine, including his immediate boss Leonardo, Justin from Shannon's, Pete the caretaker at Chatham Towers, and Paddy Morgan, the caretaker at Sampford House who had found Marlena's body. There was nothing as yet to indicate the direct involvement of any of these, and the usual procedure would have been to conduct informal interviews elsewhere or invite them to attend Charing Cross police station by appointment. But Vogel had them picked up and brought in for formal questioning. He'd taken his kid gloves off and thrown them away.

There was one exception. Tony Kwan. Vogel wasn't yet ready to summon the Triad boss to the police station, and he certainly wasn't going to send a load of plods to pick Kwan up. Apart from any other consideration, if you started something with a man like Kwan, if you appeared to be taking him on, then you had better be prepared to finish it. Or else. And Vogel didn't like to think about the 'or else'.

A few years previously a couple of Met detectives based at West End Central had been investigating an upmarket protection racket centring on some of the major Oxford Street stores. They found evidence of blackmail, coercion and the use of extreme aggression, all of it pointing to Kwan. Somehow, Kwan got wind of the fact they were closing in on him. Threats were made; the detectives were warned that their families' lives would be in danger if they didn't back off. And fast. One of them, DC Leonard Smith, even claimed to have spotted a man armed with a sniper rifle on a roof overlooking the Savile Row entrance of the Mayfair police station. The top brass had dismissed the detective's claims as pure fantasy, and ultimately both men had taken early retirement from the force. Vogel knew that Len Smith, with whom he'd been friendly, had suffered a nervous breakdown from which he had never recovered. The case was ultimately closed due to lack of evidence. To Vogel it seemed the Met had done what it had been told to do. Backed off. The whole matter had left a nasty taste in his mouth.

It was hard to blame those within the force who had taken the decision not to proceed. Kwan's reputation was such that he was generally regarded as untouchable. Vogel did not know whether that was true. He did not operate at that kind of level within the Met. He did know that he was afraid of Tony Kwan. Very afraid. Anyone with half a brain would be. Vogel was a family man. He had a wife and a daughter. A vulnerable daughter. He wasn't the gung-ho, have-a-go-hero type. He would have liked nothing better than to forget about that particular entry in Greg Walker's phone, to accept Walker's glib explanation of a simple purchase of whisky. But he couldn't. As was often the case, he found himself resolved to follow a course of action he knew he might live to regret. Or did he just hope he might live to regret it? Vogel told himself off for letting his imagination run riot.

He was going to Soho to see Tony Kwan, and that was that.

It was almost 10 p.m. when he arrived, alone, at the Zodiac gambling club. Like Greg, he knew that Tony Kwan operated out of an office in the club. Unlike Greg, Vogel had never set foot inside the building. But he knew enough about Kwan to be confident that he would still be in his office. According to the legend that meandered its way around the bevied echelons of the Met, there was a sumptuous bedroom at the rear of the private office where Kwan frequently entertained whichever of the acquiescent young women who surrounded him might currently be taking his fancy. Kwan only returned to the gated complex at Virginia Water – his official residence and that of his wife, his sons and his daughters-in-law and their children – a couple of nights a week, and for Sunday lunches when he presided over a veritable banquet of dim sum and played at being the benevolent and doting head of his personal dynasty.

The two dinner-jacketed heavies on the door stepped forward and blocked Vogel's way when he approached the entrance. With his horn-rimmed glasses, crumpled cords, and diffident manner, Vogel might not have looked much like most people's idea of a policeman, but these men were trained to spot a copper.

Vogel introduced himself and asked very politely if he might see Mr Kwan.

The smaller of the heavies spoke in a high-pitched voice which somehow added to his menace, as did his distinctly London accent.

'The boss don't see no one without an appointment,' he announced.

'I wonder if you could ask him if he might make an exception in my case,' said Vogel, obsequious now. There was, however, an edge to his next remark: 'We have matters to discuss which may be of mutual interest.'

The heavy subjected him to careful scrutiny, then stepped back into the doorway and began to speak quietly into the radio mike clipped to his lapel.

There was considerable noise in the street and coming from inside the club. Vogel couldn't make out what the man was saying. The result, however, was that the doors opened and Vogel was escorted through the club to the private door at the back, then up the rickety staircase to Kwan's private offices on the third floor. The same route that Greg had taken just days before.

Vogel should not have been surprised by the lavishly appointed interior, having been forewarned by colleagues. Nevertheless his jaw dropped.

The ever-courteous Kwan got up from behind his desk and came towards Vogel. He stopped a few feet away and bowed his head very slightly. Vogel did the same.

'And so, Mister Vogel, we meet at last,' said Kwan.

Obviously the doorman would have supplied his name, but Kwan's choice of greeting implied that he already knew about Vogel.

'Indeed,' he replied.

He'd often wondered what it would be like to meet Tony Kwan. He had wondered if he would be intimidated. Particularly on the man's own territory. Oddly, he felt no fear. So far, at any rate, he remained intent on his mission.

As if aware of Vogel's thoughts, Kwan continued: 'And how is your dear wife, and your daughter? In better health, I hope?'

Vogel felt something then, all right. He hadn't expected Kwan to know anything about his personal life, especially given the fact he'd arrived unannounced, so Kwan had not had the opportunity to do any homework. A chill ran down Vogel's spine. He was especially sensitive to any reference to his daughter. How did Kwan know she was anything other than entirely well? Was this just his way of displaying the depth of his knowledge of the Met in general and Acting Detective Inspector Vogel in particular, or was it a veiled threat? Only one thing was certain, thought Vogel: it was not a simple enquiry after the welfare of his family. Nonetheless he responded as if he had taken it that way.

'They are both quite well, thank you, Mr Kwan,' he said, struggling to keep his voice level.

'To what do I owe this great pleasure?' enquired Kwan softly.

'I understand you know Greg Walker,' responded Vogel, making a huge effort to put all other considerations out of his mind.

Kwan nodded almost imperceptibly.

'Ah,' he said. 'I believe you are heading the inquiry into the recent murder of two women in this area, both of whom have a connection with Mr Walker, I understand.'

'Indeed,' said Vogel again.

Then he waited, aware that Kwan was taking control of their meeting. Vogel didn't mind. All he wanted was to find out what Kwan knew. And he sensed that the Triad boss had every intention of telling him.

Kwan cut right to the chase.

'You did not come here this evening to enquire whether I or my people had any involvement in this?'

'Of course not,' lied Vogel.

'Of course not,' repeated Kwan. 'We do not cut up old women and remove their reproductive organs.'

Vogel didn't speak. The gruesome details of Marlena's killing had not been released to the media. Miraculously, they hadn't even been leaked on the net. If anyone else had divulged such knowledge, it would have aroused his suspicions. In Tony Kwan's case, however, it was only to be expected. Both Marlena and Michelle had died within Kwan's domain. The Triad leader was protective of his territory. He kept himself informed of any villains unconnected with him who were bold enough to operate on his patch. He would want to know who was behind such brutality, and why. Or that's what Vogel was banking on.

Vogel waited for Kwan to continue. The Triad took his time.

'My people have been making enquiries, on my instructions,' said Kwan eventually. 'We have our contacts, people you may not necessarily have dealings with, Mr Vogel . . .'

Kwan stroked his sleek black hair with the manicured fingers of one hand. Vogel thought he might be wearing clear nail varnish. His face revealed nothing. Vogel tried to appear equally inscrutable. He suspected he did not do it terribly well.

'We also, Mr Vogel, have our own methods. Methods that are neither appropriate nor available to the Metropolitan Police.'

Kwan stretched his lips back from his teeth. Vogel assumed the man was trying to smile. He made his own attempt in response, but his mouth was so dry he feared he was unsuccessful.

Kwan turned and walked back to his desk. Suddenly he raised a clenched fist and smashed it down on the glass with such force that Vogel flinched, fearing the glass might break. It didn't.

Kwan raised his fist again and held it up towards Vogel almost in a fascist-style salute. The part of his hand that had struck the desk was already beginning to swell. Still Kwan gave no sign of discomfort, but his face contorted in anger.

'I have learned nothing! My people have found nothing!' he shouted. 'I know no more than the police. Nothing!'

Kwan spat out the word 'police', loading it with contempt. Vogel winced.

Then as abruptly as he had flown into a rage, Kwan sat down. Vogel could see the man was making a supreme effort to compose himself. He swallowed nervously, hoping that his anxiety didn't show.

Kwan held out both his hands, palms upwards, as if in resignation.

'I know nothing, Mr Vogel,' he repeated, but this time in his usual quiet and courteous voice. 'I have heard nothing. Neither have my people. It seems we may have a madman on the loose. You and I are on the same side here, Mr Vogel, I assure you. I am in business. I understand business, and the unpleasant necessities it sometimes brings. But this is something different. Something is happening under my nose, yet I cannot see it. Do you appreciate what I am saying?'

'Oh yes, Mr Kwan, I most certainly do,' said Vogel.

Tony Kwan saw these crimes as a violation of his domain. Moreover, people feared him in part because they thought him omnipotent, that nothing escaped his attention. Yet his efforts to identify the person responsible had been no more successful than Vogel's. This was an intolerable personal affront.

Vogel, too, was a proud man. He had no illusions about his own omnipotence, but his failure to identify the killer had delivered a severe blow to his pride and he felt it keenly.

'I am not happy, Mr Vogel, I am not happy at all,' said Kwan.

'And neither, Mr Kwan,' replied Vogel, 'am I.'

twenty-one

In their respective homes, the various friends struggled to come to terms with the aftermath of arrest and incarceration.

Tiny and Billy clung to each other, mentally and physically, seeking comfort.

Suddenly, Billy broke free of his partner's embrace and asked: 'Why did you go looking at puppies without telling me, darling?'

'I told you, I told you as soon as we left the police station,' Tiny replied. 'You'd said you weren't ready yet for another dog. You were quite definite about that. I had this crazy idea that if I found some gorgeous little puppy, and maybe showed you a photograph or something, you wouldn't be able to resist. I don't just *want* another dog, sweetheart, I feel like I *need* a dog about the place again. Surely you understand?'

Billy pulled away from him.

'Look, Tiny, I'm sorry, but this has been on my mind all evening,' he said. 'You did go to Uxbridge, darling, didn't you?'

Tiny stared at him for several seconds. Tears formed in his big brown eyes.

'I can't believe you're asking me that, Billy,' he said. 'Not you, you of all people.'

Murder creates many victims. There are grieving friends and relations of the deceased, the neighbours, colleagues and casual acquaintances shocked by the proximity of such violence. Then there are the suspects, not only those arrested and questioned as part of the official investigation, but those who fall under suspicion from their own family members and friends. And even if they have no doubts about each other's innocence, there is always the question of blame. Would the young woman murdered after a night out with a group of mates still be alive if one of them had taken the trouble to walk her home? Could a child's life have been saved if the parent or sibling or friend who was supposed to be looking after them had been more vigilant? Should we somehow be able to spot the paedophile, the rapist, the psychopath in our midst before they commit some terrible crime?

In the face of such guilt and recrimination, relationships that hitherto seemed rock-solid suddenly slide into a quagmire of doubt, fear and grief. Successful careers flounder. Men and women who have held down demanding jobs, led productive lives, cease to function. Children and young people who have previously been promising students, happy and fun-loving, lose the ability to learn or play. Decent human beings of all ages go off the rails, dropping out, running away, turning to violence. Those who have only dabbled in drink or recreational drugs, lose the ability to keep their habit in check.

Lives are wrecked, beyond all hope of retrieval.

Bob spent the evening alone, unable to eat, drink or sleep. He wanted to pick up the phone, to at least speak to another human being, to call a friend. But he couldn't trust his friends any more, could he? He wanted to phone his son, only it had been so long since he'd spoken to Danny that he couldn't just call him, out of the blue, and pour his heart out. And his friends, the little group in which he had once been so grateful to be included, were murder suspects, who, just like him, stood accused of killing one of their own. Bob felt totally alone. What had been done could not be undone. He could see no reason to carry on living. If he had the courage, he thought, he would find a way to end what passed for his life. But he didn't have the courage. So instead he paced the perimeters of his cramped flat and the terrace which usually brought him solace but offered him none tonight. Only at dawn did he fall into a fitful sleep on his sofa.

Ari locked the door of his apartment, ignored the pleas of his mother and the fury of his father, lifted his bathroom cabinet from the wall, removed a small panel of plaster from behind and took from the cavity his reserve stash of crack cocaine. To his relief, a full-scale police search had failed to locate it. Then he snorted his way to oblivion.

Alfonso also spent the night seeking oblivion, which, apart from his brief and unsuccessful attempt to return to work and carry on as if everything was normal, had more or less been his only aim in life since being released from Brixton Prison. He too had locked himself away, in a far less salubrious bedroom than Ari's, at his mother's Dagenham home, with a litre-bottle of supermarket whisky. He had sunk into drunken depression, made worse by his mother's near-hysterical response to all that had happened. She seemed to have barely stopped crying.

George also shut himself away in his flat. He passed the evening tending his orchids, trimming back any dying stalks, giving them feed. George loved the way orchids responded, sometimes quite spectacularly, to just a little TLC. He wondered if he were getting like Bob, who often gave the impression that he preferred plants to people. Certainly George wanted no other companionship that night. He felt utterly drained.

Greg and Karen had barely spoken to each other since their release. Karen was no longer in tears. She just seemed angry.

Very angry. Mostly with Greg. It didn't occur to Greg that Karen could have had anything to do with the death of their two friends, but she was now making her suspicions of him quite clear. He understood that she must feel wounded, and indeed have doubts about him, since learning details of his past life that he had never previously revealed to her. But she appeared to suddenly believe him capable of almost anything, as if their many years of happy fruitful union meant nothing to her. Or that was the way Greg saw it. And he found that far more distressing than having been arrested and held in custody.

As soon as they arrived at their flat Karen called her mother, who was both babysitting and dog-minding, and asked if she would keep dogs and children for another night, and take the kids to school in the morning. Karen fielded her mother's questions and expressions of concern and ended the call summarily. Then she turned her attention to her husband.

'I want to know everything that's going on,' she stormed. 'Why didn't you tell me about this Mr Kwan? Am I married to a gangster? Is that the truth of it?'

'Of course not,' Greg responded, stricken. 'I'm no gangster. I could have become one, though. You know the sort of kids I was running with back then. But once I met you, that was it. All I wanted was you and our kids. To become a decent family man. And I've done my best. You must know that.'

'All I know is what you've told me,' Karen replied, her voice loud and shrill. 'And I don't know what the hell to believe any more.'

She began to weep, unstoppable tears of rage and despair. Greg tried to console her, to reassure her. Desperate to get things back to the way they had been, he tried to explain.

'Look, Kwan got in touch with me, not the other way round. I hadn't seen him or heard from him for years. He wanted me to do something for him – I still don't know what. I told him no. Then my tyres got slashed and there was the brick through the window. I reckoned it had to be him, that's why I kept telling you it had nothing to do with all the other stuff. To get him off our backs, I went to see him, told him I'd do whatever it was he wanted. He hasn't called on me yet and chances are, he won't. That's how he operates. The whole thing could've been a test, a way of putting me in my place. You never know with Kwan. But I had to go along with it, Karen. You must see that. I was afraid for you, and the kids.'

'Don't you try to put the blame on me!' Karen shouted. 'None of this has got anything to do with me. Why didn't you go to the police, you stupid idiot?'

'You don't understand—'

'Oh yes I do. Leopards don't change their bleedin' spots. I knew you'd been a bit of a wild one, but I thought you'd changed. And I never knew you were involved with them Chinese gangsters.'

'Look, I'm not—'

'Yes, you bloody are. And if you think anything of me and our kids, Greg, you'd better get in touch with that man Kwan right now – right now, d'you hear – and tell him once and for all that you want nothing more to do with him.'

Greg opened his mouth to explain that he didn't dare do that. That she had no idea what Kwan would do to someone he regarded as one of his own who turned his back on the Triads. But he knew Karen wouldn't listen. There was nothing he could say that would make her understand, any more than anything he could say would console or reassure her.

Automatically he reached into his pocket for his mobile phone. Then cursed under his breath. It was still impounded. He picked up the house phone, dialled directory enquiries and asked for a number for the Zodiac Club. The number he was given was the public one, not the private number for Kwan's office. It rang a few times, then he was connected to a message service.

Conscious of Karen's eyes on him, he began to speak:

'This is a message for Mr Kwan from Greg, I mean Gregory Walker.' Greg paused, desperate to find the right words, aware that there were no words for this situation. For this man.

'I, uh, just wanted to apologize, to say, I'm sorry,' he continued. 'But I'm afraid I will not be, um, available to work for you after all. Not in the near future, that is. I have, uh, family problems, you see. I hope you will understand, Mr Kwan. I know what a great family man you are. And, uh, well, I just want to say how sorry I am.'

He ended the call.

'Why don't you grovel a bit?' asked Karen.

Greg held out his hands. 'I've done what you asked, haven't I, doll?' he pleaded. 'What more do you want?'

'Too little too bleedin' late. What I want is some honesty from my alleged husband.'

'"Alleged husband" – what the fuck are you going on about?'

The row escalated. Greg's phone call to Kwan seemed to have done nothing to defuse the situation. Karen remained furious. Greg became furious. They argued on and on. The neighbours to one side knocked on the wall. Several times. Neither of them even heard the knocking.

'You can't seriously believe that I murdered Marlena and Michelle?' asked Greg, incredulous.

'Can't I?' Karen shouted the words at the top of her voice. 'Why the hell not? Maybe Tony Kwan told you to do it. Maybe you enjoy killing women. Maybe that's something else I don't know about—'

Greg took a step towards her. She was the love of his life. She was his life. He had never looked at another woman since he'd found her. She had always been his rock, supporting him in everything he'd ever done or attempted to do. Until now. Over and over, she kept telling him he wasn't the man she'd thought he was. And he'd tried so hard to be that man. But apparently he'd failed. What did that make him? Did she genuinely believe he was capable of murdering Michelle and Marlena? No, she couldn't, she had to know him better than that. She had to. Surely she was just trying to hurt him.

He reached out a hand, his eyes pleading. He touched her gently on one cheek.

She pulled back, swatting his hand away.

'Don't come near me! Don't you dare touch me, don't you ever touch me again, you evil bastard,' Karen yelled.

Something snapped in Greg. Without realizing what he was doing, he slapped her. He had never in his life hit a woman, let alone his beloved Karen, but it was done before he knew what had happened.

She cried out, just once, and looked at him in horror. Tears formed in her eyes. She wiped them away with the back of one hand, and drew herself up, looking him in the eye as she did so. It was as if she was determined not to break down, not to show any weakness.

For what seemed a very long time neither of them spoke. It was Greg who broke the silence, horrified at what he had done.

'I'm sorry, love. I am so sorry.'

All he wanted was to hold her close, and go on holding her all through the night. But the slap had changed everything.

Curiously, Karen's anger seemed to evaporate. When she spoke, her voice was quiet and calm, but her eyes were cold as ice.

'I'm going to bed,' she said. 'Don't try to follow me into the bedroom. I think you'd better sleep out here on the sofa, don't you?'

Greg just stared at the floor. He didn't look up until she'd left the room. Soon afterwards he heard the key to their bedroom door turn. The lock he'd installed so they could ensure privacy from the kids, keep their sex life going strong. And some of the best sex had been make-up sex, after a row. But that wasn't going to happen tonight.

He so wanted to hammer on the door, beg Karen to let him in, try again to explain everything. At least get her to forgive him for hitting her. To make her believe it would never ever happen again.

But he had enough sense to know that would only make matters worse. If they could be any worse. So instead he took a blanket from the airing cupboard and curled up on the sofa.

Unable to sleep, afraid to move in case she heard him and in doing so he angered her further, he lay there in the sitting room and waited for morning, when he hoped he might be able to begin to put things right.

twenty-two

That next morning Vogel was at his desk at 7.30 a.m. in spite of having been late home the previous night.

He checked through his messages and scanned the reports that had been filed overnight. There had been no progress, no sign of a breakthrough. Forensics had drawn a blank. The computer boys had got nowhere.

An hour later, as Vogel was devouring the organic egg sandwich his wife had packed for him, DC Parlow burst in, flushed with excitement.

'Guv, I've been through electoral registers, employment and immigration records, the lot,' he announced. 'I've found three Carla Karbuskys in the UK. One is sixty, one's a ten-year-old child, and the third, probably about the right age, lives in Cardiff. Only she swears she's never heard of George Kristos and—'

'Right,' Vogel interrupted, about to issue further instructions. Parlow, positively pink with excitement now, didn't give him the opportunity.

'I haven't finished, guv. I just got word on that pay-as-you-go phone. We tracked it down, and you'll never guess what . . .'

'Get on with it, Parlow,' snapped Vogel. 'I'm in no mood for guessing.'

'Sorry, guv. The phone was purchased by George Kristos. It's his bloody phone. If you ask me, that girlfriend of his doesn't exist. He made her up. It's all a great big lie, and if he can lie about something like that, what else is he lying about, eh guv?'

'Calm down, Parlow. One step at a time,' said Vogel, even though it was all he could do to keep calm himself. He could feel that familiar buzz somewhere in his solar plexus that always occurred when he was on the brink of cracking a case.

'Could the network tell us anything else?' Vogel continued.

'You bet, guv. They've just emailed me a list of calls and a transcript of recent messages. Not a lot of activity, but what there is is all from Kristos's other phone, the one we detained. He was sending text messages and leaving voicemails for this woman who probably doesn't exist, on a phone that is actually his. What d'you suppose that's all about, guv?'

Parlow handed Vogel a sheet of A4, the contents of which he was able to swiftly assimilate.

There were only two messages, both left on the same Sunday evening a couple of months earlier, just before the start of the chain of events which had culminated in the deaths of Marleen McTavish, known as Marlena, and Michelle Monahan.

Hi, Carla darling, it's me, read the first one. *I'm calling from Johnny's – I'm with the gang, Sunday Club. Like I told you about. Don't suppose you can join us, can you? I'd love to see you and so would the rest of the bunch. If you can bear it, do come. Love you, baby. Kiss kiss.*

The other message had been sent half an hour or so later on the same night, when George had again claimed to be attempting to contact his girlfriend.

Oh dear, I'm still getting your voicemail, baby, and I soooooo want to speak to you. Please come to Johnny's if you can. This lot are driving me mad. They're desperate to meet you. But don't be put off. They're all right, honest. All my love, baby-face. More kisses.

Vogel folded the piece of paper and put it in his pocket. Then he looked up at Parlow.

'What are you waiting for?' he asked. 'I'll put Clarke in the picture, you get us a couple of uniforms and organize a car. Then let's bring Kristos in. We need the devious bastard to tell us exactly what he's up to.'

Parlow beamed. 'You bet, boss,' he said, taking off at a run to do Vogel's bidding.

Vogel called after him. 'One more thing, Parlow.'

The young man looked anxiously back over a shoulder.

'Bloody well done,' said Vogel.

Vogel called his superior officer, who had not yet arrived at Charing Cross, on her mobile to bring her up to speed. Then he rushed out of the station to catch up with Parlow, who was already behind the wheel of a CID car.

It took them only minutes to get to George's apartment block. George was dressed, in jeans and a black sweater. There was a bag of pastries on his kitchen table. He said he'd been out to buy them fresh, and was about to take them round to his neighbour Marnie, as was his habit.

At almost exactly 9 a.m. Vogel again formally arrested George, who seemed more baffled than angry.

'Why are you doing this?' he asked. 'You only released me yesterday afternoon.'

'We will discuss that during a formal interview back at the station,' said Vogel.

Greg finally dropped off at dawn, though it was more of a doze than proper sleep. He was woken by Karen going into the kitchen just after nine. Usually they were both up much earlier, getting the kids off to school and themselves ready for work. He wondered if she had really slept until then, or lain fitfully awake for most of the night as he had done.

He listened to the usual morning noises, the clatter of crockery and cutlery, the hiss of the kettle. It all sounded so normal, even though this horrible morning was anything but normal. Then he heard Karen talking on the phone. He couldn't catch what she was saying so he had no idea who she might be speaking to. He decided he would just stay put rather than risk inflaming matters by making the first approach. Eventually Karen came into the sitting room. There was a faint pink mark down one side of her face. Greg felt ashamed of himself. It had been unforgivable for him to strike out at her, and he still couldn't believe what he had done.

Karen was carrying two mugs of tea, one of which, rather to his surprise, she handed to him.

He felt momentarily encouraged. Maybe things would turn out OK after all.

He couldn't have been more wrong.

'I think we need some time to ourselves. I do, anyway, while I sort myself out and decide what to do next,' she said. 'I certainly don't want to be with you right now, Greg. So I'm going to spend the day with Sally.'

Sally was Karen's sister. She lived with her lesbian partner in Hounslow. Karen would have said she was the last person in the world who could ever be accused of being homophobic; she had gay friends, and was totally opposed to any kind of prejudice based on people's sexuality. Nonetheless Greg suspected that she'd never quite come to terms with her own sister's sexuality. The two women weren't entirely comfortable with each other. And yet, on the very first occasion there had ever been a problem in their marriage, it was to her sister that Karen now turned.

He knew better than to argue. He tried to remain calm, to appear affectionate and concerned without attempting to get close. But he hated the thought of Karen discussing their differences with her sister rather than him. He wished she would stay at home so that they could sort things out together, just as they had always done.

Karen, it seemed, was not interested.

She showered, dressed, spent some time putting on rather more make-up than she usually wore, and an hour or so later bade him a cursory goodbye as she prepared to leave the flat.

She was wearing her best, and tightest, jeans, with the shiny black ankle boots he had given her for Christmas, and that chunky black leather waistcoat with the little steel spikes on the shoulders which was quite butch, yet, Greg reckoned, somehow made her appear all the more feminine.

She had washed her spiky red hair and it gleamed in the morning sun. Greg loved Karen's retro punk look, and he thought she looked even sexier than usual. Certainly her appearance betrayed nothing of the events of last night and the previous day.

Irritated by this, he stood in the doorway, blocking her exit. 'Won't you at least try to talk things through for a bit, before you go?' he asked. 'We could go across the road to Starbucks, if you like. Their cappuccinos always give you a lift, don't they? A change of scene might do us good. What about it, darling?'

'No,' said Karen. 'Right now, Greg, I'm not up for a cosy chat with you over a cup of coffee.'

Greg's irritation grew. All he wanted was to put things right. And he had tried. Really tried. He'd even made that phone call to Kwan in an effort to appease her, totally against his better judgement. He was prepared to do anything, risk anything, for the good of his marriage. But Karen didn't want to know.

Perhaps because he was afraid, he allowed his temper to get the better of him again.

'Oh go fuck yourself,' he said.

Vogel conducted the interview with George himself, backed up by Parlow, who sat to his left in the small, windowless interview room. George sat opposite Vogel, alongside his lawyer, Christopher Margolia, who'd arrived at the station within half an hour of his presence being requested by George.

Vogel stared hard at George while Parlow went through the preliminary formalities of stating the names of those present, and the time of the start of the interview, for the video record.

Could this be their murderer? Vogel thought George still looked more bewildered than anything else. From the moment of his second arrest he had proclaimed his total bafflement, insisting he had done nothing to warrant further questioning, and that he had no idea what could have led Vogel and his team to re-arrest him. At least he appeared to have shed his earlier arrogance.

Now he sat in his recycled paper suit looking around the interview room, waiting for the interview to begin. He did not appear unduly distressed. He certainly wasn't in a panic. Indeed, he seemed quite calm.

Vogel once more placed the photograph found in George's wallet in front of him.

'Would you please tell me again, Mr Kristos, who this young woman is?'

A flicker of annoyance passed over George's face, but when he replied his voice was level and conversational. 'My girlfriend, Carla,' he said.

Vogel then placed in front of George a piece of paper bearing the printed phone number George had earlier pointed out on his impounded phone.

'And do you recognize this phone number, Mr Kristos?'

George nodded.

'So would you like to tell me whose number it is?'

'I told you already, it's my Carla's.'

Was it Vogel's imagination or was Kristos blinking more rapidly than was normal? He wasn't sure.

'Mr Kristos, we have managed to trace that number, and presumably you will not be surprised to learn that it is the number of a pay-as-you-go mobile phone which you bought last year with your Visa credit card, the last four digits of which are 5006. We have also traced a later payment you made for that phone from the same card.'

George shrugged. Vogel noticed that he was frowning.

'Would you like to comment on that, Mr Kristos?'

George seemed to be making an enormous effort to look nonchalant.

'So what?' he asked eventually.

Vogel kept his manner easy.

'Mr Kristos, it would seem that this phone does not belong to the woman you say is your girlfriend. Moreover, we have reason to believe that Carla Karbusky does not exist. We have made extensive enquiries and been unable to trace the young woman whose picture you keep in your wallet. Perhaps you would like to clear this matter up for us?'

George's frown deepened. He remained silent.

'My client does not wish to answer that question at this stage,' said Margolia.

Vogel ignored him. It was his turn to frown.

'Mr Kristos,' he persisted. 'I do not believe that this photograph is of your girlfriend. Perhaps you do not have a girlfriend.

And perhaps you would like to tell us who the woman in this picture really is? Would you do that for me, Mr Kristos?'

George leaned forward in his chair and looked down at the photograph on the desk before him. It was almost as if he were seeking inspiration from it.

Margolia seemed about to interject again, but George suddenly looked up at Vogel and said, 'OK, I suppose I'd better tell you. I don't have much choice, do I? Carla doesn't exist. And I don't have a girlfriend. People tell me I'm a good-looking bloke, but I never seem to be able to keep a girl for more than five minutes. All the Sunday Clubbers, my mates, they tease me rotten about it. Have done for ages. So last year I thought I'd put a stop to it. I invented Carla. I bought the pay-as-you-go and programmed the number into my own phone so I could be seen to be calling my girlfriend, leaving her messages and so on. It wasn't as if I could bring her to meet 'em, could I?'

George's cheeks had turned pink. He looked flustered. But then, he was an extremely proud young man. Indeed, Vogel had found him arrogant. Perhaps, having gone to such lengths to create a fictional girlfriend, Kristos was simply embarrassed at being caught out.

Vogel looked down at the photograph on the desk. He'd been frustrated by it from the start. He still had a feeling that he knew the young woman, but he was no nearer to recalling who she was.

'So who is this woman in the photograph, Mr Kristos?' he asked.

George held out both hands, palms upwards. 'I've no idea. I cut it out of some magazine, scanned it into my computer and reprinted it. That's all.'

'Which magazine did you find the picture in?'

'I don't know. I don't buy magazines, so it must have been one I found somewhere. Probably someone left it lying on a seat on the tube, or a bus.'

'I see. Why this particular picture?'

'No reason. I thought she looked nice, that's all.'

'So you gave her the name of Carla and built up all this pretence around her, even to the extent of buying a second telephone so you could call this non-existent person. All because you wanted your friends to believe that you had a girlfriend when you didn't. Is that so, Mr Kristos?'

'That's about the size of it, yes.'

'Mr Kristos, could you tell me please where you were in 1998?'

Vogel had changed tack without warning and he watched the reaction of his interviewee extremely closely.

'What?' asked George. He just looked puzzled.

Vogel repeated the question.

'Uh, 1998.' George did some counting on his fingers.

'I was in college, studying drama,' he said eventually. 'I left in 2000.'

'Could you tell me the name of this college?'

'The Willesden Academy of Performing Arts,' he said. 'Manchester.'

Manchester, thought Vogel, getting on for three hours away from London's King's Cross in 1998. Those kind of logistics obviously did not mean that Kristos couldn't have been responsible for the earlier murders, but it did make it more unlikely. Vogel continued to study George carefully. The other man continued to look merely puzzled. Vogel would get it checked out, of course, but he suspected George was telling the truth.

'I think you'll find the place has closed down,' said George, almost as if he were reading Vogel's mind.

'You haven't asked why I wanted to know where you were in 1998,' said Vogel.

George shrugged. He did quite a lot of shrugging. 'I assumed you'd tell me when you were good and ready,' he said.

He has not totally lost his arrogance, thought Vogel.

'Two young women were murdered in the King's Cross district of London in October and November 1998,' he said. 'We have reason to believe that their killer may also have murdered Marleen McTavish, and perhaps Michelle Monahan.'

George raised both eyebrows.

'So you thought you might try to pin that on me too, did you?' he asked. 'Just because I claimed to have a girlfriend when I didn't.'

'It's a bit more than that, Mr Kristos,' said Vogel, unsure whether it was or not.

'I think you are clutching at straws, Detective Inspector,' said George.

You really are an arrogant little bastard, thought Vogel. But unfortunately you're not far wrong.

'You should realize that everything you have told us concerning your fabrication of the fictional Carla Karbusky will be fully investigated,' said Vogel, trying to ensure that neither the tone of his voice nor his facial expression gave any indication of his inner frustration.

'I don't see what the big deal is. OK, so I invented a girlfriend to get my mates off my back. I know it was daft, but it made me feel better about myself. But, it's not a crime to say you have a girlfriend when you haven't. It's not illegal, is it Mr Vogel?'

George seemed ingenuous enough. But there was something unnerving about him, as if, even when under arrest, he was playing a game. Vogel didn't know what to make of it all.

'No, it's not illegal,' he replied evenly.

'No. And it doesn't make me a murderer, either, does it?'

'No,' said Vogel again. And with that he got up from his chair and walked out of the interview room, leaving Parlow to complete the formalities.

Kristos was dead right. The man's behaviour was curious. A little weird even. But that didn't make him a murderer. And Vogel had no real evidence against him. Not yet anyway.

He marched resolutely into the large office which had been designated for the use of MIT. Vogel had a feeling about George Kristos. His gut instinct told him they could very well have found their man. But his gut instinct wasn't going to persuade a judge and jury.

'I want Kristos's flat turned over again,' he said. 'Get the SOCOs there, and tell them to take the floorboards up, I want them over everything like a rash. And let's dig into his background. Where are his parents? Are they alive? I want everyone in his life spoken to. Let's go right back to his drama school days, and before.'

Vogel surveyed his team. There was a palpable excitement in the air at the prospect they might just have their man in custody. But excitement could be dangerous in these circumstances. It could lead to some vital clue being overlooked. He was determined that no such mistakes would be made in this case.

'If we don't come up with some hard evidence, we will have no option but to release George Kristos. And I do not want to be responsible for putting a killer back out there on the streets.'

twenty-three

Two hours later, just as he was considering having another crack at George, Vogel heard that Karen Walker had been killed.

The first report was that she'd thrown herself in front of a train at Leicester Square tube station and had died instantly.

PC Jessica Harding in Command and Dispatch phoned Vogel with the news as soon as the response team first on the scene called in their report. Karen's body had been identified by the contents of the wallet removed from her handbag. The body itself, Harding told Vogel, was in a condition which would have made any other immediate identification almost impossible.

Vogel was stunned. He did not believe for one moment that Karen had committed suicide. His immediate reaction was that she too had been murdered, presumably by the same individual who killed Marlena and Michelle Monahan.

'When did this happen?' he asked PC Harding. 'Presumably as Karen Walker went under a train, we have a precise time of death?'

'Yes, guv,' answered Jessica Harding. 'Transport police have logged the incident at 10.25 a.m. this morning.'

Vogel leaned over his desk and buried his face in his hands. Had he really got everything so wrong? He and Parlow had arrested George Kristos at 9 a.m., and he was still in custody.

Kristos could not possibly have pushed Karen Walker under a train at 10.25 a.m. For the second time a suspect would have to be released because he was in police custody when a murder occurred. The investigation seemed to be going round in circles.

Vogel reconsidered the possibility of suicide. Karen Walker had been extremely distressed by recent events, not least by her own and her husband's arrest the previous day on suspicion of murder. Even so, she'd seemed so devoted to her children that he could not imagine her leaving them motherless. And in spite of the anger she was feeling towards her husband after discovering that he'd had dealings with Tony Kwan, Greg and Karen had previously enjoyed a good and solid marriage.

No. The detective still did not believe that Karen Walker had committed suicide.

As Vogel saw it, he'd failed once more. The killer had claimed a third victim. And that victim was female, like the previous two – or four, if you counted the 1998 murders. The removal of the reproductive organs certainly indicated that gender was a factor. Should he have arranged for Karen Walker to stay at a safe house instead of returning home?

His thoughts were interrupted by the arrival of Nobby Clarke. She told him to get himself to the scene, leaving her to handle the deployment of the rest of her MIT. Vogel ordered Parlow to commandeer a CID car, for the second time that morning, in order to rush them both to Leicester Square.

In the car he steeled himself for the task ahead. He had once before attended the scene of a train death, and the sight which had presented itself, that time on an over-ground line, remained with him still.

As Vogel had expected, Karen Walker's body was in a horrific state. Both legs had been removed from her body when the train hit her. Worse still, she had been decapitated.

Her body had already been tented off by the time Vogel arrived at Leicester Square station, and the platform closed. It seemed that the British Transport Police were accustomed to such events and handled them with an efficiency born of tragic familiarity. Three BTP officers were on sentry duty stoically preserving the scene. The Home Office pathologist was not yet there, but the SOCOs, who had apparently arrived just before Vogel, were already beginning to go about their business.

The first thing Vogel saw inside the tented area was Karen Walker's head, distorted and discoloured, like a watermelon on a bloodied stem. It lay several feet from the torso to which it had once been attached. And its bulging eyes seemed to be staring at Vogel.

The detective felt his stomach lurch. His head began to spin and he felt sure that this time he would pass out and fall over onto the railway, or maybe onto a bit of the body. The more he tried to fight the disorientating giddiness rising within him, the more consuming it became.

He decided he had no choice but to beat a fast retreat. He backed quickly out of the tent and hoisted himself up onto the platform, trying to breathe deeply and evenly. It was probably half a minute or so before his head stopped spinning, and only then did he become aware of Parlow standing alongside him. The detective constable had obviously taken the opportunity to emulate his superior officer's exit. His skin was a sickly shade of green, and Vogel noticed that he was wiping his mouth with a paper tissue. He glanced down at the grey concrete. Parlow had been sick.

'Sorry, sir,' said the DC.

'Not to worry,' Vogel told the embarrassed officer. 'Could have been much worse. I knew a rookie PC once who, first time on a murder, threw up right over the corpse. SOCOs weren't at all pleased.'

'Bloody 'ell,' said Parlow.

Vogel smiled. 'Right, let's go back in and get this over with,' he said, just as Dr Fitzwarren arrived.

'Good morning, gentlemen. Everything under control?' she asked, glancing pointedly at the mess on the ground by Parlow's feet.

Vogel waited 'til she was out of earshot then told Parlow to take no notice.

And it was with some satisfaction that, as they returned to the tented area, this time following the pathologist, he became aware that even her detachment and iron control seemed to falter when she took in the scattered parts of Karen Walker's body spread across the track.

'First impressions?' he asked.

'Don't be ridiculous, Vogel,' she replied.

'Things are not always as they seem,' said Vogel.

'How very cryptic,' responded Patricia Fitzwarren. 'Have you ever considered compiling crosswords for a living?'

'Yes,' said Vogel.

He didn't know why they were indulging in banter in the face of such horror. But perhaps it was because of it. This kind of behaviour was a common reaction among police officers, doctors, and indeed the staff of all emergency services.

'I bet you have, too,' responded the pathologist. 'Look, we don't need to ponder too much on the cause of death, do we? It's more a question of did she jump or was she pushed – and looking at the state of the poor woman I doubt we'll be able to throw much light on that. But I'll do what I can here, then we'll complete the post-mortem back at the morgue. D'you want to come?'

'I don't think that will be necessary,' responded Vogel, who found post-mortem examinations even more disturbing than crime scenes and preferred to avoid attending. 'I'll wait to hear.'

He left then, Parlow at his heels, wondering why he'd rushed to Leicester Square tube station in the first place. He wasn't sure he had learned anything, and he'd certainly been of no assistance at all.

There was another even more unpleasant task to be performed for which he had absolutely no appetite. The one every copper dreads. The death call.

'Right, Parlow, we'd better go see Greg Walker,' he said. 'Break the news.'

Unless he already knows, Vogel pondered to himself but did not add. For he could not yet rule out the possibility that Greg Walker had been the one who'd killed her.

Greg was in no danger of finding out anything. After his wife had left he'd gone back to his makeshift bed on the sofa and laid there, enveloped in misery. He supposed it was his own fault that she'd walked out on him and left him in this state. He should have entrusted Karen with the truth about his past when they'd first met. But he hadn't been able to. And as the years had passed it had become more and more impossible to do so. He'd told her he'd messed about with gangs and been involved in the odd punch-up down the market, and that his pal Wiz had died following an accidental fall. The reality had been far worse. The punch-ups down the market had been knife fights. Wiz, another young Triad recruit, had been shot by a couple of Kwan's henchmen after being caught out in some act of betrayal or disloyalty. Greg had never been told the details. But because it was known that he was Wiz's friend, he had been ordered to help dispose of the body. Kwan's heavies had stood over him giving orders as he dismembered Wiz's corpse and placed the body parts in bin bags. He'd then delivered the remains to an East End pet-food factory run by Kwan's uncle. As Kwan intended, the horrific experience had proved a most effective warning, one Greg had never forgotten. His participation had given Kwan a hold on him, and made him terrified of the consequences if he ever tried to break free.

Karen's anger and frustration when she learned of Greg's association with Kwan had been understandable. But she had no idea what Kwan was capable of, so it was incomprehensible to her that Greg couldn't just turn his back on the man. The miracle in Greg's life was that he'd been allowed to move on as much as he had. Yet the shadow of the Triads had never really gone away, and it never would. How could he explain that to Karen without telling her everything, forcing her to share with him the dreadful burden of what he had done?

Unable to face going to work or even getting up off the sofa, Greg had stared up at the ceiling trying to figure out a way to salvage his marriage. His phone rang twice shortly after Karen's departure. He checked the display panel just in case it was her who was calling. Or, heaven forbid, Tony Kwan. But the first call turned out to be from his dodgy whisky supplier and the second from Bob. He had no wish to speak to either of them, particularly Bob, so he ignored both calls. He supposed later that he had heard the whine of police sirens and the noise of ambulances arriving at the tube station a couple of streets away, but such sounds were a normal part of city life. He paid them no heed. After an hour or two of torturing himself about both his past and his now uncertain future, the sleep Greg had denied himself in the night finally overcame him and he drifted into blissful nothingness.

He was woken by the entryphone. With a start, he sat bolt upright on the sofa. Maybe Karen had come back. She had her own keys, but she could have forgotten them. Especially given the state she'd been in. He hurried to the phone and spoke into it hopefully.

He was disappointed to hear Vogel's voice.

'We need to come up and see you, please, Mr Walker. I'm afraid there is something we have to speak to you about.'

Greg felt no particular sense of foreboding. He was merely irritated. He assumed the detective had more questions, and that was the last thing he needed right now.

But he opened the door to find Vogel grim-faced. And an equally grim-faced CID man accompanying him.

'I think you'd better go and sit down, Mr Walker,' said Vogel.

Greg led the two policemen into the living room and perched himself on an upright chair at the table by the window. It was obvious that Vogel had something important to say, but the policeman seemed to be having difficulty finding the words. Alarm bells were now ringing loud and clear in Greg's head. This was serious, he thought, very serious. Yet it did not occur to him that this latest police visit concerned his wife until Vogel spoke again.

'I am afraid I have some bad news, Mr Walker,' said Vogel.

It was like being struck by a bolt of lightning. Suddenly Greg knew. Beyond any doubt, he knew.

'Karen,' he said. 'Karen. She's dead.'

It wasn't a question. He didn't need to ask a question. It was a statement.

Vogel nodded. 'I am afraid she is, Mr Walker,' he said. 'And I am so sorry to be bringing you this—'

'How?' Greg interrupted, his voice unnaturally high. 'Was

346

she murdered? If she was, I'm going to get the bastard. You lot can't do it, that's bloody obvious. But I will. I'll get the bastard.'

'Mr Walker, we do not know yet whether your wife was murdered, not for sure anyway.'

'What happened? Just tell me, will you. Tell me exactly what happened to my Karen.'

Vogel did so. He explained that while the cause of death seemed clear, it was not known exactly how Karen came to fall under the wheels of a train, that inquiries were ongoing, CCTV footage was being checked, and so on.

'What do you mean, you don't know how she came to fall? She must have been bloody pushed. I mean, after what happened to Marlena and Michelle it's obvious she's been murdered. It's not fucking rocket science, is it?'

'Clearly we are investigating that possibility,' said Vogel.

Greg stared hard at him. He sensed that the policeman believed Karen had been murdered. All this business about keeping an open mind was just Vogel playing it by the book.

'We can't rule out at this stage that Mrs Walker's fall was accidental. And then again, it could have been . . .' Vogel paused to take a very deep breath. 'It has to be possible, I'm afraid, Mr Walker, that your wife may have taken her own life.'

'What? My Karen? Top herself? No fucking way, mate,' said Greg.

Vogel glanced pointedly at the sofa. There was a pillow at one end and a crumpled blanket tossed carelessly across the middle. It was obvious someone had been sleeping there.

'May I ask if you and your wife had a recent disagreement, Mr Walker?' Vogel asked.

'Oh my God,' said Greg. 'You seriously think my Karen went and topped herself because we had some bloody silly row? Is that what you're saying? That's rubbish. Rubbish, do you hear?'

Vogel seemed to take pity on him. Certainly his reply was uncharacteristic in that it revealed more information about his own attitude than might have been prudent at that stage.

'Actually, that isn't what I think, Mr Walker,' he said. 'I believe, in all probability, and given the circumstances involving other recent incidents with which you and your wife have connections, that Mrs Walker was murdered. But our inquiries are still proceeding, and I must say again that we do have to investigate all possibilities.'

Greg simply nodded. He felt drained. For the moment, it didn't matter how Karen had died. All that mattered was that she was dead.

'And I am afraid I need to ask where you were this morning, at 10.25 a.m., when your wife died?'

Greg wanted to scream at Vogel. No one in their right mind would believe he was capable of killing his own wife, the only woman he'd ever loved. But he couldn't summon up the energy. He had no fight left in him.

'I was here, just lying on the sofa most of the time,' he said.

'On your own, sir?'

'Yes, on my own.' Greg spoke wearily rather than in anger. He had gone beyond anger.

Vogel glanced again at the sofa, with its pillow and blanket. 'Were you sleeping?'

Greg shrugged. 'Some of the time. Not at first. But I hadn't slept for most of the night, so yes, I did drop off eventually. I was asleep when you—'

Greg stopped speaking abruptly. He supposed he might be arrested again now. On suspicion of his wife's murder. He stared apprehensively at Vogel, waiting for the detective to speak again. To issue a caution, perhaps.

Instead Vogel asked, 'Do you have anyone you could contact,

someone who could be with you, Mr Walker? You've had a terrible shock, you shouldn't be on your own.'

Greg shook his head. He supposed he was relieved that he wasn't going to be arrested. But he didn't care what happened to him. Not now.

Vogel continued, 'I could arrange for someone—'

'No,' Greg cut him off. 'I don't want anyone with me. Not family, not friends, and certainly not a copper.'

'As you wish, sir, but—' Vogel began.

'I want to see her,' Greg said suddenly. 'Will you take me to see her?'

'Mr Walker, your wife was hit by a train. Her injuries are . . . They are extensive . . .'

'Look, doesn't she have to be formally identified? Isn't that what happens?'

'Yes, but not necessarily by you, Mr Walker. You may prefer to remember her as she was.'

'No,' Greg insisted. 'She's my wife. I should be the one to identify her. And I want to see her. You can't stop me.' He looked at Vogel questioningly. 'You can't, can you?'

Vogel shook his head. 'I can't stop you, Mr Walker,' he said gently. 'Nor would I wish to, if that is what you want. But I must warn you that you may find it upsetting. Upsetting in the extreme.'

Greg drew himself up, visibly steeling himself for whatever lay in store.

'I have to say goodbye to my Karen,' he said. 'I have to. For her. For me. And for our kids.'

Back at Charing Cross police station minor pandemonium awaited Vogel in the shape of a rampant Christopher Margolia. Nobby Clarke had instructed the front office staff to make him wait for Vogel's return, and the lawyer wasn't best pleased. Neither was Vogel. His workload seemed to be growing with every passing minute, and he needed to focus all his powers of concentration on the three violent deaths he was dealing with, not waste his precious time fending off angry lawyers.

Somehow Margolia had learned of Karen Walker's death, and he seemed to think this meant George Kristos should be released at once. Vogel sighed to himself as the lawyer pontificated as if he were grandstanding in front of a crowded courtroom instead of one unimpressed detective. Kristos had been very much Vogel's own personal prime suspect, so he supposed it was fair enough that Nobby Clarke had delegated this tiresome business to him. All the same, he could have done without it.

'You had no cause whatsoever to re-arrest my client in the first place,' stormed Margolia. 'How Mr Kristos cares to conduct his personal life is not a police matter. And now it emerges that while he was detained in police custody another murder was committed. In light of the fact that Karen Walker was the only surviving female member of Sunday Club, there is every reason to suppose her death was the work of the same person who killed Michelle Monahan and Marleen McTavish. Is that not so, *Acting* Detective Inspector Vogel?' Margolia put emphasis on the word 'acting'. 'Or are you one of those police officers who ignores the overwhelming evidence against him and tries to pass it off as a coincidence?'

Vogel did not reply to that. He wasn't one of those police officers. Nor was he one of those officers who was led by hunches rather than hard facts. But he had been so sure that Kristos was guilty. He'd honestly believed it would be only a matter of time before some genuine incriminatory evidence was revealed. Unfortunately, it appeared he was running out of time.

'Mr Margolia, we are still investigating your client and we wish to continue questioning him. We have thirty-six hours, as you well know, and then we can if we wish apply to a court for an extension.'

'Well, you certainly won't get it,' snorted Margolia.

Vogel thought the lawyer was probably right, but he said: 'That would be for a court to decide, and would obviously depend on how our inquiries are proceeding.'

'I am asking for my client to be released immediately on police bail,' insisted Margolia.

'No, sir,' said Vogel, quite forcibly for him. 'I intend to keep your client in custody for as long as I am legally allowed.'

And with that he turned his back on the lawyer and marched off in the direction of the MIT room.

Much as they would have preferred to devote their energies to building a case against Kristos, Clarke and Vogel knew they had no option but to pursue other avenues of inquiry. They immediately set about assigning teams of officers to question the rest of the friends as to their whereabouts at the time of Karen Walker's death.

Bob had returned to work, trying to carry on as normal. A pair of MIT detectives tracked him down to a boutique hotel off Covent Garden's Broad Court, where he was attending to the small garden and window boxes. He seemed stunned by the news of Karen's death. But he was once more able to satisfactorily account for his movements. He had arrived at the hotel just before nine and had remained there ever since. There were a number of witnesses who could vouch for this. He was not re-arrested.

A second team found Ari, near comatose on cocaine, at his home. It proved impossible to ascertain his movements earlier in the day. They therefore arrested him on two accounts, the second as instructed by Vogel before they paid their visit. Suspicion of murder and possession of class-A drugs.

'If he's got any coke on him, then let's do him for it,' Vogel had said. 'Sticking a drug charge on him will allow us to keep him in custody, whether his lawyer likes it or not.'

Alfonso had not returned to his job at the Vine, having been told by the management to stay away until the matter was cleared up. In any case, he would have been in no fit state to walk let alone wait on tables. Previously only a moderate drinker, he was now hell-bent on drinking his way to oblivion. He was found in an alcoholic stupor at his mother's home in Dagenham. His mother affirmed sadly that he had been drunk all day, and had not left his bedroom except for calls of nature. She had taken him breakfast and then sandwiches at lunchtime, but he was not interested in food, she'd said. Just alcohol.

Alfonso was not rearrested.

Billy, who had been suspended by Geering Brothers until, or unless, he was formally cleared, and Tiny, who was so distressed he couldn't even think about work, and in any case whose duties were almost exclusively nocturnal, were both at home when two detectives arrived. They claimed to have been at home at the time Karen Walker died, and indeed to have been at home together all day. But their only alibi was each other.

They were re-arrested. And along with Ari they were detained at Charing Cross overnight.

Around noon on the day after Karen Walker's death Greg was finally escorted to the morgue at University College Hospital to see his wife's remains and to formally identify her body. DC Parlow, as a recently qualified family liaison officer, had been assigned to support and monitor the bereaved man.

Greg couldn't get over the fact that his last words to her had been 'fuck off'. He hadn't told the police that. They were already investigating the possibility that Karen had topped herself. But Greg knew better. He hated himself, though, almost as much as he hated the man he believed had murdered his Karen.

The previous evening, Greg had visited his children, who were still staying with Karen's mother. He'd come away feeling, if possible, even worse than before, having been unable to answer their questions or to provide any comfort. He couldn't begin to think about how his little family was going to face a future without Karen. He couldn't think about anything but the fact she was dead and the person responsible was still living.

The staff in the morgue had made Karen Walker look as presentable as possible, her amputated limbs and decapitated head had been arranged in such a way that the body appeared intact underneath the white sheet. The orderly who pulled the sheet back so that Greg could see his wife's face was careful to reveal nothing below chin level.

Greg knew though. He had guessed from Vogel's reaction, and the way the detective and his team had tried to persuade him not to see his wife's body, that she had been decapitated. It had seemed obvious somehow.

The head, in spite of the attentions of the morgue staff, was in any case shocking to look at. Discoloured and distorted. But it was his Karen lying there so horribly mutilated. Greg didn't flinch. He leaned forward and kissed her poor bloated forehead. Then he left, declining all offers of assistance from DC Parlow, and refusing to allow the officer to accompany him further. But it wasn't grief that was consuming Greg now, it was anger.

After breaking the news to his children and Karen's mother he had returned to the home they'd once shared and spent a long sleepless night formulating a plan to deal with the man he held responsible Karen's death. The prospect of taking revenge was the only thing keeping him going.

The police might think that Karen had been killed by the same individual who murdered Michelle and Marlena, but he knew better. He'd said all along those acts of vandalism directed at him and his family had nothing to do with the attacks on the other Sunday Club members, but no one would listen to him. They were all too scared of Tony Kwan. The police had wasted no time hauling Greg and his friends to Charing Cross nick, throwing them in cells and questioning them for hours on end, but you could bet they wouldn't try that with Kwan. It would be like every other police investigation into his activities: the case would be dropped due to lack of evidence. Well, Greg didn't need bloody evidence. He knew it was Kwan. The bastard had picked up that voicemail Karen made him leave, refusing to work for him. The message which said he was sure Kwan would understand, being a family man. Kwan had understood, all right. Knowing how much Greg's family meant to him, he'd targeted Karen. No beating, no torture his heavies could have inflicted on Greg would have been worse than losing the woman he loved.

But Kwan had made a fatal mistake. Because Greg was now quite mad with grief.

Greg took a cab from Agar Street to his Waterloo lock-up. He went straight to the workbench at the rear of the building and, using a screwdriver for leverage, began to prise a wooden peg from one section of the bench. The moment the peg was removed, Greg was able to easily push the apparently solid workbench to one side exposing the wall behind. One of the bricks was not cemented in place; Greg pulled it free, revealing a small rectangular hiding place recessed into the wall. He reached inside with one hand and lifted out an object wrapped in a soft oily fabric, which he placed carefully on the bench. Then he unpeeled several layers of protective cloth to expose a handgun which his squaddie father had taken from an Argentinian prisoner and brought home from the Falklands. It was a semi-automatic Browning 9mm Hi-Power, standard international army issue at the time. There was also a box containing magazines and cartridges.

Greg had wondered whether the police who'd searched both his workplace and his home would find his hidey hole and the illegal weapon it contained. Fortunately, they hadn't.

He picked up the pistol and stroked it. He'd only been four or five when his father first showed him the gun, telling him he must never mention it to anyone, and that he should never touch it. Even now he could clearly remember the way his father used to take the pistol out to clean and oil it before wrapping it in the cloth and hiding it away again.

Greg had hero-worshipped his father. If it hadn't been for Ted Walker abandoning his family, running off with his wife's younger sister when Greg was fifteen, he would never have got involved with Kwan. Instead his dad's departure had marked the beginning of Greg's wild period and his involvement with the Triads, culminating in Karen's murder.

Greg hadn't seen his father since the day he'd walked out. He wasn't even sure if the old man was still alive. His mother had never got over the betrayal of her husband and sister. She just seemed to pine away, her health gradually declining. Not long after Greg had married Karen, she died. Her heart had given up, the doctors said. Greg knew it hadn't so much given up as been broken.

While clearing out the family home, Greg had found his father's gun hidden away at the back of a cupboard. He had no idea why his father hadn't taken it with him, or why his mother had not disposed of it. Maybe she hadn't known how to.

For reasons he did not entirely understand, Greg had decided to keep the gun. Perhaps it reminded him of the happy times he'd shared with his dad. It brought back memories of those times whenever he took it out of its hiding place to clean and oil it, just the way his father had shown him.

He picked up the gun and peered into the barrel. It was gleaming. As far as Greg knew, the pistol hadn't been fired since his father had brought it home. But that was about to change.

He loaded several of the cartridges into a magazine and inserted it into the handle of the pistol, just as he had seen his father do. Greg was quite confident that the gun was up to the task ahead. He only hoped he was too.

Late that afternoon George was released. Vogel had attempted to persuade Nobby Clarke that an appeal should be made to magistrates court for a further period of detention. Under the Police And Criminal Evidence Act, magistrates have the power, when it can be effectively argued that a suspect's further stay in custody is both necessary and potentially productive, to authorize detention in police cells, without charges being brought, for up to four days. But Clarke and her superintendent at Homicide Command refused even to apply for a magistrates order, saying it would be a waste of time. They had no evidence that could convince the court there was sufficient cause to detain George Kristos a moment longer. Vogel had no choice but to concede defeat. In truth, he knew his superiors were right, but he felt he had to at least make the attempt.

George went straight home. He made no attempt to contact any of the remaining friends. Unaware that some of them would have been unable to take his call in any case because they had been re-arrested, he simply assumed they wouldn't want to speak to him. Any more than he wanted to speak to them. Besides, the police still had his mobile phone. He did, of course, have a house phone, and it started ringing soon after he returned to his flat. He ignored it. George was in a state of shock. He felt tense and, for perhaps the first time in his adult life, threatened. He needed time to himself. Space to think things through. He was aware that he had become Vogel's prime suspect, but he had no idea what influence this third violent death would have on the detective's thinking. After all, there was no way anyone could accuse him of killing Karen Walker. Not when he'd been banged up in a cell at Charing Cross nick when it happened.

There had been times in the past when I felt that God had deserted me, turned his back on me in my hour of need. My faith had been tested, it had weakened, but He had never forsaken me. For the righteous cry, and the Lord heareth, and delivereth them out of all their troubles.

Despite my best-laid plans, I had made mistakes as I sought to fulfil my mission. Mistakes that had resulted in my being delivered unto my enemies and looked set to allow those enemies to reveal me for what I was. That man Vogel, the one poor little Michelle so revered, thought he had the measure of me. But he'd understood me not at all. He thought he was so clever, and yet he had failed to spot so much.

But neither he nor I could have foreseen the divine intervention that lay in store. For He was watching over me. After all, I am His instrument of destruction. Through my flesh His will is channelled and implemented irrevocably. And so He brought me forth, He delivered me, for He delighted in me. What other explanation could there be?

Thanks to the hand of God, I was now beyond suspicion in

the eyes of Vogel and his self-important cohorts in the Murder Investigation Team. And that was how I hoped to remain.

The deed was done. I had been avenged. There would be no more pranks, no acts of vandalism afflicting the shattered and scattered remnants of the ill-fated Sunday Clubbers. There would be no more muggings, no more murders.

It was over. I am a creature apart and will stay that way. A creature it is impossible for others to grasp. I am, it seems, as elusive as ever. My very being is impenetrable. I wonder if they will ever find me now. But in any case, it doesn't matter. I have triumphed. His power and His glory abide with me.

Not long after George's release Vogel received the telephone call from Dr Patricia Fitzwarren which changed everything. She had begun the post-mortem examination on Karen Walker immediately after Greg Walker had left the morgue. She now had the results.

'I've checked and double-checked, Vogel,' she said. 'It seems quite incredible in view of all that has happened, but there's no doubt about it: Karen Walker was not pushed and neither did she jump.'

'How can you be so sure?' said Vogel.

'Mrs Walker suffered a massive subarachnoid haemorrhage, caused by an aneurism in the brain,' Pat Fitzwarren announced. 'You know what an aneurism is, don't you, Vogel? A bulge in an artery, a swelling. It can cause headaches but generally there are no symptoms significant enough to cause alarm, no warning signs. Indeed, an aneurism doesn't cause any trouble worth mentioning unless it bursts. And that's what happened in this case.'

'So are you saying she died of natural causes?'

'No doubt about it. Mrs Walker's aneurism burst, resulting

in a fatal brain haemorrhage, enough to kill her almost instantly even if she hadn't been unlucky enough to collapse onto the track in the path of an oncoming train. It may not be possible to ascertain whether she was actually dead when the train hit her, but I guarantee she was as near as damn it.'

'My God,' said Vogel.

The implications of the pathologist's verdict were immense. George Kristos had been released from custody not only because of a lack of hard evidence but because it was believed that there had been another murder, one for which he couldn't have been responsible.

Vogel was still trying to assimilate what it all might mean, when Parlow came into his office.

'What are you doing here?' Vogel demanded. 'You're supposed to be on family liaison duty with Greg Walker.'

'I know, guv. But he didn't want me with him. Said he needed time on his own.'

'Parlow, for God's sake, didn't they teach you anything on that fancy course you went on? What Greg Walker does or doesn't want isn't the bloody point. The job's not just about playing nursemaid to the bereaved. It's a watching brief. The man's already threatened to take the law into his own hands. And now it seems his wife wasn't murdered after all. You'd better go find him. Fast.' Vogel sprang to his feet and hurried towards the door. 'First though, let me get Nick Wagstaff – you're going to need some back-up.'

'Right, guv.'

Chastened, Parlow followed Vogel into the outer office. Not seeing Wagstaff seated at any of the desks, Vogel shouted his name. A head turned.

'Yes, guv,' it said.

Vogel frowned, confused. For a split second he had no idea

who was addressing him. Then light dawned. It was Wagstaff. But his former grey hair was now a rather unnatural bright and evenly coloured brown.

'Bloody hell!' said Vogel. 'What have you done to your hair?'

Wagstaff flushed. 'It's the missus, guv,' he said. 'Reckoned I was looking old.'

'Right. Well before you retire to your vegetable patch, I need you to team up with Parlow. He'll fill you in.'

Despite the enormity of unfolding events, Vogel couldn't help smiling as he turned towards his office. It was hard to believe that a simple change in hair colour could so dramatically change Wagstaff's appearance.

At the door, Vogel turned suddenly. 'Wagstaff, don't you usually wear glasses?' he asked.

Wagstaff paused, his arms half in and half out of the coat he was pulling on. 'The missus again, guv,' he said. 'Got contact lenses now. Damn things are bloody irritating to wear too, and if you ask me . . .'

Vogel had nothing more to ask Wagstaff. He had stopped listening.

He returned swiftly to his desk and from the top drawer removed the photograph that had been bothering him. He scanned into his computer the picture of a young woman George Kristos claimed to have found in a magazine, then opened it in Photoshop, where he began to adjust the hair colour from blonde to black, then brown. He played with the colours, darkening and lightening them. He added a touch of red, removed it, and settled, for the moment, on a kind of mousey brown. It looked right somehow. Then he changed the style of the hair, made it less contemporary, longer, with some width. He made it curly. That seemed wrong. Didn't suit the face. He waved it, just a bit. Added a fringe. Removed it. Put it back in again.

The eyes were blue. He changed their colour too, turning them hazel, then dark brown.

Finally he added spectacles, experimenting with different kinds of frames. Wire ones, round ones, oval, black ones, red ones. Then he tried tortoiseshell.

A frisson of excitement began somewhere in Vogel's lower abdomen and expanded slowly through his body. His mouth was dry. His fingers were trembling. He had it – or at least part of it. He knew who that woman was. And she certainly wasn't a Polish wannabe student.

He printed his doctored version of George's photograph, googled a name, brought up another picture, printed that too, and used the Met's recently acquired facial recognition software to make the final comparison.

Then he hurried along the corridor to find Nobby Clarke.

The DCI was on the phone when Vogel barged through her door. Clarke looked up, unimpressed. Vogel didn't give a damn.

'It's urgent, boss,' he said.

Frowning, Clarke ended her call. Vogel slapped the three photographs onto her desk: the original photo taken from George's wallet, the version he had just photoshopped, and, uncannily similar to the second, the third which he'd just downloaded. He tapped it with an extended forefinger.

'Alice Turner,' he said. 'Remember her?'

Then he pointed to the photograph he had doctored. 'An amended version of the picture of George Kristos's alleged girlfriend,' he said.

Light dawned on Nobby Clarke's face.

'Bloody hell!' she said. 'I remember Alice Turner. Who doesn't?'

She glanced down again at the pictures before her.

'And that photograph. It was iconic. In all the papers. My

God, I can't believe none of us saw this before. These are pictures of the same woman.'

'Yes, and facial recognition software backs it up. The proportions and so on are identical.'

Vogel would have bet his life that Clarke would remember Alice Turner. There were images that stuck in your mind forever. The criminals evil beyond comprehension. Myra Hindley, half-pouting, staring challengingly at the camera. Fred West, plump-cheeked and boyish. And then there were the innocent victims, their lack of foreboding making their eternal pictorial presence all the more poignant. Little James Bulger, holding the hand of one of his killers. Milly Dowler doing the ironing. Beautiful Anni Dewani, murdered on honeymoon, in her Indian wedding dress. And Alice Turner. Even after twenty-three years, her face was instantly recognizable.

Vogel supposed it was the same for everyone, but he always felt these things meant more to police officers. Maybe they cared that bit more. If not, why would you join the police force? Vogel glanced down at the picture. Alice Turner's kindly eyes seemed to gaze reproachfully back at him. But what happened to her had not been Vogel's fault. It hadn't been anyone's fault, really, except the young bastard who'd attacked and maimed her.

Alice had somehow survived, but was unable to cope with her terrible injuries. Two years later she committed suicide.

Vogel had been a probationary PC when it happened, a new recruit. He guessed Clarke must be three or four years older than him, in order to have been a contemporary of Forest's, and therefore almost certainly a serving officer at the time. The Alice Turner story had sent shockwaves through police forces nationwide. People in all walks of life had been shocked, of course, but the general public had been spared the gruesome details.

Alice Turner had been brutally attacked at her Edinburgh

home. Her tongue had been hacked off and both her eyes gouged out. Her attacker had pounced in the early hours of the morning while she was asleep in bed. Without the advantage of surprise, he would have struggled to overpower her, for he had little physical strength. He was after all, just a boy. A boy ten years old.

It had been 1990, three years before poor James Bulger was abducted, tortured and murdered by two ten-year-old boys. In 1990 the police and the great British public had found it hard to believe that a ten-year-old child could be capable of such violence. The horror of it had transfixed the nation, and Alice Turner's photograph had featured on every front page and news bulletin. The 'before' photograph, that was. And it was impossible to look at it without imagining what the 'after' must resemble.

The press were forbidden by law from revealing the identity of the child responsible. Not only could they not name him, they were prohibited from publishing any details that might lead to him being identified. This meant they could not reveal that the boy in question was Alice Turner's foster son. But Vogel had known. It had been common knowledge throughout the police forces of the United Kingdom. Even amongst rookies like him.

'And this picture that none of us can forget, albeit significantly altered, was in George Kristos's wallet?' mused Nobby Clarke. 'Turned into the fictional Carla Karbusky. She looks a bit younger than Alice does in the un-doctored photo.'

Vogel nodded. 'Alice was forty when she was attacked. I reckon Kristos has deliberately made her look younger and more contemporary. Turned her into someone suitable to be his girlfriend. Also someone you wouldn't immediately recognize as Alice. But Alice all the same.'

'Pretty damned twisted,' muttered Clarke.

'No doubt about that, boss,' agreed Vogel.

'What was the name of the boy? Something Scottish, as I remember . . . Rory, Rory something?'

'Rory Burns,' said Vogel. 'As I recall, he'd been badly injured in a motor accident when he was very young. His mother had been killed in the crash and his father couldn't cope, so little Rory was put into care and eventually fostered by Alice Turner and her husband. He'd been with the couple for about six years and seemed quite settled. I don't think they ever found out what made him turn on her.'

'"Like a rabid dog" – that was how the prosecution counsel described the boy,' murmured Clarke. 'It's all coming back to me now. Edinburgh High Court, wasn't it?'

'Yes, boss. Just like Venables and Thompson, the Bulger killers, Rory Burns was tried in an adult court because of the severity of his offence.'

'Didn't he say something quite chilling when he was arrested, something biblical? It came up in court and was quoted everywhere.'

Vogel looked down at a report of the trial which he'd just printed out.

'*And thine eye shall not pity, but life shall go for life, eye for eye, tooth for tooth, hand for hand, foot for foot,*' he recited.

'Shit,' said Clarke.

'After the attack, the boy just stayed in the house waiting for Alice Turner's husband to get home,' Vogel continued. 'He worked shifts, apparently, and she very nearly bled to death. Poor man found her upstairs. Burns was downstairs, covered in Alice's blood.'

'The boy was mentally ill, surely?'

'It was decided that he was sane enough to have known what he was doing and to stand trial,' said Vogel. 'But whereas at the close of the trial of Venables and Thompson the judge ruled that their names should be released in spite of their ages, Rory Burns' anonymity was preserved. It leaked locally, though. He spent eight years at a young offenders' centre, and when he was released there was a public outcry in Scotland, though nothing like the furore over Venables and Thompson.'

'What happened to him?' asked Clarke.

'He was released on licence and sent to some kind of halfway house in Edinburgh . . .' Vogel paused. 'That was in 1998, the year of the King's Cross murders.'

Clarke looked thoughtful. 'So it could have been him. He just had to get himself to London and back.'

Vogel nodded his agreement. He referred again to the printout: 'For almost a year Burns reported to his parole officer according to the terms of his licence and appeared to behave impeccably. Then he vanished. Completely and utterly. Off the face of the earth.'

'And he's never been rediscovered?'

Vogel shook his head. 'There's a school of thought across the border that some relative or friend of Alice Turner's caught up with Burns and knocked him off. She had a brother who's a bit of a toughie, ex para, always said he'd get him for what he did to his sister.'

'But you don't think he's dead, do you, Vogel?'

Vogel shook his head again.

DCI Clarke stared at her second-in-command.

'You think George Kristos is Rory Burns.'

It was a statement, not a question. Vogel answered it, nonetheless.

'Yes, I do, boss,' he said.

'Didn't we check out his background?'

'Kristos was born in Edinburgh to Greek Cypriot parents. Scottish police told us his family were believed to have returned to Cyprus some years ago. There was nothing to arouse suspicion. He went to school in Scotland and then drama college in Manchester. It all checked out. He has a passport, national insurance number, tax record, driver's licence – everything. All in the name of Georgios Kristos. And no criminal record, obviously. He's an Equity member as George Kristos, and is generally known as George. So he'd anglicized his name, but that didn't seem suspicious either. Particularly not for an actor.'

'What about his alibi for the time of Michelle Monahan's murder? Didn't his neighbour say she was with him?'

'Yes, boss, but she's an old lady and she's not well. I think we should double-check it.'

DCI Clarke nodded. She remained silent for a few seconds. Then she clenched her fist and banged it on the desk in front of her.

'Go get the bastard, Vogel,' she said. 'And this time we're going to nail 'im.'

'Yes, boss,' said Vogel, over one shoulder. He was already on the way to the door.

Clarke immediately called in the key members of her team.

'I want everything there is on Rory Burns and Georgios Kristos,' she demanded. 'Every spit and fart. Photographs – I want every available photograph. Tell forensics I need an expert to run photos of Rory Burns through age-progression software. Get on to Scotland: we need the complete court records and the statements of everyone involved. And we need to find Kristos's parents in Cyprus, or wherever the hell they are.'

George seemed unsurprised when Vogel and a team of officers arrived at his flat to arrest him for the third time, even though he had only recently been released from custody. It was almost as if he had been waiting for them.

He unlocked the door and stood calmly with his arms extended as he was handcuffed.

'I was half-expecting you to turn up again,' he told Vogel. 'But you're not as bright as you thought you were, are you?'

Vogel ignored that. He formally arrested George on suspicion of two counts of murder.

George's eyes seemed to glaze over as Vogel cautioned him.

'Anything you do say may be given in evidence,' the detective concluded.

'*God is jealous and the Lord revengeth, the Lord revengeth, and is furious,*' said George.

'I'm sorry, sir?'

'*The Lord will take vengeance on His adversaries, and He reserveth wrath for His enemies.*'

'I see, sir,' said Vogel, noting that George was now speaking with a distinct Scottish accent.

He and two of the uniforms led George to the waiting squad car and bundled him in. George grabbed Vogel by the arm. His eyes bore into the policeman. Vogel had not noticed previously how cold those eyes were. Maybe they hadn't been that way before.

'*The Lord will not acquit the wicked, the Lord hath His way in the whirlwind, and in the storm and the clouds are the dust at His feet,*' said George.

twenty-four

I didn't care. I had completed my task. It mattered not to me what happened to my apology of a body. My soul is omnipotent. I am as He is. And will be for ever and ever. Amen.

My table thou hast furnished me, In presence of my foes, My head thou dost with oil anoint, And my cup overflows.

I supposed it was inevitable that eventually I would be discovered. Although, as I had fooled so many for so long, I did wonder, had almost come to believe, that I might yet escape.

But sometimes I was not even sure I wanted to. There was a part of me that yearned for them all to know what I had done and why I had done it. Perhaps that was the reason I had chosen to carry a picture of my non-existent girlfriend, knowing it could conceivably lead to my being discovered. A doctored picture of the woman who had been my foster mother.

Now they would know. The whole world would know what I had done.

There was another reason why I chose to carry with me that doctored picture of Alice Turner, even before I learned about Marlena. Alice was the only woman I had ever really loved. The only human being I ever loved after my mother was taken from me. Along with my mother, I lost all hope of a future, any chance of a normal life. And I was only three at the time, too young to understand. Too young to hate. My father, my weak bloody father, claimed to have suffered a nervous breakdown. Said he couldn't cope, and gave me away. Just gave me away to the state, asking that I be taken into care.

He *couldn't cope?* What did he think it was like for me, having to cope with what I had become?

But Alice. My dear sweet Alice. She had nurtured me, cared for me, soothed me, made me feel that I was normal in spite of everything, and that to her I was precious. I'd yet to think about growing into a man, and what that might mean. As a child, with Alice, I felt safe enough. I had perhaps dared to believe I was just an ordinary little boy. And to her, to Alice, a special boy.

Then I witnessed her betrayal. A quite casual betrayal.

I overheard her one day, talking to a social worker in the kitchen. They thought I was in the garden, kicking a ball around with the boy from next door, but I'd come back into the house to find a plaster because I'd cut my knee. I was in the hall when I heard the words I shall never forget.

'He was such a disturbed child when he came here,' said the social worker. 'And he's doing so well now.'

'Yes,' replied Alice. 'But I can't help fearing for his future. He's always going to be a freak, isn't he, out there in the big wide world? My dear, darling little freak . . .'

I didn't make a sound. It was as if I was frozen. Then I turned, crept along the hallway out of the house.

They never even knew that I was there.

She might have known later though, in the early hours of the following morning. I've often wondered if she ever realized what had sealed her fate. What she had done. How she'd left me with no choice but to deal with her disloyalty, her nonchalant derision, in the way that I had.

I took no notice of the other words she used, not 'my', nor 'dear', nor 'darling'. All I heard was 'freak'. I was a freak to her, as well as to the rest of the world. My sweet Alice thought I was a freak. And that one throwaway comment, never intended for my ears, meant that I would always be a freak to myself. How could I ever regard myself as anything other than that after hearing Alice, lovely Alice, speak of me in that way?

I never told them. Not any of them. Or not in so many words. If they'd been cleverer, they might have guessed.

Alice was the second woman to have destroyed my life. I could do nothing about the first evil bitch. Not then. But I could destroy Alice. I could make her life every bit as dreadful, as empty, and as wasted as I knew mine would be. I was only ten, but I had the power. The vengeful God of the Bible I kept always at my side was with me, bestowing upon me steadfast resolution and a will beyond my years.

I took her eyes so that she would never again see me. And I took her tongue so that she would never again speak of me.

Alice had been more than a foster mother to me. I'd loved her in a way I do not remember loving even my real mother. But then I have no memories of the time before my devastation. It was Alice who seemed to have been always there for me. She'd been everything to me. Until she betrayed me. The shock of it made me capable of what others might regard as a quite heartless brutality. It wasn't that. I was not the evil one. Alice had proven herself to be shallow and craven. I did have a heart, then, but she broke it. I knew at once what I had to do. Alice left me no choice. My destiny lay before me. It was written in The Book.

'And thine eye shall not pity, but life shall go for life, eye for eye, tooth for tooth, hand for hand, foot for foot.'

Ironically it was Alice who had sent me to Sunday school. I quickly became a star pupil. I was a clever boy, particularly good at memorizing verse from the Bible. And I took an intense pleasure in the Old Testament. I avidly devoured the messages it held for me. I gloried in them. I knew beyond doubt that so many of them were directed at me alone. They had been written in another age, by prophets and by saints and by scholars, for me to seize upon, to grasp with my whole being, and to obey.

My one true friend is the Bible. The Good Book has an answer for everything in my world. It tells me that my God will supply every need according to his riches in glory in Christ Jesus. That has always been and always will be so. For ever and ever. Should my heart be troubled He provides solace. Should I ever, for a second, question my destiny, He enhances my resolution. He lifts me from despair and gives me vigour in all that I endeavour. I am and will always be His avenging angel.

Vogel travelled to Charing Cross in the back of the squad car with George. He wanted to be close to him. He was appalled and captivated by him. If George spoke, if George moved a muscle, if George crossed his legs, scratched his nose, touched his ear, sneezed or coughed, Vogel wanted to know.

George Kristos, né Rory Burns, did not look like a monster. Yet he was undoubtedly the most monstrous creature Vogel had ever encountered.

Kristos did not speak again during the ten-minute journey, nor did he speak in the custody suite. It was only when he was asked to step into an anteroom with an officer in attendance and remove his clothes for forensic examination that he spoke.

'*And you shall make them linen breeches to cover their nakedness, from their loins even to their thighs they shall reach,*' he said. And he smiled. A wide gentle smile that did not reach his eyes.

Vogel felt a shiver run up and down his spine. Clearly George Kristos was some sort of religious maniac. Vogel wasn't sure that modern psychology recognized such a condition. But the label certainly fitted.

He waited until George reappeared, now dressed in the regulation paper suit made of recycled materials, which was standard custody issue. Then he instructed the custody officer, Sergeant Andy Pierce, to arrange for George to be placed in a cell where he would be detained until they were ready to interview him. Vogel knew that Clarke and the rest of the MIT team would have been working flat out on the case in his absence, and he wanted to familiarize himself with any new information before proceeding with a formal interview.

George smiled again. It was a knowing smile. Vogel looked away. He couldn't wait to see Nobby Clarke and learn what progress had been made.

When he arrived at the DCI's office she was engaged in an animated discussion with Pam Jones and Joe Carlisle. Clarke looked up at him, pausing mid-sentence.

'Scotland have done some digging for us. The real Georgios Kristos died when he was seventeen,' she said.

'Jesus,' said Vogel.

'And you are not going to believe the rest of this, Vogel,' she said.

Vogel thought he might. He said nothing, waiting for her to continue.

'We now have details of the road accident in which Rory Burns' mother was killed and he was injured. Apparently, mother and son were walking across a bridge when a motorcyclist who'd been going way too fast suddenly lost control and ploughed into them. The mother was catapulted into the river and swept away on the current. They found her dead body washed up downstream a couple of days later. The boy ended up straddling the front wheel of the bike. It seems the motorcyclist carried on across the bridge until the boy eventually fell off. A witness said the biker just sped off – didn't even stop to see whether the kid was still alive. The boy suffered appalling injuries to the genital area and lower abdomen. Surgeons had to perform a penectomy and his testes were also removed.'

'Jesus Christ,' said Vogel. 'He has no penis and no balls. No sexual organs. That would explain why Marlena's sexual organs were removed – same thing with the two King's Cross victims.'

'Revenge,' said Clarke. 'Revenge for what happened to him.'

Vogel nodded. 'Was the motorcyclist caught?'

'Disappeared without trace. The only witness was a fisherman down on the riverbank, a couple of hundred yards away. It was dusk, and he wasn't close enough to give a description of the biker. Rory Burns was three years old – too young and too traumatized to be of any help. All they could get from him was that there'd been a big wheel and a pink lady.'

Clarke looked down at a report in front of her, freshly emailed from Edinburgh. '"The pink lady went away," he said. His mother had been wearing a pink coat, so the cops thought the boy must have been talking about her. I think they should have listened more carefully. I think the motorcyclist may have been a woman. I think she may have been the pink lady.'

Vogel thought fast.

'You think the pink lady was Marlena?'

Clarke passed a photograph to Vogel. It showed a young Marlena standing alongside a pink Norton motorcycle.

'The SOCOs found it in that suitcase of memorabilia in

Marlena's flat, but nobody thought it had any significance. Do you remember seeing it?'

Vogel shook his head. 'Even if I had, it wouldn't have meant anything to me 'til now.'

'Well, it turns out Marlena's father was from Edinburgh, so she may have had other kin up there. There can't have been too many female motorcyclists in the early eighties, not riding proper grown-up machines.'

'But wasn't she supposed to be living in France throughout the eighties, supplying the great and the good of Paris with young women of ill repute?' asked Vogel.

Clarke picked up the mug of tea on her desk and took a sip. She pulled a face. Vogel guessed she'd probably let the beverage go cold.

'Maybe she was just visiting Scotland. That would explain why they never caught up with her. A day or two after the incident a couple of uniforms were called to an explosion at an old municipal dump. Someone had set light to a motorcycle. The tank had been full of petrol, so there was damn all left of it. The number plates had been removed and the vehicle identification number destroyed, either during the fire or before. The local plod believed it was the bike involved in the incident that had maimed Rory Burns and killed his mother, but they couldn't take it any further. The evidence literally went up in flames.'

'But if Marlena had been riding that bike, how did Kristos find out? And when? The Sunday Clubbers had been meeting at Johnny's Place for two years. He couldn't have known from the beginning surely. Why would he have waited so long for his revenge?'

Vogel paused, reflecting on this. 'That's what we're talking about here, isn't it, revenge? And if this theory holds together, it was all about Marlena from the start. Kristos planned to murder her, and all the other stuff was a smokescreen.'

Clarke agreed. 'Poor Michelle Monahan was onto something, I reckon. That's why she had to die.'

'You know what, boss,' Pam Jones interjected. 'When Michelle was attacked in Brydges Place, she could well have just come from Kristos's place. It's just off the top of St Martin's Lane, so she'd have had to pass that alleyway to get from there to here.'

'There were lock-picking tools in her pocket,' interjected Carlisle. 'Remember?'

'Shit,' said Vogel. 'Perhaps she thought he was out and decided to break in. He could have walked in and found her there. But then, why didn't he kill her there and then?' He tried to picture the scene in his mind. 'Maybe he was at home all along. In bed asleep, or in the shower.' He nodded to himself. 'Yes, if she'd surprised him, caught sight of him naked – a man with no dick and no balls – she'd have known. And it would have given her a chance to make a run for it.'

'You're getting carried away, Vogel,' said Clarke. 'We haven't got evidence for any of that.'

'We could at least try checking out whether Marlena had ever talked about having a pink motorcycle,' said Vogel. 'And if she did, did they all know about it? Did Kristos know? That would be something.'

Clarke nodded. 'We've got three of 'em here already, haven't we? That leaves another three, including Greg Walker. We need him too, but go gently. Ask all three to come in. Don't arrest 'em, not this time. We need them on our side. Tell them we would like to share certain information before it becomes public knowledge and ask them to come here soon as poss. And tell the three we've got banged up – Ari, Billy and Tiny – that they're about to be released on police bail but we need a final chat. Tell them all that they may be able to help us finally settle this.'

'Right, boss,' said Vogel.

'Then get a doctor here,' instructed Clarke. 'I want Kristos or Burns or whatever his fucking name is fully examined before we go any further. If we're right, his physical condition should confirm that he's Burns. Custody are about to get the hairdrier big time. Twice now they've had him undress and taken his clothes away. You'd think they might have noticed he didn't have a dick.'

'You know how it is, boss, the prisoners always turn their backs, and nobody looks really,' said Carlisle, who had been a custody officer before his transfer to CID.

Clarke flashed him a stony look.

'I don't give a damn how it is, Carlisle – and when I want your fucking opinion I'll ask for it,' she said. 'Neither do I want any more fucking mistakes, right? And let's get our prisoner's genitalia, or what remains of it, photographed and put on record.'

'Right, boss,' said Vogel again.

'Oh, and go see the bastard in his cell. Tell him what's happening. Let him realize his big secret is about to be revealed. Let him stew. We've still got bugger-all in hard evid—'

Carlisle giggled.

'Oh, for fuck's sake, grow up, Carlisle, or I'll have you back in uniform,' said Clarke, glowering at the DC.

'Our best hope is a confession,' she continued. 'Proving Kristos and Burns are the same person will be straightforward enough. Apart from his lack of genitalia, we can run a comparison between the DNA samples we took when Kristos was first arrested and the samples taken when Burns attacked his foster mother back in 1990 – luckily for us, they pulled out all the stops on that one; if it had been a routine case they wouldn't have bothered with DNA samples back then. We'll prove he's Rory Burns, no question of that. But it's going to be a lot tougher pinning four murders on him. The evidence for the two King's Cross victims, Marlena and Michelle – it's all circumstantial. So far anyway.'

'It's got to be him,' said Vogel.

'Yep. You know that and I know that. But first the CPS have to be convinced and then a jury. We've checked out his alibi for Michelle's murder, by the way – the neighbour, Marnie. You were right: when pushed, she couldn't be sure when Kristos was with her that day. Said he usually came round about nine, sometimes before. He banked on that, I reckon.'

'Well, that's something, boss.'

'Not enough. Just go put some fear into the bastard, Vogel. He's too damned cool for my liking.'

'Yes, guv,' said Vogel.

He was getting up to leave when Clarke's desk phone rang. She listened for a few seconds, then gestured for Vogel to wait.

'We've had a call from a woman who works in the Covent Garden Veterinary Surgery,' she said. 'Apparently she's only just seen a newspaper report mentioning that Michelle had been mugged and her face disfigured not long before she was murdered. Says she put two and two together and reckons it was Michelle, wearing heavy make-up, dark glasses, and with a baseball cap pulled down over her face, who visited the surgery on the morning of her murder. She was asking about the medical history of George Kristos's dog.'

Vogel looked at Clarke enquiringly.

'The dog was terminally ill, Vogel. And Kristos knew it. He'd been taking the creature to the vet regularly. It had cancer of the liver.'

'Christ, so Kristos was about to lose his dog anyway. This is getting better, boss.'

'Yep. But still not enough for a conviction. Let's just see if we can't break Kristos. Clinch it.'

Vogel left the room, taking Joe Carlisle with him.

He told Carlisle to get a doctor to the station to examine Kristos as soon as possible, to contact Bob and Alfonso, and to pass on DCI Clarke's message to Ari, Billy, and Tiny in their cells.

Hoping that Parlow and Wagstaff would call in soon with news of Greg Walker, Vogel was just about to head off to the cells to begin the process of trying to break Kristos when Carlisle halted the phone call he was making and called after his DCI.

'Guv, they reckon it's going to be a couple of hours before they can get a doctor here,' said the DC. 'Apparently there's been some sort of emergency . . .'

Vogel set off for the cells, cursing under his breath. On the bright side, a two-hour delay would give him time to talk to the Sunday Clubbers. And it would mean Kristos would have plenty of time to stew.

When the detective entered his cell, George Kristos was sitting bolt upright on the stone bench that served as a bed. His eyes instantly fixed on Vogel's. It was as if he had been staring at the door, waiting.

The cold gaze unnerved Vogel. He had to remind himself that he was the one who was supposed to be doing the unnerving. It wasn't going to be easy, but Vogel had an idea of something that might intimidate Kristos far more than the prospect of being tried for murder.

'We have arranged for you to be seen by a doctor,' he said. 'Information has come to our attention that makes it necessary for you to undergo a full medical examination before we formally interview you again.'

He knew that his language was stilted and awkward. It was deliberate. Vogel studied Kristos carefully. Was there just a flicker of something indecipherable in his eyes? Was the man blinking a little more quickly?

'Unfortunately it could be as long as two hours before an appropriate doctor can attend. Until that time you will be detained in this cell. Food and drink will be brought to you at the requisite intervals. Is that clear?'

Kristos inclined his head slightly. Were his hands trembling? Vogel wasn't sure of that either. Perhaps he had begun to imagine things.

'I shall see you later then, Mr Kristos,' said Vogel as he left the cell.

This time there was no reaction at all.

I will never allow myself to be violated again. The surgeons were as bad, in some ways, as the woman who had destroyed me. I still found it hard to believe that they could not have saved some part of my manhood.

I read, many years later, of transplants and reconstructions, but after what I had been through I would never again put myself at the mercy of the medical profession. They had left me like this. Not even half a man. And as I had grown into what would have been puberty, in a young offenders' centre, with vandals and rapists and idiots, neither they nor anyone else knew of my inner agony. They did not realize that I too had sexual feelings. That the torture of adolescence was also mine. Testosterone raged inside me, just as it did in the bodies of my fellow inmates who passed for normal.

The last time I saw a doctor was when I was seventeen, the year before I left the young offenders' centre. The ignorant bitch sat there in her white coat and stethoscope and told me that as I had lost my testicles as well as my penis, I would not suffer from any sexual desires I may be unable to satisfy.

Was she not aware that it is not only the testes which produce male hormones? The adrenal glands also do so. Not enough to deliver any sort of sexual satisfaction – especially in one who lacks the required equipment – but enough to drive me mad with sexual frustration. Particularly in my teens.

I have not been near a doctor since. My knowledge of my condition, and the drugs I have used to manage it, have all come from the Internet.

When they let me out of that dreadful institution, a place where everyone knew what had happened to me, where the staff and the inmates all knew that I was a freak, I vowed that I would reinvent myself. I would learn how to pass for normal. I thought if I could become an actor I could teach myself to perform off stage as well as on.

And, indeed, my whole life since I was eighteen has been a performance.

But first I had to acquire a new identity. As long as I remained Rory Burns I would always be the freak with no balls and no prick. I would never be able to get beyond that.

The whole time I was in the Edinburgh halfway house, I was just awaiting the right opportunity, obeying my licence to the letter, reporting like a good boy to my probation officer, behaving myself perfectly – apart from the small matter of my two visits to King's Cross.

Although I had no money, I was clean and tidy and well-mannered, so it was easy enough for me to hitch-hike to London. I'd read about King's Cross and how the prostitutes lurked there, wanton and lustful, worthless in the eyes of the Lord. Unable to find the one who had been responsible for my destruction – the evil bitch Marlena having yet to be revealed unto me – I needed to release the anger within. I needed to vent my wrath, to worship at the altar of retribution. With my sacrificial blade I violated their secret places and ripped out their womanhood. And then I returned to the halfway house.

It was only after I sacrificed my second victim that I found out she was not a prostitute. She was a student nurse from Sweden who had strayed into that place of depravity by accident. I watched the girl's parents on television, weeping as they told of how she'd wanted only to devote her life to God. She had been pure – a virgin as I was and would always remain.

God showed me His wrath then. I began to have violent headaches. I would wake up in the night in a terrible sweat and quaking with fear. Sometimes pains would course through my whole body. I knew that God was punishing me for causing the death of one of His chosen children. I listened to His voice. I vowed I would never again give in to my base urges. There must be no more wanton killing. Instead I would dedicate my life to becoming someone else.

One day in the local paper I read about a Greek Cypriot couple who ran a kebab shop in Muirhouse. Their seventeen-year-old son, Georgios Kristos, had died suddenly of meningitis. Broken-hearted, they were selling up and returning to Cyprus. It was perfect. The boy was just a year younger than me. I would turn myself into Georgios Kristos. And I knew exactly how I would set about doing so.

I'd read the book, The Day of the Jackal. It had all seemed too simple to be true. Surely it was only in a novel that this method of building an identity could work? But work it did. In 1998 anyway.

The authorities had found me a job in the packing department of a chicken factory. Not exactly appropriate for someone who had committed a violent crime, but nobody seemed to notice. It paid little, but I saved all I earned. Then I realized that I could earn far better money by actually killing the creatures. I applied for overtime whenever possible. It caused me no concern to watch these poor hairless battery hens die. After all, their lives were as full of pain and despair as mine had so far been. And I too had sometimes thought that I would be better off out of my misery.

But suddenly I had a real purpose. I saw my chance to become a new person, somebody who could at least seem to be normal – and I grasped it.

The newspaper report most obligingly supplied the date of Georgios Kristos's death. I was able to obtain his death certificate. That supplied me with his date of birth, and I was then able to obtain a birth certificate. The report also told me which school Georgios had attended. It seemed he had been a precocious student, and at seventeen had already passed four A-levels, including English and, most fortuitously for me, Drama.

I waited until Georgios would have been an adult. On his eighteenth birthday I left my halfway house one morning and never returned. Neither did I ever see my probation officer again. I was no longer Rory Burns. I was Georgios Kristos. I dyed my reddish blond typically Gaelic hair a Mediterranean black, acquired dark-tinted contact lenses, and took to using sunbeds and fake tan.

I have learned well how to pretend to be something that I am not. Indeed, anything at all that I am not. I was not drawn to acting by a desire to become a star of stage or screen. Though I have found, curiously perhaps, that I enjoy performing before an audience. I chose acting because it seemed the ideal craft for a man who was to live entirely by subterfuge.

The principals of the Willesden Academy for Performing Arts were impressed by my false academic qualifications. And it turned out that I was a natural. While I was there, I learned to drive and acquired a driving licence, I acquired a passport in the name of Georgios Kristos, I opened a bank account, and I was able to join Equity.

I had succeeded in creating a new life for myself. And I wanted to live it. For my God. In order to keep my vow that there would be no more killings, I researched medications and therapies, and overseas suppliers who did not concern themselves with prescriptions and legalities, eventually settling on a cocktail of anti-psychotic drugs that allowed me to keep my anger in check.

Sometimes I almost forgot that I was acting on and off stage. Playing a role. I travelled to London, found myself work, acquired somewhere to live in the heart of the city and nurtured my new life. I kept it up for thirteen years. Thirteen unbelievable years. There was one little lapse. But only one in all that time. And I doubted anyone would ever find out about it, even now, for it took place in another country. Not realizing that it would react with my medication, I decided to sample marijuana. My hard-won control evaporated and I was again overwhelmed by the urge to take revenge. But I did at least make sure that my victim was a prostitute. An evil woman without morality. And God did not seem to mind. The terrible pains in my head and my body did not return. And I never smoked marijuana again.

God rewarded my efforts. I achieved happiness of a sort. Enough acting engagements came my way to fund my modest needs, supplemented by the various odd jobs I undertook. There were bit parts on TV, pantomime, a couple of commercials, fringe theatre and occasional provincial tours. I worked out in the gym as a diversion for any sexual energy, and to build up muscle and improve the appearance of my body. With the help of enhancing jockstraps I became an expert at creating a satisfactory crotch bulge.

I was George Kristos, handsome young man-about-town. I could have any girl I wanted. Or so everyone thought.

For the first time in my life, I made friends. Each week, I would look forward to Sunday Club. I kidded myself I was fond of the others and they of me. Then I learned that I had been sharing a table with the woman who had brought about my destruction.

My pink lady was Marlena. Or rather, Marleen McTavish.

And it was then I rediscovered my own true identity: Rory Burns.

Now the whole world will know. I have been found out. But that is no matter. I have fulfilled my destiny.

And there shall be no retribution levelled against me except that of my Lord God Almighty.

Parlow and Wagstaff approached Vogel just as he arrived back at his desk.

''Fraid we can't find Greg Walker, guv,' said Parlow.

'What!' snapped Vogel. He glanced at his watch. 'It's taken you long enough to not bloody find him, hasn't it? What the fuck have you been doing?'

'We went to his flat, then to his mother-in-law's place in case he'd gone there to see his kids. That's up towards Camden, sir. She hadn't seen him all day, so we drove to Waterloo to check out his lock-up. He wasn't there either, but there was a bloke in the lock-up opposite who said Walker had been there all afternoon and had only just left.'

Vogel grunted, bored already with what was beginning to sound like a succession of excuses for failure.

'I don't suppose this bloke had any idea where Walker was going?'

'Not really, guv. He said Walker got in a taxi and he thought he heard him ask for an address in Soho, but he couldn't catch exactly what he—'

Vogel barely hesitated. He turned and ran for the door, yelling for Parlow and Wagstaff to follow.

'Have you still got that CID car outside?' he asked breathlessly.

'Yes, guv,' said Wagstaff.

'Thank God,' said Vogel, still running. 'We need to get to the Zodiac on Lisle Street. Parlow – on your radio! Call for back-up. And get an Armed Response Unit to meet us there. I reckon we're gonna need 'em.'

Wagstaff, proud holder of a police advanced driving certificate, jumped behind the wheel, and with Parlow in the back seat and Vogel next to him shouting instructions, took off with a screech of rubber.

Greg Walker was at that moment climbing out of a black cab outside the Zodiac. The Browning was tucked into one pocket of his leather bomber jacket. It wasn't yet cocked. Nonetheless the gun's close proximity to his abdomen caused Greg to break into a sweat. He kept one hand in his jacket pocket, holding the pistol in place, almost as if he feared it might leap out of its own volition and shoot him in the foot.

It was early evening. The Zodiac opened at lunchtime seven days a week and stayed open until three or four the following morning, but it was seldom busy at this hour. There was only one security doorman on duty, whom Greg recognized from his

385

previous visit. Greg approached him without hesitating. He was beyond fear.

'I'm sorry to come unannounced,' Greg said. 'I have some information for Mr Kwan. I wonder if he could possibly find time to see me?'

The doorman turned slightly away from Greg, bending his head towards his radio mike, clipped, as usual, to the lapel of his black jacket. As he reached with one hand to switch it on, Greg stepped forward, removed the pistol from his pocket, cocked it by pulling back the top-slide thus springing a cartridge from the magazine, and thrust the barrel into the man's midriff.

'Take me in,' he muttered, 'or you're a fuckin' gonner.'

To Greg's surprise, the bouncer made no attempt to knock the gun out of his hand the way Greg had so often seen it done in movies and on the telly. Instead he led the way through the main gaming room, where only a few dedicated punters were playing the tables. Greg walked close to the doorman and kept the gun tucked into the man's side, hoping nobody would notice it. No one did. The gamblers were intent only on their own activities.

Perhaps because of the time of day and the relatively small number of punters on the premises, there was no second security operative at the rear door which led to Kwan's offices. Greg gestured to the doorman to open the door, which he did at once, tapping in a security code. Greg pushed him through.

As soon as they were on the other side, the doorman made his move. Greg was pulling the door shut, which put him slightly off balance. The man kicked out, catching Greg with a mighty blow at the top of one thigh, then wrapped his leg around both of Greg's, behind the knees, causing him to topple backwards, crashing heavily to the ground. It was expertly done. Unfortunately, as Greg fell he inadvertently squeezed the trigger of the Browning in his right hand.

The bullet hit the doorman straight between the eyes. The tac vest he was undoubtedly wearing was therefore of no use. He died instantly.

Greg scrambled uncertainly to his feet, stunned but determined to finish what he had begun. He ran up the stairs to the third floor. The door to Kwan's offices was shut. Greg fired three rapid shots at the lock, then gave the door a shove.

Tony Kwan was sitting at his glass desk, just as he had been when Greg had made his previous visit. But this time he did not rise to greet Greg. He did not move. He just sat there, unblinking.

Greg aimed his pistol at Tony Kwan's head. He had no idea whether or not Kwan wore a bulletproof tac jacket, but he was taking no chances. He wanted to shoot the murdering bastard right between the eyes. As he had the doorman. Only this time it would be deliberate. He began to squeeze the trigger.

The subsequent bang was therefore not a surprise. Then he became aware of a terrible pain in his lower arm. He looked down and saw that his right wrist and hand were a bloody mess of shattered bone and sinew. His pistol lay at his feet. He had been given no opportunity to fire it at Kwan. He'd been shot. Worse, he'd failed. He'd let his Karen down.

But what had he expected? Greg wondered, as the world started to go hazy and he slumped to the ground.

One of Kwan's goons, holding a still-smoking revolver, stepped forward and kicked Greg a couple of times in the ribs.

Greg howled in agony. There was little doubt that at least one rib had been broken. But then, that too was only to be expected.

With lights flashing and siren blaring, Wagstaff got Vogel to Lisle Street in four minutes. As they approached the Zodiac all three policemen heard gunshots. Vogel threw himself out of the car before Wagstaff had brought it fully to a halt. They did not know then, but the first four shots had been fired by Greg Walker at the security doorman and then the lock on the door to Kwan's office, and the fifth was the shot fired at Greg by Kwan's henchmen.

Vogel moved at speed across the pavement to the now un-supervised front door, which stood ajar. He rushed inside. The place was empty, all the gamblers having fled the moment the first shot was fired. Vogel ran past empty gaming tables, Carlisle and Parlow trailing in his wake.

'Shouldn't we wait for the back-up, guv?' asked Parlow lamely.

'Yeah, we need those armed response boys,' Carlisle called after the DI.

Vogel ignored them both. The door at the back of the club which led to Kwan's private offices was closed but unlocked. Vogel pushed the door and it opened, but not completely. He squeezed himself through the gap, his pulse quickening as he saw the dead doorman lying at his feet. He stepped over the body and ran upstairs.

The third-floor door to Kwan's office was also open. Having been decimated by the blast of gunfire administered by Greg Walker, it would no longer close.

Vogel burst through. He just had time to take in Tony Kwan, still sitting at his desk, a bleeding Greg Walker slumped on the floor, and a Kwan henchman holding a handgun stepping threat-eningly towards him. Thanks to his police firearm training, Vogel registered that the gun, doubtless illegal, was a revolver of the type favoured by bodyguards and so-called security staff because, although it could not be fired as rapidly as a semi-automatic, it didn't jam.

The henchman fired. The revolver didn't jam. Vogel felt a burning sensation in his left shoulder.

He staggered but managed to stay upright.

'Put that gun away, you fool!' Tony Kwan shouted at his henchman. He was almost screaming, apoplectic with rage. 'You've shot a cop!'

Vogel's knees were beginning to buckle. His legs felt like jelly, and the burning sensation in his left shoulder had become a searing pain. His mind remained absolutely lucid. He'd behaved like a fool, but perhaps the consequences were not entirely without merit.

'Yes, indeed Mr Kwan,' he said, managing a small smile. 'Your goon has shot a policeman. And in your own office. Looks as if we've got you bang to fucking rights at last.'

Then he fell to the ground alongside Greg Walker.

twenty-five

Parlow and Wagstaff, who were making their way up the rickety staircase, heard the shot that had felled Vogel and instinctively stopped climbing.

'Shit,' said Parlow.

Wagstaff, still fired up from his manic drive, recovered fastest. 'Come on,' he said, taking another step upwards. 'We gotta get our guvnor.'

Parlow grabbed his fellow DC's arm.

'No,' he said. 'We could have a dead copper up there. Nobody wants another one. An ARU should be here any minute.'

As if on cue, a tall Chinese heavy with a gun in his hand stepped out of Tony Kwan's office onto the third-floor landing and peered down the stairwell at the two detectives. He looked as if he was thinking of making a run for it.

Parlow gulped.

'Fuck,' said Wagstaff.

Fortuitously for both men, the henchman seemed to change his mind and retreated back into the office. And armed response did arrive within minutes.

Wagstaff and Parlow were ordered out of the building. The ARU boys proceeded cautiously upstairs. No further shots were fired. Kwan was arrested, along with the security man who had shot Greg Walker and Vogel, two of Kwan's sons, another security man, and the three young women who were found cowering in the bedroom.

Once the premises had been cleared and declared safe, a paramedic team was allowed in. Greg Walker, who'd lost so much blood he was by then barely conscious, was swiftly loaded into an ambulance.

Vogel turned out not to have been seriously injured. After the paramedics had removed his jacket and cut away the sleeve of his shirt it was revealed that he'd suffered only a flesh wound. The bullet had passed through the fleshy part of his shoulder at the top of his arm, avoiding any bone or major ligaments. It hurt like hell, but Vogel refused point-blank to be dispatched to A and E.

'I'm in the middle of something that won't wait,' he said. 'I have work to do.'

He seemed more worried about his horn-rimmed spectacles than his injured shoulder. The glasses had fallen off when he'd collapsed after being shot. They were duly retrieved and handed to him.

'Thank God for that. Thought I was going fucking blind,' Vogel muttered.

He then draped his damaged jacket over the temporary dressing on his shoulder, wincing as he did so, then ignored the protests of the paramedics as he walked out of the building.

Wagstaff and Parlow, still hovering outside in Lisle Street, were mighty relieved to see him.

'Thank God you're all right, guv,' said Parlow.

Vogel grunted. 'Take me back to Charing Cross,' he instructed Wagstaff.

As he reached to open the door of the CID car his jacket

slipped off his injured shoulder, revealing the recently applied dressing through which blood was already seeping.

Wagstaff hesitated.

'Get on with it, man!' Vogel ordered.

Once in the car, he examined his jacket. It was corduroy and had seen better days, but now the left sleeve was stained with blood and there was a hole in it.

As they all climbed out of the car at Charing Cross, Vogel turned to Wagstaff.

'Take your jacket off and give it to me,' he ordered.

Wagstaff hesitated.

'Give me your coat, man,' said Vogel. 'I have interviews to conduct. I can hardly turn up with blood all over me, like some fucking *Casualty* extra, can I?'

Somewhat reluctantly Wagstaff handed over his light grey suit jacket and helped Vogel put it on. Parlow watched as the necessary manoeuvring of Vogel's arms and upper body caused the DI to turn even paler than he had been before. Wagstaff was about the same height and of similar build to Vogel, but he was very slightly slimmer. The jacket was a tight fit, which did not help matters.

'Are you sure you shouldn't go to hospital, guv?' Parlow asked.

'Shut up, Steve,' said Vogel.

He led the way into the station. DCI Clarke was waiting for him.

'Vogel, I know this case is your baby, but you belong in hospital,' she said.

Vogel glowered at her. 'So everyone keeps telling me,' he replied. 'And I will go there, boss, as soon as this is over.'

Nobby Clarke studied him for a moment and gave a resigned shake of the head. 'All right, Vogel, against my better judgement, you can carry on,' she said. 'But you're going to the hospital later, whether everything's sorted or not.'

'Thanks, boss,' said Vogel, thinking he'd argue about that 'later' if necessary.

'Bob Buchanan's come in, but Alfonso Bertorelli was so pissed when Carlisle spoke to him on the phone there was no point in even trying to get him here,' Clarke continued. 'I've got Buchanan and the three Sunday Clubbers we already had in custody waiting in the big interview room. Best to talk to them all together this time, I reckon. Might jog each other's memories.'

Vogel made his way there, pausing to ask Parlow to go get him some paracetamol. Not that it would do much good. The pain in his shoulder was beyond the remit of non-prescription drugs.

DS Jones took the chair next to Vogel. Bob, Tiny, Billy and Ari were sitting in a row of upright chairs like a bunch of kids in detention, Vogel thought. Not one of them had asked for a solicitor to be present.

'I want to know if any of you are aware of Marlena ever having owned or ridden a motorcycle,' Vogel asked.

Ari glanced towards Bob. 'She did say something,' he said. 'Didn't she, Bob?'

'Yeah, the last time we played The Game. It would have been—'

'What game?' interrupted Vogel.

'Our version of the truth game,' said Ari. 'One of the group would ask a question of the others. The idea was to get everyone talking, to have a laugh . . .'

'Only that wasn't how it panned out that particular Sunday,' said Billy. 'It all got a bit too serious, for some reason.'

'"What was your biggest life-changing moment?"' said Tiny. 'That was the question. Karen was the one who asked it.'

'Yes,' agreed Billy. 'And we nearly had a domestic, Michelle ended up in tears—'

'I got maudlin about my boy,' Bob cut in.

'And Marlena told us her life-changing moment was when she had an accident riding her motorbike,' said Ari. 'It made her grow up, she said. Seemed a bit strange to me, now I think of it, but Marlena always came up with something unexpected.'

'That was it though: a motorbike accident, a long time ago,' confirmed Bob. 'And I remember that she said it was a pink motorbike. Well, you wouldn't forget that, would you?'

The hairs on the back of Vogel's neck were standing on end. This was it. This was really it, he thought. Marlena on her pink motorbike – little Rory Burns' pink lady. She had to be. No doubt about it.

'Was that the first time any of you had heard about Marlena's motorcycling days, the first time she had spoken of it?' Vogel asked.

'I think so,' said Billy. 'It certainly came as a surprise to me.'

'Can you all remember when this took place? You said it was the last time you played that game?' Vogel continued.

'It was the end of February, wasn't it, when the weather was so cold?' offered Tiny.

'I can tell you exactly,' said Bob grimly. 'It was my son's birthday: February twenty-fourth.'

'And that was well before any of the incidents, wasn't it?' enquired Vogel.

'Oh yes,' said Billy. 'The Mr Tickle thing with George happened in mid-March. I remember because he didn't come to Sunday Club right afterwards, and that was the weekend we went to your mate's wedding on the Saturday, Tiny . . .'

Billy paused. A thought had obviously struck him.

'Where is George, anyway?' he asked. 'We know Alfonso's on the sauce, but where's George?'

Vogel did not answer the question.

'And where's Greg?' asked Bob. 'Though he must be half out of his mind, poor bastard.'

Vogel passed no comment on that, either.

'Can any of you tell me if George Kristos was present at Sunday Club the night Marlena talked about her motorbike and the accident which changed her life?' he asked.

'Oh yes,' said Bob. 'He was there. We all were, which was unusual . . .'

His voice tailed off. Then he spoke again.

'What's happened to George?'

Vogel thought for a moment. He decided to tell them the bald facts.

'Mr Kristos has been arrested on suspicion of the murder of Marleen McTavish and Michelle Monahan,' he said. 'And we expect to charge him, probably within the next few hours.'

Four shocked faces stared at him. Nobody spoke.

Then Bob pointed at Vogel's shoulder.

'You're bleeding, Mr Vogel,' he said, looking even more shocked.

Vogel glanced down. Blood was seeping through Nick Wagstaff's jacket. Flipping thing would be pale grey, Vogel thought, wondering if he'd end up having to buy Wagstaff a new suit, and if so, whether he'd be allowed to claim it on expenses.

'Don't worry about that, it's nothing,' he said dismissively.

Without further explanation he told the four men that he had more questions for them, several points he needed to clarify, and he would be grateful for their continued assistance.

They had questions for him too, once they'd recovered from their initial shock, but he could not provide answers. All four men would be called as witnesses in due course, and the last thing he wanted was to see the case thrown out of court because something he'd divulged had prejudiced the defendant's right to a fair trial. He did tell them that Greg had been injured, but avoided the details.

He spent half an hour or so going over what the men knew about George, and what they knew about Marlena, the meetings between them and so on, and then there was a knock on the door and Parlow stuck his head in.

'The doc's here, guv,' he said, discreetly passing Vogel a packet of paracetamol.

'About time too,' said Vogel, checking his watch. 'Right, get him set up and go fetch Kristos.'

He returned his attention to the four.

Five minutes later Parlow burst through the door without knocking. His face was flushed and he was in a state of panic.

'You'd better come quick, guv,' he gulped.

Vogel immediately got to his feet and hurried to the door. Whatever had spooked Parlow, he didn't want him blurting it out in front of the four witnesses.

As soon as he'd closed the door behind him, he turned to Parlow. The younger man was trembling.

'It's Kristos,' he said. 'Looks like he's topped himself.'

Vogel raced to the cell block, ignoring the pain in his shoulder. He pushed through the crowd of police officers who'd gathered in the custody suite and stopped in the cell doorway. George Kristos was lying on the bed, covered in blood. It was obvious that his throat had been cut. A stunned Sergeant Andy Pierce stood over him.

Vogel stared in horror. Then he thought he heard a gurgling

sound. That surely meant the man was still breathing, didn't it?

He leaned forward and felt George's pulse. Was there a flicker of life? He wasn't sure.

'Get that doctor in here, for fuck's sake,' Vogel shouted to nobody in particular.

'I've sent Jenkins to fetch him, sir,' said the custody officer. Vogel turned to him.

'How could this happen, Pierce?' he asked. 'Don't you guys check prisoners?'

'I looked in every half-hour, I swear it,' replied Pierce. 'The prisoner was lying down, wrapped in his blanket. I couldn't actually see him because the blanket was pulled up over his head. I just assumed he was sleeping.'

'You assumed,' growled Vogel. He turned his attention to the prisoner.

'How did he do it? What did he use to cut his own fucking throat? You did search him, I presume?'

The custody officer ignored the last remark. Instead he pointed to the bloodied half of a razor blade which lay alongside George on the bunk.

'Seems he smuggled it in, guv,' said Sergeant Pierce.

Again he pointed. This time to a small cylindrical object with some sticky tape attached to it. Vogel recognized it as the curved end of a cigar container. He didn't need to ask how George had smuggled the half-razor in. He had inserted it in his anus, and an anal search is not a routine part of custody procedure at British police stations.

'He must've had that damned thing up his arse when we arrested him,' muttered Vogel. 'He had it all planned. He knew exactly what he was going to do if we came to get him. He was one step ahead of us, the bastard. Just as he's been all along.'

Vogel shook his head angrily. 'How can a man cut his own throat?'

George's eyes were closed. Vogel moved closer and lifted one eyelid. A pale blue eye stared at him, presumably the man's natural iris colour. Having decided to end his life, Burns had finally abandoned all pretence and removed the tinted contact lenses that had been part of his George Kristos disguise. The cold blue eye was full of hatred. Vogel stared into it. He could see a kind of triumph there too, he was sure of it.

Then Burns' entire body convulsed and he spewed black blood from his open mouth. Vogel let go of the eyelid and stepped back.

At the same moment the doctor arrived in the cell and rushed to Vogel's side, bending over the blood-covered man.

After a couple of minutes he stood up and turned to face Vogel.

'There's nothing I can do,' he said. 'I'm afraid your prisoner is dead.'

Vogel's gaze remained fixed on the prisoner. Who had beaten who? Vogel was not sure. He did wonder, however, how many questions would remain unanswered. All hope of a confession was gone. There would be no cross-examination in a court of law. They could only guess at what had motivated him, and they might never be able to determine exactly how many victims he had claimed.

Vogel allowed his eyes to wander around the cell, taking in the volume of blood and the crumpled blanket, which he assumed had been pulled off the dying man by the custody officer.

Kristos had removed his police-issue paper suit and folded it neatly on the bottom of the bunk. He lay now with his naked-ness exposed, which presumably had been his intention. His body was almost hairless, presumably because of his emasculation. Between his legs there were no recognizable genitalia. No testes and no penis. Just a jagged scar and an almost vaginal opening which had presumably been fashioned in order for him to urinate.

Vogel shuddered. What a secret to keep, he thought.

Then the piece of cylindrical cigar casing caught his eye. Was there something in it still? Vogel thought so. He reached for it carefully. Using only the tips of one forefinger and thumb he removed a neatly folded piece of paper.

It bore an inked message, rather beautifully handwritten and resembling medieval biblical script, Vogel thought.

Thus saith the Lord: Though I have afflicted thee, I will afflict thee no more.

epilogue

DCI Nobby Clarke waited until seven days had passed before visiting Vogel at his home. He was on mandatory sick leave. His upper arm and shoulder had become infected, almost certainly due to his refusal to undergo proper treatment until several hours after he was shot.

Vogel's wife, Mary, greeted the DCI warmly and ushered her into the living room of the Pimlico apartment.

Clarke took in the abundance of pink, the floral wallpaper and curtains, and the predominantly feminine air of the place. For some reason, Vogel, sitting on an ornately covered settee with luxuriously deep cushions, seemed to fit in perfectly – but then, why shouldn't he, in his own home?

Next to him was a young girl, in her early teens, Clarke thought, holding a purple Nintendo Game Boy. She waved one arm awkwardly. All her movements seemed awkward.

Vogel stood up and shook Nobby Clarke's hand.

'Thanks for coming, boss,' he said. Then he gestured to the girl.

'This is my daughter, Rosamund,' he said.

'Hello,' said Rosamund. She spoke in rather a slow, stilted way, but her smile was captivating.

Clarke found herself smiling back. Then she returned her attention to Vogel. He was wearing, or half wearing, a large white cotton shirt, the sleeve hanging loose over his left arm and shoulder.

'How're you doing, David?' she asked.

'OK, the antibiotics appear to be doing their stuff,' Vogel replied.

'Good,' said the DCI. 'You know you're bloody lucky to still be in the job, don't you? Blundering into a gunfight as if you're a sheriff in a very bad western. Against every damn regulation.'

'Yes, boss,' said Vogel.

'Anyway, I managed to bring the brass round. They're convinced you're some kind of hero now.'

'Thanks, boss.'

'Must say, I never expected this sort of trouble from you, Vogel. Thought they called you the Geek?'

'Yes, boss.' Vogel was staring at Nobby Clarke with a wicked gleam in his eye. 'But names can be very inappropriate, can't they?'

'Don't even go there, Vogel,' growled the DCI.

'No, boss,' said Vogel, just as his wife walked into the room carrying a tray bearing teapot, cups and saucers, and a large round fruit cake, yet to be cut.

'Any further news about Kristos?' Vogel asked, changing the subject and getting on to the topic he was really interested in.

'No more than you know already,' said Clarke, accepting a cup of tea. 'Kristos and Burns checked out to be the same person. There was a load of stuff found in Kristos's flat that none of the idiots searching it previously had thought important – hair dye, medication, jockstraps, that sort of thing. And, of course, the original photo of Alice Turner was on his hard drive, along with the one he'd doctored, the one that was supposed to be his girlfriend Carla. All circumstantial, as evidence goes. So perhaps it was a good job he topped himself.'

'Surely nobody could doubt his guilt?' said Vogel.

'A bloody court of law could,' muttered Clarke. 'We have, however, officially closed the investigations into the King's Cross murders, the two Sunday Club murders, and all the other Sunday Club crimes, major and minor.'

Vogel had expected that. 'What about Amsterdam?' he asked.

He might have been on sick leave, but contacts within MIT had told him about the murder of a prostitute in the notorious red-light district of De Wallen in 2007. It had not previously been linked with the 1998 King's Cross murders, even though the young woman found dead in the cabin she rented in order to ply her trade had been strangled and then repeatedly stabbed and mutilated in the same manner as the London victims. The Internet had still been in its infancy in 1998, in Europe at least, and information, both official and unofficial, did not cross international boundaries as freely back then.

'Well, we were able to inform the Dutch police that Kristos/Burns was in Amsterdam at the appropriate time,' said Clarke. 'Filming a walk-on role in a commercial for a budget airline, it seems.'

'Don't think they'll be repeating it then,' murmered Vogel.

'No. Anyway, we just heard that the Dutch have officially closed their murder investigation.'

'What else could they do?' Vogel asked. 'It all seems so unfair on the victims and their families though. No proper closure.' He looked Clarke in the eye. 'And speaking of unfair, it seems very hard on Greg Walker. If only I'd been quicker off the mark, I might have stopped that shooting.'

'Hmmm, and if you'd been a bit slower, Walker would be dead. I know it doesn't seem fair that he's facing a murder charge, and I don't give a damn about Kwan's goon, but there's no alternative, is there? Walker set out with a loaded handgun, intent on killing a man – and that's just what he did, albeit the wrong man.'

'So what about Kwan and his mob?'

'The goon who shot you and Walker is being done for GBH. I'm trying to get Kwan on a conspiracy charge, but the bastard's wriggling like a maggot on a fish-hook.'

'Well, if anyone can make it stick, boss, it'll be you,' said Vogel.

'I'll take that as a compliment, Vogel,' said DCI Clarke. 'But there's really no need to arse-lick . . .'

She stopped, remembering Vogel's daughter was in the room.

'Sorry,' she said, to nobody in particular.

'She's heard worse,' said Vogel.

'Anyway,' Clarke went on. 'What I mean is, I've already fixed it for you to drop the "acting" and become DI on a permanent basis. And, even though you've caused me so much trouble, I'd like to keep you on my MIT. I always have been perverse.'

Vogel grinned broadly.

'Thanks, boss,' he said. 'Much appreciated.'

He glanced almost imperceptibly towards his daughter.

Nobby Clarke ate two slices of fruit cake, which was extremely good, and drank two cups of tea before leaving.

Mary Vogel showed her out. The DCI noticed a wheelchair in a corner of the hall. She must have walked straight past it on the way in.

As she opened the front door, Mary paused. 'Rosamund adores her dad,' she said. 'Don't know what she'd have done if he'd got himself properly shot. I've given him a right telling-off.'

'Me too,' said Nobby Clarke.

Vogel's wife smiled. 'He'll never say, but for the first time in his life he really wanted this promotion. He's not one to think much about money, you see. But Rosamund's getting to an age when she needs all sorts of things. Her dad wants to be able to do a bit more for her . . .'

'I understand, and I'm delighted it's worked out,' said DCI Clarke. 'You do know your husband is an exceptional officer, don't you, Mrs Vogel?'

'Oh yes,' said Mary Vogel, beaming with pride. 'I know.'

Nobby Clarke was preoccupied as she wandered off in the general direction of Pimlico tube station. She was almost certain Rosamund Vogel suffered from cerebral palsy. Clarke had a friend with a son who had CP. Yet there'd been no mention in Vogel's file of his having a disabled child, and she'd never heard it mentioned. Typical, she thought.

David Vogel wouldn't want anybody to know anything about his personal life, if he could avoid it. He was the most private of men. And a rather surprising one too, it seemed.

About a month later the remaining Sunday Clubbers met for what they all knew would be the last time.

Marlena, Michelle, Karen and George were dead. Greg was out of hospital, but had been remanded in custody until his trial.

The five who were able to do so gathered at Tiny and Billy's flat. None of them could face Johnny's Place, even though Johnny had made a point of calling them to say they would always be welcome. So Tiny and Billy had offered to lay on a light supper at their home – and on a Saturday evening, not a Sunday. The boys were still together, and still living in the same Covent Garden flat. But they had not acquired another dog, and didn't intend to. They were, however, the proud owners of a large silver cat.

Alfonso was drunk when he arrived and immediately announced that he was leaving the country.

'I can't face this fucking city any more,' he said. 'The Vine don't want me back. I'm going to Italy. I have a cousin with a restaurant in Naples. He's taking me on.'

'And your mother?' asked Billy. Tiny kicked him under the table.

'Oh sherrup,' said Alfonso, pouring himself a large glass of wine.

The other friends wondered sadly if he would ever sober up enough to be able to hold down a job. Particularly in catering.

Bob too was planning to emigrate. But his was a happier story.

'I'm going to New Zealand to be with my boy,' he said. 'There's nothing left for me here now. Danny heard about what happened because it was all on the Internet. He phoned me out of the blue. Said he was sorry we'd fallen out of touch. I have a granddaughter now, as well as a grandson. My Dan's doing brilliant. Lives in Auckland in a big house with a chalet in the garden. Said I could have it, if I liked, and there's a lot of people he knows want gardens looked after – including him! So I'm going. What the hell, eh!'

'Glad shumbody's got a happy fucking ending,' muttered Alfonso.

'That's great news, Bob,' said Ari, glowering at Alfonso. 'I'm delighted for you.'

Alfonso turned towards Ari.

'And what about our poor little rich boy?' he asked, not very pleasantly.

'I've got some news too,' responded Ari levelly. 'I'm getting married.'

'Jeshus Christ,' said Alfonso.

'Congratulations, mate,' said Bob.

'Yes, congratulations,' echoed Tiny and Billy.

'Hope she likes the white stuff,' said Alfonso.

'Shut up, Fonz,' said Bob.

'No, it's all right,' said Ari. 'She's a good Muslim girl. She doesn't do drugs, and neither do I. Not any more. Dad said I had to sort myself out or else. And I knew he was right.'

'I give it five minutes,' said Alfonso. 'The coke *and* the marriage.'

'Oh, shut up,' said Bob again.

'Let's keep it cool, guys,' said Tiny. 'We've been through enough, haven't we? All of us.'

The large silver cat was sitting on his lap, as she had been through most of the evening.

Bob reached to stroke her neck. He'd known this reunion of the surviving Sunday Clubbers was always going to be tricky. Alfonso, drunk and somewhat belligerent, was making it worse.

'What's the cat's name?' Bob asked, seeking any sort of diversion.

'Lola,' replied Tiny.

'Isn't that what the cops told us Marlena was called in her other life?' asked Ari.

'Yep,' Billy replied. 'Madame Lola, after the Marlene Dietrich song, we reckon. *Lola, Lola, they call me naughty Lola.* Dietrich was Marlena's heroine, after all. Lola is our tribute to Marlena.'

'I see,' said Bob, looking as if he didn't.

There was an awkward silence, filled eventually by Ari.

'Look, we can't get over George, can we?' he said. 'I mean,

he seemed so normal, one of us. How did he keep that act up for so long?'

'He was a trained actor,' said Tiny.

'He was also a raving lunatic and a psychopath,' said Bob. 'And none of us noticed. Ari's right. I'll never get over it. Never.'

'Four of our little group dead, two horribly murdered, and poor Greg banged up for taking the law into his own hands.' Billy blinked rapidly. 'How can any of us ever get over it?'

Alfonso poured more wine, slopping some of it on the table.

'I think we should raise our glasses in a toast,' he said. 'To absent friends.'

The five stood up, Alfonso rather unsteadily.

'To absent friends,' they repeated,

'All except one,' said Tiny.

extracts reading groups
competitions books new
discounts extracts
competitions
new
books
events
extracts
new titles reading groups
interviews
discounts
new books events
events new
discounts extracts discounts
www.panmacmillan.com
extracts events reading groups
competitions books extracts new